Nefarious, Minacious Hound

A Hound Series Novel

Nefarious, Minacious Hound

A Hound Series Novel

JD McIntire

Nefarious, Minacious Hound

Acknowledgments

I would like to thank Debbie Sadowski, Di Freeze, Dr. Charlie Weiner, Gary Schueman, Gjelard Karrica, Emily Crutchfield, and Carla Crutchfield for their help in making this book a reality.

1

Carmella had been married to Roberto Sanchez for almost a year. As Roberto had promised, he and Carmella were now living in Oakland. She would begin attending Berkeley University the next month, in January 1971.

Carmella had provided Hound with a phone number where he could reach her. She had also provided him with specific dates during the month she'd be available to receive phone calls or meet. He called her before he left Saigon. His arrival in Oakland would coincide perfectly with the time of the month she was available. She became overjoyed and excited to learn of his early discharge and they could see each other again sooner than expected. She was overcome and began to cry.

It was midmorning when Hound arrived in Oakland. Carmella had been waiting, anxiously anticipating his phone call. When the call finally came, she was once again overcome with joy and began to cry.

"Carmella, is everything all right?" Hound asked. "You said it would be OK to call. Is it?"

"Oh, my sweet gringo boy! Of course, it's OK! I told you it would be."

"Well, because you're crying, I wasn't sure."

"God damn it, Hound! I'm crying because I'm so fucking happy about getting to see you again!"

"I'm happy about seeing you again as well."

"How long will we have together before you have to return to Louisiana?"

"I have the rest of the day today and tonight, all day tomorrow and tomorrow night."

Carmella gave Hound the suite number and name of the exquisite hotel where she'd meet him in an hour.

"Hound, the food at the hotel is divine," she told him. "We can have dinner in the suite and talk about everything needed to bring each other up to date on the happenings in our lives since we last saw each other."

"That sounds wonderful, Carmella, but are you sure it's safe for us to be in a hotel suite? What if someone you know sees you and tells Roberto? Are you sure he's not having you watched while he's away? Are the phones in your home bugged?"

"Hound, I assure you there's nothing to be concerned about. What about Jo? Doesn't she expect you to come directly home?"

"She knows I'm being discharged but knows nothing regarding my time of departure, travel itinerary, or time of arrival back in New Orleans. I'll take a cab from the airport to her parents' home when I get back. I'll say I wanted my arrival to be a surprise."

"What if she finds out about the time you spent in California?"

"I have an excuse if that happens."

"What excuse do you have?"

"I promised a very fine superior officer I'd pay a visit to his wife and daughter who live in Oakland. I intend to keep my promise. That will be my legitimate excuse."

"What's the officer's name? What are the names of his wife and daughter?"

"General Charles Hughes is the officer. His wife is Carolyn. Rebecca is his daughter. General Hughes is a splendid human being in every way. He told them about me in a letter. I'm curious to know what he said."

"Hound, I'll see you in an hour. The hotel is easy to find. Just follow the directions I gave you."

"I'll be there. See you soon."

Hound was purposely 10 minutes late arriving at the door of the hotel suite. He wanted to increase the chance of Carmella being inside before he arrived. The door of the suite opened before he completed his soft knocking on the door. Without saying a word, Carmella grabbed his hand and pulled him quickly inside. Her passionate kiss and embrace were long in duration. She then stepped back from him a distance sufficient to allow each of them to view the other from head to toe.

What Hound saw standing before him was a woman whose beauty could be described as remarkable and extraordinary. Her dark skin was soft, smooth, and flawless. Her dark brown eyes were piercing as she gazed at him. Her black hair was straight, thick, shiny, and reached a length even with her hips. The dress she wore was pale yellow. It conformed perfectly to her hourglass shape and accented her large, well-proportioned and rounded breasts.

"Carmella, you're more beautiful than ever," Hound said softly. "When I last saw you, I thought you could never become more beautiful, but I was wrong. You've exceeded perfection."

"And you're still the most handsome, sexy, and desirable gringo boy ever born! I still love you with all my heart, Hound! I always will! I want you to always know and remember that!"

"Carmella, I do, and I will."

Carmella had provided a variety of beverages and hors-d'oeuvres. After their initial greeting of each other, they sat down to partake of them and visit for a while. Hound realized she was burdened and very anxious to have a serious conversation with him.

"Hound, I desperately need to get some things off my chest," she told him. "Will you let me do that? Do you mind?"

"Of course not. Talk to me about anything you wish. Why would I mind?"

"You just got here. We haven't seen each other in a long time. I didn't want to begin our visit in a way that would disappoint you. I want you to be glad you came to see me. I don't want you to feel I'm trying to make my problems yours. I don't want you to feel sorry for me. I don't want you to feel obligated to or responsible for me."

"Carmella, tell me what's on your mind."

"Hound, I truly believe you once loved me, that we could someday, somehow be together, and then I really fucked up! I was nothing short of crazy when I got involved with that God-dammed prostitution! When I did, I lost your love and your respect! Thank God, I didn't lose your friendship! I need to know if it's possible to win back your love and respect. Can you ever forgive and forget what I did? Please tell me the truth. Can I earn a second chance?"

"Carmella, everybody on the face of the Earth has made a mistake at one time or another? Shit! I know I have! If there was any need for me to forgive you, then I would have judged you. I don't have the right to judge you or anyone else. There's no need for me to forgive you, because there's nothing to forgive as far as I'm concerned."

"Oh, Hound! I wish I'd never met Roberto! I should never have let him into my life. That's made the distance between us even greater! I gave up and stopped fighting for us much too soon. At least that's what I've come to believe! God damn it, Hound! I've waited a long time for a chance to meet face-to-face and tell you these things!"

Carmella was growing more excited and anxious. Hound knew she was suffering emotional pain. He also knew she was sincere regarding what she was saying.

"Carmella, I want you to relax, settle down, and listen very carefully to what I say," Hound said tenderly. "You've never lost the love I've always felt for you. You prostituted yourself for money. I prostituted myself for money, and other things as well. I realize that now. You're married to someone who likely loves you very much, but you don't feel the same way about him. You married Roberto because you got in too deep with him with no way to refuse what he wanted. I've come to realize my relationship with Jo may be much the same. I'm not ready to marry anyone, but situations and circumstances have presented me no other choice. I'll marry her shortly after I return home."

Carmella seemed to be somewhat calmed by Hound's confession. He was a bit surprised.

"Now that we've cleared all that shit up," Hound said, smiling, "I'm hungry! These hors-d'oeuvres are OK, but I need some real food. Where can we get something to eat around here?"

"They're keeping everything warm and ready for us in the hotel kitchen. As soon as I call room service, our food will be delivered to the suite. I took the liberty of ordering steak and lobster for two, along with wine that will complement both."

"Carmella, that sounds great. You ordered my favorites. You remembered."

"There's nothing about you that I don't remember. I cherish every memory of you, every moment we ever spent together. Hound, why did you wait so long, until now, to tell me those things?"

"I took time to do a lot of thinking and soul-searching while I was in Vietnam. I made myself a promise regarding what I'd say when I saw you again."

As they enjoyed a delicious dinner, Carmella wanted to ask Hound many questions about his tour of duty in Vietnam. She quickly realized it wasn't a topic he wanted to discuss.

"It really must have been terrible for you there, sweetheart," Carmella told him tenderly.

"I suppose so, but certainly not as terrible as it was for many others."

"I'm so thankful to God that you made it back safely and you're here with me now."

"I'm not sure God had anything to do with it. I saw no evidence of his presence anywhere over there. South Vietnam was a God-forsaken piece of real estate."

For a long time after they finished their meal, Hound and Carmella sipped wine and conversed on many topics. It was getting very late in the afternoon when he asked what time she needed to be back at her home.

"There's no specific time, day or night, that I have to be home during the time Roberto is away," she replied.

"Doesn't he call you by phone?"

"No, never."

"That seems odd. Why not?"

"He doesn't want any evidence available that would prove where he was during his time away. Phone records would provide that type of evidence. He doesn't allow me to know the places where he goes. All he tells me is when to expect his return."

"Does he ever come home sooner than he tells you he will?"

"No. He never returns earlier, or later, than 15 minutes of the time he tells me."

"Carmella, how does it feel to be married to a cartel boss?"

"I must admit his profession allows me to live a most luxurious life. I enjoy the best of everything."

"What time are you going home?"

"I plan to spend the night here. I hope you'll do the same."

This was the first time since Hound arrived that Carmella had even slightly indicated a desire for him sexually. He concluded the desire was there, but her desire to talk and unburden herself was priority.

"Carmella, don't you think it a large risk to stay away from home all night, in a hotel suite with me?" Hound asked. "What would Roberto do if he found out? Are you sure you're willing to take that risk?

"I'm certain he'd be greatly offended. He'd punish me severely. However, you should know and understand he'd punish you worse. Are you willing to take that risk?"

"Well, yes, I suppose I am."

"Well, then so am I. I'm certain Roberto fucks other women. Even though he likely cares a great deal for me, I'm also simply a trophy for him to display when such is needed."

"You're his wife, extremely beautiful and desirable. Why would he ever present you simply as his trophy?"

"I've always felt that way. Had I not been blessed with exceptionally attractive and desirable physical features, he'd never have wanted to marry a former whore."

"So, Roberta knows about that part of your history?"

"Yes, I told him shortly after we met."

"Why did you feel it necessary to tell him?"

"He's the kind of man that would want to know such things. Besides, I knew he'd check me out. I was well-aware he knew the right people and had the resources to find out anything he wanted about me."

"Well, Carmella, then don't you think it reasonable he'd keep an eye on you while he's away?"

"I have two bodyguards who used to report my every movement to Roberto when he wasn't with me, but for just a short time now, I haven't had to worry about that."

"Why not?"

Carmella was hesitant to answer Hound's question but had decided long ago to always be completely honest with him.

"Hound, it was very important that I be able to spend time with you whenever the opportunity presented itself," Carmella began. "To remove the bodyguards as obstacles preventing my freedom to do that, I seduced each of them separately and discreetly over a period of time. Neither of them knew I was seducing both of them. Each thought I was only interested in him. As fearful to do so as they both were, I eventually was able to fuck each of them in the master bedroom of my home, where Roberto and I sleep. I secretly placed a hidden camera in the bedroom. I recorded audio and video of everything. Now, both bodyguards, not wanting their cock and balls cut off and shoved up their ass, will always deliver positive reports about me to Roberto. Hound, please don't be upset regarding what I just told you! I only did what was absolutely necessary! I had no choice. There was no other way available to me."

"Naturally, I wish there had been some other way, but I'm not upset with you. Not at all. I understand completely. Perhaps someday you'll decide to divorce Roberto. Even though you have everything money can buy, you also seem very unhappy with the world he's put you in. Carmella, you're smart enough to have your own business and become very financially secure without Roberto."

"Hound, where would I get the money to start such a business? Certainly not from Roberto. Besides, he'd never allow me to divorce him. The only way I could ever be free of him was if he were to die."

"Well, Carmella, there's a solution to every problem. It may not be easy to find or carry out, but one is always there. If you truly want Roberto out of your life, then I'm sure you don't have to wait until he dies. I'd be willing to loan you all the money needed to get started and live on until your business started turning a profit."

"If I were ever to leave Roberto, then it would have to be his idea. He'd punish me if I left without his permission. He might even kill me."

"Is he fucking insane?"

"When it comes to hurting his pride and ego, I suppose he is. Hound, do you remember my dream of someday becoming a partner in business with you?"

"Yes, I do, but I'm not talking about a partnership. You should be the owner and CEO of your own company. You should be free to make all the decisions."

"You never wanted me as a partner, did you?"

"No, but it had nothing to do with you. I was never interested in partnership with anyone."

"Do you honestly think there's a way to get Roberto out of my life without having to fear his retribution?"

"Yes, I honestly do. Like I said, there's no problem that can't be solved with proper research, planning, and patience. Unfortunately, you've never practiced any of those things. You've always been in too much a hurry to consider what the outcome of your actions could be."

"Hound, I believe you're absolutely right. As long as I've known you, you've always seemed to be right about everything. Will you help me?"

"In any way I can, short of killing Roberto!"

"You know I would never ask, or expect, anything like that from you!"

"Yes, I know."

Carmella finally decided everything had been discussed with Hound she wanted him to know and had waited so long to tell him. She was now interested in spending time with him that was more enjoyable and satisfying. She stood from her chair and walked slowly to Hound, who was already standing. He was dressed in his Army uniform. She again kissed and embraced him tenderly. She began to slowly remove his clothing until he was completely nude. She than began, slowly and seductively, to remove her clothing. Her sexual arousal became intense as she watched him become fully erect. She took him by the hand and slowly led him to the bedroom.

"You're my sweet, darling gringo boy," she said softly. "We're both in need of something that only we can provide to each other."

"Carmella, I really should take a shower first."

"I don't want to wait a minute longer to feel your love and experience your body close to mine again. We can take a shower together later."

Carmella achieved her first orgasm sooner than Hound expected. He was unable to quiet her extremely loud verbal response to the intense pleasure she was experiencing.

"Carmella, you probably need to be a bit quieter," Hound said with a chuckle. "We don't want any of our neighbors calling the front desk to complain about the very loud and vulgar way you express sexual pleasures."

"Don't worry, baby. I read the description of our suite. The rooms are completely soundproof."

Their initial time in bed together that afternoon lasted over an hour. When it ended, both declared their complete sexual satisfaction. It had been nothing less than a sexual rodeo.

"Hound, you're still a sexually superior man!" Carmella said sincerely. "But you're also a son of a bitch for spoiling me. No man except you can provide me with complete satisfaction."

"Well, thank you, Carmella. That's a wonderful compliment, but are you sure you're being completely honest?"

"Fuck you, gringo boy! You know God-damn well I'm being honest! You've known it since the first time you fucked me in the barn so many years ago. Do you remember our first time?"

"Vividly, Carmella. All guys vividly remember their first time. Do you remember another time we were enjoying some fun in the barn and Hunter started howling in response to sounds you were making during your orgasm?"

Carmella began to laugh uncontrollably. "Hound, over the years, I've often thought about what Hunter did that day," she said. "You really loved that old hound, didn't you?"

"I still love him. I miss him a lot. I guess I always will. He was a very special kind of friend."

"Are you ready for that shower now, gringo boy?"

"Absolutely. Then let's go back to bed, cuddle up, and sleep until we wake up."

"You won't get any argument from me."

When Hound and Carmella woke from their nap, it was almost

9 p.m. They ordered dinner from room service. After dinner, they had sex until well after midnight and then once again fell asleep in each other's arms. It was almost noon when they finally got out of bed.

They ordered coffee from room service and decided to have lunch at a restaurant about six blocks from the hotel. Hound put on his dress uniform for his visit with Carolyn Hughes later that afternoon. He left the hotel several minutes ahead of Carmella. He walked to the restaurant and sat down at a table to wait for her arrival. The restaurant was a medium-size establishment, nice, but not fancy. Many local businessmen and women were patrons in the restaurant when he arrived.

It was a little after 1 p.m. when Carmella entered the restaurant. She located where Hound was seated and began walking to join him. The restaurant was still serving lunch to numerous customers. From the time she first entered the restaurant, Carmella received glances from those customers on a consistent basis. Both men and women alike were impressed by her beauty. Hound received equal attention and admiration. He was indeed a most handsome young man. His appearance was further enhanced by the uniform he wore. When Carmella reached his table, she greeted Hound with a kiss. This convinced everyone they were a couple, very much romantically involved. They both ordered the same thing from the menu. It had been highly recommended by their waitress.

"Well my sweet gringo boy," Carmella said, sipping from a glass of iced tea. "Where do we go from here? What's next for us?"

"Carmella, I guess from now on we will both have to be satisfied with simply living our lives from day to day. We have both complicated our lives to such a degree we have no other choice, at least until such time those complications might be eliminated."

"Do you think they will ever be eliminated?"

"Live life one day at a time. Anything is possible, but it will take time. Perhaps a great deal of time."

"Hound, do you remember promising me we could live together for a year after your return from Vietnam? I wanted that year to prove to you we were meant to be together. I was absolutely sure I could prove that to you. Did you ever intend to keep that promise?"

When he made the promise, Hound knew he would likely not be able to keep it even if he had wanted to. Perhaps for a few reasons he did want to keep the promise. Now, Carmella's marriage to Roberto offered him the opportunity to avoid answering the question truthfully without telling her an outright lie.

"Carmella, I have never broken a promise," Hound replied. "Unfortunately, it was broken for me when you married Roberto."

"I only married him when I found out you were engaged to Jo!"

"I only agreed to marry Jo when you told me you had married Roberto. It's true that I had considered it, but while in Vietnam I decided to honor my promise to you. Had I known of your plan to marry Roberto and why, then I would have made every effort to inform you of my intention to keep the promise."

"OK, but now you are definitely going to marry her. Right?"

"Yes, that's right."

"You should marry her only if you're deeply in love. I don't think you are. Are you?"

"No, honestly I'm not, but I do have special feelings for her."

"Hound, if you are not deeply in love, then why get married?"

"Carmella, last October in Vietnam I beat and severely injured a superior officer. He almost died. I was charged with attempted murder and incarcerated at a detention facility in Saigon. I was to face a court-martial the first week of December. The probable outcome of that court-martial would've been a dishonorable discharge from the Army and several years in prison. Jo's father evidently has connections with some very powerful and influential people in Washington, D.C. I don't know who those people are, but I do know they're responsible for getting the charge of attempted murder dropped along with my early, honorable discharge."

"Are you marrying Jo as a kind of payment for the help you received?"

"Yes, I suppose so."

"Hound, if you're not in love with Jo, then please don't marry her!"

"Were you in love with Roberto when you married him?"

"Surely you must know by now I wasn't!"

"So, you married him because you felt obligated? Like you had no choice."

"Like I told you, he isn't a man to take no for an answer. He could be dangerous if he didn't get what he wanted."

"I rest my case. He and Jo seem to have that in common."

"Hound, I've never known you to be afraid of anything. Are you saying you're afraid of Jo?"

"Yes, I guess I am."

Carmella was right. Hound had never been afraid of anything or anyone, but he decided to lie in order to better justify his intention to get married. He knew he had no fear of Jo or her father. However, he did have great respect for them. He also had a great sense of responsibility and obligation to pay his debts. It was because of that respect, responsibility, and obligation that he'd keep his commitment to Jo and marry her.

"Besides, I feel certain you'll remain married to Roberto," Hound told Carmella. "You'll never be free of him, will you?"

"Hound, I have to stay with him. I've already told you that, and why. He's too powerful and dangerous to do otherwise, especially after all he's done for me."

"Carmella, it seems our lives are currently being controlled by a similar set of circumstances. Would you agree?"

"Yes, Hound. As much as I hate to, I have to agree. We've both managed to really fuck up our lives! Do you really think it's possible to someday get our lives back on track?"

"Day by day, Carmella. Live life day by day. Make the most of what you have today and use it wisely to make tomorrow better."

"Hound, what time are you leaving tomorrow?"

"I have reservations on a direct flight to New Orleans that leaves at noon."

"When can we see each other again?"

"It may be possible on a random basis for us to get together a day or two when Roberto is away. However, I don't want to be seen together around the San Francisco and Oakland area. To do so would greatly increase the chance of Roberto finding out. You may be safe regarding your bodyguards, but other people who know you and Roberto also present a risk. During the time Roberto is away, does he ever visit Las Vegas or Reno?"

"No. He's most often out of the country, usually Mexico or Colombia. On infrequent occasions, he does visit Las Vegas, but he always takes me with him. Why do you ask?"

"I plan to gamble in Reno, Vegas, or possibly both for a few days each month beginning in January. I could plan my trips during the time of the month Roberto is away. You could catch your flight and meet me wherever I am."

"Oh, hell yes! I'd love to do that, but there's a problem. Roberto provides me with a very generous allowance to spend any way I choose. However, he always verifies everything I spend it on. I could never purchase airline tickets to Reno, Vegas, or anywhere else."

"That won't be a problem, Carmella. I'll always be able to take care of your airfare. Naturally, I'll take care of all expenses while we're there. I suppose you'll need me to reimburse the money for our suite?"

"No, sweetie. I've been saving a little bit for quite some time so I could pay for our suite. Roberto will never notice."

"Are you and Roberto known by many people in Vegas or Reno? You know that could be a problem."

"Only a small few."

"How safe is it for us to be together there?"

"Extremely safe. I know how to avoid being seen by any of

them. I know where they all hang out and the places they never go."

When they left the restaurant, Carmella drove to her home where she would remain until it was time to once again meet Hound at the hotel that evening. Hound took a taxi to his scheduled visit with the wife and daughter of General Hughes.

Carolyn Hughes was an attractive, intelligent, and most delightful lady. General Hughes had told her absolutely everything about Hound, setting the stage for a more informal, comfortable initial meeting. Rebecca Hughes was a 21-year-old senior at Berkeley majoring in mathematics with a minor in political science. She was 5 foot 9 inches tall, with shoulder-length, curly blonde hair, blue eyes, and a very attractive figure.

Hound's first impression of her was that she was bold, beautiful, and intelligent. Rebecca was immediately attracted to Hound's striking good looks and physique. She knew he was extremely intelligent. Her father had made mention of that in his letter. She created the opportunity to let Hound know her attraction to him before the visit concluded.

Rebecca was also aware of his engagement and pending marriage. General Hughes had reported that in a recent phone call. Rebecca's behavior toward Hound showed no concern over his engagement. Afterall, he wasn't married yet. Mrs. Hughes was somewhat embarrassed by her daughter's forward behavior and made polite and subtle innuendos to deter it. However, she supported Rebecca's insistence to personally drive Hound to the destination of his choice after the visit concluded.

Rebecca took Hound's arm and escorted him to her new 1970 Corvette parked in the four-car garage.

"Where would you like to go, handsome?" Rebecca asked flirtatiously.

Hound told her the name and address of the hotel.

"Wow! You're staying at the finest hotel anywhere in the area," she said.

"That's what I've been told. My suite is certainly elegant."

"Who recommended the hotel to you?"

"A friend who lives in the area."

"Would your friend happen to be a female?"

"Maybe. Why do you ask?"

"I'm naturally a curious person. Is she staying in the hotel with you?"

"That's a bit personal, don't you think? Why do you ask?"

"If you're staying with a woman and she's not your fiancée, then that proves what I think about you is true."

"Miss Hughes, you don't know me well enough to think anything about me. You shouldn't be the least bit interested in my private life. Why are you?"

"I don't believe you're ready to get married. I certainly don't believe you're in love. OK, Hound, I can see that you're certainly not immature, or naïve. I know you're extremely intelligent. You're also extraordinarily handsome. You're likely the most desirable man I've ever met. You have the looks and charm to sleep with any single woman, and very likely any married woman you'd desire. That would certainly not contribute to a guy your age wanting to be tied down in a marriage. Therefore, I think other things are motivating you. That being the case, I think you won't be a faithful husband, at least not very long. That would cause you, and certainly the woman you're going to marry, heartache that neither of you want or deserve. By the way, call me Rebecca, not Miss Hughes."

"Well, Rebecca! You're really something! But, for some reason I like you. However, I'll be damned if I'm sure I know why! You're definitely nosy, intrusive, and forward, but I'd also have to say perceptive, intelligent, and without a doubt very beautiful. I too have good instinct and perception. I believe you're intrusive and forward for reasons other than your concern for me and my fiancée. What has really motivated all the behavior you've displayed toward me? I feel your purpose is to manipulate me for some reason."

"What reason could I possibly have for wanting to manipulate you? Manipulate you to do what?"

"I think you play games to win trophies. After each trophy is won, you look for the next appealing challenge, and then you again play your game to conquer the challenge and claim the next trophy. I don't play such games. I have no need of trophies. My ego and self-esteem don't require such and my character would never permit it. Besides, I've never experienced sexual frustration."

"What does sexual frustration have to do with anything you're talking about? What the hell are you saying to me? I don't understand what you're saying regarding manipulation, games, trophies, and sexual frustration. Perhaps you could provide me with some clarification?"

"I think you search for men you're attracted to. You play a game of seduction and take them to bed. When they're unable to satisfy you sexually, you simply consider them a conquest and regard them as a trophy. That's your way of compensating for not being able to reach orgasm. If you wanted to fuck me in hopes I might be the one to end your constant sexual frustration, then you should've been honest regarding your wants and needs. If you would have simply asked, then I would have been pleased to help you discover the total number of orgasms you can achieve. Unfortunately, you've deprived yourself of that. You perceived me as a possible trophy rather than the man who could definitely end your frustration and provide you with what you so desperately want and need. The game you play is insulting to a man like me. Especially when I know what I'm capable of sexually."

Rebecca was greatly shocked, surprised, and became extremely angered by what Hound had said.

"Hound! You're an arrogant, pompous, crass, rude, and insulting son of a bitch!" Rebecca screamed.

"Rebecca, you forgot to include extraordinarily handsome, honest, absolutely correct in my perception of you, and very well-endowed sexually. Never mind the endowment. You have no way of knowing how big my cock is."

Rebecca took her eyes off the road for a moment to respond and offer Hound a nasty look. She gasped when she saw the much longer and wider girthed than average penis he'd removed from his trousers and caused to become fully erect. She returned her attention and focus to driving when the car veered off the road onto the right shoulder and the sound of tires rolling over gravel began. Both Hound and Rebecca remained silent as she continued to drive.

Rebecca at first decided to stop the car and put Hound out on the side of the road. After further consideration, she decided to drive on and deliver him to the hotel. When they arrived at the hotel, she pulled into the side parking lot and parked the car in a vacant space. Hound could see her anger had subsided. A calm demeanor and sincere, intentional desire to be respectful and courteous had replaced it.

"Hound, will you be making another trip here sometime?" Rebecca asked in a soft, calm voice.

"I suppose it's possible, but unlikely. Why?"

"Hound, I feel like I owe you an apology. I believe we got off on the wrong foot and it's my fault. If you'll accept my apology and give me another chance, perhaps we can start over on a more positive note. If we could, then I believe the worst thing that could result would be a genuine and honest friendship. I truly hate to admit it, but I believe you might be right regarding the things you said about me. I know you're right about some of them."

Hound smiled and accepted her apology. He also accepted her phone number she wrote on a small piece of paper and offered to him. He told Rebecca goodbye, thanked her for the ride, got out of the car, and began walking away.

"Hey, Hound!" Rebecca shouted when he'd walked only a short distance. "Is your sexual performance really as good as you say?"

"Absolutely, Rebecca! Satisfaction is guaranteed! Would you like me to honor my guarantee sometime in the future?"

"Indeed, I would, Hound! Absolutely! Hey, don't you feel I'm also deserving an apology? Wouldn't you agree some of the things you said, and especially did, weren't those of a gentleman?"

"Rebecca, you gave me your phone number and the invitation to enjoy you sexually at the earliest possible time. There's no way in hell I'd ever apologize for making that happen."

Rebecca laughed loudly at Hound's response and then drove away. She laughed again at random times during the drive back to her home. In the short time she had known him, Hound managed to leave a lasting impression on her. A very positive impression. She'd never met anyone like him before. She wanted to see him again as soon as possible. She hoped he'd want that too. She'd never believed in it before, but she wondered if it had been love at first sight when she met him.

As soon as he was back in the hotel suite, Hound showered and dressed in casual civilian clothes. Carmella arrived an hour later. They would again enjoy a nice dinner provided by room service. It would be there last time together for possibly several weeks. After satisfying their sexual desires, later that evening, Carmella lay snuggled in his arms.

"How was your visit with the Hughes family?" Carmella asked.

"Surprisingly interesting and rewarding."

"So, you're glad you went? It was everything you hoped it'd be?"

"It was a bit more interesting than I anticipated."

Carmella and Hound bid each other goodbye the next morning at 10:30 a.m. Carmella departed the hotel first and drove home. A taxi was waiting in front of the hotel to drive Hound to the airport. When he arrived at the passenger area where he'd wait to board his flight to New Orleans a half hour later, an unexpected visitor was waiting for him.

"Rebecca, what in the world are you doing here?" Hound asked, surprised to see her.

"I just wanted to see you again before you left. Do you mind?"

"I suppose not, but how did you know what time to be here?"

"I checked the schedules of all direct flights to New Orleans. There was only one. I hoped you'd arrive early enough for us to visit awhile before you left. I wish you'd showed up sooner. I've been here for over an hour."

"Well, Rebecca, I'm very flattered by your gesture."

"Would you be more flattered if I asked you to stay one more day? You could change your ticket and leave on the noon flight tomorrow if you wanted to."

"I guess I could, but why should I? Why would I want to?"

"The simple truth is I'd love to spend more time with you. My mother has gone to Los Angeles to visit a friend and won't be home until tomorrow evening. We'd have the whole house to ourselves. I'd prepare a very nice dinner for us. It might surprise you, but I'm an excellent cook. Hound, we both know it's very likely I'll never see you again. I just want to spend as much time as possible with you. I know you're engaged to be married, but I want you to know, and please believe that my invitation isn't because I see you as a challenge or trophy. Today I'm simply a young woman asking a special young man, while he's still single, to spend some time with me. Time that I desperately want and need."

Hound knew Jo had no idea when he'd arrive in New Orleans. He also knew he needed to call her as she would be expecting to hear from him by now. He called and informed her he'd be arriving in New Orleans the following evening. Although Jo sounded happy and relieved to finally hear from him, Hound could tell from the sound of her voice something was wrong.

"Jo, is everything all right?" Hound asked. "You don't sound like yourself. Are you ill?"

"I guess I'm a little under the weather, sweetheart, but I'm all right. I'm relieved you finally called. I was beginning to get worried about you. Are you all right?"

"I'm fine, Jo. I couldn't be better."

"Where are you, sweetheart?"

"I'm in San Francisco. At the airport. I just arrived."

"If you're in San Francisco, then how come you won't be home until tomorrow?"

"I have an appointment to meet with the wife and daughter of General Charles Hughes this evening. I promised him I'd call on them for a visit."

"Well, sweetheart, you're certainly obligated to keep your promise to the general. I'm well-aware of how fond he is of you. After waiting so long already, I guess I can wait one more day to see you."

Hound didn't press the issue with Jo, but he knew something other than being under the weather was wrong with her. He felt that if she wanted him to know exactly what, then she would've told him.

Hound had no trouble exchanging his airline ticket for one the next day. Rebecca was delighted with his decision to accept her invitation to be a most welcome guest at her home. While walking from the airport terminal to her car, Hound and Rebecca engaged in casual conversation regarding a variety of topics. As soon as they left the passenger waiting area, Rebecca took Hound's hand and held it gently as they walked. She didn't release it until they reached her car.

They'd been standing in the large living room of her home for a short time when Rebecca inquired if Hound was hungry.

"No, Rebecca," Hound replied. "I ate a late breakfast. Are you hungry?"

"Not at all. May I give you a tour of my home?"

"Take me to your bedroom, Rebecca. I'd very much like to enjoy you sexually." Rebecca knew Hound was very aware she wanted to be sexually intimate, but she found herself blushing. Neither of them spoke as she led Hound up the staircase and then down the hall to her bedroom. They entered and she shut the door behind them.

Hound removed all his clothing as Rebecca sat silently on

the edge of her bed watching. He moved slowly to her and began removing her clothing. As he did, she began to tremble.

"If you're having second thoughts, then we don't have to do this," Hound said to her softly.

"I'm not having second thoughts. I'm just concerned you might be disappointed. I've never been with a man as well-endowed physically as you are. The size of your cock may be too much for me to accommodate."

"I'm larger than average, but not too large. If you're concerned about me hurting you, then don't be. I'll provide you with only pleasure. Never pain."

Hound was sincere and convincing. Rebecca immediately felt more comfortable. She began to relax. Hound positioned her on the bed and began providing all the things he knew she'd enjoy. When she achieved her first orgasm, her verbal and physical reactions were indicative of a most intense feeling of sexual ecstasy. The duration of her orgasm was longer than Hound had ever seen a woman experience.

Only a brief period of time passed after the first orgasm ended and before the second began. The time between orgasms began to lengthen after the third, but neither the intensity of pleasure nor her response to it changed during the nine she achieved before becoming too exhausted to continue.

She soon fell fast asleep while holding Hound tenderly and she lay quietly beside him in his arms. He soon joined her in sleep. He was far from exhausted but completely satisfied. Two hours later, he was awakened by Rebecca as she began performing oral sex on him. He quickly became fully erect.

"Would you mind if I enjoyed your body again?" she asked softly, showing eager anticipation.

"Rebecca, you can enjoy me as much as you want, for as long as you want."

Rebecca was far beyond the point of absolute satisfaction when she finally decided to stop enjoying what Hound was providing. She once again lay beside him, positioned herself in his arms, and fell fast asleep.

It was a little after 6 p.m. that evening when Rebecca awakened. When she discovered Hound wasn't beside her, she went to search for him. She found him sitting in the dining room sipping a cup of hot coffee he'd made for himself. When he looked at her, she smiled.

"Hound, why did you let me sleep so long?" she asked, somewhat embarrassed. "I should've started preparing our dinner an hour ago."

"After all the energy you exerted this afternoon, I knew you needed the rest. I thought we might go out for dinner."

"That sounds fine, but only if you let me pay. It's the least I can do after failing to prepare the dinner I promised you. Hound, I can't find the words to tell you how wonderful I feel."

"May I assume the sex was to your liking, and satisfying?"

"Oh, my God! Surely you know the answer to that! I enjoyed it immensely! Satisfying doesn't begin to describe it! You were correct in believing I'd never had an orgasm. You're right about everything."

"Well, Rebecca, you beautiful, sweet, young lady. I think you did a damn good job of catching up. What do you think?"

"I sure tried, didn't I?"

"You sure as hell did, but I enjoyed every minute of it."

"I always thought there was something wrong with me. Now I know it was just the men I was with. I have you to thank for that. You're definitely some kind of man! All man! As good as the best and better than the rest! It wouldn't surprise me if you were the best of the best! I sincerely mean that."

"I believe you do. That's quite a compliment. I greatly appreciate it."

Rebecca took Hound to a small but very nice Italian restaurant for dinner that night. They enjoyed sex one more time after they returned home before sleeping through the night. Rebecca drove

Hound to the airport the next day. She allowed him privacy while he called Jo to inform her of the time he'd be arriving in New Orleans. She gave him a passionate goodbye kiss and watched him board his flight and take off. She watched his plane until it was out of sight, hoping she would somehow, somewhere, someday, sooner than later, see him again.

2

Jo was excited and happy about Hound's homecoming. When his phone call to her ended, she quickly relayed the news to her parents. She then placed a phone call to Hound's parents, who wasted no time in beginning their trip to New Orleans. They wouldn't arrive in time to meet Hound at the airport but would arrive at the O'Malley estate as soon as possible to welcome their son home.

Jo had talked with John and Linda by phone on a regular basis but hadn't visited with them in person since Thanksgiving Day when they had dinner with her and her family at the O'Malley estate. When she'd completed delivering the good news to John and Linda, Jo began to sob intensely. This was a result of mixed emotions she was experiencing over Hound's return. She was overjoyed that he'd soon be safely home again. However, she'd been suffering from almost unbearable episodes of depression and anxiety.

The onset of her symptoms had occurred three days prior when a visit with her personal physician confirmed she was approximately six weeks pregnant. Both her mother and father were aware of her condition and situation. Jo hadn't been with Hound sexually since they were together in Hawaii during his R&R leave last June. She'd very soon come face-to-face with the man she truly loved with all her heart, body, and soul. A man who was returning to her after going through a special kind of hell and surviving. Her thoughts raced as she considered what the answer might be to several very important questions.

How would she be able to tell Hound what had happened? She could only imagine how it would hurt him. Did he love her enough to forgive her? Did she deserve his forgiveness? Even if he did forgive her, would he still love her the same? What if he couldn't love her and all? What if he left and she never saw him again?

Jo was engaged in personal emotional battle of paramount proportion. Ken and Sandra O'Malley knew and understood how she felt. Her father exerted all possible effort to support her and lessen her burden any way he could. They sat together in the den on the day Hound was returning home and discussed Jo's situation.

"Oh, Dad! What am I going to do?" Jo asked as she began to cry. "The love of my life will be coming home to me later today! How can I face him and tell him what's happened? I can't bear to think how he'll feel, or what he'll do!"

"Honey, what happened wasn't your fault. You never intended for anything like this to happen. When you explain everything to Hound, I'm certain he'll be understanding. Naturally, he'll be hurt, but he'll understand. He's extremely intelligent and very strong emotionally. I think you'll be amazed how much understanding you receive from him and how quickly it's offered. The emotional wounds he receives will heal over time. Because he's strong emotionally, that time should be minimal."

"I should get an abortion and never tell him!

"Jo, we've talked about that. We're of the Catholic faith. Abortion could never be an option. You have no choice but to tell

Hound the truth about what happened. Besides, your character and conscience would never allow you to deceive him. He knows how much you love him. He also knows how much you and I have done to pull his ass out of the fire. If he hadn't had your love, he would've never received the help he desperately needed during specific, crucial times of crisis in his life. He owes both of us a great debt. Supporting and being there for you during your critical time of need may be required of him as at least partial payment of that debt."

"Dad, I could never require or expect Hound to stay with me if his love for me was lost. I didn't ask you to help him because I wanted him to owe a debt to me or you. I wanted him to be safe and happy because I love him with every ounce of love within me that I have to offer a man. If he chooses to forgive me and stay with me, then I want it to be because he loves me in an equal way."

"So, if he chooses not to marry you and walks out of your life forever, you're willing to let him go without using anything and everything in your power to stop him?"

"Yes, Dad. I wouldn't want you to try stopping him either. Promise me you won't."

"Jo, I'm not sure I can promise you that. Even if I did, I'm not sure I could keep the promise."

"I need you to promise! I need you to promise and swear before God you'll keep the promise! Please, Dad, promise me!"

"All right, sweetheart. I promise! You shouldn't be getting so upset. You're going to make yourself sicker than you are. Calm down. I'm sure everything will work out fine. The son of a bitch that took advantage of you and put you in this hell needs to pay for what he's done. Why won't you tell me who he is?"

"Because I know what you'd probably do to him. I don't want that. If I decide he should be punished, then it will be my hand, not yours, that punishes him."

Jo's problem was created about six weeks prior to the conversation she was having with her father in the den early on that afternoon Hound was finally coming home. She had insisted on traveling with her father to Washington, D.C. The purpose of the trip was to assist Hound in escaping consequences likely to be imposed by his court-martial. Her father didn't need her assistance, but she felt compelled to meet with the powers that be and participate with her father regarding the advocacy on Hound's behalf. She and her father attended a very discreet dinner with the senator from Louisiana, another senator, and a congressman who had intervened to help Hound in the past.

Unfortunately, Jo was permitted to participate in only a portion of the meeting. She wasn't allowed to hear the particulars of how Hound's problem would be resolved. A short time after everyone had finished their meal, Jo was asked politely by her father to excuse herself and return to the hotel where they were staying. The hotel was only a short walking distance away from the restaurant. Naturally, Jo wanted to know everything regarding the plan to assist Hound, but she fully understood the reluctance of her father and the three powerful politicians to allow her to have that information.

Jo's consumption of alcoholic beverages had always been on a very infrequent basis. When she did drink, it was always small in volume. That night at the restaurant, she exceeded her limit. Had she been less anxious and stressed over Hound's situation, then she would've never consumed more than one cocktail. She'd become too inebriated to walk. The Louisiana senator provided his car and driver to deliver her to the hotel.

Jo entered the large lobby of the hotel and began walking toward the elevators. Her walk took her past the entrance to the hotel's small night club. A popular local band was playing inside. She recognized the current song being played as one greatly favored by she and Hound. She entered the club, walked to the long bar, and took a seat on the only bar chair that was vacant. She'd just finished her second vodka martini when an older gentleman seated next to her, with whom she had made casual conversation, paid his bar bill and left. A tall, dark, well-dressed and very handsome 31-year-old man quickly took over occupancy of the vacant chair.

"Hello, miss," the man said to Jo. "My name is Steve Cooper. If it's not too forward of me, may I ask your name?"

Jo turned to look at the man speaking to her. She was astonished by what she saw. Although Steve wasn't as handsome as her true love, his height, physical build, and mannerisms greatly reminded her of Hound.

"I'm Jo," she replied in a somewhat slurred speech. "It's nice to meet you, Steve."

"It's nice to meet you as well, Jo. I'd bet Jo is short for Joanne."

"Good guess, Steve. I bet Steve is short for Steven."

"Nope. I'm just a Steve. Jo, I've been coming here for a long time. This is the first time I've seen you here."

"Well, Steve, this is my first time to come here. This is my first time in D.C."

"What brings you here? Business or pleasure?"

"My father is here on business. It seems I just came along for the ride."

"Can I buy you a drink?"

"I think I've had enough to drink tonight, but thanks anyway."

"Come on, Jo. I hate to drink alone. Have just one more with me."

"Well. OK, but just one, and then I have to go to my room and get some sleep. We have to be at the airport early in the morning to fly home."

"It's good you're staying at the hotel. You shouldn't be driving."

"No shit, Steve! I'm having a hard time walking! I apologize for my language. I've had a bit too much to drink. You've probably noticed that. I don't usually drink a lot. Unfortunately, I've had a rough day and needed to relax a bit. Actually, my days have been rough for many months. I guess today was just my breaking point."

"Do your rough days have anything to do with a bad marriage?"

"I'm not married, but my fiancé has been in Vietnam for several months. That's the reason for my bad days."

"What branch of service is he in?"

"He's a captain in the United States Army."

"I guess it can be tough being engaged to a career Army officer. It won't get any easier once you're married."

"He's not a career officer. He only has a two-year hitch. It's my sincere hope he'll be discharged and come home in January."

"It's unusual as hell to hold the rank of captain and have only a two-year military service obligation. How did that happen?"

"My fiancé is a very unusual man. Steve, I really don't care to talk about this anymore. To do so would only upset me more than I already am."

"I understand, Jo. Let's talk about something else. What would you like to talk about?"

Jo and Steve talked for about an hour longer. During that time, she consumed more martinis. Steve learned what her profession was at LSU. She discovered he was a special agent with the FBI assigned to the D.C. office. He showed her his identification to prove it. When she absolutely refused to have just one more drink with him and tried to get up and walk to her room, she was unable to do so without assistance. Steve almost had to carry her as he escorted her to her room. He opened the door with the key she provided. The room began to spin as he sat her on the side of the bed. She passed out for a moment. When she came to a short time later, she was in the bed, completely nude, lying on her back. Steve was also nude and had just moved atop her.

He used his legs to push hers apart. She was able to realize what was happening. She began an attempt to say no and resist as best she could as he pushed his penis inside her. As she continued to try verbalizing her non-consent for what was happening, he began to increase the intensity of his thrusts. He knew she was doing all in her power to physically and verbally resist what was happening. He simply didn't give a damn. He wasn't going to stop doing what he knew was nothing less than rape. He continued the act for a long time after Jo once again passed out. When he'd indulged himself as much as he wanted, instead of leaving, he rolled off her and fell asleep.

When the hotel wake-up call Jo had requested began to ring at 7 a.m. the next morning, she opened her eyes for the first time since she'd passed out the final time. It quickly came to her mind what had happened the night before. The shame she felt seemed unbearable. Steve had spent the entire night with her. However, he needed to be at work early that morning. Naturally, he'd decided not to wake Jo and say goodbye, or anything else, before he left. He did, however, leave a business card where Jo was sure to find it. On the back of the card, he'd written a short message indicating he'd be more than delighted to come visit her in Louisiana if she was interested in seeing him again. He ended the message by thanking her for a most enjoyable and exciting time, and he hoped she'd be as excited to see him again as he was to see her.

Jo began to sob intensely. She became nauseated and rushed to the bathroom to vomit. She had been raped but felt certain there was nothing legally she could do about it. She decided to do nothing. She would say nothing about it to anyone. Her parents would be the first to learn of it, but only after she confirmed her pregnancy. She wouldn't tell anyone else unless it was absolutely necessary.

Hound would be arriving in New Orleans within an hour. Jo couldn't compose herself and continued sobbing intensely.

"Oh, my God, Dad, I can't go to the airport and meet Hound in my condition," she told her father. "What can I ever say or do that will allow Hound to get past what has happened? I can't imagine what John and Linda will think when they find out."

"Don't concern yourself with John and Linda at this time. Concern yourself only with Hound."

31

"I should've never stopped using birth control, but with Hound away, there was no need for it. Besides, I wanted to start a family as quickly as possible after he returned home and we were married."

"You and Hound can still have children of your own."

"Maybe, but will he want to? Oh, Dad! My relationship with Hound could never be the same again. How could it be? Even if he had his own children, having to raise a bastard, always being around a child that didn't belong to him would be a constant reminder of what happened. It's going to be a reminder to me as well."

"Hound is adopted. Don't you think that would make him more willing to raise a child that didn't belong to him, especially when the child is part of you? I truly believe what he'll consider the most isn't the fact you became pregnant, but the circumstances by which you became pregnant. Jesus Christ, Jo! You were raped! You didn't become pregnant because of a voluntary and careless act of infidelity! Sweetheart, I know it would break your heart to lose that young man. God damn it! I will never understand why he didn't accept my offer to keep him out of the military. If he had, this would never have happened. In that respect, he's partly to blame."

"Dad, you know that's not true. Hound has no blame in what happened to me. He felt it would be dishonorable to accept help in avoiding the draft while so many other men had no such help and were forced to serve. He felt a responsibility and obligation to do what he thought was right."

"Maybe so, but what about his responsibility and obligation to keep his ass out of trouble? I suppose he felt it would be dishonorable not to almost beat Colonel Westerman to death and be charged with attempted murder by the United States Army. Son of a bitch! If he hadn't gotten himself into that shitload of trouble, then we wouldn't have been in Washington D.C. and you wouldn't have been raped! Jo, don't tell me he has no blame in this! He damn well does!"

"Dad, regardless of the reason we were in D.C., I'm to blame for what happened to me. I shouldn't have drunk as much as I did, but I did. I should've gone straight to my room when I returned to the hotel, but I didn't. I shouldn't have done any of the things that I did after I left you at the restaurant. If I hadn't, then what happened to me would've never happened and we wouldn't be having this conversation. We should leave for the airport now. I don't want Hound to arrive and not be waiting to welcome him home. I suppose I should tell him what's happened as soon as possible. It won't take him long to know something is wrong. He's very perceptive."

"Jo, it might be better to allow him some time to adjust to being home before you tell him. You should certainly wait until John and Linda return home."

"You're right. What's happened will certainly impact them as well. He should be the one to tell them whatever he wants them to know. He needs time to process all this and decide what he's going to do without being influenced by anyone else. My body isn't showing evidence of the pregnancy, so he'll have no idea until I tell him."

Jo was remarkably composed as she stood with her parents at the airport terminal gate when Hound arrived. As soon as she saw him, all thoughts of the pregnancy temporarily left her mind and she rushed to kiss and embrace him. No soldier returning from Vietnam could have experienced a more loving or enthusiastic welcome home than he received from her.

"Oh, my darling Hound," Jo said tenderly. "You can't imagine how happy I am that you've safely returned home to me."

"Angel, you'll never know how happy I am to be here."

"Welcome home, son," Ken said sincerely as he shook Hound's hand and then hugged him. "I'm sure as hell happy to see you again."

"Hound, we all dearly love you and have missed you very much," Sandra told him as she gave him a hug and kissed him on the cheek when it was her turn to welcome him home.

After a short period of time, Ken reminded everyone that John and Linda would soon be arriving at the estate. He suggested they all leave right away so Hound would be there when they arrived.

After everyone had exited the airport terminal and were walking toward the parking lot, Jo once again became overwhelmed by the reality of her situation. She began to sob uncontrollably. Hound became concerned and immediately inquired as to what was wrong. Jo explained her tears were those of joy over having him home again.

Hound sensed she wasn't being truthful but said nothing. He knew her tears were those of extreme emotional distress rather than joy. During the drive to the estate, Jo once again regained her composure. She moved as close as possible to Hound in the back seat of the car. She gently held his hand and laid her head on his shoulder.

"Hound, I love you more than life itself," she told him softly. "I want you to always know and remember that will never change."

"Jo, are you all right?"

"Yes, my darling. I'm fine."

John and Linda were waiting at the estate when Hound arrived. Linda began to cry as she embraced him. John took his turn embracing and welcoming his son home.

"It's good to have you home, son," John told him. "You look well. Are you well?

"I'm fine, Dad. It's wonderful to see you and Mom again."

"You've lost a lot of weight," Linda said.

"I know, about 20 pounds."

Well, I'm not worried about that. I know Jo is a great cook. She'll put that weight back on you in no time."

Hound spent the next couple of hours sitting in the living room and talking with everyone. He wanted to be informed about everything that had happened during his time away. Everyone quickly became aware that he didn't wish to discuss what happened during his tour in Vietnam. They felt he wanted to put everything he experienced over there behind him as soon as he could. No one would ask, but everyone wondered if he'd be able to.

Hound had his own question he wasn't yet ready to ask. He'd wait for the appropriate time to ask Jo what was troubling her. Maybe he wouldn't have to ask. Perhaps Jo was just waiting for an appropriate time to confide in him. He was now certain whatever was upsetting her couldn't be trivial.

Everyone enjoyed a specially prepared dinner that evening.

"Hound, how long will it be before you visit the farm again?" John asked during dinner.

"Jo and I will be returning to Baton Rouge tomorrow. I'll take a couple of days to settle in and then I'll come to visit you."

"The farm hasn't changed much since you left. We've added a few more cattle to the herd, also more hogs. We built the new hay barn and bought a new tractor."

"Jo told me farm profits have been really good."

"This has been the best year ever."

Dinner had almost concluded. Everyone had enjoyed the meal and especially the conversation. Linda found it impossible to control her extreme curiosity regarding what life was like for Hound during his tour in Vietnam.

"Hound, it must've been terrible for you there," Linda said. "I know it must be hard for you to talk about. However, I'm sure you realize how much we all want to know how you've been affected by what you experienced. We all love you very much and want to help. You have all of us to talk with anytime you feel the need."

"Mom, I have absolutely no need or desire to talk about Vietnam. Why do you think I would? I don't want anyone to worry about the effect my experiences have had on me. I assure you I'm quite well, physically and emotionally."

"Hound, I believe your father and I have been informed regarding most if not all the significant events you experienced during your time over there. No human being, not even you, could experience those events and not be affected emotionally, at least to some degree. I'm your mother. Nobody knows you better. I feel, and to a point can see, that you've changed."

"Mom, how do you feel I've changed?"

"Hound, you've always looked older than you were, been more mature physically and emotionally. You're still very handsome, but you look and behave older than ever before. I'm sure you have changed emotionally. I simply sense it. It's my mother's intuition."

"Well, Mom, I've been away for a while. I'm older since you last saw me, so you'd expect to see some changes. Service in any branch of the military naturally increases one's maturity level and changes perceptions of life. I freely admit that serving as a combat field commander accelerated my growth in maturity and change in perception, but I don't believe in a negative way. Personally, I feel I'm better in every way because of my experiences in Vietnam. Even though I'm telling you the truth, I freely admit the majority of those experiences were most unpleasant. That's why I don't care to talk about them now, or ever again. To do so would simply serve no purpose to better me or anyone I discussed them with. I know everyone is curious to know everything that happened in Vietnam. My time there is over. I wish only to put things that happened there behind me. I haven't been emotionally damaged, even though many of my fellow soldiers were. I'll tell you one thing about the war in Vietnam, the United States isn't going to win it. All of the soldiers who died or became disabled over there did so for nothing."

Linda wanted to keep the conversation with Hound regarding Vietnam going, but John took her by the hand under the dining table. He gave it a gentle squeeze, signaling her the conversation was over.

Shortly after dinner, Hound suggested he and Jo take a walk alone together. He felt it was time to find out what was troubling her.

"Jo, I think it's time you told me what's wrong with you," Hound said as they walked holding hands.

"What makes you think something's wrong with me?"

"You know I've always been able to tell when you're upset. What's going on? Tell me. I have a right to know."

"Hound, there's something I need to talk to you about, but I prefer to wait until a more appropriate time."

"Why is now not an appropriate time?"

"Hound, you just got home. I'm extremely happy about that and want to celebrate it. I want only to talk about happy things. Your parents will be leaving tomorrow. We'll talk about this again after they leave."

"We're alone. We can talk now. Obviously, you feel what you have to say will upset me and cause me to upset everyone else."

"Yes, I suppose so. Please allow me the courtesy to tell you tomorrow after your parents have gone."

"All right, Jo, if it's that important to you, then I'll wait until tomorrow."

Hound was now certain he wouldn't be happy to hear what Jo needed to tell him. Whatever it was, Jo didn't want his parents to find out while they were at her parents' estate.

Hound and Jo hadn't seen each other for almost six months. Later that night, Jo once again became overwhelmed by her situation. She made no attempt to visit him in his bedroom. He allowed her the alone time she obviously needed and made no attempt to visit her bedroom. She cried herself to sleep that night thinking of the conversation she would have with him the next day.

As he lay in bed on his first night home, Hound began to listen closely to what his instinct was telling him. He listened for only a short time and then closed his eyes and fell fast asleep. He slept soundly through the night and didn't awaken until 8 a.m. the next morning.

Hound enjoyed another nice visit with everyone during breakfast. He devoted most of the conversation to his parents, who would be leaving to return home before noon. As soon as they'd finished eating, Jo and her parents left the dining room to allow

Hound and his parents some private time together. The excessive stress Jo was feeling quickly became apparent to everyone during breakfast, but no one said anything.

"Jo seems extremely upset about something," Linda said. "She's been very stressed all the time we've been here. Hound, do you have any idea what's wrong with her?"

"I have no idea, but I'm sure she'll tell me sooner or later."

"I certainly hope it's nothing too serious. It does, however, seem to be. I don't believe I've ever seen Jo so obviously upset."

"I'm sure there will be a solution to whatever problem she's having. Don't worry about her. She'll be fine."

"Please let your father and I know when she's feeling better. Let us know if there's anything we can do."

"I will. Like I said, I think she'll be fine."

After his parents had left, Hound once again approached Jo for some answers. She told him they'd discuss everything during their drive home to Baton Rouge. They departed her family's home a little after 11:30 that morning. Jo was driving and remained silent for the first half hour of the trip.

"Sweetheart," Jo began reluctantly. "I'm about to tell you something I wish with all my heart I didn't have to. Before I do, I want you to know I love you so very, very much!"

Jo gave him a complete and truthful account of everything that had happened while she was in Washington D.C. with her father. She completely lost control of her emotions as she told him of her pregnancy and had to stop the car on the shoulder of the highway.

"I'm unable to describe how terrible I feel, or how sorry I am!" Jo said as her crying became more intense. "I've been living a nightmare ever since I woke up in D.C. the next morning and realized what had happened to me! The nightmare became absolute hell when I discovered I was pregnant! All I've been able to think about is what a horrible, despicable thing I've done to you! To us! I've constantly hoped and prayed you'd be able to forgive me! Can you, Hound? Can you ever forgive this horrible mistake I've made?"

Hound was silent for a moment, as he viewed the pain Jo was experiencing.

"Of course, I can forgive you, Jo," he replied in a soft, compassionate tone of voice. He told her he'd drive the remainder of the trip back to Baton Rouge. After stating the forgiveness Jo so desperately needed, Hound said nothing else for 15 minutes.

Jo finally decided to initiate more conversation. She hadn't yet confirmed all she wanted to know. She'd managed to better compose herself and was better able carry on a less emotional conversation.

"Hound, what happens now?" she asked. "Where do we go from here?"

"Do you plan to keep the baby, or get an abortion?"

"I wanted to get an abortion, but when my parents reminded me that I was Catholic and abortion wasn't an option, I wanted to put the baby up for adoption as soon as it was born. They quickly told me that wasn't an option either. My father told me that despite the circumstances, the baby was still my child and his grandchild."

"Jo, do you realize how absolutely fucked up all that sounds to me?"

"What do you mean?"

"You and your family honor and celebrate your faith only when it serves your purpose! Most generally when it serves your father's purpose! None of you are devout regarding your professed religion! You're all a bunch of God-damned hypocrites and your religion is absolute bullshit! I don't want to discuss this any further now!"

Hound and Jo arrived in Baton Rouge before either spoke another word.

"Jo, I've got some personal business to take care of," Hound told her as soon as they arrived home. "I'm not certain how long I'll be gone, but I'll return as soon as I can."

He hurried into the house, obtained the keys to his car, and was preparing to leave.

"Hound, what are you talking about!" Jo said anxiously. "We just got home. We still have much to discuss. You can't just leave with everything up in the air like it is! I desperately need to know what's going to happen next between us! Can't your personal business wait at least until tomorrow?"

Hound offered no response. He got into his car and drove away. Jo sat on the sofa in the living room and again began to cry. Hound had offered her his forgiveness, but he hadn't said the forgiveness included no separation from her. Jo became terrified she might never see him again. She knew Hound's forgiveness was sincere, but she realized it might not be void of consequences. Jo was aware that Hound's ability to conceal his true feelings was remarkable. Not knowing what his true feelings or intentions were began to seem unbearable. She would force herself to embrace Hound's philosophy of never crossing a bridge until that was reached.

Hound was able to reach every bank where he had money secured before they closed that evening. He gathered all funds in safety deposit boxes, checking and savings accounts. The safety deposit boxes still contained a substantial amount of money. Just before dark that evening, he began driving to his family's farm and arrived shortly before his parents went to bed.

John and Linda were happy but surprised to see him.

"Can I sleep in my old room tonight?" Hound asked, smiling.

"Of course, you can, son," John replied. "What's wrong? Why aren't you with Jo tonight?"

"I'd rather not talk about anything right now, if you don't mind."

"We don't mind, son. You can tell your mother and I all about it later. Are you hungry?"

"A little bit."

Linda prepared Hound something to eat. He engaged in casual

conversation with them for about an hour and then they all went to bed.

Hound ate an early breakfast with his parents the next morning. Soon after breakfast, he excused himself and drove into town. He waited in the parking lot of a bank until it opened. He placed five thousand dollars of his money in a checking account. He left one hundred thousand dollars in his car. The remainder of his money, he secured in the largest safety deposit box available.

He was wearing the only clothing he'd brought with him. After leaving the bank, he visited various stores to purchase a new wardrobe. He returned to the farm in time for lunch that day. During lunch, he told his parents he was going to take a vacation road trip.

"I feel like I need some time away," he told John and Linda.

John was quick to respond. "Hound, your mother and I know something is terribly wrong," he said in a concerned way. "What is it, son? What's going on? What's wrong? You've just returned home from fighting in that awful war. Now, you're suddenly leaving the people that love you. Son, would you agree that's not normal?"

"Not necessarily. Perhaps I'm just not ready to be home yet. I realize that probably doesn't make any sense."

"Son, it makes no sense at all! Does it really make sense to you?"

"With all things I've considered, it makes perfect sense to me."

"What about Jo? Does it make perfect sense to her? Don't you think you should discuss it with her?"

"What makes you think I haven't already discussed it with her?"

"Because she called your mother and me last night after you went to bed. She said not to wake you, but to ask you to please call her as soon as possible today. She assumed you'd come here when you didn't return home to her last night. She said there was much you and she needed to talk about. The poor girl has no idea what's on your mind or what you're planning to do next. What's going on between you two?"

"What did she tell you?"

"Nothing. She's as secretive about what's going on as you are. She did, however, sound extremely sad and upset. Son, I think you should call her. I think she's afraid you're not going to return. Is that your plan? She's completed plans and preparations for your wedding. Have you decided not to marry her? Jesus, Hound! What's happened?"

"Dad, nothing has happened that you and Mom should be concerned about. Everything always works out for the best. I'll stop on the road somewhere and call Jo."

John and Linda were very opposed to what Hound was planning, but they realized it was no use to try and change his mind. Both were concerned that what he'd experienced in Vietnam might now be causing his seemingly irrational behavior. He wouldn't say where he was going, how long he'd be gone, or what he'd be doing. All they could do was wish him a safe journey and a quick return home. When he was ready to leave, Hound told his parents goodbye, gave them a hug, and then got in his car and drove away.

3

Hound took his time driving to reach his first destination. He reached Las Vegas three days after leaving the farm. He hadn't yet called Jo when he arrived. He wasn't sure if he would ever talk to or see her again. He was neither angered nor hurt by what she'd told him. He considered that unusual given the fact he did have strong feelings for her. He was, however, very happy with his current emotional state.

He acquired a luxury room at Caesars Palace, took a nap until 6 p.m., enjoyed a nice dinner at 7 p.m., and began gambling at 8 p.m. He was delighted to discover his skills at Blackjack hadn't diminished. In fact, he felt they had improved.

Hound's stay in Vegas lasted a full week. During that time, he gambled in all the major casinos. He left Vegas early on a Monday morning and drove to Reno. He spent three days and nights in Reno before leaving. He would've stayed longer in both Vegas and Reno, but the amount of money he won was drawing unwanted attention from casino managements. When his tour of gambling ended, Hound had cashier's checks from all the casinos he had gambled at in both Vegas and Reno. His net winnings after taxes were paid totaled $3,500,000. He considered that a very nice early Christmas present. When he left Reno, Hound decided to make his next destination Oakland, California. Because it would soon be Christmas, he placed a phone call to his parents. They weren't surprised when he told them he wouldn't be home for the holidays. They did their best to change his mind, but it was no use.

When Hound arrived in Oakland, he secured a suite in the same hotel where he and Carmella had stayed only a short time ago. Because Roberto's travel schedule would be uncertain until after the new year arrived, he wouldn't risk contacting Carmella until then.

He placed a phone call to Rebecca shortly after he'd checked into his suite. She was overjoyed to hear from him and discover he was back in town. She agreed to meet him in the hotel restaurant later that evening for dinner. Hound spent his time before dinner depositing the Reno and Vegas winnings in four separate Oakland area banks. After he'd completed his business at the banks, he decided to buy a new car. He used his old car as a trade-in and paid cash for the balance due on a new Corvette.

Hound was seated at the table he reserved in the restaurant when Rebecca arrived at 7 p.m. She greeted him with a tender embrace and passionate kiss. It was obvious to all who witnessed it that she was excited to see him.

"Hound, it's so wonderful to see you again, but what are you doing here?" Rebecca asked. "Tomorrow is Christmas Eve. Shouldn't you be home with your family?"

"Maybe, but I've decided to spend Christmas in Oakland."

"Do you have relatives or friends here that I don't know about?"

"Only you and one other."

"Well, which one of us do you want to spend Christmas with?"

"With you, if you're extending an invitation."

"Of course, I'm extending an invitation! That is if you can put up with my mother and a few other relatives and guests."

"I don't want you to feel obligated or pressured to invite me. I certainly don't wish to intrude."

"Don't be silly! You'll likely be the most welcome guest there. I know mom would be delighted."

"Who are the other guests?"

"Just a couple of aunts and uncles, a few cousins and close friends of the family."

"Is General Hughes not going to be home for Christmas?"

"We were all hoping he would, but unfortunately he won't."

"That's too bad. I would have greatly enjoyed seeing him again."

"I know he would've enjoyed seeing you as well."

"I assume there's a dress code for Christmas dinner?"

"Unfortunately, it's coat and tie."

"I don't have anything but boots and jeans. Can you suggest a store where I can purchase more appropriate attire? Tomorrow is Christmas Eve. Do you have a place in mind that's open?

"I do. Would you like my assistance?"

"I'd appreciate it. I'm sure you have good taste in men's clothing. I certainly want to be as well dressed as possible."

"I guarantee you will be. The store I have in mind is expensive. How much money did you want to spend?"

"Whatever amount necessary. I'm pretty sure I can afford it. What time shall we go shopping tomorrow?"

"Would you like to have breakfast together? Then, we could do your shopping and spend the rest of the day doing other things."

"That sounds good to me."

Hound assumed Rebecca was anxious to ask about Jo. He wasn't quite certain why she hadn't. During dinner, he asked her.

"I didn't want to pry," she told him. "I assumed you'd tell me what was going on if and when you wanted me to know."

"It's really very simple. You were correct when you said I wasn't ready to get married. It didn't take me long after I got back home to realize that."

"I suspect there's more to the story than you're telling me. I'm sure you have your reasons for not doing so. You've answered the question that most concerned me."

"What question is that?"

"You're no longer engaged and planning to get married. You might be interested to know I brought a change of clothes with me tonight."

"Is that right? Well, why did you do that?"

"You know very well why. I wanted to be prepared in case you invited me to spend the night. Naturally, I don't want you to feel obligated or pressured to do so."

"I suppose it would be more convenient for you to spend the night. You wouldn't have to get up so early in order to drive here and meet me for breakfast."

"Asshole! Stop teasing me. You know I have another reason for wanting to spend the night with you."

"Well, I hope so. I'm in complete agreement with your reason. I have very much been looking forward to being with you again."

"So have I, Hound. I hoped I'd see you again but felt certain I wouldn't. You can't imagine how happy it makes me that you're here."

"Do you think your father would approve of us being with each other?"

"Maybe. Maybe not. However, it doesn't matter. I'm going to be with you as much as you'll allow."

"Rebecca, how much has your father told you and your mother about my tour in Vietnam?"

"Quite a bit, but perhaps not everything. Why?"

"Please tell me what he said about me."

"Dad said you were a remarkable young officer. He said you were a brilliant field commander and leader, well-liked and respected by all the men under your command. He told us that you were the youngest officer to ever reach the rank of captain, and that the rank was achieved as result of a battlefield commission.

He was impressed how fierce and fearless in battle you were. He was very proud when you were approved to receive the CMH and saddened when that approval was reconsidered and then denied."

"Did he tell you why it was denied?"

"He said it was due to politics. He also said it should've never been denied."

"General Hughes really said that?"

"Indeed, he did. I'm sure you feel the same way."

"I'm not sure. I'll never be sure. I do know your father is a fine officer and gentlemen. That can certainly not be said of all officers. Rebecca, did your father tell you anything about Base Camp Bravo, or Delta?"

"I've never heard of either one. What about them?"

"Never mind, Rebecca. It's not important."

For almost an hour after they had completed their dinner, Rebecca and Hound continued to talk about a variety of things. Rebecca smiled and agreed when Hound suggested it was time to retire for the evening. They held hands and continued to talk as they walked to his hotel suite.

After reaching her first orgasm, Rebecca laughed and apologized for her loud verbal expressions of sexual pleasure. Hound smiled and assured her there was no problem. He informed her the walls in the suite were soundproof.

The next morning, Rebecca suggested they have breakfast at a restaurant that was famous for its pancakes. Hound insisted they use his car for the day's activities. Rebecca was very impressed with his new Corvette.

"I now understand why you weren't concerned about the expensive clothing store I plan to take you too," Rebecca said, smiling. "Your new car is top of its line and you're staying in a very high-dollar hotel. You're not by chance wealthy, are you?"

"I wouldn't say wealthy. I'd simply say comfortable for the moment. However, I do plan to become extremely wealthy in the future."

"I assume you're not involved in a career at this time. You haven't been back from Vietnam long enough to already be working in a good paying career, have you?"

"No. Not yet. I don't know for sure what type of career I want."

"Surely, you must have some idea."

"Not really. I'm going to take my time and consider many important things so I can make the right decision."

"What does your father do for a living?"

"I'd call him a combination rancher and farmer. He raises commercial livestock and produce on 750 acres of prime farmland in Louisiana."

"That sounds like a profitable business. Have you considered following in your father's footsteps? You could take over the family business someday."

"I have no desire to be a farmer, or rancher. The family business earns a good living but not good enough to satisfy me."

"Hound, I don't see you as a man motivated by wealth and the material things wealth can provide."

"I certainly can't say material things aren't important. Everyone wants the most comfortable life possible. However, I can say that material things aren't the primary reason for me wanting to be as wealthy as possible."

"What is the primary reason?"

"It's power, Rebecca. Wealth is the power behind any throne."

"So, someday you want to sit on a throne, be in some type of leadership position. Perhaps you'll be a politician. I could envision you as a congressman, senator, or maybe even president."

"Hell no! I'm not interested in being any kind of politician. I don't want to sit on any throne. I want enough power to determine who does."

"That would require a tremendous amount of wealth."

"You're absolutely correct."

Jo placed a phone call to John and Linda midmorning on Christmas Eve. Her emotional well-being was continuing to decline.

"Can you tell me how Hound is?" Jo asked John, who answered the phone. "He hasn't called me yet. I haven't heard from him since he left. If he's at home now, would you ask him to please speak with me?"

John could tell from her voice how distraught she was. "Sweetheart, I'm terribly sorry. Hound isn't here," he told her reluctantly.

"Do you know when he'll return?"

"I don't know. We haven't heard from him since he left."

"When did he leave?"

"About two weeks ago. Soon after you last called."

"Do you know where he is?"

"No, sweetheart. I'm sorry, I don't. However, he did call to tell us he wouldn't be home for the holidays. Jo, he never said what happened between you and him. What did happen, sweetheart?"

"John, I hope you'll forgive me, but I'm not ready to talk about it with anyone but Hound. He may never wish to talk with or see me ever again."

"I guess whatever happened must be pretty serious."

"Yes, John. I would say so."

"Jo, I understand why you don't wish to talk about it. That's OK. I'll ask Hound again to contact you the next time he calls. I hope you and he can work out whatever the problem is. Linda and I will be praying for both of you."

"Thank you, John. I'll be hoping and praying as well."

When Jo completed her conversation with John, she sat down to visit with her father in his den.

"Were you able to find out anything about Hound?" Ken asked.

"John believes him to be well, but he has no idea where he is."

"I'll contact some people and start looking for him whenever you're ready for me to do so. Are you ready?"

"I don't know what good it would do to find him. He won't talk to me until he's ready."

"Honey, what if he's never ready? What if you never see or hear from him again?"

"I have to keep hoping he just needs some time to process what's happened and loves me enough to want things to work out between us."

"What will you do if he's unable to deal with what's happened and decides he doesn't want to work things out?"

"I have no idea what I'd do if I lose him forever. I don't believe I could ever forgive myself. It's for certain I could never love another man the way I love him."

"You know there are ways of forcing him to return to you. Release me from the promise I made to you not to influence his decision and I'll make that happen."

"I know, Dad, but forcing him wouldn't be fair to him or me. I desperately want him back, but only if he loves and wants to be with me."

"Have you decided whether or not to contact your baby's father and let him know the situation?"

"Jesus, Dad! Why would I ever want to see or talk to that dirty son of a bitch ever again?"

"If you're not going to allow me to deal with him in other ways, then at least the bastard can pay financially for what he's done. We could make that cost extremely high for the next eighteen years. I promise you we can break him financially and destroy whatever career he has. Just tell me who he is, and I'll get all that started."

"Dad, you're pulling a con on me. You'd kill him if I told you who he was. Surely you know I'm smart enough to know that. We've talked about this before. If and when he should ever have to answer for what he's done, then it will be me and me alone that he answers to."

"All right, Jo. I'll continue to support any decision you make. Whatever you want, I want. Honey, I truly wanted Hound to be my successor in the family business."

"I know that. Hound is perfect in every way for that position, but Dad, you know he was never really interested in being involved with the family business in any way. He wants to build his own empire, one that he alone is responsible for."

"Yes, I suppose you're right, sweetheart. I certainly have to respect him for that. However, I still feel he owes the family a great debt. You and I have done much to help him in the past."

"Dad, Hound is not the kind of man to ever let a debt remain unpaid. I'm sure the day will come when he'll pay his debt in full, with interest."

"You're probably right, honey. However, I'm still not ready to give up the hope of him becoming my protege and successor."

"Dad, we should both follow Hound's philosophies."

"Which one's? He has many."

"There are only two that are important to me right now. There is a solution to any problem. It may be difficult to find, but not impossible. Never give up until you find it, and never cross a bridge until you get to it. If you never reach it, then you'll never have to cross it."

After she completed the visit with her father, Jo went to her bedroom to rest for a while. She drifted off to sleep and began to dream of the relationship she used to share with the young man she loved dearly. She felt fortunate to have such dreams. Having them were the only times she was happy and at peace.

Spending Christmas Day with Rebecca and her family was an enjoyable experience for Hound. Everyone made him feel very welcome. His natural charm and charisma quickly made him popular. His intelligence and knowledge, along with his speaking ability, allowed him to have intelligent, individual conversations with everyone on the topic of their choosing and interest. When Rebecca's mother invited him to spend the night, he accepted.

When Mrs. Hughes found out Hound was no longer engaged to be married, she wasn't disappointed to learn Rebecca planned to spend a great deal of time with him.

General Hughes called from Vietnam around 9 p.m. that evening. He was delighted to discover Hound was a guest. Like his wife, he was happy for Hound to spend time with his daughter. He spoke with Hound briefly over the phone and wished him a happy holiday season and the best of luck in the future. Neither General Hughes, his wife, nor anyone else inquired of Hound as to the reason he wasn't spending Christmas with his family in Louisiana. This surprised Hound, but he greatly appreciated it.

Hound was provided the largest guest bedroom in the house. Rebecca informed him she would be visiting him in his room as soon as everyone was asleep.

"Rebecca, that's not a good idea," Hound whispered in her ear. "I don't wish to disrespect your parents. I'm certain they both believe I'll behave in an honorable way while I'm a guest in their home."

Rebecca smiled at Hound's remarks. She joined him in his bedroom around midnight and remained there until 6 a.m. She took special care not to offer loud verbal expressions during orgasms. She knew Hound's bedroom wasn't soundproof.

Hound and Rebecca were together constantly until January 2 of the new year, 1971. She made reservations and took him to the most elegant nightclub in San Francisco on New Year's Eve. Hound became so impressed with everything about the club that he began to consider building one of his own. He envisioned the one he would build as being absolutely the largest and most elegant to be found anywhere in the country. When he disclosed his thoughts to Rebecca, she laughed, thinking he wasn't serious. He agreed it was only a daydream at that time, but one that might hold some significance regarding his future career choice.

On the morning of January 2, 1971, Hound announced to Rebecca he had some personal business to take care of and would be leaving for a while. When she asked what type of business, he told her it was of a financial nature. Feeling it wasn't her place to inquire further, she refrained from asking more questions.

Early that afternoon, Hound boarded a flight for Las Vegas. Carmella was again free for a time and would meet him there that evening. She took a taxi from the airport in Vegas and joined him in his hotel suite.

"It's wonderful to see you again, my darling gringo boy!" Carmella said with enthusiasm when he opened the door and she entered his suite.

"It's good to see you too, Carmella."

"I bet I've missed you more than you've missed me."

"Well, you might just lose that bet."

"What excuse did you use to get away from Jo?"

"No excuse was needed. We're no longer together."

"Bullshit! You're joking with me! Right?"

"No bullshit, Carmella. I'm telling you the truth."

"Well, I'll be damned! What the fuck happened?"

"I simply decided I didn't want to get married."

Carmella was speechless for a moment. "Shit! I don't know what to say," she said in a low voice. "Are you OK? Don't you think you might change your mind?"

"Not likely. Honestly, I feel exceptionally good about the way things have worked out between Jo and I."

"Well, it seems like you've solved a large problem. I wish I could solve mine, but I know solving my problem with Roberto will be a much more difficult task. You're now free to do as you please and be with whomever you wish. I'm the prisoner of a marriage I should've never allowed to happen. All I ever wanted was the time to come when I could be with you. Now, that time is here and because of my stupidity and impatience, I've made all I ever wanted impossible."

"Carmella, karma and fate solved my problem. When the time is right, I believe they'll solve yours as well. Let's talk about more pleasant things. How would you like to spend our time together in Vegas?"

"Well, it's not safe for us to be in the casinos. There's a chance I might run into someone who knows Roberto and me. Even if that didn't happen, I certainly don't want evidence of my being in Vegas recorded by security cameras."

"I plan to gamble four to six hours a day. I'm sure you can find something to occupy your time while I do. I'll gamble during the day so we can have the evenings free to do other things that aren't under a camera's eye."

Hound and Carmella were together during the morning. They'd enjoy breakfast together and then go sightseeing, or shopping, which was something she enjoyed doing very much. They'd have lunch around 1 p.m. He'd begin gambling around 2 p.m. He kept his winnings on a daily basis in each casino at a substantial amount, yet specific and reasonable as not to draw excessive attention to himself.

He'd continue to visit Vegas and Reno on an approximate monthly basis and didn't want to be recognized and labeled as a professional gambler with techniques that cost the casinos mega bucks on a consistent basis. It was his plan to earn a lot of money during his career as a gambler, but in acceptable amounts each time he visited. At some point in the future, he'd conduct one final gambling tour to win as much money as possible before retiring from gambling altogether. Based on the amount of money he planned to win during that final tour, he was certain to be denied gambling privileges in the casinos thereafter. It would be a long time, if ever, before he could gamble in Vegas or Reno again. Perhaps he'd employ his skills in Atlantic City, or maybe in casinos outside the United States.

On their last night together in Vegas, Hound and Carmella decided to share a lobster dinner for two at a highly recommended restaurant. "Hound, what will you be doing until I see you again?" Carmella asked as their conversation over dinner began.

"I'm going to do a bit of traveling. I've decided to build a nightclub. I want to explore and find the ideal location to build the best in existence anywhere. If I'm satisfied with the money I earn, then I may consider building more in other locations."

"Hound, I've pictured you as many things, but never as a nightclub owner. It somehow doesn't seem to fit you."

"I know what you mean. I've considered that. Building a nightclub might just be a steppingstone to other things. However, for a while I'll enjoy it."

"Surely you must have some idea where you'd like to build it?"

"None whatsoever, but I feel I'll know the place when I see it."

"The kind of nightclub you're talking about will cost a lot of money to build. Do you have that kind of money? How much do you think it will cost? I know you must have researched that."

"The club will be large. I want at least 40,000 square feet under roof. Its construction and furnishings will be the best money can buy. I want at least 15 acres of land to build on as to allow for plenty of parking, elegant landscaping, and plenty of additional land I might want to use for other things. Based on what I believe to be a reasonable estimate, it should take a minimum of four million dollars to build what I have in mind."

"Where are you going to get that kind of money?"

"I already have over half of it. I'll have all I need by the time I'm ready to start building. I've got more than enough to buy the land as soon as I find it."

"You said the club might be a steppingstone to other things. I'm certain it will be. Do you have any idea what those things might be?"

"It's likely land and real estate development will be one of them."

"Why are you interested in that?"

"Land is a good investment. There's only a limited amount in this country and around the world. No more will be added in the future."

"Hound, you've accomplished and experienced a lot to be only 21 years old. I suppose your accomplishments have all been good, but your experiences certainly have not all been good."

"I think that's true for both of us. I think it's true for everyone. Don't you?"

"I suppose that's true for everyone. You can bet your ass it's true for me! I've made up my mind about something."

"What?"

"As I've told you before, marrying Roberto was one of the two biggest mistakes I've made in my life. The other was becoming a prostitute. I've decided to end my marriage without incurring the consequences resulting from Roberto's wrath. How do you think I can do that? You've always said there's a solution to any problem. What's my solution?"

"I also told you the solution might be difficult to determine, and you might have to be patient during the time you search for it. What do you honestly think Roberto would do if you tried to divorce him or he found out about us?"

"I'm not completely sure what he'd do to me. Killing me will certainly be a consideration. If he didn't kill me, then what he might do could be worse. I am, however, absolutely sure he'd kill you. That's something I cannot bear to think about happening! Hound, please tell me what to do!"

"Aren't you supposed to begin classes at Berkeley this month?"

"Yes. Next week."

"I think you should proceed with your plan to get a college education. Roberto has provided you the opportunity. I think you should take it."

"Are you saying I should stay with Roberto?"

"No. I'm saying you should make the most of a bad situation until you can correct the situation. It will take time, but I'll do all in my power to help you devise a plan to get away from him without having to face any consequence."

"I hadn't thought about that. Perhaps you're right. I hate to say this, but the longer we continue to see each other, greater is the chance Roberto will find out. I was serious when I said he'd kill you. I was also serious about not being able to bear the thought of that. It would seem the only solution right now would be for us to stop seeing each other until I can somehow safely free myself from Roberto. However, I'll still need your help to come up with a plan. You can do that without putting yourself at risk by being with me. You're the only person I would trust to help me."

"Carmella, I don't like talking about anything to do with Vietnam, but I'm going to talk to you about it. I feel it's significant regarding Roberto being a threat to me. I lived through my tour there suffering only a few minor scrapes and scratches. With the exception of only a few days during my time in Vietnam, the enemy was trying to kill me, but they never succeeded. To some degree, that was due to nothing more than pure luck. I believe to a major degree; however, it was due to destiny and how I assisted it with instinct and intelligence. I also came to realize I didn't fear death. When I realized that, then I realized I feared nothing. I lost count of the number of enemy soldiers I killed. I was able to kill them rather than be killed by them because I was simply superior to them in the ways that counted most on the battlefield. The success of my survival in Vietnam is based on the same philosophy I'll embrace regarding Roberto, should the need to survive him ever arise."

"What is that philosophy?"

"It's very simple. Always, and I mean always, be prepared in advance to kill the enemy before he kills you, when the only choice you have is kill or be killed. Should Roberto ever make an attempt to harm me, then I'll definitely kill the mother fucker. I'll consistently rely on my intelligence and instinct to assist my destiny. I know being killed or harmed in any way by Roberto isn't included in my destiny."

"Hound, you've convinced me regarding you, but what about me? It's not possible for me to embrace that philosophy. I'm not you."

"Can you think of any circumstances, should they occur, that would influence Roberto to allow your separation from him?"

"I believe the only possible circumstance would be if he found someone he'd rather be married to than me. However, even then he'd likely want to keep me around to share his bed anytime he so desired."

"Is Roberto really that big a piece of shit?"

"I didn't think so when I married him. Of course, I knew he was a criminal, but I thought he wanted a true marriage and would show me the love and respect due a wife. He didn't start showing what he was really like until after we were married. I only learned then he was really that big a piece of shit! I truly believe the only way I can ever be free of him is if he were to die."

"I hope that's not true, but I guess it might be if you think so."

Hound was very aware of what Carmella was thinking. She wanted Roberto dead and him to devise a plan to get what she wanted.

"Carmella, we can talk about this again the next time we're together," Hound told her. "For now, let's just enjoy our last evening in Vegas together."

He reimbursed her the money she spent on airfare. The next day, they took separate flights back to San Francisco. Carmella's left at 10 a.m. He booked a flight leaving at 7 p.m. that evening. He gambled for the rest of the day until it was time to leave for the airport and catch his flight.

Rebecca was waiting at the airport for Hound when he arrived. She'd volunteered to drop him off at the airport when he left and pick him up when he returned. He had told her the reason for his trip was financial business. She knew he'd gone to Vegas, but she had no idea his financial business was gambling. She was clearly happy he was back. The way she kissed him upon his arrival clearly indicated it.

"Hi, Rebecca," Hound said when her kiss ended. "Wow! That was some kiss! It made me feel like you're really glad I'm back."

"I'm really glad you're back. I've missed you terribly. It seems like you've been away longer than you were. Did you miss me?"

"Of course, but you should know that."

"I never take anything for granted. I needed you to tell me. Did you have dinner before you left Vegas?"

"No. Have you eaten yet?"

"No. Are you hungry?"

"Actually, I am. How about you?"

"Absolutely. Do you want to have dinner somewhere?"

"Of course. Where would you like to go?"

"I know a nice place. I think you'll enjoy it."

"All right. Let's go."

Rebecca drove them to a small, quaint, but very nice restaurant a few miles from the airport. Hound was fond of Rebecca and enjoyed spending time with her. He was, however, becoming concerned that she was beginning to require more of his time than he wanted to give on a consistent basis.

"I came to spend the night with you," Rebecca told him during dinner, "if you want me to."

"Rebecca, a man would have to be blind, crippled, and crazy to turn down such an invitation. Of course, I want you to spend the night."

"Hound, I need to talk to you about something important and I need you to be completely honest with me."

"Well, all right. What's on your mind?"

"I've only known you a short time, but in spite of that, I'm in love with you. With all honesty, I can say it was love at first sight. I knew you were the man I wanted to spend the rest of my life with when you first came to visit at my home. Knowing you were engaged to be married created panic in me. I know now that's the reason I made such an ass of myself regarding the things I said to you during our drive back to your hotel. I became more than addicted to you sexually the first time I experienced you in that way. You did not simply fuck me — I felt you were making love to me. That's probably the main reason you were able to satisfy me sexually in such an extraordinary way. I guess I just need to know if at this time you think we might have a future together. Do you?"

"Rebecca, you're absolutely everything a man like me could possibly want a woman to be. Everything about you physically is perfection. You're honest, trustworthy, and highly intelligent. I'd be lying if I said I could see no possible future for us. However, I would also be lying if I were to offer any guarantees or promises at this time. You, as well as anyone, should know I'm not prepared to enter into a committed relationship. There's much I have to do before I allow that to happen. I believe that you love me. You would've never said you did if it wasn't true. You've flattered and honored me greatly."

"You're telling me your feelings for me aren't the same as mine are for you. Am I correct?"

"Rebecca, I feel a huge fondness for you. I enjoy being with you. I want to see you whenever possible while I'm preparing for my future, but that may not be as often as we'd like for a while. I'm going to be traveling a lot. I have to decide where I'm going to make my home. I'm certain it won't be in California. I've decided to build my nightclub. There's a perfect location for it somewhere. I don't know how long it'll take to find it, but I'll search until I do."

"I appreciate your honesty. Thank you. When will you be leaving?"

"Sometime tomorrow. I have some business at the bank to take care of in the morning, and then I'll be on my way."

"Don't you think it's very likely you'll build your club and make your home in Louisiana?"

"I suppose it's possible, but right now I consider it very unlikely."

"Where would you go first after you leave California?"

"Arizona, I think. I want to explore Phoenix and surrounding areas."

"Will you please keep in contact with me? I'd like to know where you are, and how you're doing. Will you come visit me and allow me to come visit you as often as possible?"

"Of course, I will."

"Do you still want me to spend the night with you tonight?"

"Of course, I do. Why wouldn't I? Do you still want to? I'll understand if you don't, but I certainly hope you do."

"You know I do. I'll always want to be with you whenever I can."

Hound obtained traveler's checks from the bank the next morning. He made sure to secure an amount adequate to meet his needs for at least three months. He was optimistic he could locate a suitable area and location to make his home, and eventually build his club, in that period of time.

By 11 a.m., Hound was driving toward the border of California on his way to Arizona. Before leaving Oakland, he placed a phone call to his parents. He told them everything was fine and not to worry. They were disappointed to learn he didn't know when he would visit them again. John gave him the message from Jo and asked him to please contact her. Hound briefly paused his conversation. John felt this was an indication Jo might not be contacted.

"Son, regardless of what has happened between you and Jo," John said, "she's obviously very worried about you and greatly troubled about something. I fear her health might be failing. She at least deserves to hear from you, even if it's for the last time. Please call your mom and me every chance you get and come home again as soon as possible."

Linda was participating in the conversation on the phone in the kitchen. She asked for Hound's promise to contact Jo and come home for a visit in the shortest time possible. He promised to do both.

4

It was early in the evening that day when Hound arrived in Phoenix. He located a suitable motel and rented a room. He sat down on the side of the bed in his room, lifted the receiver from the phone sitting on the nightstand, and dialed Jo's number at her home in Baton Rouge. Jo immediately began to sob when she discovered it was Hound calling.

"Jo, you'll have to stop crying if you expect us to have a conversation," Hound told her in a compassionate and understanding way. "My parents told me you deserved at least a phone call. I agree. I should've called before now. I sincerely apologize for not doing so. It would be ridiculous to ask how you are. It's obvious you aren't doing well. If there is anything reasonable I can do to make things better for you, I'll be happy to do it."

"Oh, Hound! Sweetheart! You can't possibly know how terrible I feel, and life is for me now. I hardly sleep, can't eat, and it's all I can do to complete my work daily at the university! What's happened between us is absolutely more than I can bear! I'll do anything in my power to make things right between us again!

Please tell me it's possible to somehow do that!"

Hound began to experience sadness, and even pity, as a result of Jo's situation. It was obvious her disclosures of experiencing a horrific emotional burden weren't under-exaggerated. He felt certain such a burden was affecting her physical health in an extremely negative way. He decided to say everything possible over the phone that might provide her some degree of relief.

"Jo, I think you're being harder on yourself than you deserve," he told her tenderly. "Everybody makes mistakes, but life must go on. You have to start thinking about the welfare of a child you're carrying. You have to get your emotions under control and take care of your health. The baby will suffer for it if you don't. You aren't the kind of person to let that happen."

"The only way I can do that is if you come home! That's the only thing that will make me better! Sweetheart, please come home! Give me a chance to make this horrible mistake I've made right between us! I know it's in my power to do so if you'll just give me a chance! I know I can help you forgive me!"

"Jo, I forgave you the second you told me what happened. After everything you've done for me in the past, forgiving you came easy and quickly. Actually, there was really little to forgive. Afterall, what happened wasn't altogether your fault. Unfortunately, forgetting what happened will not come so easily and quickly. Surely you can understand that. Can't you? I don't know if it will be possible for me to ever forget."

"Oh, my love! Of course, I can understand that! Neither of us will likely ever be able to forget, but if you'd just come home, we can help each other learn to live with it. Over time, the pain we both feel now will decrease to a level we can bear, and we can be happy together again in spite of it."

Hound paused for a moment to consider what he would say next. "Jo, perhaps what you're saying has some merit. Time does have a way of healing emotional wounds."

"Oh, my darling! Are you saying you're willing to come home

and give time a chance? Please tell me you are! If you'll come back to me, I promise you won't regret it."

"Jo, I'm terribly sorry, but I'm not prepared to come home at this time. I don't want to. Maybe in time I will. Maybe I won't. I just don't know right now."

That wasn't what Jo wanted or needed to hear. The moderate degree of composure she'd been able to achieve was quickly lost. She began to sob hysterically. Hound made special effort to once again calm her, but it was no use. He eventually told her goodbye, that he would call her again at a later date, and ended the phone call. He sat on the side of the bed a few more minutes giving careful thought to his conversation with Jo and how it had ended. He began to remember the things he'd experienced with and because of her, beginning with the first time they met.

During good times and bad, she had always been there for him. He knew she was owed a great debt for everything she'd done. She'd been undefeatably driven as she unselfishly welcomed and was always successful acting as his guardian angel. This had created a debt he felt would likely be impossible to repay. However, perhaps at some appropriate time in the future, he'd get an opportunity to try. Returning home to Jo now might pay his debt, but he didn't consider now to be the appropriate time. He decided to stop thinking about Jo and focused his thoughts on other things. He took a shower, put on a fresh change of clothes, and left his room to locate a nice restaurant for dinner. After dinner, he drove around the city to see some of Phoenix after dark.

Hound's random exploration of Phoenix that night consisted of driving down one street and then another. He drove in one direction for a time and then would turn right or left and drive for a time in another direction. He maintained the slowest speed of travel legally permitted as he carefully surveyed things to be seen on the right and left side of the street.

As his sightseeing tour continued, he realized he'd departed the inner city downtown area and now was in a less desirable part of town. This was indicated by the apparent construction and condition of homes and businesses in the area. The majority of others driving in the area clearly displayed the appearance of not being above the poverty level financially. Most who were driving newer and more expensive cars were likely in the area to transact some type of illegal business.

Pimps and prostitutes were easily identified standing on street corners or walking on the sidewalks. Drug dealers were selling various forms of illegal drugs to the unfortunate souls who bought them. Hound considered a drug dealer among the worst kind of predators. He noticed a few unfortunate souls being victimized by these predators were wearing a piece or two of military issued clothing. He wondered how many of them might be former soldiers that had served in Vietnam.

For a time, his thoughts focused on the men he'd served with and commanded during his Vietnam tour. He wondered how many who survived and came home were walking the streets at night in various cities all over the United States. He envisioned them buying drugs and wearing tattered and dirty remnants of military clothing. He wondered if anyone who hadn't experienced the horrors of Vietnam would understand or give a damn about these men. If that were the case, then it would forever be a God-damned shame and disgrace.

It was after midnight when Hound looked down the inside of an alley as he drove by it. A small streetlight burning in the alley allowed him to see what appeared to be one lone man being attacked by four other men. It appeared the lone man was engaged in hand-to-hand combat to remain alive. All the men were tall and large in physical build. The largest was defending himself against the other four.

Hound had no idea what or who had prompted the fight. He didn't bother to consider if the lone man was a good guy or bad. It made no difference to him. The odds of four against one automatically made the one a good guy. Instinctively, Hound turned quickly into the alley, brought his Corvette to an abrupt stop, got out, and quickly joined in the fight. During the officer-training phase of his military service, Hound had been taught and learned well the techniques of hand-to-hand assault and defense. Had it not been for those skills and the fact he'd practiced them religiously since they were learned, he likely wouldn't have fared as well in the fight as he did. The men he had challenged were at least two inches taller than him. Each outweighed him by at least 25 pounds and were all tough, mean, and very skilled in the art of street fighting.

When the fight could finally be considered over, Hound stood beside the man he'd entered the fight to assist. Even though he was looking at the four unconscious men lying on the ground, Hound wasn't ready to declare that he and the man standing beside him were the absolute victors. They were certainly the ones standing, but both were badly bludgeoned and bloody. Hound's nose was bleeding profusely, but fortunately wasn't broken. Portions of his face were also bleeding from numerous scrapes and cuts. His left eye was swollen shut and now the color of an 8 ball.

His newly found comrade standing beside him shared a similar fight aftermath appearance. They assisted each other to reach the outer wall in the alley where they slowly sat down and leaned their backs against the wall. Hound's new comrade was 6 feet, 4 inches in height and weighed 280 pounds. He had an obvious beer belly but was otherwise solidly built and very strong. Fire engine red hair bordered the top of his balding head. After a moment, the big man was first to speak.

"Thanks for the help, partner," he said to Hound. "I could've probably handled a couple of those mother fuckers, but four was just too God-damned many! I don't know why you decided to jump in, but I'm sure as hell glad you did. Those bastards meant to kill me. We don't know each other, do we?"

"That's not likely. This is my first time in Phoenix."

"Why did you decide to jump in? You sure as hell took a beating because of it."

"I'm not completely sure. I guess four against one pissed me off. You don't look any better than I do. How badly are you hurt?"

"Oh hell! I'm OK. I've survived worse beatings than this. How about you? Anything broken?"

"No. I don't think so. How do I look?"

"You look like you just got the shit beat out of you. How do you feel?"

"Honestly, not too bad. I guess not as bad as I look."

"Well, by tomorrow morning, you're going to feel exactly like you look. Those four other guys are sure as hell gonna feel worse than we do. What's your name, partner?"

"My name is John Smith, but everyone calls me Hound. It's a nickname I've had most of my life. What's yours?"

"Charlie Wyman, but everyone calls me Bear. It's a nickname I've had most of my life also."

"Bear, not that it's any of my business, but what was the fight about?"

"You're right, partner. It's none of your business. On the other hand, seeing as how you likely saved my life, I kinda like you and feel you can be trusted, so I'm going to tell you. However, I'm not going to tell you right now. We need to get the hell out of here. I don't know how bad those other guys are hurt. Hell! They may be dead. None of them have moved since the fight ended. Cops don't patrol this area much, but it would just be our luck if they showed up. I don't know about you, but I don't need that. Besides, both of us could use a little medical first aid sooner than later."

"You're probably right. Where's the closest hospital?"

"Shit, partner! We ain't going to no damn hospital! We're going to the clubhouse. We keep ample first aid supplies there. There should also be a couple of ladies hanging around the clubhouse that can patch us up."

"What kind of clubhouse?"

"You'll find out when we get there. Get in your car and follow me."

Hound watched Bear walk over and retrieve a large duffel bag that had been lying in the shadows. He brought the bag to Hound and asked him to transport it back to the clubhouse.

"I toted this damn bag here on my bike," Bear said, "but I sure as hell don't feel like toting it back to the clubhouse. It's a heavy mother fucker. I'm tired and feel like shit!"

Bear also retrieved a leather jacket he'd taken off and thrown on the ground before the fight began. When he put it on, Hound noticed it bore the name and colors of the biker club Bear was a member of.

"What's in the duffel bag?" Hound asked.

"What's in the bag caused the fight," Bear said and then walked to the back of the alley where he'd parked his Harley-Davidson motorcycle behind a large garbage dumpster. The alley filled with a loud roar when Bear started the Harley's engine. Bear rode the bike from the alley to the street, turned right, and rode away with Hound not far behind. It was five minutes later when the first of the four lying in the alley started to regain consciousness. Ten minutes later, all were up on their feet staggering and trying to regain proper balance. Unlike Hound and Bear, a visit to the nearest hospital emergency room was mandatory for them.

Bear was a ranking member in the Phoenix chapter of a well-known, major, and infamous biker club on the West Coast. Hound followed Bear for a few miles until he rode his bike through the open gate of a twelve foot high, heavy gauge chain link fence. Bear stopped and parked his Harley beside several others in front of a large building. The building resembled some type of manufacturing facility. The grounds surrounding the building were covered in car and truck bodies, giving the definite appearance of a salvage yard. Bear signaled Hound where to park his Corvette and then escorted him through the front entrance of the large building.

Inside the building was nothing like the outside. Its design and décor very much resembled a honky-tonk country western bar.

The furnishings weren't elaborate, but nice and adequately fit the theme. Everything appeared spic and span clean. A mahogany bar thirty feet in length was located near a rear wall that separated the bar area of the facility from a variety of other type areas located farther within the building. Hound would learn later these areas included, but weren't limited to, bedrooms with private baths, storage rooms, and a large conference room. A large open area at the rear of the building was a garage used for auto and truck paint, and body work and mechanical repair. Providing these types of services was a legitimate business conducted by the club. They also served as a front for other businesses the club was involved in that were nefarious.

The bar area of the facility was constantly stocked with a wide variety of beers, liquors, and wines. Each table in the large bar could seat up to six individuals. Two hundred fifty individuals could easily be accommodated before additional seating had to be provided. There were about fifty individuals in the bar when Hound and Bear arrived. One of these individuals was tending the bar. Two young women hurried to get first aid kits while everyone else began to inquire about what had happened.

Hound and Bear sat down at a table. Bear introduced Hound as his newly found friend and disclosed the circumstances under which they had met. Bear told everyone that Hound had likely saved his life. As Bear gave a detailed and accurate account of what had occurred, everyone listened intently.

Bill Tillman and Jim Johnson were seated at a table with two other men. They left their seats and came to join Hound and Bear at their table. Bill was president of the Phoenix chapter. Bear was considered to be his second-in-command and next in line to be president should Bill no longer be able to serve. Jim was next behind Bear in the chain of command. Jim also had a nickname. He was introduced to Hound as Pony Johnson. Bill was a tall, slender, blond-headed man. He was 35 years old and had been president for two years. Although his build with slender, Bill was very muscular.

Pony was 33 years old, heavyset, with shoulder-length brown hair. He was 5 feet, 9 inches tall, with a beard approximately half the length of his hair.

"God damn, Bear! You two fuckers look like hell!" Bill said, smiling. "However, I'm glad you won the fight and brought the duffel bag back. I'd assume the guys you fought look worse than you do. Am I right?"

"Hell yes, you're right! I'd bet they feel a hell of a lot worse too. Shit! I can't say for sure they're all still alive!"

Hound hadn't yet said a word when the two women returned with the first aid kits and began cleaning and treating the wounds he and Bear had received.

"Hound, you have the gratitude of the entire club for lending Bear a hand," Bill told him, "but why in the hell did you decide to get involved?"

"Like I told Bear, I didn't like the odds."

"Maybe it's partly because you like to fight. Do you?"

"Not particularly. In fact, right now I'm somewhat sorry I came to Bear's rescue."

"Why is that?"

"You told me a minute ago I looked like hell. Well, I'm beginning to feel exactly the way I look."

"Hound, even if you don't like a fight, you're damn good at it," Bear said, joining the conversation. "You have skills superior to those of the best street fighter. How did you learn them?"

"Out of necessity, I suppose."

"Bear, how good is he?" Bill asked.

"He's as good as and likely better than I've ever seen."

"Well, Hound, Bear would never say that about a man unless he believed it was true. You must be one mean, tough son of a bitch. Are you?"

"I really don't know, but if I am, its only if and when I have to be."

"Hound is a cool nickname. I really like it. How did you get it?"

"I had a hound dog named Hunter when I was a kid. Hunter and I were good friends. He's the reason I got the nickname."

"How do you think Pony got his nickname?"

"I have no idea. How?"

"Because he has the same size cock as a Shetland pony. He can only fuck a woman that has an extra large, deep pussy. All women not meeting that criteria avoid him like the plague."

The longer he remained at the club, the more convinced Hound became that all its members, both male and female, were a brother and sisterhood of the most crass, vulgar, and even dangerous citizens of the United States he'd ever expected to meet. However, in spite of that, he sensed if he should be accepted as a trustworthy friend of the club and all its members, then they wouldn't hesitate individually or as a group to assist him during any crucial time of need.

After the first aid treatment on him had been completed, Hound was invited to join Bill, Bear, and Pony for a drink and some further, more private conversation in Bill's office. Bill picked up the heavy duffel bag and carried it with him. Once inside his office, he put the bag on his desk and opened it. Before the meeting proceeded any further, Bill asked Hound if he could be trusted to keep his word once it was given. Hound said yes.

He was then asked to give his word he would never divulge to anyone at any time any information of a nefarious kind he might learn about the club or its members during his visit there that night, or any other time he might learn such information. Hound gave his word. It was made crystal clear what would happen to him should he ever break his word. Hound felt certain his trustworthiness was being tested for a specific reason but thought it extremely unusual he was being tested so soon. Afterall, he had met Bear only a short time ago. He had met Bill and Pony less than an hour ago. Hound wasn't surprised to discover the duffel bag contained several fully automatic rifles and rounds of ammunition.

Bear began to disclose what had caused the fight between him and the four men in the alley. He told Hound the men had placed an order to buy the automatic rifles and ammunition. A price had been agreed upon before Bear took them to the alley for delivery. When Bear arrived in the alley, the leader of the four men stated he was only prepared to pay less for the weapons then previously agreed. When Bear refused the offer, the four men attempted to take the weapons and pay nothing. The fight had only just begun when Hound arrived on the scene to assist by improving the odds.

When Bear completed his story, Bill once again entered a conversation with Hound. "Hound, where are you staying in Phoenix?" Bill asked.

"I have a room at a motel."

"It will be a day or two, maybe more, before you start to feel better after the beating you took. We have bedrooms here at the club that are as nice as any motel. Why don't you stay here until you start to feel better? Also, it wouldn't hurt you to look a little better before you start to mix and mingle with the public again. You haven't looked in a mirror yet. When you do, you'll see what I'm talking about. The club has a well-equipped kitchen. There's always a lady or two around that would be willing to cook meals for you while you're here, and we'll have more time to get better acquainted. What do you say?"

"That's very kind and generous of you, but I certainly don't want to impose."

"It wouldn't be an imposition. Consider it a gesture of appreciation from the club, me, and Bear personally, to thank you for assisting one of our own."

"Well, all right. I'm happy to accept your invitation, but I'll have to go back to my motel and get my belongings."

"Don't worry about that. Give me your room key. I'll send one of our members to get your stuff. Don't worry. None of your belongings will be missing when they arrive here."

"Why would I be worried about that?"

"Hound, I'm sure you've realized by now we're a group of outlaws, but we'll always treat you with proper respect and courtesy. So far, you've earned it. It will continue as long as you deserve it. We don't steal from, mistreat, or otherwise harm anyone who has earned our respect."

"Bill, I believe that. However, you didn't have to tell me. I already knew it."

"How do you know?"

"I consider myself a smart guy. I also have good instinct and insight regarding people. I know you're an outlaw. I know all of you are, but I also know when you give you word, you honor it."

"Hound, you're right about that. I believe you'll always honor yours."

Hound was given a room in the club adjacent to the one Bear would be staying in. His room was large, adequately furnished, and actually more comfortable than his motel room. The first thing he did after arriving in his room was take a look at his face in a mirror. He was feeling a great deal of pain. The image he saw in the mirror gave a clear indication of the reason why. The pain grew more intense when he took a shower, but he was determined to clean himself.

Pony had volunteered to retrieve Hound's belongings at the motel. Hound waited until those belongings were delivered to his room before going to bed. There was no doubt in his mind Bill had instructed Pony to inspect all his belongings for identification, or any other indication he might be a threat to the club and its members. He smiled knowing the main concern would be if he were an undercover cop, maybe a federal agent. Bill would certainly want to be cautious regarding that possibility.

Hound felt certain Bill's decision to show him the automatic weapons in the duffel bag was just part of the plan to help verify his reliability. Bill was an intelligent man. He had watched for telltale body cues from Hound when he displayed the duffel bag's content and allowed Bear to tell his story regarding the cause of the fight in the alley. Bill also knew showing the weapons and hearing the story would never be any type of evidence that could be used. Even if Hound was some type of undercover law enforcement, he had no physical evidence to present. Any testimony he might give would simply be his word against the word of every club member.

The club had experienced such several times in the past. No charge was ever brought against, or arrest warrant issued, for any individual club member, or the club chapter itself as a defendant organization. Hound knew he was being tested. He wasn't yet completely sure why. He could only assume perhaps he'd made an impression that led the club's leadership to believe he could be a valuable asset. Maybe they were interested in nothing more than inducting him into the club as a common member with common rank and status. Maybe they had other ideas in mind. Maybe they were interested in nothing more than making sure he wasn't undercover law enforcement. He would just have to be patient and wait to see what happened next.

After Hound went to bed, his pain grew more intense. When he heard a knock on the door of his room, he struggled to get up and respond. It required effort and time, but he eventually reached the door and opened it. When he did, Bear entered his room.

"Hound, how are you feeling?" Bear asked. "I figured you might need something for pain. I sure as hell did. I brought you something, if you want it."

"You figured right! What did you bring?"

"Fuck! What difference does it make if it kills the pain and doesn't kill you?"

"I guess it makes no difference. What did you bring?"

"A shot of morphine. I've also got some pills. I preferred the shot of morphine. It works a hell of a lot better for me than any damn pill."

"How much morphine should I take?"

"How much do you weigh?"

Hound disclosed his weight and waited as Bear filled a syringe with a specific amount of morphine. Bear injected the drug into a vein in Hound's arm. They talked for a while as the morphine started doing its job.

"Hound, have you ever taken morphine before?" Bear asked. "I would guess you've never taken any narcotic."

"Why would you think that?"

"You don't strike me as being the type to indulge in such things simply for pleasure."

"You're right. I'm not that type. However, I am the type to indulge for the purpose of reducing excruciating pain. I know morphine is good for that. I saw it ease the pain of a lot of wounded soldiers. I also saw it make dying a lot easier for more of them than I care to remember."

"I thought you might have been in the military. In what branch did you serve?"

"I was in the Army."

"I assume you must have served in Vietnam."

"I did."

"When were you in Nam?"

"I shipped over June 27, 1969, only a week after I completed officer training. I arrived at my first combat duty assignment in the field on July 27. I was discharged and sent home in December of last year."

"Son of a bitch! So, you were an officer. What was your rank?"

"Captain."

"Captain! You advanced in rank from second lieutenant to captain in only sixteen months. How in the fuck was that possible?"

"My promotions to first lieutenant and then to captain were both due to a battlefield commission."

"You must have done some real heroic shit, more than once, for that to happen!"

"I don't know. Maybe. Maybe not."

"If you went to Officer Candidate School, you must've signed up for a long hitch. Maybe you planned to make the Army a career. You were discharged early, so you must've been wounded and disabled in some way. What happened?

"Shit no! I had a two-year hitch. I was drafted. I was never wounded. The short version of my story is I got in a shitload of trouble. I managed to get an honorable discharge from the Army after being demoted back to first lieutenant and barely escaping a court-martial."

"I'd bet the long version of that story is very interesting and worth hearing."

"Maybe I'll tell you sometime, but maybe not. I don't really like to talk about the things I saw and experienced in Vietnam."

"Neither do I, brother. Most of us who were really in the shit over there don't like to talk about it. Did you see a lot of combat?"

"Yes, Bear. I did. It sounds like maybe you did too. How long were you in Nam?"

"I shipped over in January 1966 and came home in February 1967. I saw and experienced some dark shit over there. Several of the current club membership served in the military. Not all, but many of them, were sent to Nam. Bill and Pony were over there. Shit! We all got drafted around the same time. We didn't serve together, but we all suffered in that fucking hell. We were all wounded too, but not seriously enough to be discharged early. I guess we should be grateful for that. At least we're not disabled in any way. Well, except we're probably a little fucked up in the head. I'm pretty sure I am. You're probably a little fucked up too. Are you?"

"I don't feel like it, but I probably am. Did you serve under decent officers?"

"Some were decent, but most were assholes. You were likely not an asshole, were you? By God, I can almost guarantee you weren't."

"I hope I wasn't. I tried hard not to be."

When the morphine reached its full threshold of effect, Hound felt his pain begin to subside. He told Bear it was time to get some sleep. After Bear left his room, Hound quickly fell to sleep. It was early afternoon before he awakened. He got dressed and left his room to visit the kitchen area, where he'd been told someone would be available to prepare him something to eat.

Shortly after he arrived in the kitchen, a moderately attractive woman joined him. Jane was about 35 years old. She had volunteered to cook for him and Bear. Jane informed him Bear visited the kitchen much earlier and had already eaten. She asked what he'd like for her to prepare for him. He told her anything would be fine. She prepared a breakfast that consisted of fried eggs, ham, hash browns, homemade biscuits, fresh fruit, and the best coffee he'd tasted in a long while.

Immediately after finishing his breakfast, Bear participated in a meeting with Bill and Pony.

"Bear, where's Hound?" Bill asked.

"He was sleeping like a baby when I looked in on him about an hour ago."

"What's your opinion of Hound, beyond the fact he came to your aid and took a pretty good beating helping to save your ass?"

"Well, that alone is enough to make me like and respect him, but my gut feeling tells me I would have liked and respected him anyway."

"I know what you mean. There's something about him that causes me to feel the same way you do. However, we don't know a damn thing about him. We need to be cautious. Because of what he did for you, I'm all for him staying here a couple of days until he feels better, but we need to be careful not to show or tell him anything regarding the club's business operations that he isn't already aware of. It wouldn't be the first time the feds have tried to slip an undercover prick into our organization. They've been trying to get evidence on our illegal business activities for a very long time. We have to maintain extreme caution. The feds aren't stupid. I wouldn't put it past them to allow an agent to suffer a horrific beating in order to gain our confidence. You said Hound showed special fighting skills. He had to learn them somewhere. He may have learned them as part of his government training."

"Bill, I understand and support your concern, but I feel confident Hound isn't undercover. He told me earlier he served as an Army officer in Nam. Everything he told me about his time in the military, especially his tour in Vietnam, leads me to believe it's very unlikely he's an undercover agent for the feds or any other law enforcement organization. What he told me was only the tip of the iceberg regarding the whole story. I'm anxious to hear it all. I hope he tells me, but I'm not sure he will."

"What did he tell you?"

"He said he was drafted for a two-year hitch but was sent to OCS and was commissioned as a second lieutenant. In Vietnam, he achieved the rank of captain in a very short time under battlefield commission statutes. He got into some bad ass kind of trouble, was demoted back to second lieutenant, and was almost court-martialed. Even though he received an honorable discharge, he was forced out of the Army. He said he was discharged last month. If everything he told me was true, then there's no way he could be undercover."

"Maybe, but you make a very good point. How do we know everything he told you was true? Do you believe him?"

"Well, yes, I do."

"Why? What makes you think he wouldn't be lying?"

"I just have a strong gut feeling that he told me the truth."

"If he did, then that's another plus in his favor. I'll ask Maggie to thoroughly check him out as soon as possible. She'll be dropping by here sometime this afternoon. She'll be able to find out if he's lying or not."

"You're right about that. Maggie has the connections to find out anything about anybody. Do you have anything in mind for Hound if he checks out OK?"

"He might be a good candidate for club membership. He could likely be of special use to us, performing a special job."

"He might not be interested. What if he isn't?"

"Bear, all we can do is ask him. If he's not interested, then we'll respect his decision."

Maggie Mitchell was a 28-year-old, extremely intelligent young woman. She graduated first in her class from the Harvard School of Law. She was on a retainer as the club's attorney and had been since graduating from law school in 1968. Maggie could have obtained a very lucrative position at the law firm of her choice anywhere in the country had she wanted to do so. Instead, she elected to make her home in Phoenix and open a private law practice.

Maggie presented the impression she had the highest of moral turpitude and professional integrity, but her nature was pure rebel. This helped her be selected by the club as its attorney of record. The club was her first client. Because she was intelligent, charming, a subtle and successful manipulator, had graduated from Harvard at the top of her class, and was extremely attractive, Maggie had managed to develop contacts that would assist her in several useful and important ways, such as obtaining background information on individuals that might otherwise be difficult or even impossible to acquire. Naturally, this was looked upon very favorably by Bill and the biker club's other members in positions of authority.

Maggie was 5 foot, 10 inches tall, had shoulder-length dark brunette hair, and blue eyes. Her figure would be considered perfect for her height and weight. She usually dressed in a way that brought additional attention to her above average size breasts. She was extremely physically fit and religiously completed an intense physical fitness workout daily. She was also proficient in the martial arts and had achieved black belt status.

When Maggie arrived at the clubhouse that afternoon, Bill immediately escorted her to his office. He told her why Hound was invited to be a guest at the club. She told Bill it wouldn't be a problem to get the background information he wanted. She agreed to spend some time with Hound to develop a personal opinion of him. Bill valued her opinion regarding things of importance.

When Maggie met Hound, her first impression of him was positive. They sat together privately at a table in the corner of the club's bar. The lacerations, swelling, and bruises on his face showed no improvement since he acquired them. Although his strikingly handsome face was well concealed by his wounds, Maggie knew it was there. Naturally, he had no trouble instantly noticing and admiring her overall beauty.

"Well, Hound, I've heard quite a few things about you," Maggie said as their conversation began. "I was told you assisted Bear in defending himself against four assailants. Without your assistance, Bear would've been seriously injured, or possibly killed. Without you, the assailants would be the victors. Instead of you and Bear, they would have won the fight."

"We won the war but paid a huge price during the battle to win it. I suppose that's true regarding any fight."

"What do you mean? What price?"

"Just look at me, at my face. Have you seen Bear? He looks as bad as I do. We both paid the same price for our victory."

"Oh, I see. I understand and agree with you. I understand the other guys paid a much higher price."

"Bear and I paid the price for winning the war. They paid the price for losing it."

"You sound a bit philosophical. I like that. Incidentally, is that your Corvette parked outside?"

"If it's color is metallic midnight blue."

"That's the one I'm talking about. It's a beautiful set of wheels."

"Thanks. I'm very fond of it. Do you like Corvettes?"

"Hell yes, I do! You might be interested to know I just bought a new one myself. I believe mine is exactly like yours except for the color. Mine is metallic red. I was told you arrived in Phoenix only yesterday."

"That's right. I got here just in time to get the shit beat out of me."

"Well, everyone is happy you showed up in time to help Bear. I'm sure he's happier about it than anyone."

"Maybe. Anyway, I'm happy I could help him out. I don't know Bear very well, but there's something about him that rubs me the right way. I like him."

"He said close to the same thing about you. I hope you'll like me once we get better acquainted."

"I'm sure I will. You seem like a nice person. My instinct tells me you are. I have a reliable instinct."

"So do I. It tells me you're a nice person as well. What do you consider a nice person to be?"

"I guess someone who treats others the way they'd like to be treated. Are you that kind of person?"

"I'd like to think so. I hope so. Do you plan to stay in Phoenix for a while, or are you just passing through?"

"If I find what I'm looking for, I'll be staying. If not, I'll be moving on."

"What are you looking for?"

"Well, Maggie, I'm looking for the ideal location to build a nightclub."

"A nightclub? That's interesting. What do you consider an ideal location to be?"

"I'm looking for the ideal property, in the ideal city, in the ideal state. I want to build my club in an area where it will be well received and best appreciated. Its design will be the biggest, most elegant anywhere in the country. It could possibly be the first of several that I build. Naturally, I want the first to be as successful and profitable as it can be."

"I know you realize it's going to cost a lot of money to complete your plan. Do you have the kind of money it will take? I'm sorry. That question was a bit forward. I didn't mean for it to be. It's really none of my business how much money you have. If you're really serious, I'll tell you it's my opinion the Phoenix area would be as ideal as any to build such an establishment. There are a lot of people who live in Phoenix and surrounding areas that have a lot of money. There's nothing they'd like better than to spend some of it at the most elegant nightclub anywhere in the country. I know just the right people to contact that can help you locate the ideal site to build it on."

"That's good to know. Thank you. Your help would be greatly appreciated."

"Hound, if you don't mind me asking, how old are you?"

"How old do I look? It may be hard to tell because of the condition my face is in now."

"Hound, you'll have your good looks back sooner than you realize. It's not hard to see that beneath your injuries is the face of a most handsome young man. I'd estimate your age to be about 26, maybe 27. Am I close to being correct?"

"Your estimate is a few years older than I am. I'll be 22 on July 31 of this year."

"You have to be bullshitting me! Are you really only 21 years old?"

"I have no reason to lie. I'm 21. How old are you?"

"Now that I know your age, I wish you hadn't asked. Besides, you should never ask a woman her age. You know that."

"Come on, Maggie. Give it up. How old are you?"

"I'm seven years older than you. I'm 28."

"Well, Maggie, we have something in common regarding our choice in cars, but not in how old we look. I look older than my age and you look much younger than yours."

"Thank you for the compliment. Even if you're not serious, I appreciate it."

"I'm being completely serious, Maggie. Surely others have told you the same thing."

"Well, actually they have, so maybe you are being serious. Say, if you'd consider building your club a reasonable distance outside the Phoenix city limits, I know where there's some land I think might be a good location to build it on."

"Do you know how much money the owner wants for the land?"

"Not at this time, but I'm certain it would be a lot less than you'd pay for undeveloped land in the city."

"Maggie, I suppose it's worth consideration. I should at least take a look at the land."

"I agree. I think you should too."

"Are there any state, county, or local restrictions that would prohibit me from building a club on the land?"

"You could build whatever you want. Do you plan to buy a house or build one, if you decide to stay in the area?"

"I'd rather build. I want to personally design my home. Why do you ask?"

"I know where there's another piece of land ideal to build your home on. The land is only a couple of miles from where your club would be built."

"Maggie, having met you may be lucky for me."

"Having met could turn out to be lucky for both of us."

"Maybe. What makes you think so?"

"I know you're not married. You're too young and smart for that. However, you might have a steady girlfriend somewhere. One that will join you when you get settled somewhere. I hope you don't. Do you?"

"No. Actually, I don't. Why?"

"Well, maybe that's why I feel lucky having met you. That is, if you don't think I'm too old for you."

"Maggie, I don't concern myself with age. Age is only a number. I'm attracted to women based on their intelligence, character, and how they treat me."

"You left out how they look and how good they are in bed. You'll never convince me those things aren't important to you."

"Maggie, are you coming on to me?"

"Not yet, but maybe I will sometime in the future, after I get to know you better and if you turn out to be everything I hope you are."

"Maggie, I'm flattered, but just so you know, I move slow regarding things like that."

"That's good to know. So do I."

By the time their two-hour visit ended, Hound and Maggie had begun to grow fond of each other. Hound knew Maggie was more than simply a beautiful, intelligent woman with a law degree from Harvard. He was well aware Bill had an ulterior motive other than common courtesy for introducing him to her, but that was OK. He fully expected Bill would have him thoroughly investigated and knew why. He was more than convinced Maggie would play a large role in that investigation. That was OK too.

Under any other circumstances, he wouldn't want specific things regarding his past history known, especially his military history. However, it would likely work in his favor if Bill, Bear, and Pony knew those facts. He didn't want to be suspected of being any kind of threat to the biker club. He wanted to always be considered a genuine, trustworthy, and reliable friend. He felt having such a relationship with the club might at times prove to be very valuable.

Maggie's close personal and professional relationship with the club indicated she possessed a shady side regarding her use of the legal system and respect for established norms of society. She obviously had contacts that were individuals in high places. She could prove to be valuable at times as well. The fact that she was dedicated to keeping her body physically fit through intense exercise and was ranked as a black belt in the martial arts also greatly assisted her in winning his favor.

After she left Hound's company, Maggie had another meeting with Bill. This time Bear and Pony were present.

"Maggie, what did you think of Hound?" Bill asked. "What impressions did he make on you? What's your opinion of him?"

"My impression of him is positive. I think he's a genuine person."

"Genuine in what way?"

"What you see is what he is. There's no doubt he has a few skeletons in his closet that he wouldn't want publicly known, but don't we all?"

"What do you think is the likelihood he's an undercover cop sent to infiltrate the club, gain our trust, and gather evidence that can be used against the club or any of its members in court?"

"Bill, Hound is not an undercover anything. I'd be willing to bet everything I have on that being true."

"I hope you're right. However, we need to be absolutely sure he's no threat."

"I know, Bill. I agree completely. I'll have him thoroughly investigated. I'll get started on that right away. However, I'll say it again. Hound is no threat. Would any of you like to bet that I'm wrong? I'll cover the amount any or all of you wish to wager."

"Maggie, you'd likely be betting on a sure thing, but we have to be sure. We can't afford to take anything for granted. There's too damn much at stake."

"Bill, like I said, I agree completely."

When Maggie left the clubhouse later that afternoon, Hound was waiting to escort her out.

"Maggie, I want to say again how happy I am to have met you. Did you get all of your business with Bill completed?"

"Not really. I still have some work to complete for him. Why do you ask?"

"No reason. I'm just making conversation. Maggie, I'm very

impressed you're ranked a black belt. I'm very much interested in becoming proficient in the martial arts. Would you mind recommending or introducing me to an instructor who's qualified to train me if I decide to make my home in Phoenix?"

"I can definitely do that. If you decide to stick around, perhaps we could work out together on a regular basis, not only in the martial arts, but also for general physical fitness. I suspect you already work out on a regular basis, don't you?"

"Absolutely. Every day, at least six days a week."

"Are your workouts intense?"

"I think so. Are yours?"

"Extremely. Hound, how did you get your nickname?"

"My parents allowed me to rescue a young, pure blood hound dog when I was four years old. We were best friends until he died. I got the name because of our friendship."

"Bill told me something like that. I was just checking to see if it was true. I like your nickname. It probably suits you."

"I've been told that before. In many ways it probably does."

"Hound, would you like to see the land I told you about? I can show it to you tomorrow if you think you'll feel like it."

"That sounds great. I'll be sure to feel like it."

"All right. How about I pick you up here at the clubhouse around 8 a.m. tomorrow morning? We'll use my car."

"Are you driving, or am I?"

"I am. Nobody but me drives my car."

"I understand. I feel the same way about my car."

Maggie arrived at the clubhouse on time the next morning. They drove north from the Phoenix city limits for about fifteen minutes and then turned off the main highway onto another and drove west for a short time. Maggie turned off the highway to the right onto a dirt driveway, drove a short distance farther, and stopped the car.

"Well, Hound, we're here," Maggie said. "This is the piece of property you could build your club on."

They got out of the car and Hound began to survey the area. To the north, he saw nothing but desert landscape. A half mile in the distance were hills covered by an outer layer of various size rocks that could've been formed by a volcanic eruption centuries or longer ago. The hills were only a thousand feet high at the highest point but resembled a miniature portion of the Rocky Mountains in appearance.

Saguaro, other types of cactus, and mesquite bushes could be viewed as far as the eye could see. Two miles west was the beginning of a small business and residential community with a citizen population of around a thousand. To the east was nothing but desert for a distance of eight miles, where another small community began. To the south, across the highway, only desert terrain and a very few, randomly located residential homes existed for approximately ten miles. The Phoenix city limits began a short distance farther south.

Maggie showed Hound the property lines of the fifteen-acre tract of land. The property lines ran in almost a perfect square around the perimeter of the acreage.

"Maggie, I like what I'm seeing," Hound told her. "I have a good feeling about this property."

"All needed utilities are available. I know that's important. You can't operate a club without them."

"You're certainly right about that."

"Would you like to see the property I had in mind for you to build your home on?"

"Sure. Where is it?"

"Only a couple of miles west of here."

The ten-acre residential property was also laid out in a square with all four property lines almost equal in length. To the north, the hills resembling a miniature portion of the Rocky Mountains could still be seen. Hound's instinct told him the size and location of both properties were ideal for his purpose. He'd assumed it would take weeks, even months, to find the perfect location on which to build his nightclub. His search had ended only a couple of days after leaving California. He considered the additional property to build his home on as further confirmation he'd found what he was looking for. He attributed his good luck to destiny, an act of fate.

"Maggie, everything about both properties are very appealing to me," Hound said, smiling. "I certainly didn't expect to find what I was searching for so soon, but I have. I don't see any real estate signs anywhere, so I assume the properties are for sale by the owners."

"You're right, but the same person owns both properties."

"Who owns the properties? I'd like to speak to the owner as soon as possible to see if we can agree on a price."

Maggie stood silent and smiling as she looked at Hound for a moment before answering.

"Well, Hound, I own the properties," she said.

"No shit? Really?"

"Really? I can see you're surprised."

"I'm extremely surprised. Why did you wait until now to tell me? Why didn't you tell me when you first told me about the properties?"

"I felt certain you'd like both tracts of land. I wanted to see the look on your face when you found out I owned them. The look was everything I expected."

"Well, pretty lady, now that you've had your fun, how much money will it cost me to buy both properties?"

"Well, let's see, how does ten thousand dollars an acre sound?"

"That seems a bit high. Could you take less?"

"That's a bit more than it's worth right now, but sooner than later, undeveloped land in this area is going to skyrocket in price. In less than ten years, all this area will be within the Phoenix city limits. Buying the property now at the price I quoted will be a damn good investment for you. By the way, I want the money in cash."

"All right, Maggie. I'll buy the land for ten thousand per acre. Looks like I owe you two hundred fifty thousand cash."

"Looks like it. I assume you have two hundred fifty thousand cash. Do you?"

"Get started on the paperwork. I'll have the cash ready for you when it's time to sign and close the deal."

"Well, kiss my ass! I guess it's my turn to be surprised. I assumed you had some money, but I didn't think you had that much."

"Maggie, somehow I don't think you're that surprised."

"Well, actually I am. That's a lot of money for a 21-year-old to have. You must have inherited it or something."

"Or something. I sure as hell didn't inherit it."

"Did you come by it honestly?"

"I suppose that all depends on how you look at it. I would say honestly, based on where I got it."

"May I ask where you got it?"

"From the casinos in Las Vegas and Reno. I won it gambling."

"You won two hundred fifty thousand dollars gambling?"

"That's right."

"I consider that pretty damn lucky!"

"Indeed! Extremely lucky."

"So, you're not a professional gambler?"

"Not hardly."

"Was two hundred fifty thousand all you won, or did you win more?"

"More."

"How much more?"

"Just a few dollars. Not much."

"I like to gamble. Maybe we could go to Vegas together sometime."

"Maybe. Maggie, how did you acquire the properties?"

"My grandmother left them to me in her will."

"I agree the land is a good investment. Knowing that, why don't you keep it?"

"Honestly, I'd rather have less money now then wait to have

more later. Besides, two hundred fifty thousand is a good chunk of change. I have need of it at this time."

"I guess I can understand that. Maggie, do you happen to know a good contractor that would build both my home and club for a reasonable price?"

"Of course, I do. I'll put you in touch with him when you're ready to get started. Do you have any idea when that might be?"

"Likely by early spring this year, late March, maybe early April."

"Where do you plan to live until your home is built? Surely you don't want to stay in a motel until then. You might be able to remain Bill's guest at the club, but I don't think you want that either."

"I'll find a nice place to rent. One that's furnished."

"It might interest you to know I have a very nice two-bedroom, two-bath, visitors' cottage. It's fully furnished, and you'll have plenty of privacy. It's located on the property where I live, but it's a good distance away from my home. There's a separate, private driveway to the cottage. It enters through the rear side of my property."

"That does interest me. How much would you charge me for rent?"

"I'll rent it to you for two hundred fifty dollars per month, all utilities included. You can live there as long as you want or need to."

"That sounds like a good deal. I'll take it."

Hound moved into Maggie's guest cottage the next day. It took a week for Maggie to complete the paperwork needed to transfer ownership of the desert property to him. A few days later, she again met with Bill, Bear, and Pony at the biker clubhouse. She brought with her a complete and accurate report of Hound's background history. Four copies of the report were included so everyone could read and discuss it.

The pages of the report informed the readers Hound was drafted into the Army at the age of nineteen with an active duty service requirement of two years. His performance was so impressive during basic training he was recommended and accepted to OCS. He graduated first in his class from Officer Training School and shipped out for Vietnam as a second lieutenant. In less than one year, because of his leadership skills and performance during combat conditions, he was promoted to first lieutenant under battlefield commission statutes. Also, in less than a year, he distinguished himself in combat to a degree that got him recommended and chosen to receive the Congressional Medal of Honor.

In less than eighteen months, under battlefield commission statutes, he was promoted to the rank of captain. In only one month after arriving in Vietnam, he was assigned duty as a field mission commander. Shortly after being promoted to captain, he was assigned duty as commanding officer at a base camp. While there, he again distinguished himself during combat.

Things began to go downhill for him after that. In October 1970, for reasons not reported, he assaulted a superior officer, damn near beating him to death, was arrested, charged with attempted murder, and sent to Saigon to be incarcerated, awaiting court-martial. For reasons not reported, charges against him were dropped and the court-martial was cancelled. His CMH was reconsidered and denied. He was released from jail in early December 1970, given an honorable discharge from the Army, and sent home a month before his two-year hitch was up.

"Son of a bitch!" Bill said after reading the report. "Our Hound is one remarkable young mother fucker!"

"Well, I told you so," Bear added. "I had a strong gut feeling Hound was a special kind of guy and, also, not affiliated with law enforcement. I'm glad I was right about him."

"Bear, I'm also glad you were right."

"So am I," Maggie said. "Bill, aren't you glad you didn't bet with me?"

"Yes, Maggie. Both you and Bear were right about Hound.

Again, I'm glad you were. Maggie, I'm thinking about offering Hound membership in the club. I'm convinced more than ever now he could be of valuable use. What do you think?"

"Bill, Hound would definitely not be interested in a regular membership."

"Do you think the reason would be because he would object to our nefarious business operations?"

"Not at all. He simply has other career goals in mind. I mean no disrespect, but Hound would never be satisfied with a career as a regular member of your club. His personal qualifications and ambition dictate he be much more than that. However, it wouldn't hurt to offer him the honorary friend of the club membership."

"You're right. He might appreciate that. Being a friend of the club does include attractive benefits. You know that, having that membership yourself." Both Bear and Pony stated their support of the idea.

Bill contacted Hound by phone and invited him to visit the following day. The next morning, Hound met with Bill, Bear, and Pony in Bill's office.

"Hound, we've talked about it and would like to offer you a membership as honorary friend of the club," Bill told him. "How do you feel about that?"

"What would such a membership entail?"

"You'd be invited to attend all our non-business related bike rallies and social events held here at the club, or anywhere else. Naturally, you'd be welcome at the clubhouse anytime."

"Would anything be required of me I might not have time for, or want to do?"

"Absolutely not. We wanted to sponsor you for a regular full membership but somehow thought that wouldn't be appealing to you."

"You're probably right, but what makes you think so?"

"We simply assumed being a regular member would conflict with plans you've already made regarding a career."

"What career do you think I'm interested in?"

"Owner and operator of your own nightclub."

"Obviously, you got that information from Maggie. She's the only one who knows about my plan to build a nightclub."

"Well, yes. I hope you don't mind that she told us."

"Not at all. Why would I mind? You'd have eventually found out without her telling you. Bill, is my desire to pursue another career the only reason you felt I wouldn't except a regular membership in your club?"

Hound was curious to find out as much as possible about the business dealings of the club. Obviously, a substantial amount of money was required to sustain the club's existence. Also, as far as he could tell, none of the club members were employed by anyone or any business outside the club. The club's membership currently was at least two hundred men, all of whom needed to earn a sufficient paycheck. He knew for certain the club was involved in illegal, nefarious business dealings. He wanted to know what they were. However, he wasn't sure how much, if any of that, information would be entrusted with him. He was, however, certain enough time had passed for Maggie to have provided the background history on him Bill required. He thought that information might be enough to have earned him enough trust to be privy to at least a portion of what he wanted to know.

Bill sat silent for a moment considering how he'd respond to Hound's question. Hound sat patiently waiting to discover what Bill's response would be.

"Hound, how much have you heard in the past regarding the club's reputation?" Bill asked.

"Bill, I know your club has a large membership with chapters in California and other areas of the Southwestern United States. I've read about your club in the newspaper and heard its name mentioned in the news, on radio, and TV off and on over the past years."

"All right, then, I'm sure you know the club and its members don't have the reputation of being model citizens, pillars of the community."

"Is your reputation justified, or do you present a false image?"

"Shit, Hound! What the hell do you think?"

"Well, based on the story Bear told regarding his altercation with those four men in the alley and what I saw in the duffel bag, I'd tend to believe the club's infamous, nefarious reputation is justified."

"If it were justified, then how would you feel about us?"

"Bill, as long as it doesn't affect me, I don't give a good God damn what kind of business the club conducts, or what you, Bear, Pony, or any other club members do as individuals. It's none of my fucking business. How you treat me is how I judge you. How I treat you is how I want you to judge me. You've asked me to be a friend of the club. I want you to know what being a friend genuinely means to me. If it doesn't mean the same to you, then we can never be friends. We can be friendly acquaintances, but that is very much different than guaranteeing to always be loyal, trustworthy, and dependable to each other. If I accept you as a friend, then I expect you to never harm or betray me in any way. If you accept me as a friend, then you can expect the same from me. I know you felt it necessary to have Maggie verify I was worthy to be your friend. I understand why. I would've done the same thing in your place. I'm certain the information she provided regarding my past wasn't all positive. However, now knowing dark things about me, you want my friendship despite those things. Despite any dark things about the club, or its members, I can pledge my friendship as well. None of us can know at this time, but such a friendship might prove to be very beneficial to all of us at times."

The three men didn't expect to hear what Hound said, but they felt support for and agreement with it.

"Hound, how did you know I had Maggie check you out?"

"Because I'm extremely Intelligent and have excellent instinct. What did you find out about me?"

"The information I was provided began with your induction into the Army and concluded with your discharge."

"Do you know everything that happened during my time in the Army?"

"Absolutely everything."

"Why don't you have information about me before my military service began?"

"I didn't feel information prior to that would be needed."

"Is there anything else you'd like to know?"

"I'd be interested to know your level of education."

"I started attending Louisiana State University when I was sixteen years old. I completed an undergraduate degree and graduate degree in approximately two years. To achieve that level of education usually requires six to eight years. I tell you that because you might be interested to know how I was able to accomplish it. Would you?"

"That's extraordinary. Yes, how did you do it?"

"I had enough money and intelligence to put a plan into action and carry it out."

"How smart are you? What's your IQ?"

"At least 180."

"Shit! I thought I was hot stuff at 120. Your score is in the realm of genius, isn't it?"

"That's my understanding. Is there anything else you'd like to know about me? All you have to do is ask. I may choose not to answer, but I'll never lie to you."

"Actually, there is, if you don't mind."

"What do you want to know?"

"Why did you almost beat that officer to death while you were in Vietnam? Is that the reason your CMH was denied? How did you manage to avoid a court-martial and receive an honorable discharge?"

"The officer was a lowlife piece of shit. He deserved more than the beating he got. I wanted to kill the son of a bitch, but I knew

I was facing enough trouble because of the beating. I have every intention of killing him sometime in the future. Yes, what I did to him cost me the CMH. I can only assume the reason I evaded a court-martial and received an honorable discharge was because of my past service performance and just plain luck."

"Hound, I hope you don't mind me saying so, but I don't believe your past service performance and good luck were solely responsible. To get out of the kind of trouble you were in required special help from people in high places. Am I right?"

Hound felt it would be unwise, at least at that time, to confirm Bill's suspicion. Information was a form of power. He didn't want Bill to have any more information than he felt was necessary to serve his purpose.

"Bill, do you believe in guardian angels?" Hound asked.

"I've never really considered the possibility they exist. Why? Do you?"

"Well, I think I might. No person or persons in high places had anything to do with helping me. I've been helped to get out of some serious trouble a few other times in my life, trouble that I didn't think was possible to get out of. People in high places had nothing to do with that either. I can only assume guardian angels exist and I have one. Maybe I should say had one."

"Had one. What do you mean?"

"Well, even if I have a guardian angel, she may not hang around to protect me forever. There may be a code, certain rules guardian angels have to follow."

"So, you think your guardian angel is a female?"

"If I have one, then it's a female. I'm convinced of that."

"How do you know?"

"My instinct says so."

"Well, I guess I can't argue the point. I can't prove or disprove their existence."

"I suppose you're right about that."

"Hound, considering specific things, I agree having you as an honorary friend of the club might be a benefit to both of us from time to time. If you agree, then I'm ready to make it official in accordance with the club's rules regarding such membership."

"What's required to earn membership as an honorary friend?"

"I completely agree with your definition of what a friend is. To earn membership as an honorary friend of the club, you have to take an oath never to say or do anything that would be harmful to the club or any of its members. You have to understand there'll be consequences if you ever violate the oath. So, are you ready to receive the membership?"

"Yes, but I have a condition."

"What's the condition?"

"Before I take the oath, I want you to tell me every type of illegal, nefarious business the club is involved in. You felt it was necessary to know things about me. I understand the reason was to protect the club and its members. I fully agree with that reason. Now, I want to know things about the club for the same reason. If you're not prepared to comply with my request, then I suggest we shake hands, part company, and plan to never be in contact with each other again."

Hound knew he was asking for something Bill most likely wouldn't be willing to give. However, if Bill complied, Hound felt he'd be held in much higher regard than simply a common friend of the club. Bill considered the request for a moment. When he asked Bear and Pony their opinion, both were in favor of providing the information.

"Hound, we sell a variety of illegal drugs and weapons. We also fence stolen items that are sold at a profit. A very large stable of prostitutes are employed."

"I assume at least some of the stolen items are stolen by club members."

"Of course."

"Tell me how your prostitution business is operated?"

"The wives and mommas of club members function as madams

to schedule dates between prostitutes and clients. The prostitutes get forty percent of the revenue. The club gets sixty. The club also provides protection for the girls while they're working."

"Who supplies you with the drugs and weapons?"

"Why would you need to know that?"

"I was just wondering if Roberto Sanchez might be involved in some way."

"How do you know that name?"

"I heard it mentioned somewhere."

"What have you heard about him?"

"Only that he is the leader of a cartel. Is he your supplier?"

Again, Bill paused his conversation to consider the question. "Hound, I probably shouldn't tell you," Bill replied. "What possible reason could you have for wanting to know?"

Hound thought quickly to decide what response he'd give. He certainly didn't want his relationship with Carmella known.

"I might want to invest some money in your drug business at various times to make a little extra money," Hound said, "if you'd allow me to do that. Rumor has it, Sanchez provides good product."

"How much money do you think you might be willing to invest at various times?"

"That all depends on how much return I can get for my money. How much would that be?"

"That all depends on how much you're willing to invest. What amount did you have in mind?"

"Well, say a minimum of one hundred thousand dollars."

A very surprised look appeared on Bill's face. "Hound, you just paid two hundred fifty thousand dollars to Maggie," Bill said. "Do you have another one hundred thousand dollars?"

"I will at various times."

"Would ten percent return on your investment be of interest?"

"Hell no, but fifty percent would. That's what I'd require. I guess that would make us partners in my investment, would it not?"

"How come so much?"

"Bill, come on! I'm putting up all the money. It's not costing you anything to earn fifty percent of the profit it generates."

"All right."

"Well, is Sanchez your supplier?"

"Are you ready to invest one hundred thousand dollars today?"

"Yes, if Sanchez is your supplier."

"Sanchez supplies all the drugs and most of the weapons and ammo."

"How large is his business? How much territory does it cover?"

"It's my understanding his cartel is among the largest. I'm not sure of all the territory he services, but I do know California, Oregon, Washington State, Idaho, Utah, Arizona, Texas, New Mexico, Nevada, Oklahoma, and Colorado are among them. I know that because our club has at least one chapter in each of those states. In some states, we have more than one."

"Which state has the most chapters?"

"California."

"That makes sense. California is a big state."

"Texas is next in number of chapters."

"So, you don't know if Sanchez is doing business in Louisiana?"

"No, but if the territory is up for grabs, then I'm sure he will be at some time."

"What do you mean, up for grabs?"

"It's my understanding the various cartels have divided the United States into territories and have agreed which each will control. This eliminates disputes between the competing cartels. They all want to keep a low profile and make a lot of money. Going to war over disputed territories wouldn't be good for any of their businesses."

"Do you ever deal directly with Sanchez?"

"No, all business is transacted through middlemen who work for him. I guess it's only natural he wouldn't want to deal directly with anybody."

Hound took the oath required by the club to become an honorary friend. Bill informed him a jacket and vest bearing the club's colors and insignia identifying his status with the club would be presented to him as soon as possible. Hound departed the clubhouse to do other things for the remainder of the day.

It didn't take him long to discover he enjoyed living in Maggie's guest house. There were several reasons for his satisfaction, but the primary reason was the absolute privacy it provided him. Maggie's home was large and certainly of the upper middle class variety. It and the guest cottage were built on eight acres of prime real estate located in the most desirable gated residential community in the Phoenix area. Her home had been built at the front, center location of the property. The guest house had been built at a rear, center location.

Separating Maggie's home and the cottage was a distance of at least one hundred yards containing a wide variety of vegetation including, but not limited to, walkways bordered by high hedge walls, a variety of large trees, and many small, individual gardens containing plants that remained green year round and flowers that bloomed seasonally. The rear entrance to the property provided Hound a personal, private access to the cottage. The design of landscape and distance between the main residence and cottage made it impossible for Hound to observe the activity at Maggie's home. She was restricted in the same way.

From the time he moved into the cottage in late January, Hound had no contact with Maggie until his rent was due in February. It was early evening when he walked from the cottage to her home and delivered the rent money personally.

"Hello, Hound," Maggie said when she opened the front door to receive him. "Has everything been going well for you?"

"Absolutely, Maggie. How about you? Have you been doing well?"

"Absolutely, at least financially. I used the money you paid me for the land to make some damn good investments. I'm already receiving some excellent returns. It's been a month since I've seen you. Why have you been such a stranger?"

"I've been a bit busy. I'm sure you have as well."

"I have, but I would've enjoyed hearing from you before now. You could've called just to say hi."

"I suppose so. I'm sorry I didn't. I didn't get a call from you either."

"Hound! It's the man's place to call the woman, not the other way around. You know that."

"You're right. I apologize. Will you forgive me?"

"I suppose, but just this one time. Anyway, it's great to see you again."

"It's great to see you again as well. I'm personally delivering your rent check rather than mailing it only because I wanted to see you again. By the way, I don't suppose you'd tell me what you invested in?"

"You suppose right. Have you been to Vegas or Reno lately?"

"Yes. As a matter of fact, I returned yesterday from a tour of gambling in both."

"I don't suppose you'd tell me how much you won. Somehow I don't think you lost."

"You're right. I won, and I'm not going to say how much."

"Hound, do you ever lose? Tell me the truth."

"Sure, I do, but only when I choose to."

"Are you saying you sometimes lose on purpose?"

"Absolutely. It's a necessary part of my overall system."

"When are you going to take me gambling? You said you would. I'd like to learn your system of winning."

"Maggie, I said I might take you. I never promised I would, but I likely will some time if you still want to go when that time arrives. However, I'll never divulge my system to anyone. Besides, my system requires a special talent, one which I don't think you have."

"Come on, Hound! What the hell does that even mean?"

Hound didn't provide her with an answer. He only smiled. Maggie knew it was of no use to pursue the subject any further. Hound was never quick to let anyone know about his photographic memory, or the role it played in his system of winning at blackjack. His system of winning consistently involved his ability to remember all cards played regardless of the number of people playing at his table, or the number of card decks being used.

He planned to continue gambling in Reno and Vegas on a monthly basis. Each month he planned to win a net amount of no less than two hundred fifty thousand dollars. Naturally, this would afford him the level of comfort he desired in his lifestyle and allow him to save a substantial amount as well. He didn't want the cost of building his new nightclub and home to deplenish his savings below a specific amount. Maggie had already introduced him to the contractor who would build them. The contractor told him the total cost to build both home and nightclub would be approximately four million dollars.

When Hound prepared to leave after delivering the rent check, Maggie invited him into her home to share a bottle of wine and visit awhile longer.

"Hound, you're probably making so God-damned much money I should charge you more for your rent," she said, offering a short laugh. "I won't if you promise to take me gambling with you sometime in the near future."

"All right, Maggie. I promise to take you sometime in the near future. However, I'll have to take a rain check on the wine. Will you give me one?"

"I suppose so, but I can't believe you're turning down excellent wine and company."

"I'm sorry, but unfortunately, I have a previous engagement."

"I won't bother to ask you what it is."

"Good. I wouldn't tell you if you did."

Ever since Maggie had offered to rent her guest cottage to him, Hound suspected she might have an ulterior motive for doing so. He was paying much less to rent the cottage than it was actually worth. Should Maggie ever require more be paid, he'd be happy to comply. He was very fond of Maggie and found her most attractive, but he didn't want their relationship to go beyond that of friendship. He felt that to be in his best interest. She'd offered to introduce him to a master so he could begin training in the martial arts. She'd expected by now to be exercising and practicing karate with him on a daily basis, but he'd purposely avoided spending any time with her.

He was continuing to spend as much time as possible with both Carmella and Rebecca. Adding a third female to the mix, especially one like Maggie, would likely prove to be a decision he'd regret. He didn't fear her, but he certainly respected her. Based on her individual personality and capabilities, Maggie would prove to be a handful should she ever feel used or taken advantage of. He felt certain the contacts she had, not excluding the biker club, would add to the probability of her success should she ever seek revenge for any reason. Hound embraced the fact that hell hath no fury like a woman's scorn.

Carmella and Rebecca were now coming to visit Hound in Phoenix. When each would visit, they'd be his guest at the cottage and enjoy the nightlife of Phoenix and surrounding areas with him. They were both attending classes at Berkeley, so their visits were restricted to weekends or during times of break or vacation. Carmella's weekend visits occurred monthly. Rebecca tried to visit at least two weekends per month. She was eager to come more often, but Hound wouldn't allow it, telling her he was now involved in business dealings that kept him out of town over weekends on a frequent basis.

Hound hadn't told Carmella about the business relationship between Roberto's cartel and the biker club. He hadn't told her about his relationship with the club. He'd said nothing to Carmella or Rebecca about the property he'd purchased from Maggie. He'd keep his plan to build the nightclub and home in Phoenix a secret for as long as possible. All either of them knew at this time was his stay in Phoenix might only be temporary.

During the months of February and March, Hound's day-to-day existence was very common and routine. He'd already started to receive monetary return on the one hundred thousand dollars he'd invested with the club. He'd continue to make such investments on a random but consistent basis for the purpose of continuing to grow his relationship with Bill, Bear, and Pony. He insisted they be the only ones that knew of his investments. He was well liked and received by all members of the club, their wives, mommas, and the females who were on the club's groupie list, but he realized the fewer individuals who knew his relationship with the club was more than a regular honorary friend would definitely be in his best interest. Such information was power over him. He wanted that power in the hands of only individuals he knew he could trust.

The wives and mommas of club members were considered off-limits when it came to sexual relations with anyone except their husbands or boyfriends. This wasn't the case regarding the female groupies. Free drugs, alcohol, and a variety of special favors were among the benefits extended to a groupie. The criteria to become a groupie was simple. A woman had to be at least eighteen years of age. Regarding her physical appearance, she had to be at least a seven on a scale of one to ten. She had to make herself available for sex with any club member desiring such. There was always a sufficient amount of groupies hanging around. Indeed, the drugs, alcohol, and special favors enticed a certain type of woman to become a groupie, but another enticement was the club's reputation of being wild, adventurous, and dangerous. Whatever the reason, they just liked hanging out with bad boys. Some of the women in the club's stable of prostitutes were also groupies.

Hound received invitations regularly to attend social events at the club and other locations. There seemed to be some type of celebration scheduled on a weekly basis. A birthday, marriage, and occasional birth of a child were events for the club to celebrate. From time to time, Hound would attend the funeral of a club member. These deaths were seldom the result of natural causes. The funeral and wake were conducted according to club tradition. It would be quite an understatement to say this tradition was unusual. It would shock the conscience of anyone who'd never been exposed to anything but a traditional Christian funeral.

By the middle of February, all wounds Hound had received during the alley fight were completely healed, leaving no evidence that such injuries ever occurred. Because of his extraordinarily attractive physical features and winning personality, Hound was constantly sought after by the groupies. It was also a common occurrence for him to be propositioned by the wife, or momma of a club member. He always remained charming and gracious to all the women, indicating how very flattered he was regarding their offer, but always declining in ways that weren't demeaning or offensive.

Like Hound, Maggie was also subjected to unwanted propositions. Like Hound, she tried to accept as few invitations as possible to attend special club celebrations and frequently scheduled parties. Eventually, Hound and Maggie agreed it would be a good idea to attend such events together, presenting themselves as a couple romantically involved. They'd always arrive and leave together in either his Corvette or hers. The celebrations and parties usually lasted from early afternoon until late morning the next day.

Hound and Maggie never stayed much longer than a couple of hours. Neither of them ever consumed more than two alcoholic beverages and never indulged in any of the free drugs that were always available. They both understood the image they presented as being a couple was only an act that served a specific purpose. When not attending club functions together, neither of them would assume their relationship was more than good friends.

It was a little after 10 p.m. on Wednesday night during the

last week of March. Hound and Maggie were driving home after attending one of the club's parties. It was warmer than usual that night. Maggie had put the top down on her convertible Corvette.

"Hound, you know everyone at the club believes we're fucking," Maggie said, smiling. "How do you feel about that?"

"I'm happy about it. That's what we want them to think, isn't it?"

"Yes, it is, but I'd like to ask you something and I want you to give me an honest answer."

"OK. What do you want to know?"

"Hound, for a long time now I've made it very clear I'm available to you. You've consistently turned down invitations for dinner at my home and at nice restaurants, to attend a movie, go dancing, and a lot of other things. I know you realize I'm interested in more than just friendship. All you'd have to do is ask, if you wanted to take me to bed. I've never known a man that wouldn't jump at the chance to have all I'm offering to you. However, you remain seemingly without any interest in me at all. I'd like to know why."

"Maggie, I thought we agreed to just be friends."

"Come on, Hound! Don't act stupid or play games with me! I know you're not stupid and I don't like games! I just confirmed I'm interested in more than a friendship. I've done everything except lie down naked in front of you and spread my legs. Maybe that's what you want. If it is, then say so!"

"Maggie, I'd be lying if I said I wasn't attracted to everything about you. I'm just not ready to pursue a committed relationship. I feel that's the kind you'd require from me. I value you as a person and friend and don't want to do anything to disappoint or hurt you."

"Hound, the only thing I require in a relationship is honesty. I'm a mature, intelligent and realistic woman. I would never enter into any relationship believing it would be ideal or even last. However, I do believe in at least giving us a chance and see what happens. Things might work out, they might not."

"What happens if things don't work out the way you want them to?"

"I'm mature enough to handle that. Are you?"

"You know I am. Maggie, I don't disagree with what you're saying, but why don't we think about it a bit longer?"

"Hound, are you in love with someone you haven't told me about? Perhaps someone who has broken your heart. Is that why you don't want to risk caring about someone? Is it because you don't want to be hurt again?"

"Maybe. Honestly, I'm not really sure regarding either of your questions. I wonder if I was actually ever in love. I don't know if my heart was broken, or I was just extremely disappointed, and my pride was damaged. Maybe it's karma. If I have a broken heart, then maybe I deserve it."

"Well, maybe you deserve it, maybe you don't. Would it help to talk about it? I'd be happy to listen. Perhaps I could help."

"Maggie, I usually don't talk about personal things. I usually try to solve my problems personally, privately."

"Hound, maybe it's time you trusted someone enough to tell them what's troubling you. Somehow, I suspect many things may be burdening you in addition to a failed relationship. Let's go to my home. I'll brew a fresh pot of coffee and we can talk about things. I have no ulterior motive other than trying to be of help."

"OK, Maggie. Do you make good coffee?"

"Of course, I do."

Hound sat at the table in the breakfast nook of Maggie's kitchen while she prepared the coffee. They discussed casual things until the coffee was ready. She sat down across the table from him and added cream and honey to the special blend of coffee she'd prepared. The conversation remained casual for a short time longer, and then Hound began to tell Maggie about Jo. His story began at the first time he and Jo met and ended the last time he saw her. Naturally, it excluded information pertaining to specific events and individuals, such as Carlos Mendoza, Karen Thibodaux, her boyfriend Larry Trischman, and Carmella. He certainly made no mention of the O'Malley family's connection to the Irish Mafia or Ken O'Malley's position of leadership in it.

It took him almost an hour to tell his story. When he finished, Maggie asked him to tell her about his experiences in Vietnam. He was surprised to find himself willing and able to comply. It took another hour for him to tell that story. The only thing he excluded from that story was what he had done to Lieutenant Jeff Connors.

"Hound, how do you feel after telling me all that?" Maggie asked.

"You had my tenure in the Army thoroughly investigated. I probably didn't tell you anything you didn't already know."

"I certainly didn't know about your militia, Kim Li, and all the other villagers. I didn't realize how horrific your experiences really were during field missions and especially at Base Camp Bravo 127 and Delta 126. I didn't know the names of the soldiers you were close to over there that died. How has your time in Vietnam affected you emotionally?"

"I don't feel like I've been affected at all."

"Hound, there's no way what you experienced hasn't impacted your emotions, at least to some degree, in a negative way."

"Maybe, but I don't think so. If you're right, then all I need is time. Time is essential for healing, physically and emotionally."

"Jo is six years older than you. Do you prefer older women?"

"As long as the age difference isn't too great, then it doesn't concern me. Six years was certainly not a concern. I'm influenced by the individual, what kind of person they are."

"Perhaps a major reason for you selecting Jo could be because you look, behave, and feel older than you are. It seems only natural you'd prefer a woman that was older and more mature than one your own age. I'm sure older women are attracted to you because of your maturity."

"I've considered that."

"Hound, do you actually have any idea how extraordinarily

attractive you are to a woman? Not only are you extremely handsome and very physically desirable, but you're exceedingly charming, have a wonderful sense of humor, and are super intelligent. Even though you often try to hide it, I sense you're very warm and compassionate. I also sense you're a good lover. If I'm right, then you're without a doubt the perfect catch for the woman who is lucky enough to win your heart. You are a good lover, aren't you?"

"I try very hard to be good at anything I do. Are you a good lover?"

"Absolutely! Someday I hope you'll want to find out how good."

"Maybe."

It was almost 2 a.m. the next morning when Hound left Maggie's home and walked to the cottage. He went directly to bed and fell quickly to sleep. He awoke around 11 a.m. After eating a quick brunch, he contacted the contractor who was to build his home and club. Hound told the contractor he wanted to begin construction immediately on a barn type structure to be located on the same property as his home. He planned to live in the structure during the construction of his home and nightclub. He also planned to equip the structure as a small but adequate gymnasium where he could complete the major portion of his daily physical fitness workouts. In addition, the structure could also be used as a large storage area. The barn's design included a rustic but large and modern efficiency apartment in its upper level.

The barn was completed and ready for use on Tuesday in the second week of April. Hound had begun allowing himself to spend more time with Maggie. Thus far she had allowed him to maintain a platonic, friend type relationship with her. Desiring more, she had begun to grow increasingly frustrated. All she ever wanted was an opportunity to enter a more intimate relationship to see if it might grow into one that would last. He had come to view what she wanted as reasonable. To continue denying her what was reasonable would soon result in her separating from him completely.

At that time, he wasn't sure that was something he wanted.

Hound moved into his new dwelling on Wednesday. On Thursday, he called Maggie and invited her for dinner that evening as somewhat of a barn-warming party and to show her his new, temporary home. He told her if she was interested in spending the night, then she could join him for an intense workout in the barn and five-mile run in the desert the next morning before he prepared them a fantastic breakfast.

"Hound, does your invitation to spend the night include sex?" Maggie asked.

"Would you be disappointed if it didn't?"

"I'm always disappointed when you reject me, asshole!"

"Well, then the answer to your question is yes."

"Well, it's about time!"

Maggie arrived on time for dinner at 7 p.m. Wednesday evening. Hound was busy putting final touches on the steak dinner he'd prepared for them. Maggie opened the bottle of wine she'd brought, poured a couple of glasses half full, and handed one to him. She helped him with the small amount of work remaining to complete the meal. During dinner, they engaged in enjoyable conversation.

"This is ironic as hell!" Maggie said, laughing. "I've invited you to dinner many times and you turned me down each time. I accepted the first invitation you extended."

"Well, Maggie, maybe you're hungrier than I was."

"Oh, hell yes! That's the only logical explanation."

After dinner, they sat at the dining table continuing to talk and sip wine. After a time, Maggie excused herself to visit the bathroom. She returned a short time later wearing a very revealing, provocative nightie. Hound didn't say a word as his eyes surveyed her completely from head to toe. She was truly beautiful.

"Do you like what you see?" she asked him.

"Without a doubt. Maggie, you're absolutely beautiful."

"Are you ready to enjoy a little of what you see?"

"Not if it's only going to be a little."

"Baby, you can have all you want. I've got plenty to give."

Hound escorted her to the bed. She lay on her back watching as he undressed.

"Looks like you've got a lot to give us as well," Maggie said when she saw him completely nude. "Take it easy with me at first. You may not believe it, but it's been a good while since I've been with a man."

The look on her face and tone of her voice convinced Hound she was telling the truth. He joined her on the bed and began providing her the best sexual performance he could offer. Maggie was in superb physical condition. He knew this would extend her performance time. She announced her complete satisfaction after achieving more orgasms than any woman he'd ever been with. His satisfaction was equal to hers, but she far surpassed him in number of climaxes. That night, Maggie slept as close to him as possible, with his arms wrapped around her and hers around him.

The next morning, they were up early to begin their workout, which lasted almost two hours. After enjoying a hearty breakfast, they sat and talked, sipping coffee Maggie insisted on preparing. They enjoyed each other again sexually before Maggie left around noon. Hound told her he'd be leaving the next morning to visit his parents in Louisiana. He'd be away until the first week in May. Maggie wasn't happy with the news, but she understood.

"Damn!" she said, only half-jokingly. "It's not very nice to spoil me in bed and then leave me the next day to be away for so long. However, I'm glad you're going to visit your parents. It'll be good for you to see each other again. You didn't spend much time with them after you returned from Vietnam, did you?"

"No, Maggie, I didn't. I've always felt bad about that, but I also felt it necessary to get away for a time."

"Are you going to see Jo?"

"I suppose so, if she still wants to talk to me face-to-face. I at least owe her that much."

"I guarantee she'll want to see you. You're right, you at least owe her the courtesy of talking to you."

The contractor told Hound satisfactory progress would be made on the construction of his home while he was away. Every effort would be made to complete construction ahead of schedule. Hound was happy with that likelihood. He was anxious to move into his new home as soon as possible.

5

Hound boarded a flight early the next morning and arrived at the farm in time for lunch. His parents were waiting anxiously for him at the airport when he arrived. During the drive from the airport to the farm, John and Linda took turns talking in an attempt to bring Hound up to date on everything that happened while he was away. John told him the farm would likely have another record-breaking profit season that year.

Connie Newman married Tommy a little over a year ago. Their divorce was expected to be finalized sometime in May. Connie had managed not to get pregnant. Connie had told John and Linda she'd very much like to see Hound again the next time he came home for a visit.

Sherry Bentley had also sent a message she'd enjoy seeing him again. Linda said both Sherry and Connie seemed quite pleased to learn Hound and Jo were no longer together.

"Have you heard from Jo lately?" Hound asked. "Do you know how she and her family are doing?"

"We haven't heard from her in over two months," Linda

replied. "I suppose that's because the last time we talked to her she told us what happened between you two. Your father and I were devastated and so very sorry to learn about it. She's taking a leave of absence from her job at the university until the baby comes. She's moved to New Orleans to be with her parents."

"Did she say she wanted me to contact her there?"

"Yes, she did. She also indicated her father very much wanted to speak with you. I wonder what's on his mind?"

"I have no idea, but I'm sure if he wants to talk to me, he'll find a way to do it."

"Jo said he wanted you to work for him after you and she were married. Do you think he might still want that even though you and Jo will not be getting married?"

"I'm sure he still wants me to accept a specific position in his business, but he'd also want Jo and I to reconcile and get married first."

"Hound, would you consider getting involved with Jo again? Your father and I know she's still crazy about you. She and her parents might do all in their power to convince you to reconcile."

"I don't think that's likely, but even if you're right, I don't see how they could be successful."

"You had very strong feelings for her before she became pregnant. Do you still care for her?"

"You know I do, but I have strong negative feelings about her current situation. I could deal with the fact she was raped, if she really was. I can't deal with the fact she's pregnant by another man."

At that point, John decided to join the conversation.

"Son, I can understand your feelings," John said. "I don't disagree with them, but you've always agreed there's a solution to any problem regardless of how big the problem is. Once you truly love someone, then maybe you can never stop. That could be the major reason for you to consider reconciling. You're adopted, but your mother and I came to love you as if you were our own. In time, you'd come to love Jo's child as we did you. In addition, I know you and Jo would have children together."

"Dad, a different situation from mine and Jo's existed between you and Mom when I was adopted."

"Hound, whatever you decide to do is strictly your business, not mine, your mother's, or anyone else's. You must do what makes you happy. Whatever you do, your mother and I will support, but in support of Jo, there's something I want you to consider. Your mother and I weren't originally in favor of your relationship with Jo. However, over time we came to accept and respect her. There's no doubt in my mind Jo was a victim of rape. Perhaps if she hadn't been careless it wouldn't have happened, but she had no intent. If she could've prevented it, then I know she would have. Becoming pregnant only made what happened to her more traumatic. Perhaps forgiving her isn't required. Is it possible what she deserves is the kind of support and understanding that can only be generated by true love?"

"Dad, I appreciate everything you said. I'll give it serious consideration."

"The O'Malleys are a very well-to-do family. Ken O'Malley is a powerful and influential man. It's possible he could be planning to dangle a carrot in front of you. I'm sure it would be a hard one to refuse."

"Dad, that may be true, but the plans I'm currently making for my future are set in stone. They don't include being associated with the O'Malley family. At one time, Ken desperately wanted me to work with him in his business. Maybe he still does. Maybe he plans to dangle an appealing carrot, but I don't think he can make any offer that will change my mind."

"What are your plans for the future at this time?"

"I'm going to build a business of my own."

"What type of business might that be?"

Hound wasn't prepared at that time to tell his devout Christian parents he was building an elaborate nightclub in the desert on the outskirts of Phoenix. He wasn't prepared to tell him about his elaborate home either.

"I haven't decided yet," Hound replied. "I'll let you know when I do."

"Well, son, I know you'll be very successful at whatever type business you decide to build. Where do you plan to get the money needed to begin?"

Hound was certainly not prepared at that time to tell his parents about his extraordinary monetary success as a gambler.

"I'm giving a lot of consideration to that," Hound replied. "Where there's a will, there's a way. I'm currently looking for the best way."

When Hound and his parents arrived at the farm, Hector and Lupe were waiting to greet them. Hound hadn't seen Carmella's parents in over two years. They were invited into the Smith home to sit down and visit. They had only visited a short time before Hector asked Hound if he ever had contact with Carmella.

"I talk to her by phone," Hound said, "on a random, infrequent basis. Have you contacted each other?"

"Her mother and I haven't seen or talked with her since she moved out of our home several years ago."

"Hector, it's my understanding you and Lupe didn't want any contact with her after she left. Is that correct?"

"I didn't, but Lupe felt differently. I shouldn't have denied her the opportunity to keep in contact with her daughter."

"Have you changed your mind? Has your heart softened?"

"What Carmella did shamed and hurt me greatly, but it was wrong of me to treat her the way I did. Yes, I have changed my mind. Is Carmella doing well?"

"From what she tells me, I think she is."

"Do you know where she is now? How is she earning a living? Is she still selling herself?"

"Do you not know anything about her after she left?"

"We eventually found out she had moved to Mexico and was

living with her grandmother. However, when we tried to contact her there, we discovered she'd moved away. None of our family in Mexico knows where she is currently, or what she's doing. We were hoping you did."

"I do know, but I'm not sure she'd want me to tell you. However, I will tell you that she's doing well and is no longer working as a prostitute."

"Is she still in Mexico?"

"Hector, if you wish to reestablish a relationship with your daughter, then I'll be happy to tell her so. Would you like me to ask her to call you the next time I speak with her?"

"I would like that very much. Thank you. Do you know when you'll be speaking with her again?"

"I usually hear from her every month or so. I'll probably speak to her around the first week in May. Hector, I'm very happy to know you'd like to have her in your life again. I feel knowing that will make her very happy as well."

"Hound, do you think Carmella will forgive me for treating her the way I did?"

"I feel confident she will. She's always hoped you'd forgive her."

"I have. Please tell her that. I've never stopped loving her. Please tell her that also."

"I'll be sure to do that, Hector."

"Lupe and I were very disappointed with not getting to see you when you first returned home from Vietnam. We know you must be very happy to be out of the war and back in the States again."

"Very happy."

"John and Linda told us you had a rough time over there. How bad was it?"

"I'll just say it was bad enough. I don't care to discuss Vietnam any further."

It was early afternoon on Saturday. Hound had been at the farm a couple of days and decided to drive into town. He cruised the streets for a while and visited some of his old hangouts. He thought he might run into some old friends. When no old friends could be found, he drove to the café where he used to enjoy the apple pie. He occupied the table at the window where he used to always sit. He ordered a slice of homemade apple pie and a large glass of milk.

The waitress had just delivered the pie and milk to his table when an old friend from the past entered the café. Bobbi Thibodaux was five years older since the last time he'd seen her. She noticed him and he offered her a smile. As she walked toward his table to join him, Hound couldn't believe how much she'd changed. Bobbi had gained a lot of weight. She was only 21 but looked much older. The clothes she wore were clean but frumpy. When she arrived at his table, he asked her to sit down.

"Hound, it's certainly a nice surprise to see you again," Bobbi said. "Let's see, we haven't seen each other in about five years."

"That sounds about right. Bobbi, how have you been?"

"I've been better, but all things considered, I suppose I could be worse. I've changed a bit. I'm sure you noticed I've gained a lot of weight. Thirty pounds to be exact. I gained it when I became pregnant a couple of years ago. I haven't been able to lose it. It's nice to see you still look the same. You're as handsome as last time I saw you."

"Thank you. I lost quite a bit of weight while I was in Vietnam, but I regained it once I got back to the States. So, you have a baby now. Boy or girl?"

"I have a little girl."

"Who did you marry? Was it the guy you started dating when you and I could no longer see each other? You know, the guy your family thought was so appropriate for you."

"My relationship with him didn't last very long."

"Did you marry anyone that I know?"

"I've never been married. I gave birth to an illegitimate child."

"How does your family feel about that?"

"Let's just say they weren't overjoyed about it."

"Who's the baby's father?"

"Hound, I'm ashamed, but I don't know. I suppose you think I've turned into a real slut, don't you?"

"I'd be the last one qualified to judge you. I've certainly fucked up a few times in my life."

"That's very kind. Thank you."

"Did you go to college?"

"I'm in my third year at LSU."

"Are you still living with your grandparents?"

"I live on campus during the week. I stay with them every weekend and during vacations. They take care of my baby while I'm in school."

"How is Judge Thibodaux doing? Does he still have the red ass for me?"

"What do you mean?"

"Come on, Bobbi, you know he strongly suspected I had something to do with your Aunt Karen's disappearance. Does he still have that suspicion?"

"He never talks about it anymore, but I'm sure he does. I think he'll always believe you had something to do with that Mendoza kid's death and Aunt Karen's disappearance."

"How about you? Do you believe that as well?"

"Hell no. I never for a minute thought you had anything to do with either one. However, I had to pretend I did. I honestly believe my grandfather would've kicked me out of the house if I didn't. I heard you were in the Army and served in Vietnam."

"What you heard was correct."

"I'd like to know what it was like for you over there."

"How much have you heard?"

"Only that you were there. Nothing else."

"All I care to tell you about Vietnam is I was there for 16 months and then received an honorable discharge and came back to the States. I don't talk about what happened over there."

"OK. I think I understand why. Did you get married? I heard you were going to."

"No. I'm still too young to think about getting married. There's a lot of things I want to see and do first. Say, do you happen to know a girl by the name of Sherry Bentley? I think she may still be attending LSU. Sherry is an old friend of mine. She left word with my parents she'd like to see me the next time I was in town. I know LSU is a big campus and a lot of students attend. I just thought you might happen to know her."

"Sherry was very well known around campus. I saw her from time to time, but I didn't know her very well. It was highly rumored she managed a group of prostitutes. Did you know that?"

"I've never heard any such rumors. I'd find that hard to believe about Sherry."

"Another old friend of yours, I think her name was Carmella, was rumored to be a member of the group at one time. My grandfather used to talk about her from time to time. He said she wasn't around anymore. Have you seen her lately? Do you know where she is?"

"I really don't know. I haven't seen Carmella for a long time. Let's get back to Sherry. You spoke of her in the past tense."

"That's right. I'm sorry to tell you this, but she was killed in a car accident about a week ago."

Hound was saddened to hear that. Sherry may have been a prostitute, but she was also a trusted and loyal friend.

"Do you know how the accident occurred?" Hound asked.

"I heard she was very intoxicated on drugs and alcohol. She was driving very fast, lost control of her car, and ran off the road. It was raining hard at the time. I think she drove head on into a tree. Maybe it was a telephone pole. I can't remember which. Are you back in town to stay?"

"No. I'm only here for a short visit."

"Where will you be going? Will you be staying in the state?"

"I'm not sure where I'll settle, but it won't be anywhere in Louisiana."

"Maybe before you leave, we can go down to the river again. I'd enjoy that very much. I may not look as good as I used to, but I'm better at sex."

"I appreciate the offer, but I'm going to be busy before I leave. I won't have time to visit the river."

"I'm not sure I believe you. You've probably made arrangements to get all the pussy you want before you leave."

"Actually, I haven't. Honestly, I don't know of any women around here I'd want to make such an arrangement with. However, I'll keep my eyes open for some new prospects. Are there any new ladies in town?"

Bobbi was disappointed and angered by Hound's response to her proposition. He wished her the best of luck in the future, said goodbye, paid for his apple pie and milk, and then left. On his way out of town, he stopped at a pay phone and placed a call to Jo at her parents' home in New Orleans. When Jo realized it was Hound calling, she tried to control her emotions to keep from sobbing.

"Hello, Jo," Hound said softly. "How are you? I came back for a short visit with my parents. I thought perhaps we could finally have that face-to-face discussion, if you still desire to do so."

"Oh, Hound, you know I do. I hoped I'd hear from you. I was so afraid I wouldn't. How are you? Well, I hope."

"I've been fine, Jo. How are you?"

"I'm six months pregnant with a big belly. Does that answer your question?"

"I suppose so. Other than that, how are you doing?"

"As well as can be expected under the circumstances, I guess. Are you planning to come here for our visit?"

"Yes, unless you'd rather meet somewhere else. I want our visit to be private between you and me. I don't want your father intruding. What we have to say to each other doesn't concern him. He may not want me to visit you at all. Under the circumstances, he may not want me to ever see you again."

"Hound, nothing could be further from the truth. I completely agree we should have our discussion in private, but he does want to speak to you while you're here."

"All right. It's probably best I speak with him before I visit with you. That's probably what he wants anyway."

"When do you plan to come here?"

"I'll spend the rest of the weekend at the farm. There's a flight leaving here at 7 a.m. on Monday morning. I should arrive at the New Orleans airport between 8 and 8:30. I'll grab a taxi, check into a hotel, and then call you. You can let me know what time you want to meet with me at the estate."

"Hound, don't be ridiculous. You're not going to stay at a hotel. You're going to be a guest at the estate. I insist. Dad feels the same way. You won't be using a taxi either. I'm certain Dad will insist on picking you up at the airport. You and he can conclude your visit before you get to the estate."

"OK, Jo, but are you absolutely sure you want me to stay at the estate? I certainly don't want anything to become heated or awkward between you and me, or your father and me."

"Hound, that won't happen. I can promise you're as welcome here as you have ever been. None of our family resents or is angry at you. You are as much loved as ever, especially by me. Leaving is something you had to do. Not I nor anyone else in the family blames you for doing so. We are all anxious to see you again, especially me. You deserve to be treated with the utmost courtesy and respect. You will be."

"Jo, I greatly appreciate that. I look forward to seeing you Monday."

"Not nearly as much as I look forward to seeing you."

When Hound arrived at the airport in New Orleans, Ken was waiting to meet him.

"My God, it's good to see you again, son!" Ken said enthusiastically. "We're all so glad you've come. You have no idea how much you've been missed."

Hound was very surprised, but happy to receive such a warm welcome. It was apparent the welcome was genuine, but he wasn't completely sure of everything that motivated it. He was certain Ken had more in mind than just a casual visit between old friends.

"Thank you, Ken," Hound replied. "It's very nice to see you again as well. How have you been?"

"Other than being upset over your absence and missing you tremendously, I've been doing well. How about you? You look fine."

"I'd have to say life has been treating me decently."

"Jo is most anxious to see you again, but I'm sure you know that already. I thought we might go somewhere and visit a bit before going home. There are some important things I'd like to talk to you about privately. I don't want Jo to know what we discuss. Is that all right with you? The airport has a nice restaurant. We could visit there."

"Sure, Ken. That's fine."

They located a table in the most private area of the restaurant. Each of them ordered a cup of coffee.

"Hound, you're probably a bit nervous about what I might want to talk to you about," Ken said as he began the conversation. "Please don't be. I simply want to present some things for your review and consideration. Whatever you decide after you've done so, I'll accept with no hard feelings, if your decision isn't the one I hope for. Please keep an open mind about everything we discuss. Also, I hope you'll not make a hasty decision."

"All right, Ken. What's on your mind?"

"Jo is terribly ashamed and hurt over what's happened. She hasn't left the estate since her body started showing her pregnancy. Each day that passes, she becomes more depressed and withdrawn. She's remained fanatical in her determination to keep what happened to her a secret. She greatly regrets having told your parents, even though she knows their promise to say nothing to anyone will be kept. Both her physical and emotional health are quickly declining. This presents great risk to her and the baby as well. Even though she realizes this, she seems not to care. Our family physician has been adamant about her need to see a psychiatrist. He feels strongly that she has a desire to end her life. You'll be hurt and saddened when you see her. She no longer looks or acts like the Jo you remember. Before I continue, I need to ask you a very important question. Please answer me truthfully. Will you do that?"

"Of course, I will, Ken. What is it?"

"When I first met you, I truly believed you were deeply in love with my daughter. Were you?"

"Very much so."

"What happened to my daughter was horrible. Maybe it was partly her fault, maybe not, but she believes it was. She feels losing you is part of God's punishment for what happened. Hound, I truly believe Jo will die if you don't intervene and save her. I also truly believe you're the only one who can. I want you to do that for me, but especially for Jo. If she made a mistake that God feels she should be punished for, then I believe she's been punished enough. Don't you?"

"Ken, based on what you've told me, I'd more than agree, but what do you mean by intervene?"

"Hound, there are two things I want you to do. The first thing is for Jo. I want you to reconcile with her and become the part of her life you were before misfortune befell her. The second thing I want you to do is persuade her to tell you who the father of her baby is. She's kept that a closely guarded secret. Will you do for me what I ask?"

Hound suddenly felt the emotional pressure placed upon him by Ken's request. He was torn between complying to repay the debts for past assistance extended by Jo through her father and to carry on with the new life he'd begun. Ken had pledged to honor any decision he made, but his instinct told him Ken would accept only the decision that gave him what he wanted.

"Ken, I'm prepared to do what you ask of me," Hound said. "I owe you and Jo several debts from the past. We both know what they are, so there's no need to discuss them. However, with all due respect, there will be some conditions for my compliance."

Hound was gambling. The stakes were high. He could only hope he hadn't overplayed his hand.

"Hound, you've definitely got a set of big balls!" Ken said. "But that's one of the many things I've always admired and respected about you. I knew you were smart enough to realize I'd never take no for an answer. What are your conditions?"

Hound knew he needed to pad his answer in such a way Ken would be more likely to make the deal. His suspicion was great that Ken had every intention of assassinating the man who'd raped and made his daughter pregnant. That's the reason he wanted to know the man's identity. That's the reason Jo wouldn't tell him. He also knew it would still be Jo's plan to kill Carmella should she ever be found.

"Ken, I want to be free to pursue a career separate from your business," Hound began. "I want you to declare any and all debts you feel I owe from the past paid in full. In addition, Carmella Vargas is never to be harmed in any way. She's never been a threat to me. Finally, I want the privilege and satisfaction of personally killing the son of a bitch who did that damnable thing to our Jo."

Ken wasn't quick to respond. He sat calmly and quietly staring at Hound for a moment. His face was without expression, and then a smile slowly appeared on it. Hound's instinct told him his gamble had paid off.

"Hound, like I said, you've definitely got a set of big balls!" Ken replied. "Your conditions are acceptable. We have a deal. However, I have a condition of my own."

"All right. What is it?"

"I promised Jo not to use any type of coercion on you to force a reconciliation. You must never tell her I did. That's my condition. I never want her to know I broke my promise. She must always believe it was solely your idea to reconcile, because you love her. She'd never agree to it for any other reason. Do you agree to my condition?"

"I do."

"Good, then we definitely have a deal. You might be interested to know what I'm about to tell you. Sometime ago, Jo and I were discussing the debts you owed. I wasn't convinced there'd ever be a way for you to pay them. Although Jo didn't consider any debts were owed, she said there'd likely come a time when you'd more than repay them. It looks like she was right."

"Yeah, it looks like she was."

"Well, now that we've got all that settled, we should get to the estate. I know Jo will be anxiously waiting to see you."

When Hound arrived at the estate and saw Jo for the first time in several months, he realized Ken hadn't exaggerated her physical or emotional condition. Judging by the way she looked, he knew she was in real trouble. Her physical features showed no resemblance to the beautiful woman he'd left four months ago. She hadn't been truthful when she implied over the phone that she'd gained a lot of weight. She was much too thin. However, in anticipation of his arrival, she'd managed to take her first bath and groom herself in several days. When she first saw him, she began to cry.

"Oh, Hound!" she exclaimed. "I hate for you to see me like this, but I'm so glad you're here! I did so want to see you again!

Hound was overcome with sympathy, compassion, and empathy for Jo. He moved quickly to embrace her.

"I should have come sooner, much sooner!" he told her. "But I'm here now. Everything is going to be fine. I promise."

"Hound, everything isn't going to be fine. I've lost all hope of that. It's simply impossible. I just wanted to see you one last time to tell you how very sorry I am and how very much I'll always love you."

"We can talk in private later. There's something very important I need to say and ask that may convince you everything is going to be fine."

"I don't want to wait until later. I've waited months to see and talk to you again. I don't want to wait a second longer."

Ken told them to use the privacy of his den as long as they needed. Once inside the den, Jo closed the door behind them. They sat down facing each other. Jo used a handkerchief to dry the tears from her eyes and managed to compose herself. After a few seconds of silence, she was the first to speak.

"Hound, I look terrible!" she said. "I haven't been doing well since you left."

"Are you saying being without me has made you ill?"

"Do you think I'm ill? I guess I look like it, don't I?"

"Yes, I think you're ill. Don't you?"

"Hound, I know I'm ill. Very ill."

"Jo, why did you allow yourself to get in this condition?"

"You asked if being without you made me ill. Well, it did. I stopped caring about getting better. It just didn't matter anymore."

"Well, Jo, that nonsense stops right now."

"What do you mean?"

"Jo, I've missed you terribly. I've wanted to call and tell you that many times. I know that may sound strange after the way I left and only called you once. I was ashamed for the way I treated you and simply didn't have the courage to call again. I hope you can forgive me."

"You can't be blamed for the way you acted. I certainly don't blame you. You had every right to feel the way you did and do what you did. What happened was my fault. You had no part in it. However, I find it hard to believe you didn't have the courage to call me. Hound, you're the most courageous person I know. You're not afraid of anything."

"Jo, there's one thing that I'm afraid of."

"If that's true, then I have to know what it is. Please tell me."

"I'm afraid you won't let me back into your life. I'm afraid I can't live without you. Being away from you has shown me that. Jo, I'd like very much to come back, if you'll have me."

"Why would you want me back now? I'm pregnant with another man's child! Just look at me! I look like death! I may likely be close to it, at least that's what Mom, Dad, and my doctor tell me. Hound, did Dad have anything to do with you wanting to come back?"

"Absolutely not, but I know he supports it. I told him I planned to talk to you about it. He said nothing could please him more than for us to be together again."

"Hound, are you telling me the truth? Please don't lie to me. I want you back with me more than life itself, but I don't want you to come back because you pity or feel you owe me or my dad a debt. Not being able to live without me because you love me with all your heart is the only reason I'd allow you to come back to me. Now, I'll ask you again. Are you telling me the truth?"

"I'm telling you the truth. Jo, I've never lied to you about anything. I know you've never lied to me. We'll never lie to each other. Now, do you want me back or not?"

"Oh, honey! You know I do, but what about the baby I'm carrying? I need you to tell me the truth regarding how you feel about that."

"Jo, it will take time, but we'll work through that together."

"Where do we start?"

"Where we left off. Will you marry me?"

Jo suddenly began to cry uncontrollably. She stood up, pulled Hound to his feet, and embraced him. She finally composed herself enough to speak.

"Oh, my precious darling! Of course, I will marry you! When?"

"Whenever you say."

"I would say as soon as possible. Is that all right with you?"

"Whatever makes you happy, Jo."

"Would you feel uncomfortable marrying a woman that is six months pregnant? Oh Hound, I'm sorry. I know you'd prefer to wait until I'm no longer pregnant."

"I'll marry you now, or later. Whatever is best for you. Whatever you want."

"You really mean that, don't you?"

"Yes, Jo. I hope you know I do."

6

Jo and Hound left the den and joined her parents in the living room. Ken and Sandra expressed joy and excitement when they heard the good news. During lunch that day, Jo consumed more food than she had in several days. Her parents reminded her she hadn't been eating enough to keep a bird alive. They suggested consuming larger amounts of food too soon might make her sick. Realizing they were right, she stopped eating before the hunger she'd suddenly felt was satisfied.

That night Jo enjoyed her first decent sleep in four months. She awoke at 2 p.m. the next afternoon after sleeping soundly for sixteen hours. Before leaving her room that afternoon, Jo showered, and then dressed and groomed herself immaculately. She went to the living room where Hound and her parents were visiting and announced she was hungry.

She remained in the living room to visit with Hound and her father while her mother went to the kitchen to prepare her a late lunch. Everyone was amazed and delighted Jo was showing such a remarkable emotional improvement in only a few hours.

They were hopeful and optimistic her physical health would also show expedient improvement. Ken and Sandra were concerned Jo's long-term neglect of her health, and emotional dysfunction, might have a huge negative effect on her baby's health, but they didn't voice their concerns to Hound at that time. When Jo moved to the dining room to eat her meal, everyone joined her at the dining table to conduct casual family conversation.

"Jo, I'm happy to see you looking and feeling better today," Hound said, smiling. "You'll be your old self again before you know it."

"I think so too. I certainly hope so. I want to be my old self for you again as quickly as possible. Hound, are you going to accept Dad's job offer after we get married? Will you become his protégé and right-hand man in the family business?"

Hound had hoped to delay telling Jo of his current career plan and decision to decline Ken's offer. He wanted her to have more time to progress in her recovery. However, she had asked the question and deserved an honest answer.

"Jo, I've decided not to accept your dad's generous and very attractive offer. You know I've always wanted to start a business of my own. That's what I've decided to do."

Jo looked at her father, who smiled and nodded, indicating his support of and agreement with Hound's decision. She knew how much Ken had always wanted Hound to fill the second most powerful position in the family business and take over as its highest executive in the chain of command when he was ready to retire. She was greatly surprised to see her father so quickly support Hound's decision.

"Hound, what career have you decided on?" Jo inquired.

"Jo, let's discuss that later. We have much to talk about."

"All right. I'm sure we do have much to talk about."

The weather was pleasing that evening. After dinner, Hound invited Jo to take a walk outdoors. As they walked holding hands, Hound focused the conversation on a specific topic.

"Jo, I'm building a nightclub in the desert a few miles north of Phoenix, Arizona. I'm building a new home a couple of miles from the nightclub."

"A nightclub! I can't believe you'd choose the career of a nightclub owner! You've got to be bullshitting me! Phoenix, Arizona! Why in hell would you build in Phoenix, Arizona? You know my career is currently set at LSU. If your heart was set on being a nightclub owner, then why in God's name didn't you build it in Baton Rouge, or at least New Orleans? You know Dad would've helped you make it a complete success. What the fuck were you thinking? Oh, my God! You weren't planning to come back to me when you decided to build in Phoenix! Dad did have something to do with your decision to reconcile with me! He promised he wouldn't coerce, or otherwise influence you, in any way, but he did. God damn it! He broke his promise to me! Am I right? Tell me the truth! I need to know the truth!"

"Jo, sweetheart, you need to calm down. You're overreacting. I don't believe you're willing to offer understanding and be fair with me. When I decided to build the nightclub and home, I hadn't made the decision to never reconcile with you. The truth is completely opposite of that. However, I didn't want to become established anywhere in Louisiana. I certainly didn't want my business to be tied to your father in any way. Your father did nothing to influence my decision. Common sense should tell you that. If he had used coercion to influence me, then he would certainly have made sure I accepted the career he wanted for me in his business. You know how much he wanted me to accept his offer. Surely you can understand what I'm telling you is more than reasonable?"

Jo slowly began to calm her excessive anxiety, fear, and anger. She and Hound sat down on a bench in a garden at the rear of the estate.

"Hound, I do understand that what you say is rational. Perhaps I did overreact. Please know that I'm completely willing to offer you understanding and fairness in all things. I should have listened to your explanation before assuming the worst. However, I can't keep from being concerned how we can have a healthy marriage with your career being in Phoenix and mine in Baton Rouge."

"I've always believed there was a solution to any problem. I've seen it proven true many times. You know I've always embraced that belief."

"What is the solution to you living in Phoenix and me in Baton Rouge?"

"Once the club is up and running, then I'll be free to be with you in Baton Rouge on a reasonable, regular basis. It doesn't require a lot of time to travel by plane back and forth. I'd likely have been away from you more if I worked for your father. You know he'd have me traveling constantly."

"Well, you're right about that. Why did you decide to build a nightclub anyway? You know your intellect, level of education, and people skills would allow you to pursue any career you wanted. Why didn't you pursue one that was more prestigious and financially rewarding?"

"Jo, I aspire to be much more than a nightclub owner. I plan to use the nightclub in Phoenix, and others I plan to build in different locations, as steps on a ladder. My ultimate career goal lies at the top of the ladder. I simply have to climb it."

"What is your ultimate career goal?"

"I have no idea yet, but my instinct tells me I'll know what my destiny is when I reach the top of the ladder. The clubs are but a few steps on the ladder. I'm sure a number of other type businesses will be required to complete the steps needed."

"Well, knowing you'll be using the nightclub as a means to ultimately achieve something appropriate and suited to your capabilities makes it much easier for me to support you. I'll simply have to accept it as a condition of our relationship."

"Are you saying you're willing to support my decisions?"

"I believe in you and your instinct. Besides, a good wife should always be supportive of her husband, but a good husband should always be supportive of his wife."

"I couldn't agree more. I'm glad we got that settled. Do we need to discuss anything else that concerns you?"

"Hound, I know you probably don't want to discuss it right now, but I need to know how you truly feel about the baby I'm going to have in about three months. I desperately need to know. Please tell me."

"Jo, I told you we'd work through that together. Naturally, at this time I'm not happy about you being pregnant, but it's a reality that has to be accepted and dealt with. Like I reaffirmed earlier in our conversation, there's a solution to any problem. In time, I think the solution to this problem will be us no longer viewing it as a problem."

"Sweetheart, you have a way of making this heavy burden easier to bear. Is there anything I can do to make it easier for you?"

Hound considered Jo's question an ideal opportunity to gain information from her he needed but had believed would require more time to obtain.

"Jo, there is one thing you can do. There's something I need to know, something I have the right to know. I hope you'll tell me."

"Honey, what do you want to know?"

"I want to know who the baby's father is. I want to know everything about him that you know."

Jo paused at Hound's request. The expression on her face, and other body cues, indicated she was feeling concern, regret, and certainly anxiety. Hound wasn't sure Jo would grant his request.

"Hound, why do you want to know his name and other things I know about him now?" Jo asked. "Four months ago, I told you what had happened to me. I didn't bother to tell you anything about him then and you didn't bother to ask. I knew you must've had a reason for not wanting to know. I've often wondered if it was because you simply didn't care. If you didn't want to know these things four months ago, then why do you want to know them now?"

"Jo, if you expect our reconciliation to work, then you have to tell me what I want to know. I honestly don't know why I didn't ask about him four months ago."

Jo was convinced she'd have to comply with his request. She didn't want to, but she felt it necessary for the reconciliation to be successful.

"His name is Steve Cooper," she told Hound reluctantly. "He was 33 years old, a special agent with the FBI assigned to the D.C. Bureau Office. His looks, personality, and mannerisms reminded me of you. That's all I know about him — at least that's all I can remember. Hound, Dad must never know any of the information I've given you. Promise me you'll never give it to him, or even let him know I gave it to you. Promise me."

"Why didn't you tell your dad who Steve was? Didn't he want to know?"

"Hell yes, he did. I didn't tell him because I knew he'd kill Steve if I did."

"Why would that bother you? Didn't you think Steve deserved it?"

"Probably so, but if anything happens to Steve, it will be by my hand. Now, promise me you'll not tell Dad."

"All right, Jo, I promise."

"You wouldn't consider doing anything to Steve, would you?"

"No, but don't you think he deserves it? Perhaps you don't. Did he ever contact you after what happened?"

"Jesus Christ, baby! Of course not. Why would he? Oh, my God! Do you think I lied about being raped?"

"Jo, you know better than that."

"Then why would you ask if he ever contacted me? I sure as hell didn't give him my phone number or address."

"Jo, you knew it was rape, but maybe you believe he didn't."

"What do you mean?"

"You said you were extremely intoxicated and passed out. Maybe you don't remember exactly everything that happened."

"Yes, I was extremely drunk and passed out, but God damn it, I vividly remember doing everything in my power to resist what he did to me! I told him no as loudly as I could and fought him as hard as I could! The son of a bitch knew God damn well he raped me! Even after I had told him how much I loved and was devoted to you, the cocksucker raped me!"

When Jo finished her emotional statement, there was no doubt in Hound's mind she believed Steve Cooper had raped her. Hound and Jo were married three days later. The wedding ceremony was held at the O'Malley estate. The bride, groom, the bride's parents, and the priest who performed the ceremony were the only individuals present. John and Linda had no idea the wedding had been planned and carried out. Hound would inform them later. Although John had told Hound he'd support any decision made regarding reconciliation with Jo, Hound instinctively knew both his parents privately hoped a reconciliation wouldn't occur.

The wedding night was extremely difficult for Hound. It was the first time he and Jo had shared a bed in several months. He'd decided to end all ties with Jo and her family when he left four months ago. He still had feelings for Jo, but now they were much different from less complicated times in the past. He'd come to believe at least a portion of blame should be attached to Jo for what happened to her. She'd been extremely careless and naïve. All current circumstances resulting from what had happened were having great negative impact on him emotionally. It would require special effort to conceal his true feelings from her.

"Hound, how do you feel about making love to me on our wedding night, in spite of the fact I'm six months pregnant and look like shit?" Jo asked.

"Sweetie, you may be six months pregnant, but you certainly don't look like shit. I certainly wouldn't mind enjoying my wife on our wedding night, but do you feel up to it? Are you sure it won't hurt the baby? I'm more than willing to wait if you think it best."

"Of course, I feel up to it. I not only want it, my God, I need it! There's no danger to the baby, but you'll have to allow me to position myself on top of you."

Their wedding night was extremely satisfying for Jo. It provided Hound with no satisfaction, but his superb acting convinced Jo otherwise. Each night was the same for both of them until it was time for Hound's return to Phoenix.

Hound had contacted the contractor and Maggie, informing them he'd be away longer than originally anticipated. The contractor told him construction was proceeding on schedule. Maggie verified the contractor's report. She told him he was greatly missed and to return as soon as possible.

It was Monday morning. Hound was at the airport in New Orleans waiting to board his flight back to Phoenix. Jo and her parents were there to see him off. He reaffirmed with them his desire they not disclose to John and Linda that he and Jo were married. He felt the time hadn't yet arrived to tell them. Jo and her family didn't agree with the reason for his request, but they respected and complied with it. Hound had visited with his parents at the farm only twice since his return to Louisiana. During his last visit, he decided to tell them about his marriage but changed his mind.

"Hound, I wish you didn't have to go," Jo told him as he waited to board his flight. "I'll miss you terribly until it's time for you to come home again. Do you know when that might be?"

"I'd guess about a week. Maybe a little longer. I'll be back as soon as I can. I'll miss you too."

"I'm anxious to see your new club and home as soon as I feel like traveling."

"I'm very anxious for you to see them, but not until construction on them both is completed."

"Please remember to call me every day. Will you do that?"

"Of course. Be sure to keep me informed on anything I need to know, especially regarding your health."

"I will, but don't worry. I'll be fine. I have you to thank for that."

Hound was back in Phoenix by early afternoon. It was the first week of June. He arranged his schedule so he could attend Rebecca's graduation ceremony from college during that week. After the ceremony, he joined Rebecca, her mother, a few friends, and other family members for dinner at one of the nicest restaurants in Oakland. He accepted the invitation from Rebecca and her mother to be an overnight guest at their home. As prearranged, Rebecca visited his bedroom after her mother and all other guests were asleep. Rebecca waited until breakfast the following morning to tell Hound she and her mother would be touring Europe for the remainder of the summer. Hound talked and acted like he was disappointed. In reality, he was not.

Because he'd remained in New Orleans longer than previously planned, Hound had missed the scheduled monthly meeting with Carmella. This caused her to become extremely upset. She was more upset to learn that Roberto would be spending the summer in Colombia and she'd be there with him. Again, Hound displayed an act of disappointment, but he felt a degree of relief. He needed free time to complete things he wanted to do over the summer. Continuing the scheduled meetings with Rebecca and Carmella would limit the time he needed.

He'd decided not to tell either of them he'd married Jo. He was certain the marriage was doomed to failure. It was under unusual circumstances that he'd married Jo. He felt those circumstances had forced him to marry her when he didn't want to. As a result, he was already searching for a solution that would successfully end his marriage and not result in consequences for himself or Jo. He wouldn't implement any solution until Jo had sufficiently recovered emotionally and physically. He was certain the love he once believed existed for Jo was no longer there.

Unlike Carmella and Rebecca, Maggie wouldn't be away for the summer. Unlike Carmella and Rebecca, he'd tell Maggie about his marriage, along with what was safe to say about the reason for it. He knew Carmella would accept being told later. He wasn't concerned about Rebecca one way or the other. However, he had specific reasons for being concerned about Maggie. His instinct told him she could handle the truth regardless of what it was, but she would never tolerate being deceived in any manner. At the very least, he wanted to maintain a loyal and trusting friendship with her. He never wanted to anger her to the point he'd have to defend himself against her scorn.

Hound accepted Maggie's invitation to come to her home for dinner the first night after his return from New Orleans. She'd put great effort into preparing an exquisite meal. Hound had told her he had something important to talk about. She assumed it had something to do with Jo. During dinner, she allowed Hound to choose the time to deliver the information he wanted her to know. The time arrived shortly after they began eating.

"Maggie, I need to tell you something. I wish I didn't have to, but I do."

"As soon as you arrived here tonight, I could tell you were extremely troubled about something. Say what you need to. Get it out in the open so we can discuss it."

"Maggie, while I was away, I married Jo."

Hound didn't expect the smile that appeared on Maggie's face after he told her the news.

"I assumed what you wanted to tell me had something to do with Jo," Maggie said. "I never assumed it would be that you married her, but in all honesty, I'm not really surprised. I can tell you're not very happy about it. I'd be interested to know why. Tell me."

"Maggie, the reason why really doesn't matter. It doesn't change the fact that I'm married. I didn't want to delay telling you the truth."

"Hound, the reason why is very important to me. I need to know."

"Why is it important to you?"

"The reason will determine whether I continue to be with you intimately or not."

"Maggie, believe it or not, I married Jo to help her recover from a life-threatening emotional disturbance."

"I believe you. I would believe anything you told me. Hound, I trust you completely to always tell me the truth. You're the first man I've ever met I could say that to and mean it, but I suspect there's more to the story. Am I right?"

"You have excellent intuition. Yes, you're right. Unfortunately, I can't tell you the complete story. I have good reason. I hope you can accept and understand that."

"You're right, Hound. I do have excellent intuition. I'm also very intelligent and have a big curiosity. May I tell you what I think?"

"I suppose so. Go ahead."

"Jo's father is a powerful and influential man. He's connected with all the right people in high places. Some of these people include politicians in Washington. Because of Jo's relationship with you, her father used his connections to make the serious legal problems you had in Vietnam disappear. I'm convinced you married Jo for the reasons you told me, but my gut feeling tells me you also married her because you felt a great debt was owed her father. I'd assume he applied a lot of pressure on you to marry Jo as at least partial payment of that debt. I'd think Ken O'Malley can be very persuasive because he can be very dangerous. I suspect he may be connected with organized crime. He may even be a boss. How's my intuition doing so far? How close am I to being right?"

"How did you know the name of Jo's father? Maggie, did you use your contacts to investigate the O'Malley family?"

"Of course, I did. Surely, you're not surprised."

"Actually, I am. At least a little. Is there anything else your intuition tells you about Ken, or Jo?"

"Only that Jo is six months pregnant, making it impossible for you to be the father. The only reason you'd marry a woman pregnant with someone else's child is because you felt you didn't have a choice. Now, tell me if everything I said is true or not."

When Hound didn't respond, Maggie had her answer.

"Maggie, I'd appreciate it, based on the investigative information you have and your intuition, if you didn't make any more assumptions," Hound said. "I'd also appreciate you not saying anything to anyone about my marriage to Jo."

"Of course, baby. I completely understand."

"I also need you to do something else for me. I need a favor."

"I'll help you if I can. What do you need?"

"I need some information on a particular individual. A man.

"That shouldn't be a problem. Tell me his name and anything else you know about him."

"His name is Steve Cooper. He's a special agent with the FBI assigned to the bureau office in Washington, D.C. That's really all I know about him."

"Requesting information on someone in the FBI is tricky business. I'm likely to be asked why I want the information. Why do you want it?"

"It's personal. I'd rather not say."

"Fair enough, sweetie. I'll get the information as quickly as I can. By the way, would you like to spend the night?"

"Absolutely. Does that mean you intend to continue being intimate with me?"

"You can bet your sweet ass it does! I'm very fond of you, but I guess you already know that."

"Yeah, I know. I'm a bit fond of you too."

"Hound, I believe it's only fair to warn you about something."

"OK. What?"

"I'm well on my way to falling in love with you. When that happens, I'll do all in my power to create the same feelings in you about me."

"Why do you feel it necessary to warn me about that?"

"I've never been in love before. When I fall in love, I know I'll fall hard. There's absolutely nothing I won't do, short of harming the one I love, to win the one I love."

Maggie was being honest about almost everything. She had already fallen in love with him. Indeed, the fall had been hard. She decided to let the dissolution of Hound's marriage play out naturally. She was convinced it would. Hound had married Jo because of specific circumstances that he despised. She felt certain Ken O' Malley had orchestrated the marriage by coercing Hound with threats of harsh consequences that would've certainly occurred if he hadn't complied with what Ken wanted. However, despite the leverage Ken was using to coerce his new son-in-law, she knew Hound would find a way to eliminate Ken's power and control over him. She was certain Hound didn't fear Ken, but he had to respect what he was capable of. If Ken didn't have equal respect for him for the same reason, then Ken was a fool.

In her professional and personal life, Maggie had made a friend, business associate, contact, or casual acquaintance of many extremely dangerous men. She'd learned how to easily identify such personality traits. Maggie's intuition had led her to believe Hound, if pushed into a corner by a specific circumstance, would likely become the most dangerous man she'd ever met. The edge he had over most, if not all, the men she knew was his absolute fearlessness. She'd make herself available to assist him at any time, in any way she could. She and Hound were very much alike in certain ways. She wasn't completely without fear, but she had learned to control and use to her advantage the few fears she could experience.

Hound returned to the New Orleans estate the second week of June. It was almost 3 a.m. on a Tuesday morning when Jo awoke Hound complaining of severe pain in her abdomen. She was rushed to the hospital where she was diagnosed to be in premature labor. Her baby was born a short time later. It died shortly after birth. The baby was a girl.

When Jo was told of the baby's death, she showed no emotion. She remained in the hospital two more days. Jo told everyone she wanted to be alone. She asked Hound and her parents to respect her request for privacy and insisted they return to the estate. When they returned to take her home on the morning she was discharged, Jo appeared to be in the best of moods, happy to be going home.

"Jo, how do you feel this morning?" Hound asked in a soft, concerned voice.

"I feel exceptionally well. How do you feel this morning, sweetie?"

"I'm good. I'm very happy to know you're feeling so well."

"I'm anxious to get home and get something decent to eat."

"Are you hungry?"

"Very."

As soon as Jo arrived home, she enjoyed a hearty breakfast consisting of eggs, pancakes, bacon, fresh fruit, and a cup of hot tea with cream and honey. Hound, Ken, and Sandra sipped from cups of freshly brewed Cajun coffee and visited with Jo while she ate. They were all very happy to see her in such good spirits but somewhat surprised regarding her seemingly lack of emotional connection with what she'd recently experienced.

A small funeral service was held for the baby and attended by only immediate members of the family. Throughout the entire service, it was apparent to all Jo wasn't at all reverent. Nobody questioned or commented why, but everyone had their suspicions. She and Hound were back together. The one thing that would stand as a constant reminder of what happened to her and caused their separation was no longer in their lives to threaten the future of their relationship.

She sat holding Hound's hand, anxious for the ceremony to end. When it did, she smiled and made casual conversation as she walked from the gravesite to the car still holding his hand. Many of the comments she made were humorous in nature. Hound made no comments to Jo or asked any questions regarding her unexpected behavior. He assumed at some time in the future she'd talk about the baby's death. He was certain his assumption was correct.

Hound remained with Jo in New Orleans until July 1. As each day passed, Jo showed remarkable progress in her emotional and physical recovery. She spent all her time at Hound's side. It seemed she couldn't experience him enough sexually. She was eating healthy, sleeping soundly, and was beginning to exercise on a regular basis.

Each night, Hound complied with her wish to go out on the town. She relished the time they spent dining, dancing, and going to movies and other forms of entertainment they enjoyed together. Naturally, she didn't want him to leave, but she offered her unconditional support and understanding before he kissed her goodbye and walked away to board his flight back to Phoenix.

"Go pursue your destiny, my darling," she told him. "Make me proud and never forget how very much I love you. I'll miss you terribly until you again return to me."

When Hound arrived at his desert residential property early that afternoon, he found Maggie and the contractor waiting in his temporary residence to greet him. When Hound entered, Maggie stood up from the chair she was seated in and rushed to welcome him with a hug and kiss.

"Hound, I hope you don't mind that we're waiting for you inside your residence," Maggie said, smiling and obviously excited. "I knew where you kept your key, so I used it to get in. It was too damn hot to wait for you outside."

"Of course, I don't mind, Maggie, but why were you waiting for me to arrive?"

"We have a surprise for you. Your new home is completely finished and furnished. Are you surprised?"

"Hell yes! That's wonderful. What do you mean it's furnished?"

"I decided to furnish it for you while you were away. If you don't like any, or all, of the things I selected, then you'll have no problem returning and replacing them. I hope you don't mind what I did. I simply wanted to make the surprise as big as I possibly could."

"Maggie, I don't mind a bit. I appreciate the gesture. Thank you."

"You're welcome, but promise me you'll return and replace any furnishings you don't like. You won't hurt my feelings if you do."

"I promise. Now, Let's go take a look at my new home and its landscaping."

Hound's new home had a little over five thousand square foot of interior, composed of a large, spacious living room, kitchen, dining room, den, laundry room, plenty of storage closets, a pantry, large guest bathroom, five large bedrooms all with private baths, and a master bedroom twice the size of the other bedrooms. The design of the home was a combination of Spanish and Western. It was beautiful and elegant inside and out.

Maggie was delighted when Hound told her the furnishings she'd selected were perfect in every way. The landscaping of the property surrounding the home was beautiful and superbly complemented the design of the home. A stone wall, ten feet in height and two feet in width, was located on the perimeter and completely surrounded the home and property. There was a front and rear entrance to the property, both equipped with metal gates. A modern security guard house had been built at the front entrance.

"You did a fantastic job," Hound told the contractor.

"Hound, I'm happy you're pleased," the contractor replied. "I want my clients to get what they pay for. I did my best to make certain you did."

Hound invited Maggie to join him for dinner that night in his new home. She quickly accepted his invitation.

"Maggie, we need to take a trip to the store for food," Hound said. "If we're going to fix dinner, we'll need something to fix."

"I did some grocery shopping for you so you wouldn't have to when you returned. I think you'll find your refrigerator and pantry supplied with everything you'll need, at least for a while."

"That's terrific, Maggie. I truly appreciate everything you did while I was away. It's all been a wonderful surprise."

"Think nothing of it. It pleases me to do things for you. By the way, I have something else for you."

"Gosh, Maggie. Sounds like you've been really busy. What is it?"

"While you were away, I collected the information you wanted on Steve Cooper. I hope it's enough to serve your purpose."

Maggie went to her car and returned with a large legal size envelope containing the information. She gave it to Hound. He thanked her and then placed the envelope on a coffee table in the living room.

"Hound, are you going to review the information?"

"Sure, but not right now. I'll have plenty of time later to look at it."

"Hound, do you mind if I ask again why you wanted the information? I know you told me it was personal, but my curiosity is killing me."

"Maggie, in all honesty, the information isn't for me. I told a friend I'd try to get it for them."

"Why did they want it?"

"I have no idea. They didn't offer to tell me, so I figured it was none of my business and didn't ask."

Maggie took the hint and refrained from asking more questions about the subject.

"Would you like to try out the new bed in your master bedroom?" Maggie asked Hound as a mischievous grin appeared on her face.

"That's a good idea, Maggie. I need to take a quick shower first."

"Me too. How about we shower together?"

"That's another good idea."

"I have a lot more."

"What are they? Tell me."

"Rather than tell you, how about I show you, in the shower and in the bedroom?"

"Well, that sounds like another good idea."

Later that evening, Maggie and Hound enjoyed conversation as they worked together to prepare dinner. Hound knew sooner or later Maggie would ask if any new developments occurred during his last visit to New Orleans. He didn't want to tell her about the death of Jo's baby, but inevitably knew he'd have to. They had finished eating their dinner before she asked.

"Well, Hound, did anything of interest occur during your last visit to New Orleans?" Maggie asked.

"Yes, Maggie. Definitely. Jo lost her baby."

"That's too bad. Is Jo all right?"

"She seemed to be perfectly fine."

"Hound, don't you think it's highly possible she's happy about it?"

"I'm certain she is."

"Are you happy about it?"

"Actually, I'm indifferent."

"Do you think Jo might have purposely caused the baby's death?"

"It's possible, Maggie, but I'm not sure. Jo's health was terrible the entire time of her pregnancy. That was likely the cause."

"Perhaps it was her purpose to remain ill."

"Maybe, but I don't think so. If it was, then her purpose almost killed her as well."

"You make a good point, but maybe that was her plan until you decided to reconcile with and marry her. When that happened, she had to rethink everything."

"Maybe. Maggie, tell me what you're thinking. You're intelligent. You know how an intelligent woman thinks. Jo is very intelligent. Tell me what you think about the loss of her baby."

"Are you sure you want to know what I'm thinking?"

"Yes. Tell me."

"If Jo's physical condition didn't kill her baby, then she used another way to kill it."

"Why would she do such a thing?"

"As a result of what happened to her, Jo became terribly emotionally distraught. She was unhappy at the most maximum level possible. She'd lost you, obviously the center of her happiness. I believe if she hadn't become pregnant, then she would've never told you about the rape. Hound, Jo despised that baby. She made two decisions when you told her you wanted to reconcile and marry her. She became determined to regain her health so she could survive to have a happy life with you and to destroy what she believed to be the only thing that could interfere with that happy life. I'm really not telling you anything you don't already know. You're too intelligent not to know what Jo did and why."

"Maggie, I think your analysis is likely correct. My thoughts regarding the matter are the same as yours."

"Sweetheart, you have a bigger problem now than before the baby died."

"Explain what you mean."

"Any woman who loves a man as much as Jo loves you will do absolutely anything necessary to keep that man with her. Doing that will be much easier because of her father. You should've never returned to New Orleans to see Jo for that one last visit you promised her. You wouldn't be in such a shitstorm if you hadn't."

"Maggie, you're right again."

"What do you plan to do now?"

"I don't plan to cross any bridge until I have to. Hopefully when I have to, I'll have figured out a way to cross and leave it behind with no harm to myself or anyone else. I expect the first thing Jo will want now is for us to have a child of our own. I'm sure as hell not prepared for that."

"You're absolutely right. We're still thinking alike. What do you plan to do about that?"

"Maggie, what I plan to do is not think about this shit anymore right now. I'm going to Vegas. I'm overdue for a tour of gambling. I'll take you with me if you want to go. I promised I'd take you sometime. Do you want to go?"

"You know damn well I do. It's about time you invited me."

Hound and Maggie boarded a direct flight to Las Vegas early the following morning. They remained in Vegas through July 4, returning to Phoenix the following afternoon. Hound won his usual maximum amount. He assisted Maggie to win a lesser amount, but it was substantial, and she was extremely pleased.

"I can see now why you don't have to work," Maggie told him during dinner the last night they were in Vegas. "I suppose you plan to gamble the rest of your life."

"Only until sometime in the not too distant future."

"If you always win, then why would you ever stop gambling?"

"I plan to wait until a specific time and then win so God damn much money the casinos will ban me from gambling in the future."

"How much do you plan on winning?"

"As much as I can."

"I'd love to be with you and watch when you do."

"Well, Maggie, maybe you will be."

On the morning of July 7, Hound boarded another flight. This time he used the phony identification Jo had obtained for him in the past to make his reservations and purchase his ticket. He knew this was a necessary precaution he should take. He was on his way to Washington D.C. to conduct some business with Steve Cooper. He told Maggie he'd be out of town for an indefinite period of time looking at some properties out of state he might be interested in purchasing.

Maggie had no problem accepting his excuse. She told him to return as quickly as possible and keep in contact with her while he was away. This was the first time he had lied to Maggie, but he knew it to be another necessary precaution.

7

When Hound arrived in D.C., he rented a car at the airport, and then drove to the hotel where he would be staying. The location of the hotel was the closest he could find to the residence of Steve Cooper. He spent the next week following Steve from the time he left his home in the morning until he returned in the evening. He hoped Steve would not be assigned duty out of town before his business with him could be concluded.

Steve's home was in a nice upper middle class neighborhood. He was married and had two children, a 9-year-old boy, Steve Junior, and a 7-year-old girl, Stephanie. His wife, Paula, was a 32-year-old, attractive, petite blonde.

Paula was a teacher at the elementary school her children attended. She chauffeured her children to and from school daily. It soon became apparent that Steve followed a regular, predictable daily routine. He left for work by 7 a.m. each morning. With the exception of at least one night per week, he was home by dinnertime.

On the one night per week Steve wasn't home in time for dinner, he was in a nice club having drinks with friends, a woman he was having an affair with, or searching for a new woman to begin an affair with. One of the clubs he favored was the one he'd met Jo in. It was the eighth night Hound had been in town. It was the night Steve wouldn't be home in time for dinner. It was the night he'd be in the club where he'd met Jo. It was the night that would end his ever being home in time for dinner again.

On that Tuesday night, Hound followed Steve from work to his first stop, a club where he'd have a couple of drinks with buddies from the bureau. He left the club a little after 7 p.m. and drove to the club that would be his final destination ever. Hound parked as close as possible to Steve's car in the parking lot. He sat in his car and watched Steve enter the lobby of the hotel on his way to the club. A short time later, he followed.

Steve had taken a seat located about center the length of the bar. Hound took a seat to Steve's right at the end of the bar. Hound ordered a bottle of his favorite beer and sat slowly sipping it for the next hour while he watched Steve taking turns dancing with each of the three stag women he managed to join at their table. He envisioned Jo being like those women the night she met Steve. For whatever reason, maybe because he had too much to drink, Steve would have no luck bedding a woman that night.

It was a little after 9 p.m. when the last of the three women bid Steve goodnight and left. Hound assumed on the nights Steve was out late, sometimes all night, his wife believed him to be working an assignment. With no other apparent female prospects remaining in the club, Steve decided to move on to another club. Perhaps he intended to go home. No one would ever know for sure. When he left the club, Hound followed close behind.

The hotel parking lot was vacant of any individuals, except Hound and Steve. Hound surveyed the surroundings to make sure of that. Steve was fumbling with his keys, trying to unlock his car door as Hound quickly but silently approached him from behind.

Placing Steve in a chokehold he had learned at OCS, Hound decided to speak a short statement.

"Hello, Steve," Hound said softly as he made a minor adjustment to the chokehold. "Joanne O'Malley from New Orleans asked me to give you a message. She wanted you to know the consequence you'd receive for raping her was to die. In addition, she wanted you to know your wife Paula would be raped and then killed by me along with your two children."

Hound allowed Steve to struggle briefly before breaking his cervical spine at the base of his skull. He released the hold, allowing Steve's dead body to fall face down on the asphalt parking lot.

Hound walked quickly to his car that was parked a short distance away, got in, and drove away. Naturally, he had no intention of harming Paula or her children. He simply wanted what he'd told Steve to be the last thing he thought of and envisioned before he died.

Hound returned to his hotel and enjoyed a perfect sleep for the remainder of the night. He boarded his flight back to Phoenix at 9 a.m. the next morning. He was in bed with Maggie at his desert home at 4:30 p.m. that afternoon.

Steve's death was declared an accident. No evidence of any foul play could be found. It was thought Steve was drunk, simply stumbled and fell against his car in the parking lot and hit his head in such a manner as to break his neck in the specific area of his cervical spine. His wife and children might suffer his death emotionally, but not financially. Paula was beneficiary to Steve's one million dollar life insurance policy. In addition, she'd receive monthly checks for each of her children from a children's survivor fund until Steve Junior and Stephanie were 18 years of age.

The two men who had helped Hound dispose of Karen Thibodaux and her boyfriend, Larry Trischman, arrived in D.C. a week after Hound left. They'd been sent to conduct some specific business with Steve Cooper. They returned to New Orleans and reported to Jo that Steve Cooper had died from an accident. She was sorry Steve had escaped a specific type of death the two men had been sent to deliver.

Hound would remain in Phoenix another twelve days. He would return to New Orleans on July 27 to celebrate his twenty-second birthday with Jo on July 31. During the twelve days, his time was spent either with Maggie or at the biker club socializing with any of the club members that might be at the club when he was. Maggie would always try to drop by when she knew he'd be there. The friendship between Hound, Bear, Bill, and Pony was continuing to grow. Absolute trust had been established between them. Hound was forging a strong bond of friendship with all three men, but a stronger, special kind of friendship was growing between him and Bear. Both of them knew and felt this, but they never stated or discussed it. They were sitting alone at a table in the bar portion of the club drinking a beer and engaging in conversation the day before Hound returned to New Orleans.

"Hound, haven't we known each other about six months?" Bear asked.

"Yeah. That sounds about right."

"It seems longer to me."

"It seems longer to me as well."

"Why do you suppose that is?"

"I don't know how you feel about it, but I've never formed the kind of friendship I have with you in such a short time before."

"You said exactly how I feel. Just think, it all began with getting the shit beat out of us."

"It sure did. I guess friendship grows a lot faster between men who fight side by side to win a fight when winning is the only way they can survive."

"Hound, I think you're right. Hell, I know you're right. That's the way it was in Vietnam, wasn't it?"

"Yes, Bear. It was."

"I sure made some good friends there. I'm sure you did too."

"Indeed, I did."

"Several of my friends didn't survive. That was a God-damned shame. You lost a lot of good friends too, didn't you?"

"I lost all of them. You're right. It was a God-damned shame."

"Hound, I forgot myself. I'm sorry. I know you don't like to talk about Vietnam. I don't either. I don't know why I brought the subject up."

"It's OK, Bear. I have less difficulty talking about it with someone who was there than someone who wasn't."

"Me too. Hound, I'm often troubled by what I saw and did over there. I have nightmares about Vietnam more often than not. Do you suffer from anything like that?"

"Yes, I do. More often than I care to admit. Bear, I don't think we're in the minority. I believe anyone who survived a combat tour in Vietnam experience things similar or identical to what we do."

"I wonder if those experiences ever stop. Do you think they can?"

"It's my hope at some point they can and will."

"Well, fuck it! Let's change the subject and talk about something else. I'm going to drink another beer. How about you?"

"No thanks. It's time for me to go home. I've got packing to do. I'm leaving for New Orleans in the morning."

"When will you be back?"

"I'm not sure, but I'll be back as soon as possible."

"Good. I miss not having you around."

"I'll miss you too, but don't expect to ever start sharing warm showers."

Hound left to go home knowing he'd lied to Bear. He did so for the benefit of his friend. He never had negative experiences because of Vietnam. However, it was true he didn't like to talk about things that happened there.

Maggie had dinner and spent the night with Hound at his home. The next morning, she insisted on driving him to the airport. He asked her why. She told him she wanted to pick him up when he returned.

Jo was still residing at the O'Malley estate when Hound's birthday arrived. She hadn't yet returned to her job at the university. She'd told her father she might never wish to return. Ken told her she had his support whatever she decided to do.

A birthday party for Hound had been planned for quite some time. It was scheduled to begin that evening. A large number of guests had been invited. Hound didn't know most of them. After breakfast that morning, Jo asked Hound to take a walk with her on the estate grounds. Jo had continued to make remarkable progress to improve her health during the three and a half weeks Hound had been away.

"Jo, you're starting to look like your old self again," Hound told her.

"Thank you, honey. I'm starting to feel much better. Do I look well enough to be at your side during your party this evening?"

"Why would you ask me that? You look terrific."

"I don't want to embarrass you in any way. I never want you to be ashamed of me."

"I never have been, and I never will be."

"It looks to be another hot, humid day. The weather in New Orleans this time of year is horrible. Don't you think so?"

"We grew up in Louisiana. The summers have always been hot and humid. We should be used to it by now. Jo, I know you didn't ask me to take a walk so we could talk about the weather. What's on your mind?"

"I guess you do know me well, don't you?"

"I think so."

"Well, you're right. I do wish to discuss some things with you. I hope you won't mind the topics. If you do, then we won't talk about them."

"Jo, I think you have the right to discuss anything you wish with me. Even if I don't like the topic, I owe you the courtesy of discussing it at least once. However, I reserve the right to never discuss it again."

"Hound, when I lost the baby, the fact that I was pregnant became known by individuals outside the family. I'm known as an unwed mother. Everyone knows you're not the father. Nobody would dare say anything to your face, however, you should know a lot of gossip has been circulating. How do you feel about that?"

"I expected that would be the case. I really don't care what people think or say. You shouldn't either."

"I don't. I just didn't want you to be hurt or embarrassed."

"I won't be, so don't worry about it. I feel there's more you wish to discuss."

"Yes, I suppose I do. I don't know if I want to continue my career at the university."

"I thought that's what you wanted."

"I know it would've been of benefit to me. Like you're doing with your nightclub, I was using the university as a stepping-stone to bigger and better things."

"I thought it was your dad's desire that you work at the university."

"It was, at least for a specific time. After I was able to help him achieve what he wanted, then I'd be free to move on to those big and better things. However, Dad has agreed to support any decision I make."

"What do you plan to do if you don't return to the university?"

"I thought that would be obvious. My first priority is to be with you. I'm your wife. We don't need to be separated for two weeks or more at a time. If your home and business is in Phoenix, then I should be there with you. I want to start a family of our own as soon as possible. I want very much to have your children. I'm 28 years old. My biological clock is ticking. I want to be young enough to enjoy and keep up with our kids as they grow up. I assume you still want to have children with me. Is that true?"

Hound knew Jo would confront him with that question sooner or later. He'd hoped it would be later. He had to answer, but he didn't want to. He wanted to tell the truth, but he felt it wouldn't be wise at that time to do so. He didn't want Jo with him in Phoenix. He absolutely didn't want children anytime soon. He'd come to a bridge he had no choice but to cross. He had to decide how he'd answer Jo's question.

"Jo, you shouldn't try to make important decisions at this time. You should wait until you're fully recovered from all you've been through."

"Do you believe I'm not thinking clearly?"

"Jo, I can't know that for sure. You can't either. I just don't want now to be the right time to make a wrong decision. I need you to trust me. I truly believe I'm right."

"Well, what do you think we should do at this time?"

"As soon as you feel up to it, I think you should return to your job at the university. Continue your career there until you're absolutely sure you want to give it up, or keep it. It won't be long until I can arrange my schedule and be with you in Baton Rouge more often."

"How much more often?"

"Home a week. Away a week. Something like that."

"What about starting a family? How do you feel about that, now that you won't have to raise someone else's child along with your own? I know you would've never wanted children with me if the baby had lived. I also know you would've never stayed with me."

"Why do you say that?"

"Because it's true. You know it is. That's why I had to do what I did."

It quickly became apparent to Hound that Jo's statement was a slip of the tongue. Her facial and other body cues indicated her regret for saying it.

"Jo, what did you mean by that remark?" Hound asked. "What did you do?"

"Nothing you should be concerned about. Everything is as it should be. We're together again. I'm happy again. How about you? Are you happy?"

"Yes, Jo, of course, I'm happy, but I need to know what you did. I think you want and need to tell me."

"Shit, Hound! We both know your instinct is superb. What do you think I did? What have you always suspected?"

"I don't want to suspect or wonder. What did you do? You need to tell me. Now."

"You know my health was poor throughout my pregnancy. Subconsciously, I didn't want to be healthy. I didn't want the baby to be healthy. I wanted it to die. It looks like I got what I wanted. Aren't you relieved, happy about it too?"

"Maybe, I suppose so, but did you do anything else to cause the death?"

"What if I did? How would you feel about me?"

"Jo, if you did something to terminate your baby and you're happy about it, then I don't give a shit that you did it. I simply want to know what you did."

"Do you think you have a right to know?"

"Probably not. None whatsoever. Like I said, I simply want to know."

"All right. Hound, no one can ever know what I'm about to tell you, especially my parents. They'd be concerned about my soul and excommunication from the Catholic Church. Promise me you'll never say anything to anyone."

"You know I won't."

"I contacted a woman who could help me. She provided me with a liquid tonic. I took it consistently for a few days. As a result, the baby was poisoned and I went into premature labor. The woman told me if the baby wasn't born dead, then it would die shortly after birth. It did."

"Why did you wait until you were eight months pregnant?"

"Your decision to come back to me convinced me to do it. I've already told you why I became convinced. I wanted to get an abortion early on. My father forbade me to do so. I wanted to give the baby up for adoption after it was born. My father forbade me to do so. He was adamant about raising the baby. He said regardless of how it was conceived, it was still my child, an O'Malley. Fuck him! He never once considered how I felt! He never cared what I wanted or needed!"

"Jo, I completely understand. You had the right to do what was best for you."

"Thank you, my darling. I know you mean that."

Hound's birthday party began at 6 p.m. that evening. It was completely catered and held outdoors on the estate grounds. No expense had been spared to make it a memorable event. A large, temporary dance floor had been constructed so guests could enjoy dancing to music provided by an orchestra of musicians. The food served was exquisite. The alcoholic beverages were top shelf, many of them having been imported.

More than two hundred guests were in attendance. They were all associated in some way with Ken's business. All were wealthy. Ken was pleased to announce to the guests that the party wasn't only to celebrate Hound's twenty-second birthday, but also a belated celebration of his daughter's marriage to him.

Ken had only recently formed a new business relationship with one of the attending guests. This relationship had the potential of being one of the most profitable Ken had ever experienced with a single individual. Ken's political contacts in New Orleans made it possible for him to send and receive cargos through the shipping ports of New Orleans absent any inspection or other interference from local, state, or federal agencies. It was for this reason Roberto Sanchez had a meeting with Ken arranged to discuss how a specific type business agreement could be very financially beneficial to both of them.

Ken could provide a very low risk way for Roberto to get

his illegal merchandise into the United States. By virtue of his trucking companies, Ken could also provide the means by which to transport the merchandise to anywhere in the United States, also with very low risk involved. Because of Ken's status in power and influence, Roberto had decided to eliminate any middlemen and deal with Ken personally. A business arrangement was agreed upon by bosses of two powerful criminal organizations.

Roberto was among the first guests to arrive. He'd brought with him a beautiful young woman whom he introduced to the O'Malley family as his girlfriend and personal assistant. Hound softly and quietly drew a deep breath. Jo stopped breathing for a moment. The last person either of them ever expected to see at the party was Carmella Vargas, but there she stood, arm and arm with Roberto. Carmella was equally shocked to see them. She had no idea what kind of party she would be attending, or anyone that would be there. Roberto never bothered to inform her of these things.

Both Hound and Jo greeted her as though it was their first meeting. She responded likewise. All three of them knew this was the best way to handle the situation. One of the things going through Carmella's mind was that she'd lied to Hound about being married to Roberto. Now he knew she'd lied, but he'd lied to her as well. He was married to Jo.

As she smiled and shook Jo's hand when they were introduced, she thought of Jo's intention to have her killed. As soon as the opportunity presented itself, Jo quickly escorted Hound away to a place of privacy where they could talk.

"God damn it!" Jo said in a state of anger and astonishment. "This is too fucking bizarre! Absolutely fucking unbelievable! That bitch dropped off the face of the earth, and now shows up at your birthday party, the girlfriend of my father's newest, most important business associate!"

"Bizarre doesn't begin to describe the situation, but you need to calm down. We'll figure everything out later. Let's just get through tonight's party."

During dinner that night, Roberto and Carmella sat at the guest of honor table with Hound, Jo, her parents, and all other members of the O'Malley family who were in attendance. Dinner was an awkward and very uncomfortable time for Jo and Carmella, but both were able to conduct themselves in a manner that kept the truth of the situation and their feelings about each other concealed.

Hound was less anxious and concerned. He knew Carmella would do nothing to alert Roberto of their special friendship and history. Jo couldn't afford to do anything that might jeopardize the newly established business relationship between her father and Roberto. Hound knew he and Carmella would be meeting again sometime in the not too distant future. She knew that as well.

He'd offer a satisfactory explanation for marrying Jo. He felt certain Carmella would do the same regarding the lie she told about being married to Roberto. Carmella didn't want to delay having that conversation. She'd much prefer having it sometime during that evening. She didn't want to wait to find out if Hound would understand and forgive her lie. Carmella had told Hound she was married and no longer a prostitute. Now he knew she was the exclusive, well paid and maintained mistress of Roberto Sanchez — a private mistress, but none the less a prostitute.

When Roberto invited Jo to dance, she was obligated to accept. Roberto asked if Hound would care to dance with Carmella. Jo was able to conceal her intense objection but found it extremely difficult. Carmella felt this was likely the only opportunity of the evening she'd have to speak with Hound and have some degree of privacy. The orchestra was playing a waltz. When they began dancing, Carmella was the first to speak.

"Jesus, gringo boy," Carmella said in a low, soft voice. "It's sure as hell a small world, isn't it?"

"Sure seems like it."

"Hound, I would have found a way not to come tonight if I'd known what I was getting into. Roberto never tells me where we're going, why, or who will be there. I'm so sorry."

"I know. Don't worry. Roberto doesn't suspect anything. You, Jo, and I need to make sure it stays that way."

"Hound, we need to discuss some things. Wouldn't you agree?"

"Absolutely, but not here. Not tonight."

"Where? When?"

"Are you back from your stay in Colombia?"

"Yes. Roberto concluded his business a couple of weeks early. We're going back to our home in Oakland tomorrow."

"Will we be able to get back on schedule seeing each other?"

"Of course. Does that mean you want to continue seeing me?"

"Carmella, you're my oldest and dearest friend. There's nothing you would do that could change that. We both owe each other an explanation. We both know why. I know yours will be acceptable to me. I hope mine will be acceptable to you."

"It will be. You know that. So, can I assume everything is OK between us?"

"Don't worry, Carmella. Everything is fine."

"I'd think my relationship with Roberto would greatly reduce any possibility of Jo pursuing her long existing plan to kill me. Would you agree?"

"I would, but that threat was eliminated before tonight. Don't worry about it anymore, but don't do anything to antagonize her."

"How was the threat eliminated?"

"That was the main reason I married Jo."

"What do you mean?"

"Carmella, let's not discuss it now. I'll tell you when I see you again. It's part of my explanation for getting married."

"Are you planning to remain married?"

"Not any longer than I have to. Like I said, let's talk later. When we do, you can tell me if you're planning to stay with Roberto. Are you?"

"Not if I can find a way to safely separate from him. I've told you that before."

"I know. I just thought you might've changed your mind."

"I haven't. Hound, Roberto and Jo are taking turns looking at us. I think you're right about discussing all this later."

"I told you so."

When the dance ended, the two couples returned and sat down at the table. Shortly after, Roberto focused his attention on Hound and initiated conversation. Jo, Ken, and Carmella listened intently.

"Hound, it's hard to believe you're only 22 years old," Roberto said. "You look older, maybe 26 or 27."

"I guess it's true. Everyone tells me that. I've always looked a bit older than I actually was."

"That's something you and Carmella have in common. She too looks older than she really is. How old would you guess her to be?"

"I would guess mid to late twenties. How old is she?"

"My sweet Carmella is about a year older than you. Hound, you and I have something in common as well. Can you guess what it is?"

"The only thing I can think of is we both are loved by extremely beautiful women."

Roberto's response was laughter as he nodded his head, indicating his approval of and agreement with Hound's answer.

"Are you from Louisiana originally, or are you a native of another state?" Roberto asked.

Hound had no idea how much information Ken might've provided Roberto about him when the invitation to attend the birthday party was extended. Even if no information had been provided, Hound assumed if he told Roberto his home state was Louisiana, Roberto would likely ask the name of his hometown. He felt certain Roberto knew the name of Carmella's hometown. Carmella felt as though her heart was moving to her throat as she waited for Hound to answer. Hound decided to take a risk and gamble.

"Mr. Sanchez, I'm originally from Arkansas," Hound said.

"Did you wear shoes growing up in Arkansas?"

"Yes, I did. Fortunately, the rumors that people from Arkansas don't wear shoes are false. At least they were regarding me."

Hound, Carmella, and even Jo were greatly relieved when Roberto's next question changed the subject of the conversation.

"I very much like your nickname," Roberto said. "Why was it given to you?"

"I had a dog when I was a kid, a purebred hound. I earned the nickname because of the close relationship I had with the dog."

Roberto seemed to enjoy the short story Hound told about his relationship with Hunter. As soon as he finished the story, Ken focused the topic of the conversation away from Hound. He'd become suspicious that it might not be a coincidence Carmella's name was the same as the young lady Hound had successfully negotiated to never be harmed. He'd verify his suspicion as soon as possible.

The party ended a few minutes before midnight. Roberto and Carmella were the last guests to leave. A few family members were spending the night at the estate. As everyone began making their way to their bedrooms, Ken asked Jo and Hound to join him for a brief conversation in the den.

"Hound, there's something I need to know," Ken said calmly. "Is the Carmella Vargas that was with Roberto tonight the same Carmella Vargas that we agreed to terminate before she disappeared to parts unknown? I know the name isn't that uncommon. It's probably just a coincidence they both have the same name, but I need to know for sure."

"Ken, it's not a coincidence. The Carmella Vargas that was here tonight and the Carmella Vargas we once agreed to terminate are one in the same."

"Well, that's not going to happen now. I can't risk making an enemy of Roberto. Hound, you were always adamant that Carmella presented no threat to you. Do you still feel the same way?"

"Absolutely. I'm happy no harm will come to her."

Jo immediately joined the conversation.

"Dad, that's absolute bullshit!" Jo said angrily. "There are ways to kill that bitch without Roberto ever knowing, or even suspecting we had anything to do with it!"

"Jo, you'd do well to be careful what you say to me and how you say it. I've given my decision regarding Carmella Vargas. That decision is final. By God, I mean it! Never think about defying any decision I make! Do you understand?"

"Yes."

"Yes what, God damn it!"

"Yes, sir. I understand."

"Good. Jo, I'm sorry I yelled at you, but you know better than to make me mad."

Ken told Jo he wanted to speak with Hound in private. Jo told her father goodnight and retired to her bedroom.

"Hound, have you made any progress getting Jo to tell you who the father of her child was?" Ken asked.

"Yes. She told me who he was."

"Good. Now you can tell me who the son of a bitch is. I know you said you wanted to deal with him personally, but I want to help. I need to be involved. I'm sure you can understand that. What's his name? What do you know about him?"

"His name was Steve Cooper. He was a special agent with the FBI, assigned to the bureau office in D.C."

"You keep using the word was, referring to him in the past tense."

"Yes, I know. That's because he's dead."

"Are you telling me you've already killed him?"

"No, but he's dead."

"How do you know?"

"I went to D.C. to deal with him. After arriving, I found out he died accidentally."

"What kind of accident?"

"The newspaper said he fell and broke his neck."

"Bullshit! You broke the fucker's neck, didn't you?"

"I didn't have anything to do with it. If it wasn't an accident, then somebody else wasted him. It wasn't me. I wished it had been, but it wasn't."

"Son, are you telling me the truth?"

"Yes. Unfortunately, I am."

When Hound's visit with Ken concluded, he joined Jo in their bedroom. She was lying in bed awake, waiting for him.

"Hound, I don't care what Dad said," Jo stated angrily. "I'm still going to kill Carmella."

"What the hell are you talking about? You can't do that. Your dad forbids it."

"I sure as hell can. There are men employed by my dad that will help me. Dad will never know or think I had anything to do with it."

"What men? Who are they?"

"Do you remember the two men that helped you eliminate your problem with Karen Thibodaux?"

"Yes.

"They're the men I'm talking about."

"Are these men foolish enough to disobey your father's order to obey yours?"

"They'd do anything I asked. It's been that way since I was 16 years old. I recently sent them to Washington D.C. They were going to take care of some unfinished business for me."

"What business?"

"I was going to tell you when I thought the time was right. I suppose now is as good a time as any. They went there to kill Steve Cooper. I wanted that bastard to suffer in a very special, specific way for all the heartache and misery he caused us! Unfortunately, the son of a bitch had an accident, broke his neck, and died before I could carry out my revenge! Damn! I did so want to punish that mother fucker!"

"Well, at least he's dead."

"Steve's dying quickly from a broken neck was simply not

enough punishment for what he did to me, to us. He deserved to suffer a long and painful death. Would you like to know what I'd planned to do to him?"

"No, Jo, I don't want to know. The things you've endured because of him are far beyond horrific. However, you must put all that behind you. You have the rest of your life to live. You can't be happy if you continue to carry the burden he placed on you. You also have to dismiss from your life the obsession you have to kill Carmella. She doesn't deserve it. There's no reason for it. It's time to let it go."

"As long as she's alive, she's a threat to you, a threat to us. That makes her a threat to me."

"Jo, Carmella has never been a threat to me. Never. It would make me extremely unhappy and greatly anger me if you did anything to harm her in any way."

"Hound, do you have feelings for that bitch greater than a friendship?"

"Of course not, but a very strong bond of friendship does exist between us. It seemed to begin naturally when we were children together on the farm. Over the years, through all kinds of situations and circumstances that would normally destroy a friendship, ours has continued to grow."

"Hound, I've always believed the relationship you have with Carmella was much more than just a great platonic friendship. You may consider her only a friend, but she's deeply in love with you. As a woman, I know that. As intelligent as you are, I'm convinced you know it too. Because of that, she'll always be a threat to our relationship. I will not let anyone or anything come between us."

"My God, Jo! That's the real reason you want Carmella dead, isn't it? Your main concern about her has never been what she knew and could tell about the death of Carlos Mendoza. You consider her a threat to our relationship."

"Regardless of the reason, Carmella needs to be eliminated."

"Jo, I have something to say to you. I'm only going to say it once, so listen very carefully. If Carmella is harmed in any way, then I will disappear from your life and you will never see me again. I'm sick and tired of being forced to accept the desires and decisions of you or your father as they pertain to my life, how I choose to live it, and individuals I choose to protect because they don't deserve to be murdered by cowardly bullies."

Jo was both surprised and shocked by what Hound had said, and the way he said it.

"Sweetie, I can't believe you said those things to me," Jo replied. "I know you don't mean them. Obviously, you're upset. We'll discuss things further tomorrow, after we both have had some sleep. It's been a very trying evening. Your birthday party certainly didn't go the way I'd planned."

"Jo, I told you I was only going to say it once. I've told you what I wanted you to know. You know I meant every God-damned word I said. Don't ever be foolish enough to believe I didn't."

For the first time since she'd known Hound, Jo became fearful of him. She instinctively knew he'd meant every word he said. Her greatest fear was the result of one statement he'd made. He'd referred to her and Ken as bullies.

"All right, my darling. I'll honor and comply with your wishes," Jo said. "If anything ever happens to Carmella, it will not be me or my father that causes it."

"On your love for me, swear it. "

"On my love for you, I swear it!"

"Fair enough."

"Hound, is everything all right between us now?"

"Yes, Jo. On my love for you, I swear it."

"Hound, I'm sorry for the things I said. You had every right to be angry. I wasn't thinking clearly. Thank you for helping me see the light. Please don't be angry with me. Do you forgive me?"

"Jo, I'm not angry anymore. Of course, I forgive you."

"Do you feel like making love to me? I'd enjoy it very much."

"Jo, like you said, it's been a trying evening. I hope you don't mind and will understand, but I'm simply not in the mood."

"Honey, of course, I understand. I'll give you a rain check for tomorrow night."

"I'm leaving to visit my family at the farm tomorrow."

"How long will you be gone?"

"I'm not sure, but not long. Do you want to go with me?"

"Your parents still don't know we're married. They don't know I lost the baby. I think it's best you visit them alone. I'm sure you plan to tell them everything that's happened. I think it will be easier if I'm not there. Don't you?"

"Yes. That would probably be best. We can visit them together later."

Before falling to sleep, Jo lay cuddled close to Hound. She thought how very much she loved him and how for the first time since their relationship began, he had no desire to be sexually intimate with her. It was the first time she'd ever made him angry. In doing so, she'd been reminded of the dangerous beast that always lay quietly sleeping inside him, a beast that didn't like to be awakened, a beast that was unpredictable, vicious, deliberate, and undefeatable when provoked.

She would have no problem adjusting her attitude toward Carmella and would never tell her father what Hound had said to her.

8

Hound left early the next morning to visit his parents. They didn't know he was back in the state, or that he'd spent his birthday with Jo in New Orleans, so his visit would be a surprise. During the drive to the farm, Hound considered how he'd tell John and Linda of his marriage to Jo and the loss of her baby.

He didn't look forward to the task. It wasn't informing them that he dreaded; it was their response. John and Linda had pledged their support regarding whether he decided to marry her or not. However, he knew they hoped and believed he wouldn't. He anticipated they'd offer their blessing, pretending to support and accept his decision. He knew they'd be hurt and disappointed.

After first hearing the news, as expected, John and Linda were extremely upset. Naturally, they expressed their condolences for the death of Jo's baby, but they later would agree it was probably for the best. They refused to believe loving and being unable to live without her had motivated Hound's decision to marry Jo. As expected, they eventually accepted the current situation, stated their support, and offered their blessing and best wishes.

During his time at the farm, Hound spent a great deal of time down at the swimming hole. It was a quiet, private place for him to reflect on his current life situation. Changes had occurred he hadn't been prepared for. He didn't want to think about things he'd forced himself to accept and do.

He thought a great deal about Carmella and wondered what their next meeting would be like. He wondered how much truth had been in what Jo said about his relationship with her. He knew they were extremely good friends. He knew he was very fond of her. Sex with her had always been extraordinary, beyond gratifying, and hard, if not impossible, to resist. He pondered the possibility that the feelings he had for Carmella had surpassed those of only a loyal, lifelong, indestructible friendship.

He allowed his thoughts to focus on Hunter. He began to remember specific times they spent together, times when his life was less stressful, less complicated, and he was happier.

His thoughts returned to Jo. She wasn't the same person he'd loved before he went to Vietnam. He was convinced she'd forever be emotionally scarred by the tragedies she'd endured.

After a two-day visit, Hound said goodbye to his parents and returned to New Orleans. He would return to Phoenix the next day. Shortly after lunch, Ken requested another meeting with Hound and Jo in his den. Before the meeting began, Jo told Hound she'd decided against moving to Phoenix. She'd be returning to her home in Baton Rouge and her job at the university. Hound expressed his support for her decision but concealed his satisfaction with it.

"Hound, I know Jo has told you about her decision to remain in Baton Rouge and resume her position at LSU," Ken said. "How do you feel about that? I know you'd much rather have her with you in Phoenix."

"Ken, it would've been nice to have her with me, but I think the decision she made is the right one. Once my club is operating, then I can commute between Phoenix and Baton Rouge on a regular, frequent basis. It won't take long for Jo and me to become accustomed to and comfortable with that. It is said absence makes the heart grow fonder. I feel that's likely true, providing the absence isn't too long between visits."

"I agree completely. I've talked to Jo about that. She understands that if you had accepted the position I offered you in my business, then you'd likely be away longer periods of time. Naturally, the offer is still open if you're interested in making a great deal more money than can ever be made as a nightclub entrepreneur."

"I appreciate that, but I'm going to stay on my present course, at least until I see if it leads to the destiny I was born to achieve."

"Hound, do you truly believe you have a preordained destiny?"

"I can't honestly say I'm committed to such a belief now, but I'm willing to explore the possibility of its existence."

"What will you do if you discover it doesn't exist?"

"If my destiny is not preordained, then I'll simply choose the destiny I want and achieve it. I'll win either way."

"I'm certain you will. Hound, the position I offered you will always be waiting should you ever decide it's the best possible destiny you could achieve. I'll keep hoping someday you accept my offer."

"Ken, I really appreciate that. It makes me feel very special."

"Hound, you are special. You know that."

"Thank you. I've never considered myself a special individual."

"Your personal qualities make you a very special, unique man. Those qualities make you ideal to fill the position I offered. Being my son-in-law is the only thing that increases your qualifications. I truly hope you'll change your mind sometime in the not too distant future."

"Who knows, maybe I will. None of us know what the future holds."

"There's something else I'd like to talk to both of you about, if you don't mind."

"Sure. What is it?"

"I'm anxious to be a grandfather. I'm hoping you and Jo are planning to have children as soon as possible. Are you?"

Jo decided to join the conversation and be the first to respond.

"Of course, we are, Dad, absolutely," Jo said with an attitude of joy and sincerity. "Hound and I have agreed to start a family as quickly as possible."

"Jo, are you sure it's not too soon?" Hound asked. "Maybe we should wait and make sure you're healthy enough, physically and emotionally, to become pregnant again. You've been through a great deal over the last several months."

"Nonsense! My health is absolutely fine. I don't want to delay getting pregnant any longer than is absolutely necessary."

"Jo, I feel it necessary to insist your doctor give you a complete physical examination, and I do mean complete examination, before I allow you to become pregnant." Hound felt this would at least buy him a short window of time before he was forced to commit to what Jo and her father wanted.

"Hound, I'm sure that isn't necessary," Jo replied adamantly. "I'm the absolute picture of health!"

Ken's thinking was more rational than Jo's. He quickly recognized the wisdom of Hound's suggestion and concern.

"Jo, I think Hound is correct," Ken said. "You don't need to take any unnecessary risks. I understand you believe your health is fine, but you need to be absolutely sure it is before you become pregnant. You can have the examination while Hound is away this time. You both can celebrate your physician-confirmed health when Hound returns. You likely won't lose any time getting pregnant."

Jo took a moment to consider the things said to her. She knew Hound intended to have his way. With Ken supporting his suggestion, she knew the examination was inevitable.

"Well, shit!" Jo replied. "All right, I'll have the damn examination, but I know it's a waste of my time."

The next morning, Hound boarded his flight and returned to

Phoenix. Maggie was waiting at the airport to pick him up when he arrived. She drove him home and spent the rest of the afternoon and night with him.

When she left the next morning for work, Hound wasted no time calling Carmella. It was time to resume their scheduled liaisons. He knew it was best to meet her in Oakland rather than have her come to Phoenix. Maggie wouldn't be pleased to discover his relationship with Carmella, who wouldn't be pleased with the relationship he had with Maggie.

He flew to Oakland later that afternoon. He said nothing to Maggie about the trip. He decided it was time she became acclimated to not knowing every move he made when they weren't together. He hoped this could be done without angering and alienating her. He wanted to maintain a specific type of relationship with Maggie, one that suited his purpose, but one she would be satisfied with, at least for a while.

He was fond of Maggie and enjoyed her company, but not as consistently as it had become. He knew Maggie had developed strong feelings for him. He hoped those feelings would influence her to provide him the amount of freedom and privacy he required. He also knew Maggie was a very strong-willed, determined, independent, and proud woman, used to getting what she wanted. In spite of her feelings, she was certainly not a woman to tolerate being used or taken for granted if she felt such was the case.

Hound and Carmella met at a nice but secluded restaurant in Oakland for dinner. Carmella was already seated at a table in the most private area of the restaurant when Hound arrived. She stood up to greet him with a passionate kiss and warm embrace when he reached the table.

"Oh, my sweet gringo boy," Carmella said softly when the kiss ended. "I'm so happy to see you again, under much more enjoyable circumstances."

"Good to see you again as well. I completely agree about the circumstances."

"Attending your birthday party was among the most stressful situations I've ever experienced."

"I can relate to that, but it's over now. However, I'm sure you realize similar situations could occur in the future. Roberto will likely be invited to other social functions. You may be required to attend, at least some of them. There's always a possibility I'll be there. A greater possibility exists Jo will be there, even if I'm not."

"It's very ironic Roberto and Ken formed a business relationship. Don't you agree?"

"Perhaps, at least regarding our relationship. From a business standpoint, it makes perfect sense. Roberto and Ken each have something the other needs to further grow their empire."

When the waiter delivered their dinner to the table, the topic of their conversation focused on something different. There was a major question that needed to be answered by each of them.

"Hound, you must be interested to know why I lied about being married to Roberto," Carmella said. "I think it may be the first and only lie I've ever told you, but I feel you also lied to me. You told me you'd changed your mind about marrying Jo."

"Carmella, we owe each other an explanation. You go first."

"Hound, I didn't want you to know I was only Roberto's mistress. I told you I was married because I wanted you to believe I was no longer a prostitute, that I had learned from my mistake and left it behind. Even though I was married to a cartel boss, at least I was now pursuing a college education with the intention of preparing myself for an honorable, acceptable career in society and somehow separating from Roberto in the future. As a mistress, I'd still be considered a prostitute by you. I didn't want you to think of me that way anymore. Can you understand why I lied and forgive me for it?"

"Of course, I can, but you didn't have to lie. I've always believed our friendship to be unconditional but based on complete trust and honesty. When I told you in the past I had decided not to marry Jo, it was the truth. Unforeseen circumstances forced me to change my mind. I had no way of contacting you to let you know about the change, or why."

"So, you didn't lie to me at all, did you?"

"No. I'd have to agree that I didn't."

"What were the unforeseen circumstances that forced you to marry her?"

Hound provided Carmella with only part of the story. However, it was enough to satisfy her. By the time they finished dinner, their relationship was back on track, strong as ever. They spent that night and the next two days and nights together. No further conversation about Roberto or Jo occurred until the day Hound returned to Phoenix. They were having breakfast together in the restaurant of the hotel where they were staying.

"Hound, do you plan to remain married?" Carmella asked.

"Not likely. I don't plan on being married any longer than I have to. I simply don't know how long that will be. Isn't the same true regarding how long you intend to remain with Roberto?"

"Yes. I guess that's true. Hound, did you ever develop strong feelings for Jo, or was she at best only a good friend, someone who could provide you with special things no other woman could at a specific time in your life?"

"Carmella, in all honesty, I believe it was both. We weren't only great friends, but I came to care for her very deeply. Unfortunately, her feelings for me were always stronger than mine for her."

"That sounds like the feelings we share. I've always known mine are stronger than yours. Do you no longer feel anything for her?"

"I'll always have feelings for her, but not like I used to. I'll always wish her well and hope she can find a happy life. I just can't be part of it."

"What caused your feelings to change?"

"Specific events that occur in life have a way of changing anyone. That's just the way life is. If the events are positive, then the changes are positive, relationships continue to grow in a positive direction. The opposite is true when the events are negative and painful, emotionally and/or physically. Those type of events caused the change."

"Did Vietnam provide you many, if not all, such negative events?"

"Without a doubt, both directly and indirectly. A minor few, but very significant events would've never occurred if I'd responded differently to other events."

"Like what? Give me examples."

"If I'd never become involved with Jo, never allowed myself to be drafted into the Army, never gone to Officer Candidate School, never assaulted a superior officer. Those are four major examples."

"I'd think Carlos Mendoza catching us fucking in the barn that day would constitute a negative event. One you wish you'd responded differently too."

"Without a doubt. Absolutely."

"What feelings do you have for me? I want you to tell me, and I need you to be honest. I need to know finally if there's a chance you and I can have a future together."

"Carmella, I have come to the conclusion my feelings for you are deeper than I ever thought. Even though that's true, I could never guarantee we have a future together. It may be our destiny to be together. Maybe not. We just have to continue living life day by day. What will be, will be. What will not, will not."

"I can accept and live with that. I appreciate you being honest."

Hound's flight left Oakland at 9 a.m. the next morning. He arrived at his home in the desert a little after noon. As expected, Maggie was waiting anxiously for his return. She was seated on the sofa in the living room. When he entered, she quickly stood to greet him. The greeting wasn't as warm and welcoming as usual.

"You've been gone for three days," Maggie said in a way that indicated both relief and anger. "Where in the hell have you been? Why didn't you tell me you were leaving? You son of a bitch! I've been worried sick! I thought all kinds of things might have happened. I wondered if you might be sick, or injured and unable to get help! God damn it! I was even afraid you might have been kidnapped!"

"Maggie, I'm truly sorry you were worried and upset. I've been out of town taking care of some personal business. I didn't realize you required me to report and answer to you for everything I do. If such a requirement exists, then I suggest you change it. I've never reported my every move to anyone. I don't intend to start now. I'm not trying to be rude or disrespectful, but that's just the way I am."

"Shit, Hound! I don't expect you to report every move you make to me. However, I would appreciate you telling me when you plan to be away and return so I don't have to worry about something having happened to you. Is that really too much to ask?"

"Maggie, I appreciate your concern. I guess it's not too much to ask. Perhaps you care for me more than I realize."

"Hound, you know I care! I've made that very clear to you! Don't bullshit me about what you do or don't realize. What I realize is that you're an inconsiderate bastard!"

"Maggie, I guess I was inconsiderate. I didn't mean to be. I apologize."

"I'll forgive you this one time, but please don't take me for granted like that again."

"All right, Maggie."

"Where did you go?"

"Am I required to tell you where I go as well as when I'm going?"

"Is that too much to ask?"

"I suppose not. I was in Oakland."

"Why?"

"Maggie, with all due respect, that's none of your business."

"You went to Oakland to see a woman, didn't you?"

"Is that what you really think?"

"Yes, unless you tell me otherwise, and don't lie."

"Maggie, I'm not going to answer. That way you'll know I'm not lying."

Maggie's anger reached a peak. She left without saying another word, got in her car, and sped away. A week passed. Neither Hound nor Maggie attempted to contact each other. His phone rang as he was preparing to leave his home on Monday morning and drive to the airport to catch a flight back to New Orleans. When he answered, Maggie spoke in a calm voice.

"Hound, it's apparent you weren't planning to call me, so I decided to call you. Do you have a minute to talk?"

"Not really. Actually, I was just on my way out."

"All right. Can we talk later today?"

"I'll be out of town for a few days."

Maggie paused her conversation for a moment. Her desire to ask him where he was going, why, and when he'd return was great. However, she decided it would be best not to do so.

"Will you give me a call when you return?" she asked. "I think we really need to talk. Don't you?"

"What do we have to talk about?"

"I called this morning to apologize."

"What are you apologizing for?"

"For the part I played in initiating our first argument. I want things to be as they were between us before the argument. How do you feel about that?"

"I really don't know, Maggie. I don't think I'm the kind of man you want and need, at least not now."

"Hound, I think you might be exactly that kind of man."

"I'm not sure I understand what you mean."

"I've always been able to dictate to men. They always let me have my way. You don't. You don't answer to or let anyone tell you how to live your life. That's a major thing you and I have in common. I think that's one reason I was initially attracted to you. I'd like to start over, if that's all right with you. I'll never again ask you anything that doesn't concern me."

"Maggie, you know I'm attracted to you as well. Everything about you appeals to me. However, I have a lot of shit on my plate right now. You know what most of it is. I simply don't think you and I could have a compatible relationship until I resolve some issues in my life. The last thing I want to do is hurt, frustrate, or disappoint you. I certainly don't want you to think I'm using you or taking you for granted. I hope you understand."

"I understand completely. I'd never let you use me or take me for granted, but I'm sure we can reach an understanding, find some middle ground that's fair and agreeable to both of us. Can we talk about it when you return?"

Hound recognized two options had been presented to him. He could end the relationship that existed between him and Maggie and be free of any responsibility or obligation regarding her or continue and see where it might lead. He was still convinced she could prove to be a very valuable asset in the future. In addition, but perhaps a bit less important, dating her was a lot of fun, the sex very satisfying, and she was beautiful and intelligent, which were all required criteria of any woman desiring a relationship with him.

"Maggie, I think it would be a good idea to talk when I return," Hound told her. "I sincerely hope we can reach an understanding, find the middle ground you spoke of."

"I'm happy you feel that way. I'm certain we can. I'll miss you while you're away. Be sure to take good care of yourself. Call me if you can and have time."

"OK, Maggie. I shouldn't be away too long, only a few days. I'll see you when I get back."

Jo had moved back to Baton Rouge. She was waiting at the airport in New Orleans when Hound arrived. She greeted him warmly, but he knew something was wrong. They talked casually about many things during the first few minutes of the eighty-mile drive back to Baton Rouge. Eventually, Hound decided to learn what was troubling her.

"Jo, I sense something is bothering you," he said. "What's wrong?"

"I wanted to wait until we got home before I told you, but I suppose now is as good a time as any. Hound, it isn't likely I can ever have children."

"What do you mean? What makes you think that?"

"I had the physical exam you and Dad insisted on shortly after you returned to Phoenix. My doctor told me after the examination was completed."

"Well, he said unlikely, not impossible."

"I know, but I think he lied. He probably wanted to give me hope so I wouldn't be as upset."

"What did your doctor say was the reason?"

"The status of my health during pregnancy caused severe complications. I'm convinced the tonic I took to poison the baby was responsible as well."

"Did you tell your doctor about the tonic?"

"Hell no! Only you know about that."

"Jo, tell me how you're feeling now, emotionally and physically."

"I'm fine physically, but emotionally I'm a wreck. What will you do if I can never have your children?"

"What do you mean?"

"Will you still want me as your wife? You probably won't. I know how much you want children."

"Don't be ridiculous. I'd never leave you because you couldn't give me children. Besides, I don't believe the doctor lied."

"Do you really think there's still a chance we can have a family?"

"Absolutely, but we have to accept what is meant to be, whatever that is."

"You're talking about destiny again, aren't you?"

"Yes. I guess I am."

Hound remained in Baton Rouge with Jo until September 1. She resumed her position at the university the third week of August. Until he returned to Phoenix, Hound spent as much time with Jo as possible. The only time they were apart was when she was at work. He joined her daily for lunch on the university campus. They went out for dinner most evenings. Jo insisted on having sex at every opportunity. If there was the slightest chance of her becoming pregnant, she wanted to do everything possible to improve the odds.

It was Hound's intention to help Jo adjust to the news received from her doctor. He supported her hope and efforts to conceive, but he secretly hoped she wouldn't. He didn't know if he'd ever want to have children with her. He felt they wouldn't remain together. He knew there was a strong possibility he'd never want children with any woman. Perhaps that would change when he was older. His happiness currently depended upon being free to explore life and all its possibilities, feeling no responsibility or obligation to anyone.

Hound was back home in Phoenix on the evening of September 1. He hadn't been in contact with Maggie since he left. He called her at her home the following morning. She was delighted to hear from him and know he'd finally returned. She refrained from asking any questions regarding where he'd been, what he'd done, or who he'd seen. She assumed he'd been in Louisiana with Jo.

For the next two months, Hound followed a set routine. He remained directly involved in the construction of his nightclub, continued to grow his friendship with Bear and other members of the biker club, went home to be with Jo on the average of every other week, spent all his free time in Phoenix with Maggie, continued tours of gambling in Reno and Vegas, and kept his monthly scheduled meetings with Carmella.

During the time she spent in France last summer, Rebecca Hughes met a young French college professor. She decided to remain in Paris with him. They returned to Oakland in early November to be married. Hound was invited and attended. General Hughes obtained an extended leave to be home for the wedding and enjoy the Thanksgiving, Christmas, and New Year holidays with his family. The wedding was held at the church the family attended in Oakland. Rebecca called Hound in early August, prior to accepting the professor's proposal of marriage. During the phone conversation, Hound decided to tell Rebecca he and Jo were married. While sharing a dance at the wedding reception, Rebecca told Hound she decided to get married only after she learned of his marriage to Jo.

"I always hoped I'd marry you," she whispered in his ear. "I suppose it was simply not to be."

"It wasn't. Rebecca, I wish you all the happiness in the world. Your husband seems like a wonderful man."

"Thank you. He is."

General Hughes was delighted to see Hound again. When the opportunity presented itself, the general escorted Hound to a private area where they could visit for a while.

"Captain, it's certainly a pleasure to see you again," General Hughes said. "How is life treating you?"

"Sir, probably better than I deserve. It seems like forever since I was called captain. How have you been? I hope life has been treating you kindly. How is the war going?"

"Hound, the life of a career soldier never changes, especially during times of war. Do you watch the news on TV regularly?"

"Sir, every night."

"Well, that's how the war is going, and stop calling me sir. You're a civilian now."

"Sir, in my mind, you'll always be my superior officer. You've earned my everlasting respect and admiration."

"Thank you, son. You've earned mine as well. I understand you finally married the young lady you told me about before you returned to the States."

"Sir, yes, I did."

"I'm happy for you. A good man needs a good woman in his life. I'm sure she's perfect for you."

"Sir, Jo is a wonderful woman. She's much better than I deserve."

"I doubt that very much."

"Rebecca seems to have married a wonderful man."

"I think so, but I fear he isn't the man for her."

"Sir, why do you think that?"

"I think Rebecca truly cares for him, but not enough to have married him. I think she knows that. I also think she'd never have married him if she'd been able to marry the man she truly wanted."

"Sir, did she ever say who that man was?"

"Hound, it was you. Surely you know that."

"Sir, I do. Rebecca told me a few minutes ago while we were dancing. I'm very sorry. I've never led her on or made any promises I didn't intend to keep."

"Son, I know that. However, for what it's worth, it would've made me proud to have had you as a son-in-law. I believe you would've made Rebecca extremely happy."

9

The construction of Hound's nightclub was completed on November 23. Its grand opening occurred the night after Thanksgiving. The club was filled to its maximum capacity with patrons that night. Hound knew his club was destined to be extremely profitable. Without a doubt, it was the most elegant club existing anywhere in the country.

Special guests who were invited and attended the grand opening were Maggie, Bear and his wife, Bill and his wife, Pony and his steady momma, General Hughes and his wife, along with Rebecca and her new husband. Naturally, Jo and her parents were there.

John and Linda graciously declined the invitation, but they asked Hound to visit them on the farm as soon as possible. He assured them he would. Hound knew his parents wouldn't wish to attend due to the nature of his new business. Maggie and all guests from the biker club made sure not to disclose anything or behave in any way that would cause Jo to suspect Maggie's relationship with Hound. The Hughes family were equally cautious not to reveal Rebecca's former history with him. In addition to Jo, Rebecca didn't want her new husband to become suspicious.

Hound and Jo were at the farm with John and Linda from Christmas Eve until 10 a.m. on Christmas morning. They then drove to New Orleans to be with Ken and Sandra that afternoon and evening. They spent the night at the estate. They left after breakfast the next morning and returned to their home in Baton Rouge. They decided to spend New Year's Eve alone together at home. Hound would be returning to Phoenix on January 2. Jo wanted to spend as much private time with him as possible before he left and her job at the university resumed after the holiday break.

When Hound returned to Phoenix, Maggie was waiting at the airport to take him home. Shortly after they began driving, she handed him an envelope containing information he requested she obtain for him. The information was regarding Colonel Joe Westerman. Hound had never told Maggie why he wanted the information. She never asked.

Maggie had dinner with Hound at his home and stayed the night. The next morning after she left for work, Hound booked a flight leaving early that afternoon. Once again, he did so using his false identification. His destination was Joe Westerman's hometown. He returned to Phoenix on the afternoon of January 6. On the evening of January 5, Joe was found dead in the restroom at a nice restaurant where he and his wife were having dinner. The cause of his death was determined to be the result of an accidental fall that had broken his cervical spine at the base of his skull. While washing his hands, before rejoining his wife at their table, Joe looked in the mirror and saw the familiar face standing behind him. A split second later, Hound's revenge was complete.

It was 9 a.m. on Monday, the first week of February. Hound had returned to Phoenix from Baton Rouge the day before. It was two days before he was scheduled to meet with Carmella in Oakland. He was home alone when his phone rang. When he answered, Hound discovered it was Carmella calling. She'd arrived in Phoenix earlier that morning. She was calling from a motel where she'd rented a room. As she started to speak, she began to cry hysterically.

"My God, Carmella! What's wrong?" Hound asked. "Calm down and tell me what the fuck is going on!"

"He knows! He knows everything!"

"Who the hell is he?"

"Roberto, God damn it! He's looking for me now! When he finds me, he plans to kill me! I know he does!"

"Carmella, you'll have to calm down so I can understand everything you're saying."

Carmella was finally able to compose herself enough to talk rationally. However, her voice continued breaking when she spoke, indicating the intense anxiety and fear she was feeling.

"Now, tell me what's going on," Hound said in a calm, soft voice. "What does Roberto know? Why is he looking for you? Did you leave him? How do you know he wants to kill you?"

"He knows about you and me!"

"What does he know?"

"Everything, God damn it! He also knows I fucked both my bodyguard babysitters so I could blackmail them to remain silent about us. They're both already dead! Hound, you're also in grave danger! Roberto's revenge will include you! I need to be with you! You're the only possible chance we have of surviving!"

"Where are you now?"

"I'm in Phoenix, hiding in a motel room!"

"What motel are you at? What's the address?"

Carmella quickly gave him the name and address of the motel.

"Are you driving your car?" he asked.

"Yes. Why?"

"Did you register under your real name?"

"Yes. Why?"

"How did you pay for your room? Cash, I hope."

"No. I used a credit card. I wanted to keep as much cash available as possible. Why are you asking me all these questions?"

"The information you provided to the motel will make it easier for Roberto to find you. You need to get the hell out of there as quickly as possible."

"Fuck! I never considered all that shit! I'll leave right away! Where should I go?"

Hound told her the name and address of a supermarket not far from her motel.

"Carmella, I want you to drive to the supermarket," Hound said. "Park your car in the employee lot behind the market and wait for me there. I'll join you as quickly as I can."

"OK. I'm leaving now. How long will it take you to get there?"

"About 30 minutes, maybe sooner. I'll get there as quickly as possible."

"Hound, I'm frightened! Please hurry!"

Carmella quickly gathered her personal belongings, left the room, and hurried to her car. She drove away, following Hound's directions to the supermarket. Hound walked to his bedroom. He opened the top drawer of the small table beside his bed and removed two Colt 45 semi-automatic pistols, along with two reserve clips of ammunition. He rushed to his car and then drove from his property at a fast rate of speed.

The two Colt handguns were a matching set, blue steel with ivory grips. Bear had stolen them sometime in the past and added them to his collection of numerous firearms. He'd once shown them to Hound. Hound stated how much he'd like to own such a remarkable set of weapons. Bear had given the weapons to him as an early gift for his twenty-second birthday. Hound had devoted much time practice firing the weapons. He was now deadly accurate with their use.

When Hound arrived at the supermarket, he found Carmella anxiously waiting for him. She left her car in the lot and they drove away in his Corvette. Hound drove north from the city on the same highway he'd traveled south to fetch Carmella. He planned to reach his nightclub as quickly as possible.

"My God, Hound! What are we going to do?" Carmella asked immediately after entering the Corvette.

"Carmella, everything will be fine. Try to relax and remain calm."

"If you say everything will be fine, then I believe you, but what are we going to do?"

"I think the best thing now is for you to relocate somewhere where you're safe."

"Where do you think I should relocate? Is there any place that will be safe enough?"

"Of course. You may be able to stay in a location only a short period of time, but that will be temporary until I can devise a better long-term plan. Remember, there's always a solution to any problem. The more difficult the problem, the more difficult it is to find a solution, but one can be found."

"I remember. You've told me that many times. You really believe that, don't you?"

"Sure, I do. I've proven it to myself many times."

"I'm happy to know that."

"Carmella, what we need now is time. Time to think, reason, and plan. If Roberto knows about us, it's likely he'd assume you're with me. He'd also assume I'm prepared to do all in my power to help and protect you. I assume he knows I'm in Phoenix, where I live, that I own a nightclub, and where it's located."

"I agree. It's likely he knows all of that. He has all the contacts needed to find out anything he wants. However, it would take some time. It was only yesterday that I ran away."

"It's possible Roberto may have obtained needed information from my father-in-law. Assuming Roberto has already dispatched someone here to find you, I need to get you the hell out of here. Pronto!"

"Are you coming with me?"

"No."

"Why not? You have to. It's not safe for you to stay."

"My home and business are here. I still have a wife in Baton Rouge that I'm obligated to visit on a regular basis."

"Hound! I'm certain Roberto is planning to harm you. The business relationship he has with your father-in-law will not dissuade him."

"I can take care of myself. However, I'm not sure I can take care of you in the process. Right now, you simply need to hide out until I decide what to do with you long term. You're going to be all right, but you absolutely need to do everything I say. Can I trust you to do that?"

"I'd rather be with you, but I'll do whatever you say. I'll be on the run and hide out as long as it's only temporary. You know you can trust me."

"Fair enough."

"Hound, what's your immediate plan?"

"You have to stop using your real name. You can never use your credit cards again. You'll need to pay cash for everything. How much money do you have with you?"

"A little over five thousand dollars. That won't last very long, will it?"

"No. There's enough cash in the safe at my nightclub to support you for a long time. We're going to the club now. It's right on the way to where we'll be going next."

"Where are you taking me after we leave the club?"

"We're going to Flagstaff in Northern Arizona."

"Why Flagstaff?"

"You're going to take a bus from Flagstaff to your first hideout location."

"Where might that be?"

"Any large city in the Eastern United States where you can get lost in a large population of people. You can choose the city."

"I'll need some time to think about which one I should choose. I prefer one close enough to Phoenix so we can see each other on a regular basis."

"We won't be seeing each other on a regular basis for a while. Our only contact will be by phone."

"I sure as hell don't like that! Are you sure that's the way it has to be?"

"Absolutely, but I don't like it any more than you do."

"Surely you can come up with a better idea!"

"Right now, all you should be thinking about and planning is how to stay ahead of whoever Roberto sends looking for you."

"Should Roberto ever discover where I am, then he'll be coming personally for me. He'll be accompanied by two or more of his hired guns, but he'll come personally. I feel the only way to ever be out of danger, free to live my life as I choose without fear, is if Roberto dies. Unless that happens, I'll always have to be on the run. I know he'll find me sooner or later."

Hound offered no response to Carmella's expressed desire for Roberto to die. When they arrived at the club, Hound parked his Corvette at the rear in the employee parking lot. He and Carmella entered the club through the rear entrance and began walking to his office. Along the way, he gave her a quick tour of the nightclub. She was impressed with its size and elegance.

"Hound, when you told me you were building a nightclub, I knew it would be grand," Carmella said. "Your nightclub is truly magnificent!"

"Thank you. I agree completely."

Carmella sat in the chair behind his desk while Hound removed money from the safe.

"Let's get out of here," he said after putting the money in a briefcase. "We don't need to be here any longer than necessary."

"The sofa in your office looks very comfortable," she told him, smiling. "Let's get naked and try it out before we leave."

"Carmella, as much as I'd like to, that's not going to happen. We could be running out of time. Roberto's men may already be in Phoenix. If they know where my home and club are located, then they could already be on their way here, looking for you. We need to leave now. Come on, let's go."

Carmella wasn't pleased with Hound's response to her proposition. She verbally expressed her frustration, but agreed they needed to be on their way to Flagstaff. Before Hound began opening the safe, he placed the two Colt handguns on his desk. They were once again placed in the waistband of his blue jeans, under his jacket, as he and Carmella prepared to leave. Hound handed the briefcase to Carmella and they began walking to exit the club.

Once outside, they stopped briefly while Hound locked the door. He'd parked his Corvette several feet away from the rear entrance of the club. As they turned and began walking toward it, they realized another car had arrived and parked in such a manner as to block direct access to the Corvette. The immediate and surrounding areas of the club were vacant of anyone except Hound, Carmella, and whoever was inside the other car. No club employees would arrive before 3 p.m. It wasn't yet noon.

The strange car was a late model, black Cadillac. Hound and Carmella suspected the situation might not be a good one. They'd soon learn their suspicion was correct. There were two men in the front seat of the Cadillac. Another two were in the back. All four men got out of the car. All four were holding a handgun. One of the men was Roberto Sanchez.

Hound stepped in front of Carmella, telling her to remain behind him. He removed his jacket and tossed it to the ground. He placed a hand on the grip of each Colt and then stood in silence staring at the four men. He knew he was as prepared as he could be for what might happen next. Roberto stood behind the three other men. He was the first to speak.

"Hello, Hound," Roberto said, smiling. "It's nice to see you again. However, I wish it were under more pleasant circumstances."

"Hello, Roberto, so do I. What happens now? What do you want?"

"Hound, I'm sure you know what I want. I could only be here for one thing, the thing that is standing behind you. I have come for Carmella. What happens now will depend on if you give her to me, or not."

"What do you intend to do with her?"

"You know she's very special to me. I only want to take her back home to Oakland."

"I'm sorry, Roberto, but she doesn't want to go. She desires to be free of you. She has the right to make that choice and have you honor it."

"It really doesn't matter what she wants. She knows that. Now, so do you. I've said all I need to say. Give her to me now!"

"Roberto, you're a lowlife piece of shit bully. Go fuck yourself, cocksucker!"

Hound's insulting, vulgar reply sparked explosive rage in Roberto. The powerful cartel leader sprang from behind the other three men. His arm was raised, his weapon ready to fire. In the split second before he pulled the trigger, the top of his head was blown off. A split second later, the report of a high-powered rifle being fired was heard from behind Hound's position.

Assuming the assassin behind him was friendly, but having no time to verify it, Hound pulled both Colts from his waistband and began to engage the other three men in a firefight. Within brief seconds, the gunfight was over. The three men lay dead close to Roberto on the asphalt parking lot. Each of them had fired their weapons more than once. However, in their haste to be the victors, the rounds fired hadn't found their target. Hound had killed all of them with two accurate shots to the chest of each. He'd fired each of his Colts three times.

Hound turned quickly to see who the sniper was behind him. When he saw who it was, a smile quickly appeared on his face.

"Thanks, partner!" Hound said in a loud, exuberant voice.

"You're welcome, partner!" Bear replied, also in a loud voice and smiling as he walked toward Hound. "It was my plan to kill all those fuckers, but you were just too God-damned fast!"

"Bear, I'm damn glad you're here, but what the hell are you doing here?"

"I suspected you could use a little help."

"What made you suspect that?"

"I'll tell you later, but now we need to get rid of these dead bodies."

"What made you decide to help me out?"

"Well, let's just say I didn't like the odds."

10

Roberto Sanchez lay dead on the employee parking lot at the rear of Hound's nightclub. His three sicarios had fallen mortally wounded at his side. Half of Roberto's head had been blown away by the .308 caliber round fired by Bear in a successful effort to assist in the gunfight and rescue Hound from certain death. Gusts of wind began to deposit sandy dust from the Arizona desert on the parking lot.

Bear walked from his sniper position at the northwest corner of the club and stood beside his best friend. Hound lowered his arms and loosened the grip on the Colt 45 he held in each hand. He had positioned Carmella Vargas behind him before the shootout began. He wanted to protect his lifelong friend as best he could.

She was the beautiful trophy mistress of Roberto, boss of an infamous, nefarious Colombian cartel and the reason he and his men had come. She decided to break the bond of servitude he placed on her. She knew Hound was the only reliable person to assist her regardless of the cost. Roberto underestimated Hound's ability and resolve. That cost him his life.

Hound turned to face her. A soft smile appeared on his face when he was certain she hadn't been hurt, but it was apparent she was terrified. No words were shared between anyone since the ordeal ended. Hound broke the silence when he spoke to her.

"Carmella, you're trembling," he said softly. "Calm down; it's over. There's nothing to fear."

Bear was quick to disagree.

"Hound, we still have plenty to fear!" he said forcefully. "We have to make all evidence of what happened disappear. We're fucked if any witnesses happen by before we do!"

"Yes, you're right. It's still early. No club employees are due to arrive before 3 p.m."

"That's good, but we need to get busy before someone unexpected shows up."

"OK. Do you have a plan how to get rid of the evidence?"

"Hell yes. Help me put Sanchez and his men in the car they were driving. I'll drive the car to my club and take care of what needs to be done. It won't take long after we get there. You can follow me in your car and lend a hand. What about your girlfriend? She can't come with you."

"I'll take her to my home. She can wait there until I return. You can ride back with me. We'll swing by here so you can retrieve your ride."

"OK. Hound, are you sure she can be trusted to keep her mouth shut? We're fucked big time if she ever talks."

"Carmella and I have been close friends since we were children. We've been through a lot of shit together. I trust her with my life."

"Good, because that's exactly what's at stake for both of us. She's still shaking like a dog shitting peach seeds. That doesn't show much nerve."

"She's got plenty of sand. Don't worry."

Carmella composed herself and helped load the bodies into the Cadillac. Other evidence was policed from the parking lot.

After Bear left, Hound drove Carmella to his estate located a short drive from the nightclub.

"Make yourself at home," he told her after they were inside. "I'll return as soon as possible."

"OK, gringo boy. What happens to me now that Roberto is dead? Do I still need to disappear for a while as originally planned?"

"We'll discuss it when I get back. Don't answer the phone or the door. I don't want anyone to know you're here."

"Your friend is worried I can't be trusted. Should I be worried about him trying to get rid of me?"

"Of course not. I'll calm any concern he might have."

"Hound, I would die before doing anything that would hurt you. You believe me, don't you?"

"Yes, I believe you."

"I will never forget Jo wanted me dead because of what she feared I would tell about the death of Carlos Mendoza. She believed you murdered him, and I had information that could prove it."

"My wife no longer aspires to have you killed."

"That's because of the business relationship her father formed with Roberto. Now that he's dead, there's no reason to worry about my murder starting a war between him and the Irish Mafia."

There was another reason Joanne (Jo) O'Malley wanted Carmella to die. She despised the romantic relationship her husband shared with the sultry Hispanic beauty in times past and suspected had never stopped. Jo was six years Hound's senior. She began a torrid sexual relationship with him during his senior year of high school. She was 22 and his math teacher. He was 16. It didn't take long for her to fall deeply in love. She soon found herself dedicated to keeping him out of harm's way.

Using her father's power and influence as a mob boss, she contracted the death of anyone posing a threat to remove him from her life. She rescued him from a court-martial, dishonorable discharge from the Army and extensive prison time after he nearly beat a superior officer to death during his tour in Vietnam. When they were alone during times of intimacy, he often called her his guardian angel.

Jo wasn't the only one with blood on her hands. Hound's fiercely protective love for the underdog and a violent hate of bullies sometimes led him to deadly retribution. The gunfight with Roberto and his thug entourage was the most recent evidence of this.

Hound arrived at the biker club a half hour behind Bear. He hurried into the club where he was sure Bear would be waiting with Bill and Pony. Bill was president of the club's Arizona chapter with headquarters in Phoenix. Bear was next in the change of command to be president after Bill. Pony would be next. The club was nefarious in reputation. Its chapters had become infamous in major cities throughout the West, Southwestern and North-western United States. Hound found the three men seated at a table. Each was sipping a cold bottle of beer and discussing what happened. He ordered his favorite brand of brew from the bar and joined them.

"Hound, I'm glad you're here," Bill said in a concerned manner. "We have some serious shit to discuss."

"Bill, I'm sorry for what happened, but it couldn't be avoided."

"I know, but I sure as hell wish it could. The club is facing two problems and they're not small. The Sanchez cartel supplied all the dope and weapons the club sold. Those profits were major, and 90 percent of our income. We have to find another supplier fast who can provide high quality merchandise. If the cartel even sus-pects we had any connection to Roberto's disappearance, it will start a war we can't win. Why the fuck did Roberto come at you anyway? You must have done something really fucked up for him to personally come after you."

"He came for Carmella, not me."

"The woman Bear said was there?"

"That's right."

"What was she to him, and why was she with you?"

"She was his trophy mistress. She was trying to get away from him and came to me for help."

"Fuck! Why didn't you give her to him and avoid the shit storm?"

"Her leaving greatly disrespected him. At best he would have severely hurt her physically. She was convinced he planned to kill her."

"You obviously have strong feelings for her. I'm surprised. Bear said she was the most gorgeous piece of ass he's ever seen, but I never thought you would ever fall for a whore. The pussy must be pretty damn good!"

"Bill, that had nothing to do with anything. Carmella has been a dear friend since our early childhood. She was in trouble and needed my help. I couldn't deny her. She has always been there for me when I was in trouble."

"OK, OK, what's done can't be changed. We'll deal with it. Oh hell! I guess Roberto fit the bully profile. We know how you feel about that."

"I suppose. Let's move on. How do you plan to get rid of the bodies and car?"

"The car will be turned into salvage and sold as spare parts. The bodies will be cut into pieces, then put into acid and dissolved. It won't take long to complete both. We've already started."

"I'm here to help. What do you want me to do?"

"Nothing. Everything's covered, but you need to be sure your girlfriend's reliable. We're all in deep shit if she's not. What are you going to do now? Soon, others will come looking for you and her to find out what you know about Roberto's disappearance. Shit! They'll be coming here too."

Maybe not. My gut tells me only the three men with Roberto

knew they were coming to Phoenix, and why. His macho ego and pride wouldn't allow him to tell others his woman ran away. Her bodyguards were the only others who knew about me. That's how he found out. He's killed them for keeping the secret, so they're not going to say anything."

"Even if you're right, she'll be missed. Somebody will be sent to talk to her and find out what she knows. What are you going to do with her? She needs to get lost and hide."

"It might be wiser if she went home to Oakland. Roberto didn't take her along when he traveled on business. It would be normal for her to be at home when he went missing and not have a clue where he went, or what happened to him."

"That sounds reasonable, as long as nobody living knows she was here with you. It's a big gamble if you choose to believe that."

"I know, but I do. We'll hope for the best but be prepared for the worst if I'm wrong."

"What does your instinct tell you? It's always proven to be reliable."

"It tells me I'm right."

"Well OK, what the fuck! We'll back whatever you decide. That's what friends do."

"Bill, I'm happy you said that. Thanks. By the way, the cartel isn't going to fold because Roberto is gone. Someone will rise to replace him and continue to supply you with merchandise. However, in case I'm wrong, how much money does your club stand to lose without a supplier? How much, say, over a year?"

"A lot, at least a million."

"I can cover that for a year, or until you can find a new supplier, whichever comes first."

"Why would you do that? Do you have that kind of money?"

"Because that's what friends do, and yes I do."

"Well, OK! I accept but expect to eventually be repaid. That may take some time, but that's also what friends do."

"Fair enough. Bear, how did you know I might need your help

with Roberto this morning? I don't think you just decided to drop by for a visit."

"Roberto and his men came here this morning asking where your home and nightclub were located. It was the first time he ever showed up in person. I figured his business with you must be pretty damn important. He seemed angry, so I got concerned about his intentions. I didn't want to tell him anything, but felt I had no choice. After he left, I grabbed my rifle and headed to your home. When you weren't there, I hurried to your club. You know the rest."

"I'm damn glad you came. You were the edge that saved my life. I owe you one."

"Bullshit. I owed you for helping me battle those assholes in the alley the first time we met. They would have killed me if you hadn't jumped in. Do you remember what you said when I asked you why you did?"

"Sure, the same thing you told me this morning — I didn't like the odds."

Hound left the biker club and returned to his estate. During the drive, his thoughts drifted to the past and he took time to remember and reflect upon significant choices he'd made and actions taken. They put his life on a path he never intended to travel, one he might never be able to change.

He was the adopted son and only child of devout Christian parents who did all in their power to teach and model the proper path to follow. They would be heartbroken to know the path he was on, all he had done, and how he justified it. All his life he wondered if heaven and hell existed as a reward or punishment after his time on earth ended. However, his tour in Vietnam, the things he saw and did there, did convince him hell could be found on earth. He returned to the states hoping heaven might be awaiting discovery in some unexpected, secret place. He had not yet found it. Perhaps he never would. Maybe that was punishment for the path he'd chosen to follow.

When Hound arrived home, he found Carmella pacing the living room anxious for his return.

"Damn, Hound, I thought you were never going to get back," she said loudly as she hurried to kiss and embrace him.

"Sorry it took so long, but I'm back now. How are you feeling?"

"I'm afraid of what will happen now! When Roberto's people decide something has happened to him, they'll come to see me in Oakland. They'll know I wasn't with him. When they figure I'm nowhere to be found, they'll suspect I know or had something to do with his disappearance. It's important as ever now I find a place to hide out."

"Roberto's death made it necessary to change that plan. You're going back to Oakland before anyone knows he's missing. It's well known you never travel with him on business, and you never know where he's going or why. You need to go home, play stupid and keep your mouth shut. Those who knew anything are dead, including your bodyguards."

"You're right. I hadn't thought of that. Do you think I can pull it off without anyone getting suspicious?"

"You have to decide that. If you can't, you'll have to keep running and hiding for God knows how long, maybe years."

"Shit! I can do it. Being able to see you more often is all the incentive I need. How long will I be able to live in my Oakland home?"

"I know the home is paid for. Is your name on the deed with Roberto's?"

"His name isn't on it, only mine. He wanted it that way. I'm not sure why."

"God damn, Carmella! Son of a bitch! You're the sole owner of an estate worth more than a million bucks. That will help motivate your performance."

"I'll sell it and move to Phoenix! That allows us to see each other more often!"

"That would be nice, but it's not what you need to do."

"I thought you'd be happy to have me living in Phoenix. You wouldn't have to travel to Oakland or me come here for us to be together. With Roberto gone we won't be restricted to seeing each other for only a couple of days each month. When you're not in Louisiana with your crazy wife we could spend all your free time together."

"You're missing the point. I want you to complete your education at Berkeley. You always wanted that. You've paid dearly for the chance. We'll figure a way to spend time together while you finish school. Besides, suspicion would be created if you sell the estate and move away too soon."

"I agree and I do want to finish school, but are you sure we'll have plenty of time together? I've always wanted that. I still long to show I can make you happy for the rest of your life, much happier than the murderous bitch you married because you felt obligated."

"I was obligated. I owe Jo and her father a lot. She loves and needs me. I don't want you calling her things that aren't true, especially a murderous bitch."

"God damn it, Hound! She planned to have me killed over information about you that I didn't have. You made me go live with family in Mexico so she couldn't find me."

"That was a long time ago. If she planned to kill you then, she doesn't now. However, we need to make sure she never finds out we're still seeing each other."

"Jo will fear that when she finds out Roberto is gone and I'm free to do as I please. What do you think her mob boss father will assume happened to Roberto?"

"I don't know, but he won't be happy it happened. Ken O'Malley was going to make a shitload of money from the new business relationship he formed with Roberto."

"Is there a chance he would suspect you had anything to do with Roberto's disappearance?"

"Why would he? What could he think my reason would be?"

"He knows we're dear friends and that you would never allow Jo to harm me. Because Roberto brought me to your birthday party, he knows I'm connected to him. If he should suspect I ran away from Roberto and came to you for help, he might correctly assume what happened."

"Carmella, you worry too much, but that's another reason for getting you back to Oakland before any more folks find out you were here."

"I know your biker friends fear I can't be trusted. Are you sure they can?"

"I'm sure, damn it! Stop worrying. You need to relax and get your shit together if things are to go well in Oakland. Are you able to do your part? Tell me if you have even the slightest doubt."

"Baby, I'll be fine. I promise. I stand to lose everything I've hoped for all my life if I don't do my part."

"Good. I need to take you to your car. The sooner you're back in Oakland the better."

When Carmella presented a soft smile and once again kissed and embraced him, he knew what to expect next.

"Gringo boy," she said tenderly," I'm not going anywhere until you satisfy my need. The sooner you take me to bed, the sooner I'll leave for Oakland. Another hour or so won't make a difference."

Hound complied. He was ready to once again enjoy what she had to offer. They had been addicted to the extraordinarily satisfying sex first shared together in a barn on his family's farm when she was 13 and he 12. During their time of intimacy that afternoon, each offered their best performance. As usual, both were satisfied when bedtime ended.

It was after dark when Hound pulled his Corvette into the parking lot of the food market in Phoenix. Carmella left her car there when he picked her up after she arrived in town that morning.

"Hound, I'll need to know I can contact you for advice and support," she told him. "I won't be able to complete the plan without your constant help. I need to be with you as often as possible, more than I used to. How often can we see each other?"

"We'll work all that out. Don't worry or lose your nerve. Just play ignorant regarding Roberto. The less you say, the better. Follow a normal daily routine. Definitely resume attending classes at Berkeley. Call me any time, but always use a phone you know is safe."

"What if you're not home or at your club? How can I reach you during the times you're back in Louisiana?"

"Shit! Get me a safe number and I'll call you at the same time daily. Will that work?"

"Yes. That's a good idea."

She was sad to leave but gave him a passionate kiss goodbye, got into her car and began the drive to her home in Oakland. She would arrive about 14 hours later.

Soon after he got home that evening, Hound prepared dinner and ate before making a phone call to Jo in Baton Rouge. She expected to hear from him each night while he was away. When her phone rang at 8 p.m., Jo was patiently waiting.

"Hello, precious," she said. "How was your day?"

If only she fucking knew, he thought.

"It's been another normal day. How about yours?"

"Just business as usual at the university. The boss is letting me handle everything that needs to be done. Most days he comes in late and leaves early. He didn't show up at all today."

"He knows you can do the job better than he can. Besides, he retires at the end of this semester and you'll take his place as the first woman and youngest person to ever hold that title. You have cause to be very proud. You've worked hard for and deserve the position."

"Sweet baby, I love you for saying that, but you know damn well Dad was responsible for it. Anyway, it doesn't matter. Dad has decided another would be better suited for the job. I'm out at the end of this semester."

"Jo, I'm sorry."

"Don't be, sweetheart, I'm not. After my recovery, I really didn't want to resume my job at the university. My heart wasn't in it. I know now it never was. I simply felt obligated to do what my dad wanted. I guess I completed all he really needed. He saw I wanted out, so he chose a reliable person in his network of connections to replace me."

"Why did he want you in the position?"

"It was his plan to have me eventually become the school's president. He never said why. I wouldn't have found out until I assumed the position."

"What career will you pursue next?"

"I want to work in the area of business and finance."

"I suppose Ken wants you to work for him?"

"Of course. You know that."

"Are you going to?"

"Of course. You know that too. There's no other employer who would provide the title, prestige, pay and benefits Dad will offer."

"I know that too."

"Will you be coming home as usual on Saturday?"

"That's the plan, if something unforeseen doesn't happen."

"Book your flight into New Orleans. Dad has invited us to dinner Saturday night at his nicest restaurant. He hasn't seen us lately and wants to."

"I hope he's not planning to continue discussing me working for him."

"Hound, he'll never give up hope of grooming you to run the family business when he's ready to retire from the responsibility of day-to-day operations. I know he said he'd stop trying to persuade you, but he won't."

"I know."

His phone call with Jo had recently ended when Hound's phone rang. It was Maggie Mitchell calling. The Harvard graduate attorney had been out of town taking care of some legal problems for the biker club chapter in Los Angeles.

"Hi, handsome. What's up?" she said happily.

"Not much. How are you?"

"Tired. The work in L.A. wore me out. Those fucking guys get into more trouble than any other club chapter. I wish they all ran as smooth as Bill's. Did you miss me?"

"Sure."

"Did anything exciting happen while I was away?"

"It's been as dull as dirt."

"Have you had dinner?"

"Yep."

"Shit! I was hoping you'd like me to grab some carry out and head your way."

"Get something for yourself and come over, if you like."

"I like. Would you be interested in having dessert in the bedroom?"

"I don't eat carry out desert."

"Fuck you, smart ass! It's my private recipe, guaranteed to be ideally sweet."

"Can I enjoy more than one piece?"

"Darlin', you can enjoy as many pieces as you like. I'll be at your place in about a half hour."

Hound could have done without Maggie's company, but he knew she expected to see him as soon as she got back in town. He was happy she was away and didn't know Carmella had been there or especially the problem she caused. Maggie could be trusted to know what happened, but such knowledge is power, and he didn't want her to have it. She already had other information which gave her power over him but to a much lesser degree. The fact that he was sleeping with her was risky. Jo wouldn't be pleased to know, nor would Carmella now that Roberto was gone. The last thing he wanted was to get caught in a war between Jo and Maggie. Both had the power and influence to be worthy adversaries.

Maggie, as Hound expected, wanted to spend the night. He was glad when she left shortly after breakfast the next morning.

He was fond of her and enjoyed her company, but since Roberto's death he had a lot to think about and consider. He needed to be prepared to deal with whatever might happen next. All evidence of Roberto was gone, but the cartel would spare no effort or expense to discover what happened to him. No doubt a substantial reward would be offered for reliable information. He could only assume that besides himself, Carmella, Bear, Bill and Pony were the only ones who had that information, but he was very familiar with Murphy's law, having seen it at work many times.

In addition to their code of loyalty to friends, the part Bear played in Roberto's death and what Bill and Pony did to get rid of the evidence guaranteed their silence. Carmella was the only one he was concerned about. He knew his biker buddies shared those concerns. She would never tell anything, but the stress of knowing might result in physical cues causing suspicion. He told her everything she needed to do. All he could do now was hope she could keep her mind right and her shit tight.

His thoughts were interrupted when the phone rang. It was Carmella calling. Her voice indicated she was calm and in a good mood.

"Good morning," she said. "How's my sweet gringo boy?"

"Good morning to you. I'm well. Are you?"

"I'm wonderful. I can't remember when I felt this good. I believe the light at the end of the tunnel is showing. I look forward to having the kind of life I've always dreamed of."

"All you have to do is stick to the plan and act your role convincingly. Carmella, sure as death you have to do that."

"Hound, I know you're worried. I want you to focus on what you need to do and do it right. Trust me to do the same."

"So, you're not concerned about anything?"

"Hell no! Well, nothing to do with Roberto."

"Well, what then?"

What the fuck am I going to do when I spend the last of my allowance from Roberto? It will cost a lot to maintain this estate.

What about my other living expenses? I won't have enough for books and tuition next semester. I can't find a job that would pay enough. Besides, I can only work part time at best and stay in school."

"I'll provide the money you need until you graduate."

"I appreciate the offer, but I won't take any more of your money. I don't want to feel like your mistress. That's not the kind of relationship I want with you. Do you understand?"

"I do. I'll advance you money as needed until it's safe to sell me your estate, then I'll pay you market value minus the amount paid in advances."

"Hound, what need could you have for this estate? You're only creating a way to help that I will accept."

"You're wrong. The estate would be a good investment for the future. Besides, I plan to build my second nightclub in the area. I'll need a nice place to live when I'm in town. I was thinking you might be interested in working with me when you graduate. I've got an idea for another business enterprise."

Hound was saying things he knew she would be happy to hear and motivate her to stay focused on completing what had to be done. He was also being honest, intending to honor any promise he made.

"Oh, Hound! That would be great! You know I've always dreamed of working with you in business."

"I remember you talking about it when we were in high school. You wanted to find a way to afford college and get the education needed to escape having the career of a farm worker."

"I fucked up when I became a prostitute to earn the money. I should have known better. I compromised my faith, character and reputation. I lost my family. My parents won't have anything to do with me."

"That's not true, not now. The last time I saw your dad he asked me to tell you to come home for a visit. You should call your parents. Tell them you're no longer a prostitute and that you're attending college and starting a new life. Go home for a visit at spring break."

"What will I say when they ask me how I'm earning money to live on?"

"Tell them you're making excellent tips working as a waitress in an elegant restaurant. That's reasonable."

"Hound, you come up with great plans quicker than anyone, but I hate to tell them lies."

"We all have to lie sometime to protect ourselves and the ones we love from needless suffering."

"Yes, you're right."

Carmella gave him the number of a phone safe to contact her on. He would call her at the same time daily until it was no longer necessary. When their conversation ended, he felt more confident she could complete her assignment.

Hound attended the monthly employee meeting at his nightclub that afternoon. He had carefully screened and hired the best possible people to work at the club. They all agreed he was a splendid boss, being kind, caring, fair and generous. However, they also knew he was a man to never mistreat in any way. In addition to the salary and tips they earned, each received a percentage of monthly profits. Club security was staffed with several members of the biker club. Each had been personally selected and recommended by Bear, Bill and Pony. They looked like docile businessmen in their tailored suits, but they were the toughest, most formidable fighters in the Phoenix chapter. Club patrons paid them little attention as they moved about areas of the club like ninjas.

Candice (Candy) Pharr was general manager. She had been highly recommended by her best friend Maggie Mitchell. Candy was very attracted to Hound when they first met but knowing Maggie's affection for him had never acted on her attraction. She knew what her best friend was capable of if angered. Besides, she valued Maggie's friendship and was married to a captain in the detective division of the Phoenix Police Department. Regardless of her friendship with Maggie or happy marriage, she considered Hound extremely desirable. At the conclusion of each employee meeting she would meet with him in his office to discuss business not relevant to the regular staff. Candy was 29, the same age as Maggie. Both women were beautiful but shared no physical similarities. Candy was five inches shorter, with natural blonde hair and green eyes. She exercised and ate a proper diet to keep her body in shape and maintain a weight of 120.

Candy entered the office behind Hound and closed the door. They sat in their usual chairs.

"Well, Candy, is there anything I should know before I leave to visit with family in Louisiana?" he asked in a relaxed manner, smiling.

"Nothing you don't already know. No problems of any kind and profit continues to grow monthly."

"The quality of work you and all the others do is the reason for both. I hope I tell you and everyone else enough what a great job you do and how grateful I am."

"You do, but if you didn't, the ways you reward us speak volumes. Hound, can I ask you a personal question?"

"Sure, go ahead."

"Don't you get tired of traveling back and forth between here and Louisiana?"

"Absolutely! I've been tired of it since it began."

"Then, why do it?"

"I promised my wife I'd come home every other week. I also get to see my parents. I'm lucky Jo tolerates me being home every other week, sometimes less frequent."

"I'm surprised she does. Why didn't you build your club in Baton Rouge or New Orleans so you wouldn't have to commute? Why did you build in Phoenix?"

"I wasn't married or planned to be when I decided to build my home and club here."

"Why doesn't Jo move here?"

"She wants a career working with her father in New Orleans. We allow each other to pursue the career we want wherever we want."

"Don't you miss Jo while you're away? Perhaps you enjoy the company of other women."

Candy felt her heart begin to race. She couldn't believe the words that just bolted from her mouth. Her embarrassment caused her to blush and tremble.

"Oh my God! Hound, I'm so sorry!" she said loudly. "Saying that was so out of line and disrespectful."

"Don't worry about it. I'm sure others have wondered the same thing. Is there anything in particular that makes you wonder? Perhaps you don't wonder. You may know."

"It's none of my business. How would I know if you do or don't?"

Hound's instinct told him she knew because Maggie told her about their affair. They agreed not to discuss it with anyone, but he suspected Maggie confided in Candy. He wanted to confirm his suspicion.

"You know Maggie and I are good friends," he said. "What has she told you about me?"

"Nothing I didn't already know."

"So, you knew we were sleeping together before she told you. She told you, didn't she?"

Candy hesitated to respond. She realized her pause answered his question.

"Damn it!" Candy said. "I'm in the shit now!"

"Why? I'm not mad, not even upset, but why did she tell you? We agreed to maintain discretion."

"I appreciate you're not mad, but she'll be furious that you know she told me."

"I promise she'll never know if you tell me why she told you."

"If you don't mind, I'd rather not say. I've already embarrassed myself enough."

"Come on, Candy, give it up. I want to know."

Candy again hesitated before she spoke.

"I told her you were the most handsome, sexiest man I had ever known or even seen," she told him. "A man I would cheat on my husband with. She told me she was sleeping with you so I wouldn't if I got the chance. God! I'm so embarrassed. You must think I'm a terrible person."

"Bullshit! Why would I think that about a beautiful woman who paid me the ultimate compliment? Would you have sex with me if the opportunity presented?"

Candy hesitated a third time.

"Yes, but only if Maggie and my husband never found out."

"Would you tell either of them?"

"Hell no! Of course not."

"Then, they'll never find out."

Hound rose from his chair, walked to the door and locked it. He returned to Candy. She stood to greet him. He said nothing as he slowly began removing her clothing. She began to tremble slightly but offered no resistance. When she was nude, he bid her to sit on the long, wide sofa and watch as he stripped naked before her.

She began to breathe hard as she viewed him from head to toe. She paused her survey of his perfectly proportioned, muscular body and fixed her eyes on his large penis, which was now fully erect. He positioned her on the sofa and began softly kissing and caressing all areas of her body. Her breathing grew harder and faster. He moved his mouth up each of her inner thighs, then entered her with his tongue and began performing oral sex. She presented a long moan and pulled his head forward as her first orgasm began.

When she finished, he moved atop her, and she guided him inside her. As he began to thrust, slowly at first, her body required a moment to adjust to his size. After her fourth orgasm his thrusts became harder and faster. When she finished her next orgasm, he could sense she was satisfied but becoming tired and a bit sore.

He finished his second climax and then lay still. They remained in tender embrace until it was no longer safe. Their meeting had exceeded a time considered usual and normal by at least a half hour.

Candy hurried to the private bathroom in the office to put her appearance in order before leaving. Hound was dressed and waiting when she returned.

"Are we going to get away with this?" she asked in a concerned manner. "We've been in here a long time."

"Of course. We simply had more to discuss than usual. I'd bet you had no idea I would ask so many questions?"

She smiled.

"I surely didn't," she replied.

"I hope you didn't mind."

"Hound, I've never enjoyed anything as much. You are really something. All I imagined and more. I hope you enjoyed it."

"Candy, I truly did."

"Enough to do it again sometime?"

"Absolutely. I'll look forward to it, but not here. You can come to my home."

"Perfect, but be sure Maggie won't show up."

"OK."

"Damn! I understand why she's so possessive of you."

She gave him a kiss and returned to work. He would leave for Louisiana the next morning and went home to pack.

As usual, Maggie expected to have dinner and spend the night before he left. She arrived at his estate on time at 6 p.m. They enjoyed a glass of wine and talked while two porterhouse steaks cooked slowly to perfection on the patio barbecue. The weather was pleasant, so they ate dinner outdoors. A full moon in a clear sky cast a soft blue light over the desert landscape which could be seen a long distance in any direction. They saw bats and an occasional owl flying in search of their dinner. From time to time they heard coyotes howling, as if they were enjoying the perfect evening too.

"Is there anywhere more peaceful than the Arizona desert on a night like tonight?" asked Maggie.

"Probably not."

11

At 6 a.m. the next morning, Hound began his daily regimen of physical fitness training. This usually lasted about two hours. It began with a five-mile run, followed by a series of exercises designed to maintain a specific level of strength, endurance, muscle mass and distribution, body weight and proportion. Maggie joined him for the grueling workout. She was equal to his level of fitness in every area except for strength during the weightlifting portion of the workout.

"Maggie, I'm proud of you," Hound told her. "Your level of fitness is superior to any person, man or woman, I've ever known."

"Not superior to you."

"Maybe not, but sure as hell equal."

"Equal sounds good. I'm satisfied with equal."

When the workout, concluded they showered, dressed and prepared a breakfast of oatmeal, a variety of fresh fruit and fresh ground coffee sweetened with honey. She had an appointment at 9:30 and was unable to drive him to the airport.

During breakfast, Hound sensed Maggie had begun to lose her

positive, cheerful attitude. She was thinking about something that was making her angry.

"Maggie, are you OK?" he asked. "Is something wrong?"

"Will you be away longer than a week?"

"I'll be back after Valentine's Day."

"I suppose Jo has something planned that day."

"I think so. Maybe a party."

"I wish you'd get out of your marriage. You know that would be best for you."

"You know I can't do that any time soon. I have obligations, promises to keep."

"Hound, the longer you stay with her, the more obligations she and her mob boss father are going to saddle you with. Jo will always make it as hard as possible for you to leave. You'll never tell me, but I know she and her father have something they use to control you."

"Maggie, I told you I owed Jo and her father big time for saving my ass from the serious legal trouble that befell me in Vietnam."

"I would think that debt was paid by now. You married Jo because she needed your help to recover from serious physical and emotional problems. She has. How many debts do you owe? How many times has she and her father rescued you from serious trouble?"

"Maggie, we've discussed all this before. I don't want you to keep bringing it up. Everything I do serves my best interest. I will solve my problems my way, the right way. Why are you rushing me to get a divorce? I told you up front that wouldn't happen until the time was right."

"God damn it, Hound! I'm tired of sharing you. It's not necessary we get married, but I'm fed up with fucking you while your fucking another woman. I want you to get rid of that cunt bitch once and for all!"

Hound remained calm and in control but needed to make something crystal clear to Maggie.

"Maggie, this not the way I wanted our time together this morning to end," he said. "I value our relationship greatly and I'm extremely fond of you. However, if you truly mean what you said, then it's best we end our relationship. You're unhappy and need a change. Never again voice anything in my presence that even remotely demeans Jo."

Maggie had no intention of provoking his response. Ending her relationship with him was certainly not what she wanted.

"Hound, I'm sorry," she replied, "for everything I said. I don't want to lose you. Do you remember what I told you? When I fall in love, I fall hard and do all in my power to totally possess the heart of the man I love."

"Yes, I remember."

"I realize my approach was wrong, but I'm motivated by the love I feel for you. Can you forget what I said and allow us to be as we were before I went a little crazy?"

"I don't know, Maggie. You've done this before. You'll do it again. Each time you do it's always worse. We need to leave, or I'll miss my flight and you'll miss your appointment."

"OK, but promise we'll talk as soon as you get back."

Hound offered no promise. Maggie hoped everything would be all right. She and Hound had more intense disagreements in the past that always were resolved.

Hound's flight took off at 10:30. He lowered the back of his seat a bit and got comfortable for the flight to New Orleans. At 20,000 feet, he sat in his window seat looking out. It was a clear day. As he gazed at the landscape below, it somehow brought to mind his final flight home from Vietnam and his life thus far after his return. His thoughts turned to Maggie and what he would do about their relationship after he returned to Phoenix. He needed to keep his priorities straight, the people to keep happy in proper order. His first priority was Jo. Carmella was a close second because of the special lifelong bond they had and the current situation they shared regarding the death of Roberto Sanchez. Maggie was third, but could he include her without placing himself in jeopardy from her jealously and possessiveness, which were reaching an insane level. He decided he couldn't. She wouldn't take it well, but it would be harder on both of them to postpone the inevitable.

Hound arrived on time in New Orleans. Jo was anxiously waiting at the gate. She greeted him with a warm smile and rushed to his arms for a kiss and embrace.

"Honey, I'm happy you're here," she said sincerely. "Each time you're away, it seems longer before you return. Do you think there will be a time we won't ever be apart?"

"That's something to work toward and look forward to."

"Did you miss me?"

"Always. You look great. Are you feeling well?"

"Sure. I feel fine. I assume you're well. You look superb."

"Well, then I feel like I look."

Jo did look like her old self. Her appearance gave no indication that only a few months ago she suffered with severe mental problems resulting from being raped and becoming pregnant as a result. She stopped eating, became severely malnourished and looked like a walking skeleton.

Hound had called off their wedding, which compounded her emotional state. She would have died if he hadn't reconsidered and returned to marry her. He had only two reasons for doing so. It was needed to help save her life and he had been coerced by her father, Ken O'Malley. She wasn't aware of the truth as it would certainly lend to a relapse.

Ken was very fond of Hound. He was also very impressed by him. After he married Jo, Ken wanted desperately to make him his protégé and second-in-command of the family business. It was Ken's intention that Hound take over his position when the time came. Ken certainly could use coercion to get what he wanted, but that wouldn't guarantee the effort, loyalty and dedication needed for Hound to be successful.

For now, Hound was free to pursue a career as an entrepreneur. He began by building the finest nightclub in the country. Ken would never cease in his attempts to get what he wanted. Hound knew this. He had remained dedicated to avoiding any type employment within the O'Malley family business. He knew once he was in there was no easy way out.

As they drove to the O'Malley estate, Hound and Jo discussed things of significance since his last visit.

"Jo, have you seen or phoned my parents lately?" he asked. "I haven't kept in contact with them on a regular basis."

"I know. They told me. I try to call them weekly to keep in touch. I haven't seen them for some time. I think they might be a bit upset with you for not calling more often."

"I don't blame them, but they could call me."

"Like I said, they might be a bit upset."

"I'll visit them while I'm here and promise to call more often."

"That's what you should do."

"How are your parents?"

"Mom's fine, but dad's starting to get worried about his business with Roberto Sanchez. Dad never shares his concerns with mom about anything, but he talks to me about everything."

"What's going on with Sanchez?"

"Dad's holding a large amount of the cartel's product in a warehouse at the docks. Roberto is days late contacting dad about where to ship the product and pay him what's owed to date."

"What does Ken think is going on?"

"He doesn't know, but it can't be good. Roberto is the only person in the cartel dad deals with. That's part of their business arrangement. Roberto gave dad a private, safe phone number where he could be reached in case of emergency, but dad hasn't been able to reach him. What do you think is going on?"

"Shit, I don't know, but like you said, it can't be good. What is the product stored in the warehouse?"

"Weapons and drugs."

"What kind?"

"A variety of weapons. I'm not sure what kind, but the drugs are cocaine."

"How many weapons? How much cocaine?"

"I don't know how many or how much, but dad says the street value of everything is at least five hundred million."

"Holy shit! That's a lot of weapons and drugs."

"Exactly. Dad's in a hurry to ship it all out of New Orleans."

"I don't blame him. He doesn't own all the cops and politicians. He's in deep shit if the wrong people become suspicious."

"Dad's in a hurry to talk to you about the situation. I didn't tell you, but he was adamant that you come to New Orleans so he could."

"Why talk to me about it?"

"I'm not sure. He didn't say, but I suspect he needs to contact Carmella to find out what she knows. He has no idea how to do that, but believes you do. Do you?"

"Hell no!"

"Good. I'm glad to hear that."

There was no way Hound would ever let Ken, or especially Jo, know how to contact Carmella. If they knew, then it would be easy to find out where she was.

When they arrived at the O'Malley estate, Ken was anxiously waiting. He wasted no time in ushering Hound to the den for a private meeting. Hound saw Ken was extremely concerned and seemingly angry. They took a seat in their usual chairs before Ken began to speak. He wasted no time in getting to the point.

"Ken, you seem troubled," said Hound. "What's going on?"

"Don't bullshit me, boy! I'm certain Jo has told you about the situation with Roberto."

"Sure, but what's that got to do with me?"

"Not a Goddamned thing, I hope! Do you know anything about Sanchez?"

"Hell no! How would I know anything?"

"Hound, I don't want Jo to know, but Roberto called me a short time ago wanting to know how to contact you and where he could find you. When I asked why, he didn't want to say. He decided to trust me, and I became upset at what he told me. Do you have any idea what it was?"

"Hell no. What did he say?"

"It seems his private whore decided to bite the hand that fed her. She ran away. He didn't say why but was certain she ran to you for help. Did she?"

"Ken, did you believe Roberto's story?"

"What reason could he have for lying?

"I can't think of any, but I would never trust him."

"My trust in him has limits, but I believe he told the truth about this."

"Why would I help Carmella? It would put me at risk of horrific retribution."

"Because you put yourself at risk in the past to protect her."

"I suppose you're referring to Jo, who wanted to murder Carmella for having information she never had."

"Hound, be careful what you say about Jo. She's my only child, the joy of my life."

"She's my wife. I mean no disrespect, but I did state the truth."

"Maybe you remember these truths! With my blessing and assistance, Jo made it possible for you to murder and bury the bodies of detective Karen Thibodaux and her cop boyfriend because Karen was convinced you murdered Carlos Mendoza and was convinced she would eventually prove it. She was certain your whore girlfriend had information she needed. With my blessing and assistance, Jo rescued you from being convicted, given a dishonorable discharge from the Army and sent to prison for the attempted murder of Colonel Joseph Westerman during your tour of duty in Vietnam. She insisted on going with me to Washington D.C. when I was securing your rescue. As a horrible consequence to being there, she was raped and became pregnant. Because of that she almost died from the trauma and what it did to her relationship with you. My daughter loves you more than life itself. That's the truth you should focus on and cherish every day of your life. Do you dispute anything I said?"

"Of course not."

"Good. Never speak ill of Jo in my presence again."

"Fair enough."

"Now, tell me if you know anything about Sanchez."

"First, tell me if you told him where to find me. Did you give him the location of my home and nightclub?"

The look on Ken's face and his hesitation to respond provided Hound with the answer to his question. He waited to see if Ken would tell him the truth.

"I did, but quickly regretted doing so."

"I appreciate you telling me the truth. I also believe you regretted giving Roberto the information. What's the whole truth? Tell the rest of the story?"

"What are you talking about?"

"Shall I tell it for you?"

"Please do, if you think there's more to tell."

"There is. You figured if I survived Roberto's visit, I would wonder how he found me so quickly. You didn't want me to know you gave me up. You knew I was friends with the president of the biker club and his ranking officers. You met them at the grand opening of my nightclub. Roberto supplies drugs and weapons to them. You requested he visit them to ask where I could be found. I would believe they told him."

"How would I know Roberto did business with the bikers?"

"I would assume he had a reason to tell you. Probably because he wanted you to transport merchandise to them."

"That's sure one hell of a story! Can you prove it?"

"I can if it's true. The president of the biker club will tell me if any trucks from a company owned by you are delivering cartel product."

"Well shit, Hound! I should have known you would put it all

together. Your instinct and intelligence would not have dictated otherwise. You're also smart enough to know I would never be part of harming you. Roberto gave his guarantee no harm would come to you if the whore was returned to him. Because of our business relationship, I knew he would keep his word."

"What did you think he would do if she wasn't returned?"

"I wasn't concerned. You're too smart to incur the wrath of such a dangerous man to protect a slut whore."

"Ken, only a few moments ago you said I had put myself at risk in the past to help her. What made you sure I wouldn't do it again, even if I had to face a man like Roberto?"

Ken was again hesitant to respond. Hound quickly devised a new plan to deal with possible repercussions from Roberto's death. He knew he could no longer trust Ken. He had to place him in a position to suffer the same retribution as he, should the cartel discover the truth about Roberto. Ken had been willing to sacrifice Hound's life to appease Roberto so their business arrangement would not be in jeopardy. Ken's love for his business, which afforded him status, power, wealth and influence, was first and foremost in his life. Jo was his next priority, and then finally his wife, Sandra. Hound's new plan would begin when he admitted to Ken the truth of what happened to Roberto. He had decided that at an appropriate time, as soon as possible, Ken would die for his betrayal. A leopard can't change its spots. Ken would always be a rat, never to be trusted.

"You weren't sure," said Hound, "were you? It doesn't matter now. What's done is done and I'm still alive. So is Carmella. Unfortunately, Roberto and the other three bully mother fuckers he brought as backup are as dead as an old man's dick."

Anger began to rise in Ken, but Hound remained calm and in control of his thoughts and emotions, determined to stay focused on his purpose and complete this stage of his plan successfully.

"You're a crazy son of a bitch!" Ken shouted. "Fuck! When Roberto failed to show up for our meeting, I suspected something happened to him, and you were responsible. Do you have any idea what you have set in motion? The cartel won't stop until they find out what happened and who is responsible. When they do, your life won't be worth a plug nickel. They'll kill you and it won't be a quick death. They'll likely murder your parents as well."

"They'll kill Jo because she's my wife."

"I can protect Jo."

"How?"

"I'll start by getting her divorced from you."

"I thought divorce wasn't permitted by the Catholic faith. Maybe you're not as devout as you claim to be."

"This conversation is over! Get the hell out of my house and away from my daughter! Never contact me or Jo again!"

"How will you protect your life, your wife's, and Jo's when the cartel finds out you and I planned and carried out Roberto's assassination together? You should calm down and consider that for a moment."

The expression on Ken's face suddenly changed from extreme anger to a slowly changing variety of confusion, curiosity, disbelief, vulnerability and fear. He seemed to move in slow motion as he returned to his chair and sat facing Hound.

"Hound, what are you hoping to accomplish?" Ken asked in a civil manner, making every effort to still his rage. "You would never threaten me in such a manner if you didn't feel certain you could deliver on it. How would you ever prove such a lie? What is it you want from me?"

"It wouldn't be in my best interest to say how I could prove it but be assured I can. Living or dead I can. What I want is what you have wanted for some time, to become your protégé, right hand and second-in-command. I want to be groomed to assume your position when you're ready to step down and lead from the shadows. I have come to realize the size of empire and amount of power my destiny dictates can only be achieved in one way. You are the way."

"How can we possibly hope to trust each other again? We both have said and done things that can't be taken back or changed."

"We both have everything to gain as allies and everything to lose as enemies. I propose we shake hands, put the past behind us, never to be considered again, and get started doing what needs to be done."

It took only a moment for Ken to consider Hound's proposal and make his decision. He stood from his chair and extended his hand as a gesture of acceptance. Hound stood and shook the hand of his wife's father, the man who decided it was safe to trust him, the man he would never trust and would someday kill. Hound would never see Ken as anything more than an enemy. He had long since learned to never leave an enemy at his back.

"Hound, what do you think needs to be done next?" asked Ken.

"The cartel will assume Roberto is dead, but will never find out what happened, so no code of revenge will be carried out. Very soon some mother fucker will replace Sanchez and business will continue as usual. The new boss won't give a shit Roberto is gone. Hell, he'll be happy about it. We need to make sure he's pleased with the way we've represented the cartel's interests in Roberto's absence. What do you think should be done to best accomplish that?"

"Keeping their merchandise safe and secure in the warehouse until we're contacted is all we can do."

"Weren't you going to transport it to buyers?"

"Sure, but I don't know who and where they are or what to deliver. Roberto was going to give me all that information when we met this week."

"Haven't you been making deliveries?"

"No. What's in the warehouse was to be my first."

"Do you know how much the cartel charges for different products or how they receive payment?"

"Hound, I don't know a Goddamned thing more than what

I've told you! Roberto was careful to tell me only what I needed to know when I needed to know it. I should have pushed to learn more, but I didn't figure on you killing the cock sucker!"

Hound chuckled at Ken's reply and then took some time considering what to do next.

"What are you thinking?" asked Ken.

"With circumstances the way they are, I don't think it's best to wait for the new cartel boss to contact us. We need to contact him."

"Why?"

"There's a great amount of illegal shit in a warehouse you own. We need to get it the hell out of there as soon as possible. The longer it's there, the greater risk it is to us. We don't need to take any unnecessary chances. The wrong people might find out it's there. Besides, we need to show concern over Roberto missing his crucial appointment with you. If we don't, it might create suspicion you knew he disappeared, or worse, had something to do with it, which you did."

"Goddamn it, Hound! Can you at least try to say something positive! This conversation is getting more depressing by the minute! All I can think about is an army of Colombian cartel coming to cut my balls off with a dull knife!"

"You could consider yourself lucky if that's all they'd do."

"No shit, smart ass! Let's get serious and figure out how to contact the right fucker pronto! Remember, what they'll do to me, they'll do to you!"

"You make a good point."

"Have you got any ideas at all?"

"Just one. I'll contact Carmella. Maybe she'd know someone we could contact in Colombia. She's been there with Roberto."

"It would be best if I met with her in person. I'll leave on the first flight available."

"OK, but what are you going to tell Jo?"

"That I've decided to accept your long time offer to be your protégé in the family business and unfortunately you need me to take care of something for you in San Francisco, and that I'll be back day after tomorrow."

"What will we tell her I want you to do?"

"Shit, Ken! I don't know! Tell her you want me to kill somebody! Whatever, anything you like. Just make it sound important enough for me to leave immediately."

It was then a soft knock was heard on the door of the den. Jo opened it and came in.

"You guys have been in here over an hour," she said. "Are you about finished? I'd like to spend time with my husband."

"We're finished," said Ken, "but you won't be spending time with him until he gets back from California day after tomorrow."

"Bullshit! Why does he have to go to California?"

"Sweetheart, you'll be happy to learn Hound has finally agreed to accept my job offer in the family business. I'm sorry, but I need him to take care of something urgent in San Francisco."

"I'm overjoyed about the job, but what's so urgent he has to leave immediately?"

"Honey, he's going to kill a guy for me."

Hound turned his head slightly to prevent Jo from seeing the grin he couldn't subdue.

"Absolutely not!" Jo said forcefully. "You have other people to handle that kind of business! My husband's position in the family business will never include hitman as a job description!"

"Darling, I understand how you feel, but it's something I want to do. Your dad didn't ask me; I requested the assignment."

"Why?"

"Honey, there's always been a certain amount of family business conducted you didn't have privy to, things you don't need knowledge of," said Ken. "This is one of those things. Say no more about it. Be happy Hound has become my protégé and won't be doing anything in the business he doesn't want. Let him make his flight reservation and then spend all the time together you can before he leaves. He'll be back before you have time to miss him."

Jo knew what her father said was right. She had been raised to understand and accept the code of conduct and rules governing the family business. They were in place for important reasons.

Jo waited until Hound made his reservations and then discreetly accompanied him to their bedroom. She lay nude on the bed waiting for him to join her. He stood looking at her for a time. He thought how beautiful she was and of the desire she raised in him the first time he met her. It was at the party on his family farm, provided by his adopted parents for his sixteenth birthday. He was about to begin his senior year in high school. She would be his math teacher. At great risk, they began a sexual relationship that year, giving little thought to the consequences awaiting should the affair be found out. Little did he know how deeply she would come to love him and dramatically affect the course of his life.

Jo took him to the airport later. They arrived an hour before his flight was to depart. This would be the time she began an important conversation.

"Hound, what changed your mind about joining the family business?" she asked. "You've always been so opposed to having anything to do with my dad's organization."

"I suppose I've come to realize it's the best way to accomplish what I want in life. Besides, I was certain it would make you happy."

"It does, but I don't want you doing things for my dad that put you in harm's way. He would never personally carry out what you're going to do. He has associates that take care of such things. I realize this is important but promise me you'll be careful and not get hurt or caught, and never do this again."

"I promise. Jo, you were in complete agreement when your dad insisted I personally kill Karen Thibodaux and her boyfriend and then bury them in a remote pasture."

"That couldn't be avoided and was a one-time thing. Dad wanted insurance you would never tell what happened to Karen. Besides, he provided his two best, most experienced assassins to make sure everything went well. You'll be alone this time."

"Jo, I hadn't planned to ever tell you, but I've been alone several times since Karen. I know what I'm doing regarding such things."

"That doesn't shock or surprise me. I've always suspected it. When the men I sent to kill Steve Cooper returned from D.C. and told me he was already dead, my heart told me you were responsible. Did my heart speak the truth?"

"Yes, precious. Let's not speak of it again."

Hound arrived in San Francisco after midnight. He called Carmella, rented a car and drove to meet her at a café open all night in Oakland. She was up late studying and had not yet gone to bed. She was delighted he came to see her, but surprised. She didn't ask the reason for the surprise visit at such a late hour but knew it must be important. She asked no questions over the phone and hurried to dress and depart for the café. They had met there before.

When she arrived, Hound was seated at a table in a private area. She walked quickly to join him. He stood to greet her and receive a welcomed, expected kiss and lengthy embrace. He was drinking a cup of coffee. She ordered the same. They sat smiling before either spoke.

"Damn! It's nice to see you again, gringo boy," she said," but I didn't expect it to be so soon. Is everything OK? Please tell me there's no emergency regarding Roberto. Everything here has been quiet."

"No problems yet, but that's why I'm here. I need some information and hope you have it."

"OK, what do you need to know?"

"Do you know who will replace Roberto as head of the cartel?"

"Hell yes. Roberto's younger sister, Rita Sanchez. She's already called me regarding Roberto's whereabouts. She's coming for a personal visit next week if Roberto doesn't show up. Shit! Looks like I can expect company."

"Are you concerned? Are you prepared to deal with her?"

"Absolutely. Actually, I'm looking forward to her visit. We're pretty tight. I first met her in a club in Mexico City. She introduced me to her brother about a month later. She's stayed at the Oakland estate while in town helping Roberto with cartel business."

"I'm surprised to hear a woman is taking over."

"Hound, Rita is very capable. She's smart and educated, but most significant, she is one tough, dangerous and deadly bitch. Her father is the real authority. She and Roberto are his only children. They grew up being groomed to head the cartel when their father retired or died. When he retired, Roberto, being the oldest, took over as boss. With him gone, Rita is next in line."

"How old is she?"

"She just turned 26."

"Damn! That's too young to be boss."

"You will only be 23 in five months. Consider everything you've accomplished. It's pretty fucking impressive!"

"I see your point. What does Rita look like?"

"Nothing like her brother. I'm glad you and she will likely never meet. She's gorgeous."

"It will likely be necessary I meet with her."

Fuck that! Why?"

"Ken O'Malley is storing a large shipment of product for Roberto. He doesn't know where to transport any of it. Roberto never told him. We want to contact Rita and find out what to do. We don't want her to suspect we can't be trusted with the merchandise now that Roberto is gone, or we had anything to do with his disappearance. We also need to know if Rita wants to continue the business arrangement Roberto had with Ken. Do you know how we can contact her?"

"You keep saying we a lot. Why are you involved in all this? Why would you have to meet with her? You have no responsibility in Ken O'Malley's business."

"Carmella, I do."

"Fuck, Hound! Since when?"

"Since early this afternoon."

"Damn it! What the fuck have you done?"

"I've agreed to let Ken train me so I can assume his position when he's ready to retire."

"You've lost your God-damned mind! Why would you do such a thing? You said we were going into business together when I graduated from Berkeley! You know I've hoped for that since we were in high school!"

"Nothing has changed. We're still going to build a business together. What I'm doing with Ken is necessary and in my best interest."

"Tell me why?"

"I can't. I need you to trust me. You know I would never work for Ken unless I had no choice."

"Hound, you know I trust you. Just promise me you'll be careful, that we will build a business together and you won't ever change the way you feel about me."

"I promise. Now, can you help me contact Rita?"

"I have a phone number in Colombia where you can leave her a message."

"Is there anything else you can tell me about her that might be helpful?"

"Never piss her off!"

"Good to know. Thanks for the heads up. Anything else?"

"Just one thing. I know she will desire you, but never become intimately involved with her. 'Hell hath no fury like a woman's scorn' doesn't even begin to describe how far she will go to get revenge."

"Why would you think I would?"

"I told you she was gorgeous, but that's an understatement. She could likely have any man she wanted. I don't want you to be that man."

"I won't be. Are you still confident you'll be able to play your role regarding Roberto's disappearance?"

"I'll be fine. Don't give it another thought. There's plenty of other things you need to be worried about."

When their meeting concluded it was past 3 a.m. Carmella followed Hound to a nice hotel nearby. They were in bed by 4 a.m. but didn't begin sleeping until after 6. They slept until 2 p.m. that afternoon, then took a long shower together, dressed and went to enjoy a late lunch at a favorite restaurant. She asked if they would still be able to see each other on a more frequent basis. He told her yes, as soon as he completed all he had to do.

He boarded his return flight to New Orleans at 5 p.m. He arrived a little before midnight. Jo was waiting.

"Why did you wait until you were at the airport, about to board your flight home, to call and let me know you were OK?" she asked.

"That was the first chance I had. Shit, I was busy."

"OK, but remember, you're never going to do anything like that again."

"Yes, Mother."

"Baby, I'm serious! Never again!"

"Understood."

"I love you. I'm glad you're home."

"I love you too. It's good to be back."

Hound and Jo arrived at the estate around 1 a.m. and went straight to bed. Hound was up at 8. While Jo remained asleep, he showered, dressed and went to the kitchen for a cup of coffee. He knew Ken would be anxiously waiting to hear how his trip went.

Ken was pouring his third cup of coffee. Hound poured his first and they walked to the den to talk privately. Hound reported his meeting with Carmella had been positive. He told Ken what he'd learned. Ken was also surprised to learn Roberto's sister would be his successor.

"Rita must be capable, or she wouldn't get the job," said Ken.

"Carmella assured me Rita was extremely capable."

"I suppose I should call Rita immediately. What time is it in Bogota?"

"It's four hours later than our time, but you should let me call her."

"Why?"

"What to do next about the merchandise was my idea. I began the plan; let me finish it. Besides, I'm your right hand now. Let me show you how capable I am of conducting important business."

"OK. You'll probably get better results than I would anyway."

Hound sat at Ken's desk to make the call. It took a few seconds for the phone in Bogota to ring. A man answered, speaking Spanish.

"Sir, do you speak English?" Hound asked.

"Yes. Who is this?"

"My name is John William Smith. It's urgent I speak to Rita Sanchez as soon as possible. Is she there?"

"Why do you wish to speak with her?"

"My business with her is private. She wouldn't want me to discuss it with anyone but her. Please, is she there?"

"No."

"When will she return?"

"I don't know. It could be a long time, maybe never. I don't know."

Hound became convinced Rita was there, but likely screened all phone calls. If she was available, there was a sure way to coax her to the phone.

"Sir, I need to speak to Miss Sanchez about her brother, Roberto," said Hound.

It was a brief few seconds before Hound received a response.

"Mr. Smith, this is Rita Sanchez," said a new voice. "What do you have to tell me about Roberto?"

"Miss Sanchez, your brother missed a very important business meeting with my organization last week. Can you put me in contact with him? It's most urgent. I need to know if he intends to continue the business arrangement we recently agreed upon."

"What arrangement?"

"The one in New Orleans."

"Sir, I'm not aware of any such business arrangement. What are you referring to?"

Hound knew if she was telling the truth what he suspected had been verified, that only Roberto knew about the deal in New Orleans and the merchandise in the warehouse. Of course, she was likely cautious about specific topics being discussed over the phone. He quickly calculated what he would do next.

"Miss Sanchez, I don't feel it would be proper to speak with anyone but Mr. Sanchez about the business my organization has with him. I'm sure you can understand. Will you put me in contact with him?"

"Unfortunately, my brother can't be contacted at this time. He's currently indisposed and not in charge of overseeing the family business. I am, so you will have to speak with me."

"Very well, but not over the phone. It's best that we speak in person. Don't you agree?"

"The business arrangement you say exists; does it involve big business?"

"Mr. Sanchez said it would."

"How to you propose we meet?"

"I would be pleased to meet with you in Bogota if that's agreeable."

"It is. When can you come?"

"I'll book the first flight possible. I'll call and let you know the time I'm due to arrive."

"I'll look forward to meeting you, Mr. Smith, if that's really your name."

"It is, but I'm called Hound. It's a nickname I've had since I was a child."

"Hound is an unusual nickname. You can tell me how you got it when we meet. How did you know who I was and how to contact me?"

"Mr. Sanchez told me about you. He provided me with two phone numbers, one where he could be contacted and the other where you could be reached in case a problem developed and he was out of pocket."

"Did he tell you I was next in line as boss when he retired?"

"No, only to call you if a problem developed that needed to be resolved quickly and he couldn't be contacted."

Ken wasn't pleased Hound set the meeting without including him. However, a level of risk existed, and he was willing to let Hound take it alone.

Hound booked a flight departing for Miami at 11 a.m. He would depart Miami at 4 p.m. and arrive in Bogota around 8. There were some things he needed to do before he left. His plan to leave Jo again, especially to meet with the boss of a cartel, enraged her. She refused to allow it but went to her bedroom to cry in private when her refusal didn't change the inevitable.

Hound placed a call to the manager of his nightclub. He informed Candy he might not be returning to Phoenix for some time and directed her to maintain business as usual. She assured him everything would be fine and didn't ask any questions.

He called Bear at the biker club and told him about his intention to be away for a time. He asked Bear to speak with Bill and determine if all club chapters nationwide could collectively and discreetly purchase and distribute all the merchandise in Ken's warehouse. Bear said distribution within a reasonable time frame wouldn't be a problem but having the amount of money needed to purchase the products would.

Hound told him not to make that an issue when discussing it with the other chapters — he would take care of it. Bear wanted to know Hound's reason for asking the questions. Hound said he would tell him later if something he suspected was true.

Ken delivered Hound to the airport when Jo refused. However, she made sure to kiss him goodbye, telling him to be safe and hurry home. During his short layover in Miami, Hound called Carmella to secure the help he knew would be needed to confirm his legitimacy with Rita. She would not blindly accept what he told her without confirmation. She'd insure he presented no threat to the cartel.

"What do you want me to do?" asked Carmella.

"Rita will want to know I'm who I say before she'll discuss any cartel business. She'll never risk talking to an undercover agent or any enemy to the cartel. I'm going to ask if she happens to know you. When she confirms she does, I'll tell her we met for the first time at my birthday party in New Orleans last July when you and Roberto attended, and you can confirm who I am. Tell her you're aware a business deal had just been negotiated between Roberto and Ken O'Malley, that it was big, but you don't know what it involved. Verify I'm married to Ken's daughter and second-in-command to take over the O'Malley family business when Ken retires."

"Shit, Hound! What if she finds out we've been best friends for almost 20 years and lovers for 10, and that we still are?"

"Roberto didn't find out. It's likely she won't."

"Hound, you've always been right in past decisions, but if you're wrong about this, we have no chance of staying alive."

"I'm too far into my plan. I have no choice except to see it through. I believe everything will turn out OK, but not without your help. Will you continue to trust me? Can I count on you to do as I ask?"

"Yes, baby, just be careful. Remember, Rita is different from Roberto in ways that make her more dangerous. A major difference to consider is she's smarter, maybe as smart as you."

"I'll be extra cautious."

12

Hound arrived in Bogota shortly after 8 p.m. As he was told, a car and driver were waiting. The driver verified Hound was the person he was sent to meet. He placed Hound's single small suitcase in the trunk, and they departed. The driver was polite during the drive but was careful not to offer any information his boss would not approve of.

The lights of Bogota faded as they continued to drive from the city. It was over an hour before the driver turned off the main road and began to drive west on a private road. Hound had no idea how much longer the trip would take or where he was being taken. The moon was full and bright. He looked out the window and saw nothing but dense foliage.

After driving about five minutes he noticed lights coming into view ahead. Soon he saw a stone wall at least ten feet high. As he drew closer, he saw the wall extended as far as the eye could see in two directions and surrounded what he assumed was a large estate. Behind an electronically controlled steel entrance gate, two security guards stood in front of a guardhouse to receive visitors.

After the guards completed the required inspection, the car was allowed to enter. After driving for two minutes at a slower speed down a twisting, turning road, the car stopped in front an elegant mansion. The driver carried Hound's luggage and escorted him to the front entrance of the home.

There he was warmly greeted by a maid who took his suitcase and invited him to enter. He was taken to a large and elaborately furnished living area and told to make himself comfortable, that his luggage would be delivered to his room and Miss Sanchez would join him momentarily. He looked around the room and selected a high back leather chair to sit in. He had no idea what the outcome of his visit would be, but it was apparent he would be spending the night.

Hound had been seated a short time when the woman he came to see entered the large room and began walking to where he was sitting. He stood and waited for her arrival. She offered her hand.

"I'm Rita Sanchez," she said in a calm, sober tone. "Welcome to my home. Thank you for coming."

"Thank you for allowing me to come. Your home is spectacular, most impressive."

They shook hands. Rita's physical beauty was as Carmella had said. It surpassed that of any woman he had ever seen. She took a seat close to and facing him. She sat silent for a moment starring at him.

"Hound is the name you wish to be called, isn't it?" she asked.

"Yes, Miss Sanchez."

"Please call me Rita."

She was polite but wasted no time focusing the conversation on the purpose of their meeting.

"So, you have a business arrangement with Roberto," she said.

"Not me personally. It's with Ken O'Malley. I'm married to Mr. O'Malley's daughter and second-in-command of the family business."

"What kind of family business?"

"The kind that makes a lot of money, but not always by means considered proper by the norms of society."

"Why didn't Mr. O'Malley come?"

Hound thought quickly to offer the best possible answer.

"He planned to, but I convinced him to remain in New Orleans in the event Mr. Sanchez tried to contact him. I hope you're not disappointed."

"Of course not. It was the smart thing to do. I'm sure as second-in-command you're capable of acting on his behalf, but I hope he wasn't afraid he wouldn't be treated well. You don't seem concerned."

"Why should I be?"

"You shouldn't, but I would assume you're under the impression my family's business is also involved in making money in ways contrary to the norms of society. That's not the case. Even if it were true, how could I be certain you're being honest about everything you've told me?"

Hound paused for a time, as if he was thinking of a way to provide the proof she wanted.

"Do you happen to know Carmella Vargas?"

"Why?"

"She attended my 22nd birthday party with your brother at the O'Malley estate in New Orleans last July. If you know Carmella, then perhaps you can contact her. The party was a huge event. I'm sure she'd remember meeting me and Mr. O'Malley. She and your brother sat with us at our family table. We shared a dance and talked a bit."

"Hound, are you really only 22?"

"Yes."

"You look and act much older."

"People always say that when they learn my age."

"Hound, please forgive me for not asking sooner. Are you hungry? When did you eat last?"

"Actually, I am. I don't eat airline food. My last meal was breakfast."

Rita escorted Hound to the dining room and told the chef to prepare him a meal. She excused herself and left. She didn't say where she was going, but he felt certain it was to call Carmella.

Hound finished the delicious dinner he was served. He sat at the dining table enjoying a second glass of the wine that perfectly complemented his meal. When he finished, the maid ushered him back to his chair in the living area to be comfortable while he waited for Rita's return.

An hour passed before Rita joined him. She had changed the clothing she was wearing when he arrived. Her attire was now much less like that worn to create a specific first impression. Her jeans and blouse were certainly less formal and expensive, but no less becoming.

"Hound, I'm sorry to keep you waiting," she said, smiling. "Was your dinner satisfactory?"

"Absolutely. Thank you."

"I changed into something more comfortable. I hope you don't mind."

"Of course not. You look great and now I don't feel under-dressed."

"Hound, it's after 10 p.m., but if you're not too tired, I'd like to visit a bit before retiring."

"That would be fine."

"Good. I suppose you're anxious to get the problem you came to talk about resolved."

"Yes, I am."

"Tell me about the business your family has with my brother."

"Don't you know?"

"The first time I heard of it was during your phone call."

The moment of truth had arrived. Hound had to know if Rita was telling the truth or lying, setting a trap to test his honesty. He'd been watching her body cues for indications of which one it was likely to be. She was telling the truth or was the best he had ever seen, other than himself, at the art of deception. Relying only on his instinct and considering the odds regarding which it was, he made a decision.

"Ken O'Malley agreed to receive, warehouse, and then transport merchandise for your brother to buyers in various parts of the United States. The amount of product was usually large as well as the money to be made."

"Were any shipments received and transported by O'Malley?"

"The first shipment arrived and is in the warehouse. We were waiting for instructions from Roberto regarding what to do next. He was to tell us at the meeting he never showed up for."

Hound paid attention to Rita's body cues as she sat quietly looking at him while carefully considering all he had said.

"Why do you think Roberto missed the meeting and didn't notify you?"

"Rita, I don't know your brother well, but well enough to believe he'd certainly have arrived on time for the meeting or called Ken to reschedule. I hope I'm wrong, but I feel something terrible has happened to him."

"Do you think he's dead?"

"I hope not, but maybe. What do you think?"

"He's dead."

"Perhaps he was kidnapped or injured in an accident and hasn't been able to notify anyone."

"No, he's dead. He's been assassinated."

Hound felt another moment of truth had arrived.

"How can you be sure?"

"Hound, due to the type business my family is in, there's no other reasonable explanation. Three of his best soldiers and most trusted friends were always with him when he traveled in the United States. They're also missing. That's another reason I know he's dead."

"Who do you think killed him?"

"There's no way to be sure now, but I intend to find out. Maybe a rival cartel; I don't know. Roberto had many enemies."

"Rita, if you're right, then I'm truly sorry for your loss."

"Thank you, but I'm not terribly saddened over his death. I respected his position in the family, but we were never close. I didn't love him as a sister should. Truthfully, I never even liked him. Of course, my parents are devastated. I suppose you think I'm a terrible person?"

"That's not for me to judge."

"I'm happy to hear you say that. I don't like to be judged, or the people who judge me. In the short time I've known you, I've come to like you. I hope we can develop and grow a lasting personal and business friendship."

"Rita, I hope that as well. May I assume you wish to keep the business arrangement your brother had with Ken O'Malley?"

"Probably, but only after I find out everything about it. I'm not my brother. I may wish to propose changes to it. Can you tell me what I need to know?"

"No. Ken will need to do that."

"Why? Don't you know everything about it?"

"Only what I've told you."

"I would think Ken's second-in-command would know everything he did."

"I'm sorry, but I don't. I only accepted the position a couple of days ago. Ken hasn't had time to bring me up to speed on everything I need to know about the business he had with Roberto or any other areas of the family business. Besides, I'm sure at this time, under the current circumstance he'd wish to discuss business with you personally."

"All right, but I'm sure there's something we can discuss to get things started."

"What?"

"Let's talk about Carmella."

"OK. What about her?"

Hound didn't expect Rita's changing of the subject. However, he wasn't surprised she'd eventually wish to further discuss Carmella. He hoped the discussion wouldn't become an interrogation with questions he wasn't prepared to answer.

"When you met Carmella, what did you think of her?" asked Rita.

"I don't know. What do you mean?"

"Did you think she was beautiful?"

"Yes, I remember thinking she was very beautiful."

"Did you feel contempt for her?"

Hound knew Rita was likely setting a trap. He was prepared.

"Of course not. Why would I?"

"I assumed a man like you would feel that about a whore, regardless of how beautiful she was."

"I didn't know she was a whore. I assumed she was simply Roberto's beautiful girlfriend. Is she really a whore?"

"She was his mistress. That's what a private, high dollar whore is called. She was a common prostitute for a time before he took her for his mistress."

"I'd never have suspected that about her. I got the impression she and Roberto were close."

"He never said, but I'm convinced he was in love with her. Perhaps she could have returned the love if he'd treated her more like a person he cared for than a possession he paid for and owned."

"Rita, you tell an interesting story. If Roberto is dead, do you think Carmella will return to prostitution?"

"I don't think so. She convinced me that would never happen. The title to the estate she and Roberto shared in Oakland is in her name only. I don't know why, probably for security. Maybe it was a way for him to express his feelings for her. She's attending Berkeley University. I think it will be her plan to finish school and take a happier road in life. She never wanted to become a whore. She felt it was the only way to afford a college education and become worthy of the man she loved and wanted to marry. At least that's what she once told me."

"I suppose she and the guy didn't work out or she wouldn't

have been with Roberto."

"Hound, did you serve in Vietnam?"

He felt as though a noose was around his neck.

"Yes, why?" he asked.

"She told me her man served there as an officer. Were you an officer?"

He felt the noose tighten.

"Yes, I was," he answered.

"I know you feel fortunate to have survived when so many didn't. She told me the only man she wanted or would ever truly love died there."

Hound felt the noose loosen a bit.

"A lot of good men died in that shit hole," he said. "Too many. One was too many. I suppose you'll require Carmella's home be turned over to you."

"Why would you suppose that?"

"Because Roberto paid for it."

"True, but it seems he wanted her to own it. Like I said, he loved her. That's reason enough for the estate to remain hers. Besides, I'm very fond of her. She deserves the chance to have a better life. The estate is a good investment to help her get started. I'm going to encourage her to finish college, and perhaps help her financially. I know she'll need it."

"Rita, it's not for me to say, but do you feel Carmella can be trusted if Roberto is really dead? She probably knows more than she should about the cartel's business."

"Roberto would never let her know enough to make her a threat. Besides, she fears me more than she ever did Roberto. She knows what would happen if she did anything that would threaten the cartel."

Hound had learned something about Rita he liked and respected. Her willingness to allow Carmella's ownership of the Oakland estate and to assist her financially was a fair, generous and compassionate gesture.

"Rita, I presume you've already called Carmella to verify I am who I say."

"Yes. She had no problem calling to memory the extraordinarily handsome young man she met at his birthday party. Well, enough about her. Let's get back to business. Hound, we know that Roberto made the arrangement with Ken. We know the first shipment of merchandise is in Ken's warehouse, what the shipment consists of and the price Roberto was going to charge the buyers. We know Ken was to transport the merchandise to buyers and what percentage of the money paid by them he was to receive. Unfortunately, we don't know who the buyers are."

"Why would Roberto not tell you?"

"Roberto was very insecure in his role as boss. He felt keeping specific things about new business and future business ventures he had in the U.S. from being known by me and my father made his position more secure. Of course, he would tell us eventually, but not until it was absolutely necessary. That made my father and me furious."

"What are you going to do? We can't keep the merchandise in New Orleans too long. The risk of it being discovered increases as each day passes."

"We need to find new buyers quickly. If that's not possible, then shipping the merchandise back to one of our storage locations here or elsewhere will be the only option. That would present a problem for me. You might be interested to know Roberto already had a second shipment ready for transport to New Orleans as soon as Ken completed transport of the first. Without reliable buyers, my business stands to lose a lot of money. It would only be a short time until rival cartels moved to take advantage of my vulnerability. Do you have any idea how to solve the problems facing both our families?"

"Give me a minute to think about it."

Hound had already been thinking about it, and other things as well. He was damn happy he'd made the decision to tell Rita the truth about the first shipment being received and secured, the truth she knew before he told it. He was thinking what a great financial opportunity would be open to him personally if he could solve the problem. In addition, he would advance his status with the cartel and increase his personal power and influence. He wanted to secure Rita as a reliable ally, one to call upon as a last resort when the need to persuade others could only be met by the use of extreme violence.

"Perhaps I do have an idea," he said. "What is the shipment composed of?"

"Ninety percent is drugs, heroin and cocaine. Ten percent is fully automatic rifles. The street value of everything is at least 750 million."

"Holy shit! That's more than I expected."

"Does the amount frighten you? Does it ruin your idea?"

"Maybe not. It's just more than I expected."

"Hound, it's getting late. Let's get some sleep and continue tomorrow. Is there anything you need to make your stay more enjoyable?"

"I usually do a physical workout in the morning. Would I be permitted to complete a run outdoors first thing in the morning along with some exercises after the run?"

"Of course. I'll join you. I'm interested to learn how you maintain your impressive physique."

"I welcome the company."

"I welcome the competition. How does 8:00 sound to get started?"

"Sounds good."

Hound was shown to his room. It was large and furnished with expensive and elegant items. The shower was almost as large as the entire bathroom in the guest bedrooms of his Phoenix estate. He stood for a long time enjoying the streams of water hitting him from above and on all sides. He considered his meeting with Rita had gone well thus far. He was reasonably sure her trust was growing. He decided to calm his thoughts. He went to bed and soon fell into a deep sleep.

At 8:00 the next morning Hound left his room and walked down the wide hallway separating the six guest bedrooms on either side. At the end of the hall behind him was the master bedroom occupied by Rita's parents. He hoped to meet them at some point during his visit.

He walked to the end of the hall and then down the long winding staircase. A maid greeted him at the base. It seemed as though she had been patiently waiting for his arrival. She greeted him in a friendly manner and escorted him to the living area where Rita and her parents were seated and having a conversation in Spanish.

They all said good morning in English. He responded in Spanish to let them know he spoke the language. Carlos Sanchez, Rita's father, was 64. He was a handsome man, 5 feet 11 inches tall, slender build, with a dark complexion. His hair and mustache were gray. His wife Nita was 62. At 5 feet 8 inches in height, and a nice figure, she was still a very pretty woman. She surely must have been an exceptionally beautiful lady in her youth. Hound could easily see the reason for Rita's extraordinary beauty.

Her parents treated Hound like a family member. He was made to feel very welcome. Carlos seemed nothing like Roberto, in fact the opposite, but Hound was certain Carlos had been a man to step aside for in his younger days. This was probably still true.

After a short visit so Hound could meet and begin to get acquainted with her parents, Rita and Hound excused themselves and left to begin their workout. On the way to one of the home's rear entrances, Rita took time to show him the fully equipped indoor gym. They completed the run in under 37 minutes. He wasn't surprised when she remained at his side during the entire five miles. He had assumed by the look of her she was in excellent physical condition. The next hour was spent in the gym. Again, he wasn't surprised when she completed the same number of pushups, chin-ups and setups in the same length of time as he did.

When the workout ended, they went to their rooms to shower, dress, and then report to the dining room for a late breakfast. Rita's parents joined them.

"Did my daughter compete well during your time of exercise?" asked Carlos.

"I've never been challenged more."

"I know you and my daughter have discussed the business your family has with Roberto. I would like to hear the results of that discussion thus far."

Rita provided her father with a complete and accurate update. Carlos listened intently to his daughter, but never broke eye contact with Hound. Hound seemed to drift away in thought as a result of Carlos starring at him in such an intensive manner.

"Hound, you seem to be far away," Carlos said when Rita finished. "May I ask where your thoughts are?"

"I'm sorry, sir. I don't mean to appear rude or absent of interest in the current situation. I was thinking of someone else whose name was Carlos, someone I knew several years ago."

"Does he hold special meaning to you?"

"Yes, I suppose he does."

"In what way?"

"I guess he was the first of a long list of reasons I'm sitting here now."

"What do you mean?"

"I'm sorry I mentioned him. He's just a faded memory from my past."

"Do I remind you of him in ways other than my name?"

"Not yet."

"What was his full name?"

"Carlos Mendoza."

"Where is he now?"

"He's dead. He drowned 10 years ago."

It was apparent to everyone Hound didn't wish to continue that topic of discussion, so Carlos changed it.

"Hound, do you think something terrible has happened to Roberto?" asked Carlos.

"Sir, I'm sorry, but yes I do."

"What do you think happened to him?"

"I considered some possibilities, but Rita convinced me he was assassinated."

"My wife and I agree with Rita. Roberto's fate resulted from the risk people in our business take. I often told my son he took too many unnecessary risks. He was stubborn, overconfident and arrogant. He tried my patience and I was angry with him more than not, but he was my son. I loved him as did all his family. We will make every effort to find out what happened to him and who is responsible. Now, enough talk of such things. Let's focus on the important business problem both our families are facing. Rita said perhaps you had a plan to suggest."

"First, Mr. Sanchez, I'm new at this line of business. I've only recently accepted my position in the O'Malley organization."

"We know, but Rita feels you are extremely intelligent and very capable of solving business problems in any type of business. She also feels you can be trusted. Were you tempted, even in the least, to steal the product in your warehouse when Rita first said we knew nothing of it, or that any business arrangement existed between our families?"

Hound wasn't surprised by the question, but quickly considered the best way to answer.

"Sir, with all due respect, I didn't believe what Rita told me. Even if I had, it wouldn't have been my nature to steal from a business partner, especially from one my family was going to make millions. I will never lie to or steal from a friend or a partner. I expect the same from them. Also, I would never have a partner I didn't consider a friend."

"Hound, I don't know you well enough to be certain you're

everything you say, but for some reason unknown to me now, I'm willing to trust you are a man of your word. Now, how do you propose we solve our problem?"

"Sir, if your family is willing to delay receiving payment for the merchandise in our warehouse for a reasonable period of time, I can sell it all immediately."

"Are you saying you know buyers that can be trusted to pay later?"

"Yes, sir."

"Please stop calling me sir, or Mr. Sanchez. Call me Carlos. Now, are you and your family prepared to stand good for our money should your buyers not pay?"

"Carlos, I can't commit Ken O'Malley to such a deal, but I can commit myself."

"Don't you feel Ken would agree?"

"No"

"Why?"

"He'd never assume the risk of not being able to fulfill a promise to your family."

"Don't you think you should ask him? Give him a call. I'm sure he's anxious to hear from you, as is your wife. I would like to speak to him as well."

"OK."

A maid brought a telephone to Carlos. Hound placed the call to the estate in New Orleans. Ken answered. He was told the conversation was on a speaker so everyone with Hound could participate. Jo sat next to her father to also participate.

After all introductions were made, Ken and Jo engaged in pleasant, casual conversation with Carlos and Rita. When Hound told Ken of the proposal he made to Carlos, Ken paused the conversation. He resumed by saying he couldn't agree to such a bold commitment, one likely impossible to honor. Carlos understood and supported Ken's decision. Ken told Carlos he would stand ready to assist in moving the merchandise to another location desired by the Sanchez family, but respectfully requested it be moved as soon as possible. Carlos agreed.

When asked by Jo when he would return home, he told her as soon as possible. When the call ended, there was a moment of silence before anyone spoke.

"Hound, Ken doesn't have your confidence," said Carlos.

"He doesn't have my balls either."

Hound apologized for saying what he was thinking. Rita and Carlos laughed.

"Hound, you never have to apologize to us for stating a truth," said Rita.

"Hound, can you guarantee to deliver on your proposal?" asked Carlos in a serious manner.

"I guarantee to try as hard as I can, nothing else."

"Well, Rita, you are the boss now," Carlos said. "What do you want to do?"

Rita postponed her response to ask Hound a question.

"Hound, did you know Roberto had a meeting with Ken less than a week ago?" asked Rita.

Hound assumed that was when Roberto asked how to find him.

"No, I didn't," Hound replied.

"My brother placed a phone call to Ken the morning after that meeting. We feel that was the same day Roberto disappeared."

"I didn't know that either."

Hound assumed Roberto called to let Ken know he had arrived in Phoenix and gone to the biker club, as agreed upon, to ask directions to Hound's home and nightclub. Hound suddenly realized if Rita was telling the truth, then Roberto likely planned to kill him as well as Carmella and Ken knew it. Ken had given his blessing to safeguard the business deal he had with Roberto.

"Rita, is there a reason you're telling me this? Is it significant?"

"Maybe not for you, but my father and I wonder why Roberto didn't tell Ken where to transport the merchandise at the time of their meeting."

"I suppose Roberto wanted to wait until the meeting they had scheduled for that purpose."

"According to what you said Ken told you, that meeting was scheduled two days after the first meeting. Why would Roberto wait another day to get started moving the product out of New Orleans and into the hands of the buyers? We know they were waiting to get their order."

"How do you know everything you're telling me is reliable information?"

"Roberto told us. He called us daily to check in. He didn't always tell us everything, but he did tell us those things."

Hound was certain Rita was being truthful. He wasn't sure where the conversation was leading, but he had to satisfy a stressing curiosity.

"Where was Roberto when he called you the day after he met with Ken?" asked Hound.

"He didn't say, and we didn't ask."

Hound breathed a secret sigh of relief.

"Rita, I don't know anything about a meeting or phone call the next day. I wasn't present for either one. I don't know what else to say."

"I know you weren't, and you don't have to say anything more."

"Why did you tell me this? What did you hope to gain?"

"Only your response. One I hoped for. The one I got that further convinces me you can be trusted. Unfortunately, neither I nor my father feel the same way about Ken. I'm sorry."

"Why do you trust me and not him?"

"Because you're here and he's not is a major reason. Only a fool would ask for a meeting and come here after having anything to do with my brother's death."

Hound didn't see that one coming. He had no idea where the conversation would go from here, or how it would end. He was still alive, but would he be in the next few minutes?

"Shit, Rita! You can't think Ken had anything to do with whatever happened to Roberto! What possible reason could he have had for doing such a thing?"

"I'm not prepared to say at this time. Perhaps I'll tell you later, perhaps not. Let's focus on the previous topic of our discussion. How good do you feel about being able to sell the surplus of merchandise we have now, and being able to establish a steady market for future products?"

"I'm confident, but I told you nothing was guaranteed. Shit, I'm beyond confused! You suspect my father-in law was involved in your brother's disappearance, yet you want to continue doing business with him! Why would you do that?"

"I don't want to do business with him. I want to do business with you."

"How could that be possible? You know what my position in Ken's organization is. You can't do business with me without it being his business too. Shit, Rita, he's the boss! With all due respect, and at the risk of not surviving this visit, I would never compromise my loyalty while working for him, especially in the position I hold."

Hound was keenly aware what he said might seal his fate, but he decided to gamble his life on Rita expecting him to respond the way he did. She was the most intelligent woman he'd ever met. Correctly anticipating the purpose of everything she said and did was a superior challenge. She was pulling him forward on a gauntlet of carefully designed traps to test his trustworthiness to do business with her cartel.

"Hound, I know you'd remain loyal to Ken as long as you were a member of his organization," she said, "so resign and get away from him. A man such as he is destined to fall sooner or later. Don't remain and fall with him."

Rita was a very intelligent woman. She had been using well planned traps to test Hound and determine if he knew anything about Roberto. His intelligence and instinct had once again served him well. He had passed all her tests thus far and felt confident the worst was over. However, he'd never drop his guard while in her presence, or her father's. The most important thing was to never allow Rita to realize, or even suspect, he was carrying out his own plan of deception and manipulation.

It was a plan he began formulating when he decided he should make the trip to Bogota alone. He knew the plan was the biggest gamble of his life because the stakes were his life. He felt the gamble was paying off. He was close to getting the two things he had come for. A business relationship with the cartel and the timely death of Ken O'Malley were within his grasp.

Hound decided long ago that killing Ken was the only way to escape the control he had over him. However, current circumstances had made Hound an intolerable threat to Ken, one Hound knew Ken wouldn't allow to exist any longer than necessary. Hound was responsible for the death of Roberto. He had implicated Ken as a co-conspirator. There would now be a race to see which of them killed the other first to eliminate their nemesis. In using Rita as a means to be the victor, Hound needed to include in his plan a guarantee Jo and her mother wouldn't be harmed.

Rita suggested Hound join her for a walk outdoors where they would continue their conversation. It was apparent Carlos had turned over all leadership of the cartel to her. He required only to be kept advised of the status of all the business being conducted by the cartel. As they began their walk around the estate, Hound purposely appeared concerned, and intended her to notice. She did.

"Hound, you seem nervous, troubled," she said. "What are you thinking?"

"Shit, Rita! I'm wondering if you're going to let me survive."

Rita presented a soft, empathetic smile.

"Hound, I understand your concern," she said, "but you can relax. I want you enjoy the rest of your visit. If I was going to take your life, you would have already been dead."

"Well, it tickles me shitless to hear that. How do I know you're telling me the truth?"

"Because I give you my word. By the way, I like the way you sometimes express yourself. I've never tickled a man shitless before. Did you come up with that on your own?"

"Hell no, but if the shoe fits, wear it. That's not original either."

"I know. I've heard that one before."

"Rita, what happens now? Where do we go from here?"

"We do business together, if you're in agreement."

"What if I'm not?"

"Then I'll kill you."

Rita couldn't keep a straight face after making the statement. She burst into laughter.

"I'm happy one of us can laugh," he said. "I hope you always honor your word."

Rita's attitude quickly showed evidence of anger, even though she was certain his remark was made in jest.

"Hound, I always honor my word," she said forcefully. "I would die before breaking it. I hope you to feel the same way. Lying or breaking your word to me would anger me greatly. You would not welcome my wrath or the consequences that followed."

"Understood. Now what do you want from me?"

"As I said. To do business together."

"OK, but what does that entail?"

"We create and maintain a continuing market for cartel products in the U.S. One large enough to buy all the merchandise the cartel can supply."

"How much would that be, maximum, on an annual basis?"

"Two billion street value, one billion cost to the buyers in drugs only. We supply weapons on demand. When a buyer places an order, we purchase them from our supplier."

"Damn, Rita! That's a lot of drugs to market. Besides, there's competition to consider."

"I understand, but that will be your problem."

"OK, but I have another problem, a big one."

"What?"

"Ken O'Malley will never allow me to do business with you separate from his organization."

"Fuck him. Resign your position and separate from the organization."

"Rita, he'd have me killed if I tried that. He tried for a long time to get me where he wanted me. He'd never allow me to leave. I don't want to sound arrogant, but I'm the most valuable asset he has regarding growth of the family business and wealth."

"I don't think you're arrogant. I sense you have the ability to help any company prosper. That's why I want to team with you. I get the impression you and Ken aren't close."

"I despise the bastard. I don't trust him."

"Roberto didn't either, but that's another story for another time. Hound, if you were able to be free of Ken, would you accept my proposal?"

"What would you offer me financially?"

"How does 25 percent of cartel profit sound? That's 250 million per year with more to come if you do as well as I know you will."

"That's generous, and I would accept, but there's still Ken."

"Ken will be dealt with, if you don't care how."

"I couldn't care less, but I don't want my wife or her mother harmed. I require your word they won't be."

"I understand, you love your wife."

"She doesn't deserve to be hurt. Nor does her mother."

"So, you love her."

"She doesn't deserve to be hurt. I love her for all the things she's done to help me in the past."

"OK. I give you my word she won't be harmed. Do we have a deal?"

"Yes, we do."

"Would you like to go out tonight and celebrate our new business deal? What is your favorite food? I know where the best places to eat are. After dinner we'll go dancing. I know where the nicest clubs are. You do like to dance, don't you?"

"Rita, that sounds wonderful, but I need to get home and get started doing what you expect of me. There's much to do. If there's a flight to Miami anytime this afternoon or tonight, I need to be on it."

"Nonsense! You need to remain here two, maybe three more days. There's much we still need to discuss and I'm anxious to get better acquainted. What clothes did you bring?"

"The suit I arrived in, workout clothes and the casuals I'm wearing now. Why?"

"Your clothes are nice, very expensive, but you really didn't plan to stay long, did you? It doesn't matter. We can drive into the city and buy some things that will look terrific on you. If we leave now there will be plenty of time to shop."

"You're not going to let me refuse, are you?"

"Of course not! Besides, why would you want to? Can you honestly say you don't want to enjoy a night out with me?"

"Rita, I'm married, remember? Would you want your husband enjoying a night out with a beautiful woman?"

"If I had a husband, he would be too much in love to go out with another woman. You care for your wife, but you're not in love with her. Maybe at another time you did, but not now."

Hound offered no response.

"Besides, if my husband was unfaithful, I would cut his balls off, shove them up his ass and let him bleed out," she said. "What do you think about that?"

"I think my dick would remain soft everywhere except at home."

"Damn right! That's what I thought you'd say."

Hound wasn't anxious to remain in Colombia any longer than necessary, but he knew refusing Rita's invitation to stay wasn't an option. She was accustomed to having her way over the objections of, and inconvenience to, others. However, he suspected her adamancy over extending his stay wasn't entirely selfish. She was a strong woman, driven to succeed in her new position of cartel boss. She was dangerous and deliberate in the endeavor, ready to protect and preserve her family and its business by any means necessary.

However, he suspected beneath a genuine exterior of tough and deadly determination lay purposely concealed a young woman with a strong sense of honor, justice and compassion. One made dormant by a life of training to prepare for a responsibility never wanted, but now must be assumed. A woman capable of intense love and passion. One deserving of the same. Time would prove or disprove his suspicion.

They returned to the mansion to make ready for the trip into the city to shop before their night of celebration began.

"Hound, make yourself at home for a bit," Rita told him. "I need to return a phone call, and then we'll leave for the city."

"OK. Do you mind if I call my wife and let her know all is well and I'll be away a couple of days longer?"

"Of course not. Use the phone in your room. You'll have more privacy."

It was Jo who answered the phone at the estate in New Orleans.

"Hello, sweetheart," she said in a way indicative of her joy to hear his voice. "Please tell me you're on your way home. I've been worried sick about you since you left."

"Jo, I'm sorry, but business is taking longer to complete than I anticipated. I'll be here another two or three days."

"Is everything OK?"

"Everything is fine, Jo. There's nothing to worry about."

"Damn! We were together more when your nightclub was your career. I'm beginning to think accepting the job with Dad wasn't the right choice."

"I had no choice, Jo. You've always known your dad would do what was necessary to secure me as his protégé."

"You're right, honey. I'm sorry if you have regrets. All I wanted was us to be happy, but we can't be happy if you aren't."

"Don't be concerned. I'm OK with the way things have turned out. They would be a lot worse if your dad hadn't helped me in times past. Honestly, I think it was always my intention to repay Ken by giving him the one thing he wanted most from me. It was the fair and proper thing to do. Besides, I believe working with your father has always been a big part of my destiny."

"Oh, sweetie, I hope you really feel that way."

"I do."

"Have you been too busy to think about and miss me?"

"I'll never be that busy."

"Please call me every day while you're away."

"I will."

Ken had been standing at Jo's side during her conversation, anxiously waiting his turn to talk with Hound.

"Damn, Hound!" Ken said in a loud voice. "Why is business taking so long to complete? Surely you know by now what we need to do with what's in the warehouse."

"I do, but we should wait until I get back to discuss it."

"I want to know now, damn it! That shit needed to be gone from my warehouse days ago. It's risky to keep it there any longer."

"I made a new deal for us with the new boss."

"I didn't give you the authority to make any new deal! What deal?"

"Ken, you know it's not smart to discuss business over the phone. I'll update you when I get back. Don't worry, everything is fine. You'll like the deal."

"Get your ass back home pronto! I need some answers!"

"I'll see you in a couple of days, three at the most."

Hound understood Ken wasn't as anxious over the product in the warehouse as he was to find out if he'd continue doing business with the cartel. A more major concern was what the cartel suspected had happened to Roberto and what was being done to find out.

When his conversation with Ken concluded, Hound found

Rita waiting downstairs. She was just ending the phone call she'd returned.

"Return to your room and pack your suitcase," she told him. "You won't be coming back to the estate."

"OK. Where will I be going?"

"We're driving to the city. What happens when we get there will be a surprise."

The same chauffeur who delivered Hound to the estate drove them to the city. When they arrived at the private airfield a short distance from the municipal airport, Hound became curious about what Rita had planned.

"What's going on, Rita?" he asked.

"Surprise! We're flying to Miami in my private plane."

"OK, but tell me what's going on."

"There's some business in Miami I need to transact in person. Don't fret, we're still going to shop, have dinner and go clubbing. I know the best places in Miami too."

"I'd bet you know the best places in a lot of cities."

"You'd win that bet."

They arrived in Miami shortly after 6 p.m. A car and driver, along with three bodyguards, were waiting to take them to the finest hotel in the city. A VIP suite had been reserved. After they registered and spent a few minutes in the suite, Rita told their driver to take them to an exclusive men's store she'd patronized before. The articles of clothing were of superior design and quality. Rita asked Hound what his sizes were in trousers, shirts, coats and shoes and insisted on purchasing two sets of each for him as a gift. He respectfully refused. The bodyguards standing at different locations nearby grinned and looked at each other. Each of them would've been honored by such a woman desiring to offer them gifts.

"Hound, why would you refuse my gesture of friendship?" she asked.

"It's not necessary. The clothes, even though very nice, are much too expensive."

"I want you to dress a specific way for our evening out."

"Fair enough, then I'll get what you want me to have, but pay for them myself. We may offer gifts to each other at a later time, but not now. I want to build a friendship based on trust and mutual respect first."

The bodyguards waited in anticipation for Rita's response to Hound's refusal. They knew she wasn't a woman to embrace rejection of any kind. Rita smiled and showed Hound what she desired him to purchase. He couldn't be certain if she'd once again tested him but knew he'd passed if she did. He bought two pair of pants, two shirts, a lightweight leather jacket and two pairs of shoes. The cost of his purchase was $2,750.00. He paid with cash.

"Hound, you'll look very handsome tonight in your new clothes," she told him.

"I would've looked equally good if we had shopped at J.C. Penney."

"You're right. You're extremely handsome in any type attire."

Shortly after they returned to their hotel, Rita left with her bodyguards to conduct the business she came to Miami for. She told Hound she'd return in less than an hour and asked him to be dressed and ready for their night on the town. She didn't disclose the location where the business would be conducted, but Hound assumed it was nearby. She returned on time and declared the meeting had been productive.

During dinner that night, Hound and Rita sat across from each other at a table reserved for two. The bodyguards sat at a table close by, close enough to view Rita at all times, but not so close they could hear her conversation.

"I assume you always have bodyguards at your side when you travel," Hound said.

"Yes, always. Depending on where I am and what I'm doing, sometimes more are required. Do they make you nervous?"

"No, but it must present problems for you at times you require more privacy."

"Like when?"

"Where will they sleep tonight?"

"Our suite has four bedrooms. One will be awake, on duty, while two sleep in separate rooms. You'll occupy a room, and I'll have the master bedroom. I'll have all the privacy I need. Will you?"

"I'd be more comfortable in a room separate from the suite. I hope you don't mind."

"I do mind. My bodyguards are for your protection as well as mine."

"Why do I need protection?"

"Because you're with me."

"I'm sure it would stress a man to date you."

"None have complained thus far. Are you?"

"No, but this isn't a date."

"Then what would you call it?"

"Two associates celebrating their new, hopefully to be very successful, business arrangement."

"It's our first date, but you can call it what you like. I want you to know I'm never intimate with a man until I get to know him very well."

"That's the proper policy for a lady, but you know I'm married, therefore exempt from any concern."

"Hound, you're married, but you don't want to be, therefore you're not exempt from a damn thing."

"Well, you're never intimate on a first date, so it doesn't matter either way."

"That's right."

Hound hoped she was simply being sincere in her arrogant way and not providing some other test. He knew it would be a mistake to begin a sexual relationship with her type of woman. He hoped Carmella had been wrong that Rita would want to and attempt to make it happen.

After dinner they went to Rita's most preferred nightclub. Naturally it was the best to be found in Miami. They danced, talked and enjoyed the rest of their celebration until almost 4 a.m. the next morning. They went directly to bed in their separate rooms as soon as they arrived back in the suite. Hound was sleeping soundly at 6 a.m. when he was awakened by a gentle touch to his chest. Rita was lying close to him on his right side. He got out of bed and stood looking at her. He hadn't considered his custom of sleeping nude.

"Oh, my God," she said in a loud whisper. "I knew you would be beautiful in the nude, but I didn't expect such perfection."

Her eyes quickly became fixed on his large penis.

"Perfection indeed!" she said.

He quickly stepped to the bed and covered the lower half of his torso with a portion of the silk sheet.

"Rita, what are you doing?" he asked, knowing the answer. "You shouldn't be here!"

"You know why I'm here, and why shouldn't I be?"

"I thought we had an understanding this wasn't going to happen."

"I changed my mind."

"Rita, I haven't. I'm married and happily or not, I will remain faithful to my wife as long as I'm married to her."

"Really?"

Rita stood and allowed the sheer, full-length nightgown she was wearing to fall to the floor. She returned to the bed and lay on her back.

"Hound, look at me and tell me what you see," she said softly.

He couldn't resist admiring her from head to toe. He silently admitted she was the most physically perfect woman he'd ever looked upon. He became erect, clearly evidenced by the protruding area of the sheet.

"Rita, you are truly the most beautiful woman I've ever gazed upon," he told her. "I'm honored you desire me, but with all due respect, would you please leave?"

He meant everything he'd said to her, absolutely every word. She realized it.

"What is the true reason for your rejection?" she asked. "Please tell me. I need to know."

"I don't want to fall for you. I'm certain that would happen. We could never do well in business after it did."

"I could fall for you. Isn't that really what concerns you, that I would become too demanding and possessive?"

"Maybe. I simply don't want you to be hurt or angered by me."

"Hound, are you afraid of me?"

"Rita, I respect your power and what you're capable of, but let me be clear in answering your question. I'm a man who fears nothing, absolutely nothing."

With all things considered, she was surprised to hear Hound admit what she suspected was true a short time after they met. She again rose from the bed, put her nightgown on and walked to him. She delivered a soft kiss to his cheek and then turned and walked to the door. She turned and smiled.

"You're truly a special breed of man," she said. "Unique in many ways and the first to refuse my affections. Be assured they'll never be offered to you again."

Hound didn't wake until after 2:30 that afternoon. He showered, dressed and left his room to discover he was alone in the suite. A few minutes passed, and then Rita arrived unescorted by her bodyguards. She joined Hound, who was seated on the sofa.

"Well, sleepyhead," she said, smiling, "I see you finally decided to get up."

"Yes, finally. Why didn't you wake me?"

"There was no need."

"Where are your bodyguards?"

"They're waiting in the lobby. I wanted to talk with you about something important."

"OK, what?"

"I have to fly back to Bogota this afternoon. I don't want you in New Orleans for two more days."

"Why? I need to get there as soon as possible and get started working on our business plan."

"Surely you can get started while you're in Phoenix for a couple of days."

Hound was caught off guard but said nothing, knowing Rita had more to say.

"It wouldn't be unusual for you to be in Phoenix tending to important business involving your nightclub, would it?"

"I suppose not. It's operating smoothly, but an unannounced visit as a surprise inspection couldn't hurt."

"Why didn't you tell me you owned a fabulous club in Phoenix, probably the most elegant in the U.S.?"

"You didn't ask, and I didn't feel it important. How did you know?"

"I've been checking you out since you first made contact with me. You might be surprised what I know."

"I assume nothing you've discovered is objectional."

"You're still alive, aren't you?"

"Absolutely, and I plan to stay alive. Are you going to tell me why I need to be in Phoenix for the next two days?"

Rita didn't answer. Instead she handed him a one-way, first-class airline ticket to Phoenix. The flight departed Miami at 6 p.m. that evening. She said to contact her as soon as possible regarding progress being made to find a steady market for cartel products. She again kissed him softly on the cheek and left the suite.

Hound wasted no time in calling Jo to tell her he was needed in Phoenix.

"God damn it, Hound! You need to get your ass home to me," she yelled over the phone. "Fuck the nightclub. You said your manager could handle any problem that arose."

As expected, Ken was on a second line and joined the conversation.

"Jo's right, Hound. You need to get back here and let me know what the hell is going on regarding our problem. I need to know what to do next. Did the meeting end on a positive note? Are we still in business?"

"Everything is fine, better than before. That's a major reason I need to be in Phoenix. Don't worry, we'll have the merchandise ready to transport soon, and a bigger one to receive. Just relax until I get back. You'll be pleased with what's going on. Jo, if you want to join me in Phoenix, it will be fine."

"I can't. Dad needs my assistance here. Just promise you'll be around awhile once you finish in Phoenix."

"I promise to do my best, sweetie."

When Hound arrived in the hotel lobby, he found Rita waiting. This was unexpected. He thought she was on her way back to Colombia.

"I didn't know you were still here," he said. "I assumed you'd be on your way to the airport by now."

"No, I decided to talk with you a bit longer. There are things you probably need to know before you begin opening markets in the U.S. for the cartel."

"OK. By the way, where are your bodyguards?"

"Close by, always close by and watching."

Rita suggested they visit the dining room. It was almost 4 p.m. They hadn't eaten since the night before. They sat at a table that offered the most privacy.

"Hound," Rita began in a serious manner, "you know how dangerous the business we're in is. It will be especially so for you. Several factions are competing to market their products in the country. These are ruthless individuals, determined to control as much of the market as possible. You have to be careful and actually have an army of reliable soldiers to help deter the threats from competitors. Your government is already aware that illegal drugs are going to become a major problem. The threat of being caught and imprisoned will become greater as time passes and more product is introduced into the U.S. You can never be sure who to trust. The most reliable people will betray you for the right price, or due to coercion from law enforcement or rivals. When you begin to grow your market, be especially careful in the Central, Eastern, North and Southeastern part of the country. There's already big trouble brewing in Florida. Miami has already become a mini war zone. Roberto was growing a major market in the West, North and Southwest, but the competition was beginning to become a problem. That's likely what killed him."

"Do you believe he was assassinated by a rival faction?"

"Yes, but Roberto was too smart to let that happen easily. They would've had difficulty getting to him without help, likely from someone he did business with."

"Do you have any suspects in mind?"

"I have a few theories."

"Well, thanks for the advice. I'm happy to take it."

Rita gave Hound a ride to the municipal airport.

"I'll look forward to seeing you again as soon as possible," she said as he got out of the car.

"Me too. You need to visit me in New Orleans and inspect operations when I get everything squared away."

"That's already my plan. I want to visit your nightclub as well. Are you planning to keep or sell it now that you've embarked on a new career?"

"I hope to keep it, maybe build more like it someday."

13

Hound arrived in Phoenix at 2 a.m. the next morning. He took a taxi to his desert estate. The security guard on duty at the front gate was surprised to see him. He was expected to be away for an indefinite period.

He was happy to see his home again. After taking a long shower, he went to bed. He was up at 11 a.m., completed his workout, took another shower, dressed, and then drove to the nice café a few miles away to have a late lunch. After finishing his meal, he used a pay phone to call Bear at the biker club.

"God damn, Hound!" Bear said with enthusiasm. "It's good to hear your voice again. Shit! When you didn't call back to see how your proposal was received, we thought you might've fallen into some deep shit, maybe you were dead."

"I thought for a time that might happen, but here I am, still standing. How was my proposal received?"

"We shouldn't talk on the phone. Can you come to the club-house? I'm the only one here, but I've got some information."

"I'm on my way."

When Hound arrived, Bear greeted him with a handshake and hug. They got a beer from the bar and sat at a table to begin their discussion.

"All the chapter presidents are interested but want a meeting with you to get particular things explained," said Bear. "Remember, we've all been doing business with Roberto's cartel. Nobody wants to piss off the cartel by receiving a big ass shipment of maverick merchandise. They sure as hell don't want shit of less quality being sold by buyers doing business with the cartel and thinking it was provided by the cartel."

"That won't be a problem, Bear. I'm the cartel's new sales representative. The deal I proposed involved cartel product, the same shit, same quality as always."

"You've got to be fucking with me! Are you for real taking over for Roberto?"

"Well, I hadn't looked at it in that way, but yes, I suppose I am."

"Well, I'll be damned! How in the fucking hell did you pull that off?"

"It's a long story, one you probably won't believe."

"You're likely right, but I damn well want to hear it."

"Bear, I'm on a tight time frame to make this deal with all the club chapters. If they don't want the deal, I need to find other buyers to take $1,250,000,000 street value worth of cartel product off my hands, and I'll need to do it fast."

"Do you need to sell all of it at one time to one buyer, or can you sell smaller loads to several different buyers?"

"Several would take too long. I've got to move the shit pronto to make ready for more to be delivered. Can you get the presidents from all the chapters at your club by early evening tomorrow to hear the sweet deal of a lifetime?"

"You bet your ass I can."

"Buddy, I've already bet my ass on getting all the chapters to accept my deal."

"Well, then we'll just have to make it happen, won't we?"

"Yep!"

"Does Maggie know you're here?"

"No, and I don't want her to know. I don't have the time or patience to deal with her right now."

"Hound, she pulls a lot of weight with all the chapters. We all value her advice. Besides, she might be able to help in other ways."

"I can't risk her knowing I'm doing business with the cartel. She's already too damn possessive. I don't want her to know I'm up to my ass in criminal activity. That information would give her too damn much power over me. She's going to be hurt and pissed off when I break off our relationship. She could seek revenge by telling what she knows about me."

"Hound, you didn't hear this from me, but Maggie is up to her ass in criminal shit too. She just didn't want you to find out. Knowing she was the attorney of record for major criminals was enough."

"What is she involved in?"

"The sale of drugs and weapons, prostitution, money laundering, murder for hire, just for starters."

"Son of a bitch, Bear! Currently I'm involved with women that are absolutely lethal. I'm married to the daughter of an Irish Mafia boss, fucking Maggie who has fallen for me, and now I'm in business with Roberto's sister, who is the new boss of the Sanchez cartel."

"His sister! Well, I'll be damned! A woman in charge of the cartel. What does she look like? How old is she?"

"She's 26 and drop dead beautiful."

"That's very young to have such power and responsibility. Is she capable?"

"You bet. More than capable."

"I suppose you're fucking her too."

"Hell no, but I'm afraid she'll want that in the future. She's already offered. But I managed to avoid it. She said I'd never get another offer, but I don't believe her. If I sleep with her, it will be another nail in my coffin."

"Yep! You live a charmed life."

"How do you think Maggie might help me?"

"Hound, she's well connected with the right people. She's trusted by the good and the bad. I'm talking about big shots on both sides of the tracks. Local and federal law enforcement, judges, politicians, bankers, investors, and of course, among the best of the worst criminals."

"I understand, but how will she feel about me knowing all of that?"

"Don't end your relationship, allow her to make money, and she'll be fine."

Bear had no sooner completed his sentence, than Maggie walked in. Seeing Hound, she rushed to kiss and embrace him. Bear excused himself and started calling all the chapter presidents. Maggie got a beer from the bar and another for Hound. She sat down at the table with him to find out what had been going on in his life since she last saw him. She wasted no time in asking if everything was still OK between them. He smiled and assured her all was fine.

"Shit, I'm happy to hear that!" she said. "Things got crazy between us before you went to Louisiana. I was out of line. I'm sorry. I'll try to remain less childish and more like a mature adult in the future."

"Maggie, that's greatly appreciated. I'll try to do likewise."

"I hope you enjoyed the time with your family. Was everyone well?"

"Everyone was fine. Unfortunately, I saw Jo only briefly and my parents not at all. I took a necessary trip out of the country."

"What? Where did you go? Why?"

"Maggie, I'll explain as soon as Bear is free to join us. We have some important matters to discuss."

"Hound, I've never seen you look so serious. What sort of matters?"

"Let's talk about something else until Bear can participate."

"OK, babe. Whatever you say."

They focused their conversation on casual topics for a little over an hour and then Bear completed his last phone call. He pulled his third beer from the bar's beverage cooler and rejoined them at the table. He said the presidents of all existing chapters would attend the requested meeting at the Phoenix chapter headquarters the following night. To allow for all to arrive on time, the meeting was set to begin at 8 p.m. Before the situation was discussed with Maggie, Bear confessed to telling Hound why she should be informed of the dire situation, and why it was safe to do so.

"Bear, Hound must be in deep shit for you to break your word and tell him things about me I didn't want him to know," Maggie said in a surprisingly calm voice.

"Really deep. It's OK that he knows you're a fucking criminal. He's one too now, a genuine member of our family."

"OK. Now, tell me what the fuck is going on!"

Hound spent the next hour telling Bear and Maggie the particulars about his visit with Rita in Bogota. If anyone other than Hound was telling the story, it would've been considered unbelievable. He carefully explained the deal he planned to propose to all chapter presidents.

"Hound, that's a fucking mountain of product to sell, even if the chapters have a reasonable amount of time," said Bear. "By the way, what is that amount of time?"

"No specific time was agreed upon, but as quickly as possible."

"Hell yes, they will! What happens when that time arrives, and all the product isn't sold and we can't make full payment to the cartel?"

"I made the deal with the cartel. I'll suffer whatever the boss deems appropriate."

"What will the chapters suffer?"

"Perhaps a time extension, nothing unless a new deal is made and the chapters default. Naturally, the product will have to be returned if no deal is agreeable."

"What is likely the best that will happen to you for not pulling off what you agreed to do?"

"The best is a time extension."

"What's the worst?"

"Bear, it's the fucking cartel! What do you think is the worst?"

"Hound, why did you let yourself get pulled into this mess, this kind of life?" asked Maggie. "You never wanted any of the shit that's being heaped on you. I know you didn't."

"Maggie's right, Hound," added Bear. "Why did you allow it to happen? You're too damn smart for it to have been unavoidable."

"You're both right. I wanted to pursue a much different path, but I suppose I began this path many years ago. I should've made a different choice at the swimming hole on my family farm when I was only 12. You have no idea how much regret I've had over the years for making that choice. It started a chain reaction of events that's made it impossible for me to find and travel a much different path to achieve a much different destiny."

"Hound, what happened at the swimming hole?" asked Maggie.

"That's a story for another time — a time that will never come."

For a short time, no one spoke. Hound stared at the bottle of beer he was holding while Bear and Maggie starred at him.

"Hound, don't sweat the time limit," Maggie said, choosing to be the first to speak. "I've got contacts who can help if they're needed. Everything is going to work out."

"Thanks, Maggie."

Bill and Pony arrived and were given an update. They were doubtful the chapters would vote unanimously in favor of accepting Hound's proposal. However, Bill confirmed his vote would be yes. The conversation was changed to casual, like only the best of friends would share.

When their time together ended late in the afternoon, Maggie walked outside with Hound.

"Can I take you out for dinner?" she asked.

"Only if you'll come home with me after."

"All you have to do is ask. That's all you ever have to do. Why don't we stay at my home tonight? I'll fix you a special breakfast in the morning."

"Sounds good. Maggie, if you don't mind, I need to visit my nightclub and touch base with Candy. I'm sure everything is running smoothly, but I want to make a quick inspection of things. I'll meet you at your home around 8 p.m. Besides, I need to drop by my home and freshen up."

"Fine. That will give me time to finish up some paperwork for tomorrow. You're right about things running smoothly while you've been away; Bear made sure of it."

Hound drove home, took a shower and dressed for his dinner date with Maggie. He arrived at his nightclub a little after 6 p.m. It was ladies' night. All drinks served to them during happy hour were half price. He asked one of the bartenders where he could find Candy and was told she was in her office. When he entered her office, Candy presented a large smile, followed by a welcome hug.

"Hound, it's great to see you. I didn't expect you to return so soon. Is everything OK?"

"Sure, Candy. All is good. I had some spare time and decided to surprise you with a visit. How are things?"

"The club is doing extremely well. Profits have never been higher, and they continue to get better. Do you want to take a look at the books?"

"Hell no. I trust you to run the club as if it were yours. Are all the employees happy with work?"

"Absolutely. They're all making a lot of money. Hound, thank you for saying you trust me. It means a lot to me. I'll always be trustworthy and loyal."

"I know. How are things going for you away from the club?"

"Fine. Hound, can I talk to you about what happened between us in your office?"

"Sure."

"Don't take this the wrong way. You know I wanted it to happen, but it can't happen again. I enjoyed it more than you know. So much, it would confuse the feelings I have for my husband should we continue. I don't want my marriage to end because I fell in love with a man I could never have. Such feelings would affect my work performance. I certainly don't want that. I like my job very much and don't want to lose it. Do you understand?"

"Candy, I understand perfectly and agree completely. Let's put what happened behind us and move on."

"I hope I can. You're like heroin — very addictive."

"I could say the same about you, but one fix hasn't addicted either of us."

Hound pulled every employee aside one at a time for a short visit to say thanks for their good work and ask if they were still happy with the job. He told Candy he might not see her again before returning to Louisiana, but to keep him informed of anything out of the ordinary. He left the club at 7:15 and arrived at Maggie's home a minute before 8. They went to dinner at a restaurant they favored and talked for more than an hour after their meal was over.

"Hound, how long will you be in town this trip?" asked Maggie.

"I'll be here for the meeting with the chapter presidents tomorrow night, and then fly back to New Orleans the next morning."

"This new business with the cartel is going to keep you busy and hopping for a time, isn't it?"

"Yes, I suppose so."

"What does Jo think about it?"

"She doesn't know everything yet. She's going to raise hell when she finds out."

"How does Ken feel about it?"

"He doesn't know everything either. He and Jo will raise hell together."

"Do you give a damn what either of them think or do at this point?"

"I can't afford to. Certain things are only up to me. They'll have no choice but to support me. If they wish to separate from the business I have with the cartel, then they'll have to separate from me."

"Maybe Ken would separate, but Jo will stand by you."

"I'm not sure of that. Ken has a great influence over her. She seems to always do as he says when he demands it of her."

"If she won't back you, then you don't need her, she wouldn't love you enough. She may love you a lot, but certainly not enough."

"I know that, Maggie. Well, what do you want to do with the rest of our night out?"

"How do you feel about us calling it a night and going to my home? I'd really like to have you in my bed soon and for as long as possible."

"Maggie, that's exactly what I need."

Hound hadn't yet made his required daily phone call to Jo. He excused himself from Maggie and walked to a pay phone a short distance from where they'd parked. Maggie waited in the car while he made the call.

"Hound, are you coming home tomorrow?" asked Jo. "Have you completed your business in Phoenix?"

"No, but I should be finished and be leaving the day after tomorrow."

As expected, Ken was on a separate line and interrupted the conversation.

"Hound, I want you back here tomorrow. I've booked you on a direct flight leaving Phoenix at 7 a.m. Make damn sure you're on it. I need to hear everything that's going on, and I'm not waiting any longer. I'm the God-damned boss! It's high fucking time you remember that. Understand, you arrogant bastard?"

Hound felt his anger rising. He was reminded how much he had come to despise Ken O'Malley.

"Ken, I explained how important my business here is. I can't leave until it's concluded. There are two things I need you to do."

"Hound! Are you about to issue orders to me?"

"No, more like sincere requests, if you don't mind."

"Ask whatever you want but be on that flight in the morning! What are your requests?"

"Don't ever again interrupt a call I make to Jo, and never again call me a bastard, you lowlife cock-sucking bully!"

Hound ended the phone call as Jo spoke to calm the tension and Ken exploded into a tantrum of screaming and cursing.

"Dad, calm down," said Jo. "Hound hung up; he can't hear you."

"That son of a bitch you're married to is going to respect me and who I am! He called me a lowlife cocksucker! You heard him! How dare he talk to me like that in the presence of my daughter! How dare he ever talk to me like that!"

"Dad, you and Hound are both under a lot of stress. Neither of you meant the terrible things said. I certainly hope he didn't."

"What are you alluding to?"

"Dad, he called you a bully. I certainly don't want him thinking of you that way."

Ken immediately realized what Jo meant. For an instant he felt the hair on the back of his neck begin to rise. Then he considered his concern to be unrealistic. Hound was fearless and dangerous, but not stupid. He would never seek revenge that could not be carried out, knowing his life would be the price for trying.

"Jo, I think Hound and I owe each other an apology. We need to put things right between us."

"Dad, I'm sure Hound feels the same way. I'll make sure that happens as soon as he returns."

"I'll be the first to apologize when he gets here tomorrow."

"Dad, you know he won't be on that flight in the morning. He'll stay until he finishes what he started. For such a long time, you did all you could to convince him to become your protégé, your successor in the family business. Well, now you have what you wanted. He knows what he's doing; relax and let him do it."

"Jo, you're right. I just resent being disrespected and sharing my authority. It will take getting used to, but it's necessary."

"I believe we'll always be proud of everything Hound does for the family business."

"I believe that too."

Maggie had no idea of the content or tone of Hound's phone call to Jo. He returned to the car in a good mood. His performance in bed that night also showed no evidence his mind was on anything but pleasing her.

The next morning, Hound enjoyed the special breakfast promised him before he left to drive home. He told Maggie he'd see her at the biker club for the meeting that night and gave her a kiss as she continued to dress for work. She was due in court at 10 a.m. to represent one of the local chapter members who'd been arrested and charged with statutory rape. The biker was 40; the girl was 15. At his arraignment, the biker told the judge the girl may have been 15, but said she was 21 and fucked like a horny housewife of 35. The judge denied bail.

Hound stayed at his estate all day, preparing as best he could for the meeting that night. He waited until late afternoon, and then placed a call to Carmella. He knew the approximate time she'd arrive home from Berkeley. He felt certain she was waiting on pins and needles to know if his meeting with Rita had gone well and that he was safe — that they were both safe. When she answered her phone and heard his voice, she began to cry.

"Hound, my darling gringo boy!" she said as she began to control the tears of joy. "I'm so happy you're OK! You are, aren't you?"

"Yes, thanks to you covering my ass with Rita."

"I tried to do my best for you. What happened? Tell me everything."

"I'll tell you everything the next time we meet. I don't have much time, so let's talk about more pleasant things."

"I at least want to know if Rita said anything that made you think we had anything to worry."

"I think we'll be fine, but always remember what you told her and what you tell in the future. She's smart and is good at setting traps. She did say you'd be allowed to keep your estate. She also wants you to finish college and have a better future."

"Did you believe her?"

"Yes. Rita said she was very fond of you and wanted you to be happy."

"Do you think I'll hear from her again?"

"Probably, but that's likely not a bad thing. Act as you always have and be careful of those traps."

"I can handle myself around her. What did you think of her?"

"Rita was everything you said she'd be."

"Did she want to sleep with you?"

Hound knew the question would come sometime during their conversation.

"No, Rita was all about business," Hound said, grinning but sounding sincere.

"When will we see each other again? I hope it will be soon. I need to be with you on a regular basis. You promised that was going to happen."

"Carmella, it will start as soon as I get my business with Rita running smoothly. That shouldn't take more than a month. It will be much less if a meeting I'm attending tonight goes well."

Hound spent an hour on the phone with Carmella. It was after 6 p.m. when their conversation ended. He went to his nightclub at 6:30 to visit for a few minutes with Candy. They drank a cup of coffee in his office and discussed casual topics.

"Candy, I'll be returning to New Orleans in the morning," he told her. "Keep the club running smoothly. Call me if any problems arise, and I'll see you when I return."

"Do you know when that will be?"

"I never know. I'm busier than a piss ant in a forest fire lately. I hope to complete the extra work dumped on me soon so I can establish a regular schedule to be in Phoenix."

"It would be nice to see you more often. We all miss not having you around."

Hound arrived at the biker headquarters at 7:45. He assumed at least some of the chapter presidents had already arrived. Several Harleys with out-of-state tags were in a line on the parking lot. He parked his Corvette in the usual spot and entered the clubhouse.

Tables had been moved together in a line to accommodate all who would attend the meeting. At one end of the line sat Bill. To his right was Bear, and to his left sat Pony. Next to him was Maggie. A seat for Hound was reserved next to Bear. At the other end of the table sat the president of the Los Angeles chapter, which was the largest. Twenty other presidents were present. Ten were seated on each side of the table. All were drinking nonalcoholic beverages until the business meeting concluded. The clubhouse had been made secure to insure privacy.

"Brothers, the man you have all come to meet with has arrived," Bill announced as Hound walked to join the group. "He is righteous and can be trusted in all things discussed and decided tonight. Hound, all the presidents are here and eager to hear your proposal."

Bill introduced Hound to each president who stood to greet him with a smile, handshake and thanks for the invitation to meet. After introductions were completed, Bill told Hound the floor was his to present his business proposition. Hound extended his gratitude for the opportunity and began. Everyone except Maggie put on a business face to hear what Hound would say. She too was interested but presented a soft smile to support and encourage his effort.

"Gentlemen, and ladies," Hound began as he looked at Maggie and returned her smile, "I'm here tonight to present a deal on behalf of the Sanchez Cartel. I know the cartel is a major wholesale supplier of the drugs and weapons to all the chapters. Roberto Sanchez is missing and is presumed dead. He has been replaced by his sister who has convinced me to act on her behalf to expand the market area of cartel merchandise. I feel your club can assist me as I begin that task and add tremendously to your profits as a result. I currently find myself with a surplus of product that has to be sold as quickly as possible to insure a continued, uninterrupted sequence of product manufacturing and distribution. I want to divide the surplus among all your chapters to be sold in no more than sixty days. You won't pay for the product upon receipt, but in full when the sixty days is up. You will pay the same for all products as before. The fly in the ointment is the merchandise I'm asking you to sell has a street value of one billion, two hundred and fifty million dollars. If you accept, five hundred million dollars will be in your hands within a week, and the remaining seven hundred and fifty million dollars within two weeks. That's when the sixty days will begin."

Hound declared the proposal completed and asked for discussion and questions. The president of the Los Angeles chapter was the first to speak.

"Hound, first I would like to know how you got your nickname," he said.

"I got the name when I was four years old as result of a special friendship I developed with a purebred Bloodhound."

"I'd bet the story of that friendship would be worth hearing sometime."

"Maybe. I'd be happy to tell it sometime."

"Hound, what you're proposing would be a sweet deal if it wasn't for the time limit of sixty days. One billion, two hundred and fifty million dollars is a super shitload of product to sell in that length of time. Even with all the luck possible it would be hard to do. I'm sorry, but I have to decline your offer. I think my brother presidents will agree and vote the same. The last thing the chapters need is a war with the cartel because we couldn't deliver payment on time. Besides, trying to move that much product in that short period of time would increase the risk of getting all our asses busted by local or federal law enforcement."

All the other presidents voted the same way. It was then Maggie stood to voice her opinion.

"I've known all you hairy legged bad boys for a long time," she began. "In all that time, none of you has ever showed an absence of balls when it came to taking big risks to make big money. Hound is offering you a chance to collectively earn a half billion dollars in two months! God damn! How long would it take you to make that if you pass on his offer? If you don't want it, then I'll take it."

Maggie's declaration got everyone's full attention. Hound looked at her and was convinced she was serious. She seemed almost glad his offer had been rejected.

"Maggie, how in the fuck can you move that much product in two months?" asked Bill. "You're into a lot of shady shit, but not this kind of shit. I want to help Hound out, damn we all do, but the risks are too great. Hound would be the first to understand our position. We are obligated to grow the club, expand, create new chapters in other states, and increase our membership, not destroy what has already been built."

"Bill, wouldn't a half billion greatly speed up that expansion? Wouldn't the addition of risk be worth it? I have the contacts to make what Hound wants happen. I won't steal the deal if you want it, but if you're sure you don't, then I sure as hell do. I'll personally make a quarter billion off it."

"Maggie, if we take the deal and get in trouble, will you use your contacts to help us out?" asked the L.A. president.

"Only if you guarantee me a percentage of your profit if you don't get into trouble."

"How much percentage?"

Maggie paused briefly and then turned her attention to Hound.

"Hound, what is the amount you'll receive from the cartel on the deal?" she asked.

"Ten percent of their profit."

"Wow, let's see. Fuck, that's seventy-five million! Shit, I won't be greedy. I'll settle for five percent, twenty-five million."

The presidents objected to the amount, but Maggie remained firm on the amount. She reminded them of the four hundred and seventy five million dollars they would still earn. Hound's proposal was put to a second vote and unanimously accepted. The presidents felt it would be in their best interest to also accept Maggie's.

The meeting ended at 9:30. Everyone was served their beverage of choice from the bar. Hound and Maggie took their favorite beer and bumped the bottles as a toast to a successful meeting. He asked her to step outside for a time of private conversation. They leaned against the side of his Corvette and each took a sip of beer.

"Thanks, Maggie," he said. "The way you helped me get what I needed in the meeting was brassy and nothing short of the slickest moves to manipulate I've ever seen. Your skills as an attorney and your intelligence served us both extremely well."

"You're welcome, sweetie, but are you implying I intended to help myself as well?"

Maggie began to smile as an indication of agreement to what she knew he was going to say.

"I'm not implying, simply stating a fact," he replied. "You manipulated your way into earning twenty-five million dollars without having to do a damn thing to earn it. I think what you did was fucking brilliant."

"Well, I'll offer my assistance to some degree, so I don't feel completely shameful. However, I'll earn every penny if the chapters can't meet the deadline."

"Were you serious about your ability to do that? Do you actually have the contacts needed to get it done?"

"Hell yes. I would never offer a deal to my outlaw friends I couldn't or didn't plan to honor."

At 10 p.m., Hound and Maggie were back inside the clubhouse drinking and celebrating with those outlaw friends. The supervisor of the security force at Hound's nightclub walked in around 10:15. There was an expression of urgency on his face and in his quick pace.

Bear walked to meet him. Bear asked why he had left his duties at Hound's club to come there. The supervisor said Candy had sent him to see if Hound was there, and if so tell him to call her immediately. There was an extreme emergency. Candy didn't tell the supervisor what it was.

Hound was quickly given the message. He hurried to use the phone in Bill's office. Candy was waiting at the phone in her office when Hound called.

"What's wrong, Candy?" Hound asked. "What's the emergency? Are you and everyone at the club OK?"

"Hound, something terrible has happened in New Orleans. You need to call your wife right away."

"Candy, what has happened?"

"Your father-in-law has been killed. Hound, I'm so sorry!"

Hound paused and took a deep breath.

"Candy, who called you?" he asked. "Was it Jo?"

"No, it was Mike O'Malley. He tried to reach you at home and then here. I told him I might know where you were and would try to get a message to you. He said he was Jo's uncle."

"That's right. He's my father-in-law's brother. Did he say how Jo was doing?"

"He said she wasn't hurt, nothing else."

"Thanks, Candy."

Hound ended the call to Candy and dialed the estate number in New Orleans. The phone rang seven times before it was answered. Hound recognized Mike's voice.

"Hound, thank God we were able to reach you! Ken has been killed!"

"Damn it, Mike! What happened?"

"Ken, Sandra, Jo and I went to dinner at one of Ken's restaurants. After dinner, we were walking to our car parked on the street in front. As we reached the car, another pulled beside us on the driver's side. At least three gunmen opened fire with automatic weapons on Ken as he was preparing to get into the driver's seat. My brother died instantly. Jesus Christ, Hound! He was hit thirty-seven times, massacred on the street!"

"Thank God Jo and the rest of you are OK."

"Those murdering mother fuckers were professionals. They made sure Ken was the only victim."

"Where were the bodyguards? Ken never goes anywhere without at least two."

"They'd already gotten in their car parked behind ours. They fired on the rear of the killer's car as it sped away. There was little else they could do. Hound, we've got to get those cocksuckers! I want them to die a slow, agonizing death!"

"They will, but we've got to find out who they are first. I want the one who sent them too. Where's Jo? I was sure she'd be on the phone with you."

"She and her mother are heavily sedated and in bed asleep. How soon can you get here? Jo asked me to tell you, please hurry."

"I'm booked on a direct flight leaving at 7 a.m. tomorrow. No flights leave sooner that could get me there faster. I arrive at 11. Can someone pick me up?"

"Yes, I'll be there."

"OK, thanks. Mike, I'm very sorry for your loss. I know how close you and Ken were."

"Hound, he thought the world of you too. The last time I spoke with him, he told me how happy he was that you'd agreed to be his protégé and run the family business when the time arrived."

"I was excited about it as well, but I suppose that will change now."

"Not likely. Ken's successor will be chosen by Jo and her mother, mostly by Jo. Unless she wants the job, she'll pass it to you."

"I haven't been properly trained for the job."

"Jo and Ken once told me you could do the job with no training. All you needed to know was what the operations were and the names and positions of all family contacts."

"Mike, there are other things to focus on right now. Ken's successor is a topic to be discussed later."

"Of course, but the future of the family business is important to all the family."

"Mike, try and get some sleep. I'll see you tomorrow. Take care of Jo for me."

"Hound, you know I will."

Hound left Bill's office and returned to rejoin the celebration. The party had been opened to any club member who wanted to participate. The clubhouse was filled with bikers, their wives and mamas. Naturally, club groupies and prostitutes continued to arrive. Hound walked to where Maggie, Bear, Bill and Pony were gathered together waiting to hear what the emergency was. He told them.

"Fuck!" said Bear. "That's shitty news! Are you OK?"

"I'm fine, but Jo, her mother and uncle are emotionally fucked up."

"You didn't really like Ken, did you?"

"Not much. He was a piece of shit."

"What do you do now?"

"I'll go back to New Orleans tomorrow, console Jo and her family, attend the funeral of an Irish Mafia boss, and then I'll assume his position."

"Is this shit going to change the plan we agreed on to start moving the cartel merchandise?"

"No."

When Hound left, Maggie walked him out.

"Do you mind my company tonight?" she asked.

"Maggie, I always welcome your company, but not tonight. I'll see you when I get back."

"Do you know when you'll be back?"

"As soon as possible, but I'm not sure when."

"Keep in touch. You need to know how things are going with the cartel's products."

"I know, I will."

During his drive home, Hound thought of the tasks he needed to complete quickly as soon as he was back in New Orleans. Arrangements to transport the cartel merchandise in the warehouse to the Phoenix chapter would have to be made as soon as he arrived. There was no time to waste. He had agreed to transport the product to Phoenix where it would be stored in a secure location. The other chapters would be responsible for the pickup and transport of their delegated amount of each product.

This amount was based upon the size of the market in the area controlled by each chapter. When the second shipment arrived from Colombia, it would be transported to the chapter president in L.A. When that was completed, all future shipments would be picked up on the docks in New Orleans and transported by the individual buyers who had placed orders for specific types and amounts of product in advance.

If he took over leadership of the family business, he wouldn't include his arrangement with Rita as part of it. He planned to keep those profits for himself. If he didn't replace Ken, his arrangement with Rita would be maintained. He was certain it was Rita who ordered Ken's assassination. She finalized the details during the meeting she had in Florida. That was the business she had to take care of personally in Miami. She insisted he spend the time in Phoenix to keep him out of possible harm's way when the hit took place and provide an alibi should he need one. His plan to manipulate Rita into killing Ken and keeping Jo and her mother safe in the process had been completed. No longer would he have to concern himself with Ken O'Malley.

After Hound left the biker club, Maggie, Bear and Pony went with Bill to his office. They needed a break from the party that had become rowdy, and to have a private visit concerning Hound.

"I hope accepting Hound's proposal was the right thing to do," said Bill. "We're going to be in deep shit with the cartel if we can't meet the deadline."

"Stop worrying," replied Maggie. "You've got me to help out if things get hairy."

"Maggie, even with your help, things could go wrong. You know that."

"Bill, if the chapters do their best, all will be fine. Besides, I'd bet Hound has a backup plan to handle any problem except the product being stolen from us, and none of the chapters will let that happen."

"You really believe that, don't you?"

"Damn right I do! We all know he's far from ordinary, that he's a very special man, unique to say the least. We've known that for a long time."

"He sure as hell has proven it to me," said Bear. "Just think, he won't be 23 until next July, but has a graduate degree, attended OCS on the recommendation of his commanding officer in boot camp, received two battlefield commissions in Vietnam, was made commanding officer of a major base camp, and was recommended for the Congressional Medal of Honor. He built an estate and nightclub, has a major cartel and the most notorious biker club in the country as allies and is about to become a boss in the Irish Mafia."

"You make a good point," said Bill. "Fuck! Hound may be the antichrist!"

Maggie, Bear and Pony laughed at Bill's remark, and so did Bill.

"He's not," said Maggie. "Just a very special, unique man."

Hound was passing his nightclub on the way home. The parking lot was full to capacity. Many customers had to park on the shoulder of the highway in front of the club. He decided to stop and pay Candy another visit. His private parking place at the rear was the only one vacant. He found Candy doing paperwork in her office.

"Candy, sometimes you work too damn hard," he said as he entered.

"Hound, what are you doing here? I was sure you'd be on your way to New Orleans by now. I guess there were no flights."

"You're right. I can't leave until tomorrow morning."

"Hound, are you OK? The death of your father-in-law must hurt a lot."

"I'm fine. Candy, do you like your life?"

"Yes, I think so."

"What do you like best?"

"Well, my job. I really enjoy managing your club."

"Do you like your husband?"

"Of course."

"Why didn't you say you liked him best instead of your job?"

"I love him. You asked what I liked best."

"Don't you like him?"

"Sure, but loving and liking are not the same."

"Don't you have to like a person before you can love them?"

"Maybe, I suppose so. Hound, are you sure you're feeling OK?"

"Absolutely, never better. Have you been unfaithful to your husband with anyone except me?"

"What's going on? Why would you ask me that?"

"I would like to know."

"No, only you."

"Why?"

"I was tremendously attracted to you. I can't imagine a woman who wouldn't be. You're the smartest, most charismatic and physically perfect man I've ever seen."

"Would you have sex with me again if I wanted you to?"

Candy hesitated to answer. She was confused and surprised Hound was there and asking such questions with the current situation in his life being what it was. She decided to answer with the complete truth.

"Hound, I would," she said, "but I hope you won't ask."

"Fair enough."

"You weren't going to ask, were you?"

"No, but not because I don't want to."

"Why then?"

"Because you don't want me to."

"Hound, what has this really been about?"

"I suppose I wanted a normal, smart, beautiful and decent woman's honest opinion of me."

"Well, you should be pleased with mine. Thanks for the compliments."

"I am pleased, but the things you said were the least important to me. Perhaps you see me lacking in the things that are."

"What I said about you are things any man would long for, give almost anything to have. They are blessings. What else would you have liked me to include?"

"Character. The others are a double-edged sword. Perhaps a blessing, if used properly, but a curse if not."

"Hound, because I didn't include character doesn't imply yours is bad. Do you think it is?"

"I've enjoyed our chat, Candy. I'll see you when I return. Take care of my club."

He gave her a soft kiss on the cheek and left. She sat at her desk for a time pondering what might have been going on in his mind during their conversation. She silently wished him well with what was waiting in New Orleans and then returned to work.

14

Hound arrived on time in New Orleans the next day. He was surprised to see Jo waiting with Mike to greet him. Jo began to sob as she embraced him tightly. He continued to hold her as he shook Mike's hand and offered condolence to both of them.

They left the terminal and walked to where the car was parked. He kept his arm around Jo as she continued to suffer episodes of intense sobbing. They were halfway to the estate before she was able to stop crying and talk.

"Jo, you should have stayed at home. You need to rest as much as possible. I didn't expect you to meet me."

"I didn't want to spend any more time away from you. I needed to be there."

Jo began to offer a detailed account of what happened to Ken, but Hound stopped her.

"Sweetheart, we can talk about that later," he told her. "For now, try to relax. I don't want you to become physically ill."

"You mean mentally ill, don't you?"

"Honey, I don't want you to suffer either."

"Hound, it's good you're back. Things regarding the business are in chaos. The vultures are already starting to land. The family needs someone to replace my brother quickly who can calm and stabilize a lot of shit before it gets to deep."

Jo began to sob again.

"Hound, Jo and her mother have agreed you will take over as head of all family business," said Mike.

"Mike, we'll discuss everything soon, but not now."

When he arrived at the estate, Hound saw more than a dozen cars parked in a line along the driveway near the house. He recognized the only pickup truck as his father's.

"Jo, are my parents here?" he asked.

"Yes. They arrived a few minutes before we left to pick you up. I called them this morning to confirm what time you'd get here. They didn't come to the airport because of my mother. She wasn't doing well and wanted your mom to stay with her."

"How did they find out about Ken?"

"Television. It's been the news on every channel since it happened. They called as soon as they heard."

"Who do the other cars belong to? I suppose there's been a constant line of sympathizers. I was expecting that."

"That's true, but all the visitors here now have paid their respects and are waiting to see you."

"Who are they?"

"Irish bosses from major cities all over the country."

"Why do they want to see me?"

"I told them you were the new boss in New Orleans."

"Shit, Jo! Why would you tell them that before talking to me about it first?"

"There was no time. I had to tell them dad had chosen you to take over should it become necessary, or they would have decided who would replace him. They think you've been working as dad's protégé since you were discharged from the Army."

"Your dad was killed last night. How did they hear about it and get here so quickly?"

"They were already here. Dad was hosting a very important meeting with them day after tomorrow."

"What was the meeting about?"

"Dad felt I didn't need to know, so he didn't tell me, but he planned on you being there. That's why he was adamant about you getting home on time. Don't you know what it's about?"

"No, but I'm damn sure to find out."

Hound was introduced to all the bosses. He greeted his parents and then met privately with the bosses in the den. Ken had set the formal meeting to be held at 9 a.m. on February 12 in his finest dinner club. Breakfast was to be served. Hound declared the meeting would be held on schedule, one day before Ken's funeral.

He was able to glean during the discussion that Ken was going to present a deal to them that involved the sale of quality drugs and weapons. None of the bosses suspected this was the first Hound had heard of the meeting, or its purpose. They were in the den about a half hour. The bosses departed the estate when the meeting concluded. Hound began visiting with family members. His parents kept their suspicions to themselves regarding the character and employment of the twelve visitors.

It was now 1 p.m. The cook had prepared a late lunch for the family. Hound, his parents, Jo, her mother and uncle sat at the dining table and ate as they discussed the recent tragedy. Jo's sobbing as a symptom of grief was now intense anger indicative of her desire to seek the ultimate revenge on all who were responsible for the brutal and cowardly assassination of her father. Hound knew she was about to say things in front of his parents he didn't want them to hear. He asked her to accompany him to the den to calm herself and express what she was thinking to him in private.

"Jo, you can express all things you want regarding what happened to your dad, or other things pertaining to family business, to me and your family, but never to mine. I will never allow them to know anything certain about the O'Malley family business."

"I knew better; I wasn't thinking. I'm sorry. It won't happen again."

"Good. Loose lips sink ships. I will never allow my ship to be sunk."

"I want to find out who was involved in murdering my father. I want the person or persons that ordered it and those who carried it out to suffer before they're killed."

"I know. But first we have to find out who they are. Do you suspect anyone?"

"I know key people dad did business with, but he kept me in the dark about those I didn't need to know. Where will you look first as you begin your search to find those responsible?"

"At those who had the most to gain from your dad's death. I know that likely includes a lot of folks. I hope you realize that what you want and need to be done is going to take time to complete."

"I know. Hound, I'm happy and very proud of you for accepting leadership of the family business. I know Dad would feel the same."

"Jo, I don't have a choice now, do I?"

"When you accepted Dad's career offer, I thought you had made your choice."

"Jo, you know damn well when Ken made up his mind to have me as his protégé, I never had a choice. It was only a matter of time until he got what he wanted."

"God damn it, Hound! Dad's no longer an obstacle keeping you from free choices! You can do as you fucking please!"

"Calm down. If you ask me to take over for your dad, then I will, and do the best job I can."

"Why would you choose to do it for me and not for him if you feel so strongly opposed to it?"

"Because you asked out of need instead of demanding from a throne of power. Besides, I know how important keeping control of the business is to you. It's a family thing and you desire it for your father."

"Are you saying you can't refuse me because you love me and want my happiness?"

"Yes, and because you never refused to help me in my times of need. Over the years you were always there for me. Now, I'll be there for you, but you and your mother have to agree to conditions."

"What?"

"Never ask about things pertaining to business you don't need to know, and never object to or question any decision I make. Do you agree? If not, then I'll not take on the risk and responsibility."

"Speaking for myself and mom, we accept your conditions."

"Fair enough. Now, let's get back to being with family members. We need to spend time with my parents. I need to start making up for the way I've been neglecting them over the past few months. Later, I'll need to spend some private time with Uncle Mike to discuss important business."

"What business?"

Hound gave her a look she understood.

"Sorry," she said. "I don't need to know."

Jo spoke with her mother and Uncle Mike away from Hound and his parents. She felt obligated to seek final approval to turn over leadership of the family business to him. Mike had always known his forte was managing the trucking company division of the business. He had neither ability nor desire to be in charge of everything. However, he was tough, dependable, and had always been loyal to Ken, ready to do whatever was required of him by his only brother and sibling. He pledged the same to Hound.

While Jo was meeting with her mom and uncle, Hound escorted his parents and returned to the den to have his own private meeting. John and Linda welcomed the opportunity to visit with their son alone.

"Good Lord, Hound," said John. "What happened to Ken was an evil thing."

"Yes, Dad, it was."

"Does anyone have any idea who's responsible?"

"Nobody."

"Son, are you and the rest of Jo's family in any kind of danger?" asked Linda, joining the conversation.

"Of course not. Why would you be concerned about such a thing?"

"Hound, your mother and I have always suspected Ken wasn't a typical businessman who was simply smart, ambitious and lucky enough to earn the fortune his family has acquired," said John. "We thought he was involved in shady, criminal activities. Are we right? If so, you, Jo, her mother and uncle could also be targeted. What if someone has a reason to get rid of the entire O'Malley family?"

"Dad, neither I nor Jo have knowledge that Ken was involved in any nefarious business. Her mother doesn't either. If he was killed for revenge, it was motivated by something other than business."

"Like what?"

"I really have no idea."

"Are you certain you're safe?"

"Absolutely, and so are you and Mom, if you're concerned about that."

"We aren't."

Later, Jo announced that Hound was the new leader of the O'Malley empire. John and Linda presented a look of disapproval but offered him their congratulations. They remained at the estate for dinner.

Shortly after dinner, they began their drive back to the farm. Once again, Hound returned to the den for a private meeting. This time it was Mike who joined him.

"Mike, I need you to use a couple of your trucks and trailers to do me a crucial favor," Hound told him.

"Hound, you can always count on me for help at any time."

"Don't dive in until you know how deep the water is."

"OK. Tell me how deep it is."

"How much do you know about Ken's business associates and dealings?"

"I'm fully aware he was a mob boss, if that's what you're asking? Of course, he also owned legitimate enterprises. The trucking company I manage is one of them."

"Did he ever use that company to transport illegal merchandise?"

"Stolen items were sometimes shipped out of state to buyers."

"What kinds of items?"

"Cars, boats, guns, all kinds of items that he didn't want to fence within the state. Do you need me to ship something for you?"

"Mike, I need to transport a large shipment of mostly drugs, but also some weapons to Phoenix as quickly as possible. In about a week, I'll need an even larger one delivered to L.A."

"How large are the shipments?"

"How big are your largest trailers?"

"As large as legal to use without a permit and escort."

"We'll need at least two for Phoenix and three for L.A."

"I was afraid Ken would start dealing in that shit sooner or later. I need a couple of days to rig the trailers. False floors, walls, things like that."

"We don't have the time. Even if we did, it would require more trailers to move the amount of shit needed if all the space we have is in the walls and floors."

"Exactly how much cargo are we talking about?"

"Five hundred million dollars going to Phoenix and one billion two hundred and fifty million going to L.A. a week later."

"Sweet Jesus! Hound, are you proposing we transport that much illegal shit out in the open? God damn! It would be stacked from floor to ceiling the entire length of trailers!"

"I know, but it will only be that way for the two deliveries.

Chances are better than average there will be no problems."

"Maybe, but If you're wrong, some folks are going to spend a long time in prison."

"Mike, if you think the risk is too great, I understand. I'll find another way."

"Wouldn't that be difficult? Where would you find someone trustworthy at this late date to provide what you need?"

"Impossible."

"That's what I thought. I'll do it if I can convince the only drivers I trust to do the transporting."

"Have they transported illegal cargos in the past?"

"Yes, but they've never been asked to take the level of risk that's involved in this."

"I'll meet them in person and offer one hundred thousand cash to do the job. They need to see who their new boss is anyway. Do you think the money will be worth the risk to them?"

"Knowing them the way I do, I'm sure it will, but Ken never dealt directly with any of my men. It insulated him from legal threats and kept my authority established."

"I understand. Just get it done."

The next evening, trucks left the New Orleans dock en route to Phoenix carrying the warehoused products. Hound notified Rita he was ready to receive the next delivery. She was pleased. The shipment to Phoenix was delivered with no problems encountered.

At 9 a.m. on February 12, Hound sat down at a table with the twelve other bosses to have breakfast and propose the business deal they all came to hear but had no idea what it entailed. All Ken had told them was a lot of money was to be made. Hound didn't know what Ken had in mind to propose, so he would structure his own proposal. As soon as the meal was over, he stood from his chair at the end of the table and began. He saw the undivided attention being given by all his guests. He sensed they expected something very profitable to be presented.

"Gentlemen, allow me to begin by offering my love, respect and gratitude to my father-in-law, mentor and friend, Kenneth O'Malley. Ken was taken from this world in a most horrible way by cowards of the lowest kind. It will be my purpose to administer the proper retribution to all responsible. However, I now wish to act on Ken's behalf and offer all of you the opportunity to share in, and profit from, a recent business alliance I've formed with a major organization out of the United States. I can now acquire a variety of enough quality drugs on a pre-ordered basis to supply any size market you have or wish to expand in your individual territories. A variety of weapons can also be supplied, but on a less frequent basis. I will place all orders to the supplier, receive and store your orders for a reasonable period. You'll be responsible for the pickup and transportation of product after it reaches New Orleans. Payment in cash for all merchandise will be delivered to my representative at the time of pickup. To order, receive and store your merchandise, I'll charge five percent of the street value on all orders. My supplier has agreed to sell exclusively to me at a special price if I can market all that is produced. Should you decline my proposal, I can still market the volume. You're given the first right of refusal out of the respect that is due."

Hound ended his presentation and opened the meeting to questions and discussion.

"I'm sure I speak for all of us," said the boss from New York. "We would need to know who the supplier is before considering your offer."

"I'm sorry, but the supplier wishes to remain anonymous, known only to me. I'm sure you can understand why."

"Bullshit!" added the boss from Chicago. "I'm not buying drugs from a phantom supplier."

"I'm no phantom. For the reasons you're concerned, you can consider me the supplier."

All the bosses demanded to know who the supplier was.

"Gentlemen, my offer was made out respect for you and Ken

O'Malley, who called you here to make some kind of business offer. I have no fucking idea what that was going to be. He didn't get around to telling me. I suppose he planned to let me know at this meeting. I didn't want your trip here to be a waste of time, so I offered you my proposal. I understand if you reject it, but its conditions are firm and not negotiable. Please take time to further discuss it among yourselves after we leave here. Ken's funeral is tomorrow. You can give me your final answer at the conclusion of the service."

"Young man, I don't think you understand the rules of cooperation between the O'Malley and all the other Irish families," said the boss from Boston. "Perhaps I should offer them for your review and careful consideration before you declare anything nonnegotiable."

"Sir, with all due respect, what I proposed has nothing to do with the O'Malley family's Irish Mafia business. The offer comes from me personally. I offer that information for your review and consideration. I understand the muscle you can bring to bear to get what you want, but in a sense of fairness, perhaps I should disclose a very important fact. Within the borders of the U.S., I have the support and loyalty of a very powerful organization who can summon an army of the most capable of soldiers. The phantom supplier is far more superior in that capability. Between the two, I'm never absent unseen protectors. What happened to Ken will never happen to me. However, it will happen to any person or persons who represent a threat to me."

That evening, the bosses all had dinner together. The meeting they had with Hound that morning was discussed in detail.

"I think we should act to get his attention," said the boss from Detroit about Hound. "The arrogant, young son of a bitch needs to know there are consequences for certain behavior."

The boss from New York, who was seventy-five, was the oldest, and last, in the group to respond to the statement of the Detroit boss.

"Fellows, I think we can accept or reject his offer as we judge to be in our best interest. However, I judge it not to be in the best interest of any or all of us to fuck with that young man."

"If you're basing your opinion on the threat he made, then don't," said the boss from Detroit. "It was a bullshit bluff!"

"I've been in this business longer than anyone here. In those fifty years, I've learned to read men pretty damn well. Hound is young, but he doesn't bluff or make idle threats. He states facts. He's likely the most dangerous man I've ever met, and I've met many. I want him as a partner in business, not an enemy. I vote we accept his offer and make a lot of money that we would otherwise lose."

The bosses voted unanimously to accept the offer.

Ken's funeral service was held at the Catholic church attended by the O'Malley family. He was laid to rest in the family tomb at noon on the 13th of February. In addition to family friends and the Irish bosses, all of Ken's nefarious business and political contacts were in attendance. Hound was introduced to all of them during the wake held at the O'Malley estate. He made appointments to meet with the bankers, lawyers, judges, local and state politicians and high positioned individuals in law enforcement.

He spent time individually with two senators and a congressman who all returned to Washington D.C. that evening. They all assisted him in avoiding the court-martial and certain prison sentence for almost beating a superior officer to death while in Vietnam. They knew the officer had been permanently disabled by the beating and medically discharged from the Army. Had they known he was murdered after he returned to the States, they might have suspected Hound. Their suspicion would've been correct.

Hound wanted to spend more time with Jo during the wake, but she understood the importance of why he couldn't. Hound spent the entire next day with Jo and her mother. It was Valentine's Day, but nobody acknowledged it.

He slipped away to the den shortly before dinner to call Rita. She asked him to be in Bogota on the 17th. They would finalize arrangements to send the second shipment of product to New Orleans. Hound was anxious to get the merchandise to L.A. Rita was happy with the progress he had made thus far. Both looked forward to the meeting. He then called Carmella, telling her they would get together after he returned from Bogota.

Over the next two days, Hound noticed a slow but steady decline in Jo's emotional state that he felt wasn't standard for the normal grieving process. He would have to leave her again soon for his meeting in Bogota and was concerned. He hadn't told her his plan to travel the next day. They took a walk on the estate grounds.

"Jo, I know the past few days have been horrible for you," he said. "How do you feel — I mean really feel?"

"How would you feel if your dad had been massacred and you saw it happen?"

"I'd be devastated, but I don't think that begins to describe what you're feeling."

"No, I guess it doesn't. I can't put into words how I feel. Lost, empty, alone, helpless, and God only knows the countless other ways I feel. I can't stop seeing what happened. I don't want to sleep. I always dream about my dad falling to the street, blood spurting from all the areas of his body where the bullets tore into him. My God! Why did it happen? Dad wasn't a perfect man, but he surely didn't deserve that!"

"Jo, what can I do? I hate to see you like this."

"You can find the evil cocksuckers responsible! I want to be the one who kills them slow and painfully!"

"OK, but right now you've got to begin recovering. If not, you won't be in any condition to exact your revenge. Sweetie, the timing sucks, but I've got to attend a meeting out of town for a couple of days. Will you be OK?"

"Fuck! Can't business wait a few days? God damn it! I just

buried my dad! Do you ever stop to think some things are more important than business? I need you here with me for a while!"

"Jo, I'll stay if you want, but Ken started a ball rolling I need to stay in front of or it will roll over all of us."

"Would he want you to go?"

"He'd demand it."

"By all means, then go. I won't ask where you're off to this time. I probably don't need to know, so you won't tell me."

"You're right. I'm sorry."

It was 7 p.m. the next evening when Hound arrived in Bogota. This trip, Rita was with the driver and bodyguards to welcome him at the airport. They rode together in the back seat while the chauffeur drove them to the Sanchez estate. The bodyguards followed close behind in a separate car. She wasted no time in sliding close to him to kiss his cheek.

"Hound, you should give serious thought to buying a private jet," she told him. "You can afford it now. It would certainly make your travel times faster and much more comfortable."

"I'll give it some thought. Do you know where I could get a good deal on one?"

"Hell yes! You know I can hook you up with the right people. Hound, I'm pleased with the progress you said you were making. I felt you would, but the proof is in the pudding, as they say in your part of the world."

"I suppose things are good at this point, but I'll feel better after we get the next shipment safely transported to L.A. I'll feel better when all the product is sold, and you get paid."

"How long did you tell the buyers they had to sell it all?"

"Sixty days after L.A. gets their delivery."

"Damn! Is that a reasonable time? I'd be surprised if that much product can be sold in such a short period."

"I set the time to get the job done as quickly as possible. The folks selling the shit will be relieved to get an extension if one is needed."

"Do they know one will be granted?"

"Shit no! I want them busting their asses to get it done in sixty days. I want things to calm down and business to be less crucial and demanding. More risk is involved when a surplus of merchandise has to be transported and sold."

"Hound, let's focus off business until later. You've been working hard. I appreciate it, but I don't want your visit to be all work. You need to relax and enjoy yourself as well."

When they arrived at the Sanchez estate, Rita's parents, Carlos and Nita, were waiting to greet them. A few relatives and friends had arrived earlier. They were anxious to meet the special guest from the United States. A dinner party had been arranged in honor of Hound's visit. Rita escorted him to his room, where he hurried to shower and dress before going downstairs to meet those who had come to see him.

A few of the elderly guests didn't speak English. They were delighted Hound spoke their language well enough to converse with them. Dinner was elegant and delicious. During the entire meal, Hound divided his time of conversation among all present to answer all their questions about his home and family in Louisiana. When dinner was over and Rita knew he needed a break from the crowd, she excused herself and him to take a walk outside. It was a beautiful night. The temperature was made ideal by a soft constant breeze that was blowing.

He hadn't mentioned the murder of Ken seven days past. He decided it best to say nothing unless the topic of conversation presented the need to. They had just begun to walk and have a casual conversation when Rita presented the topic.

"Hound, how are things at home with Jo and her father?" she calmly asked.

"Things have been sad and in great disruption. Ken was murdered on a street in New Orleans seven nights ago."

Rita was silent for a moment, showing no emotion as she looked into his eyes.

"I suppose Jo is taking the death of her father very hard," she said.

"Yes, extremely hard."

"Will she be OK?"

"I hope so, but it will take her a long time. She was very close to her father."

"And you, how do you feel about it? Are you dealing with unbearable grief?"

"Rita, I'm sorry for Jo, but you know I feel no grief over what happened."

"Yes, I remember you saying there was intense friction between you and Ken. Are you happy he's dead?"

"You know I am."

"Do the police have any suspects?"

"I don't believe the persons responsible will ever be found, but Jo has made me promise to find them. She wants to personally torture and kill all who had anything to do with it. She'll never allow me to stop looking or find any peace until they're found and put to death in the manner of her choosing."

"The police may have no suspects, but I'm certain you do."

"I suppose so."

"How strong is your suspicion?"

"Strong."

"Well, tell me who you feel certain killed him."

Hound was now faced with another moment of truth. He had to decide quickly to lie or tell the truth. He knew she should be given the truth whenever possible. Besides, he was certain she was already aware he'd concluded who ordered the assassination.

"Rita, let's clear the air so we can move on to more pleasant conversation," he said. "I know it was you who ordered the hit. You finalized it when we were in Miami. You were insistent that I spend a precise amount of time in Phoenix, so I'd have an alibi if I needed one and not be in New Orleans when it took place so as not to be in any danger. Thank you for insuring Jo and her mother weren't harmed."

"There was no way to guarantee that, but I'm glad they're OK. Well, do you plan to keep your promise to Jo and offer me to be tortured and killed by her?"

Hound laughed.

"Rita, sooner or later, I plan to select a scapegoat to give her. It needs to be some fuckers who deserve to die, and she has to see a motive they'd have for killing her father."

"Do you have any prospects in mind?"

"Not yet, but if push comes to shove, I know twelve Irish mob bosses I can select one or more from as the ones who gave the order. I'll also need three who were the shooters that carried it out."

"I can help you with everything when the time comes, if you need it."

"Thanks, and Rita, thanks for Ken. I owe you a favor."

"Wouldn't you extend me a favor even if I wasn't owed one?"

"That would depend on the favor."

"Would you kill someone for me?"

"Only if they deserved it."

"Did Ken deserve it?"

"Ken had every intention of killing me. It wasn't necessary, but he would have anyway. So, hell yes, he deserved it."

"He deserved it for another reason too. His death gave me and my family the only degree of closure possible for whatever happened to Roberto."

"So, you're convinced Ken was involved?"

"Yes, very convinced."

"I still don't see how Ken could gain from getting rid of Roberto. He stood to make a lot of money from their business arrangement. Can you explain it to me?"

"I think Ken believed Roberto hadn't told my family of the arrangement, or that a shipment of merchandise had been stored in his warehouse. Ken saw an opportunity to steal, sell it, and keep all the money."

"Five hundred million dollars is a lot of money, but he stood to make much more over time due to the deal he had with Roberto."

"He planned to make the same deal with the new cartel boss. You really fucked up his plans."

"How?"

"Did he want you to know merchandise had already been delivered, or did you find out by accident?"

"Well, he wasn't the first to tell me. Jo was."

"Did she regret telling you, because she was told not to?"

"Yes, come to think of it, she did."

"When Ken found out you knew, he had no choice but to go along with your plan to call and come see me so I wouldn't suspect you and he had anything to do with Roberto's disappearance."

"Why didn't he simply let me in on his plan?"

"Would you have gone along with it?"

"No."

"He knew that, and so do I, now."

"When did you know?"

"When you told me the merchandise had already been received and was stored in the warehouse."

Hound's expression was one of confusion and surprise, but inside he was smiling with delight. Rita had just described the perfect scenario regarding what had happened to Roberto, created without him having to manipulate her. He was relieved it was no longer a major concern.

However, he did have a lesser, yet important concern. He decided to satisfy a major curiosity regarding Rita's motivation to form such a large and important business relationship with him so quickly. He knew her need to move the surplus product and open new markets were pressing issues, but he was certainly not her only option. It was likely she had already met with and discussed a business alliance with others before selecting him as the one individual she would deal with exclusively.

"Rita, I need to know why you chose to put all your eggs in one basket and select me to be responsible to grow, maintain and safeguard your business interests in the States," he said. "I realize your time was limited to find the right liaison, but you really don't know me well enough to have invested so much with me so quickly."

Rita wasn't surprised by the question. She looked at him and smiled as if she had been expecting it.

"Hound, do you believe in fate, in destiny that is preordained?" she asked.

"It's strange you ask, because I do."

"Well, when first we met, I sensed ours were connected in some important way. I soon came to believe neither of us could fulfill our destiny without the other playing a key role. I think you sensed that as well. Am I wrong?"

"Maybe you're right, but right now I can't support, or reject, what you believe. I believe time will tell."

"Are you a religious man?"

"I consider religion to be a way of life. In that respect, we're all religious. However, I assume you're asking if I believe in God."

"Yes. Do you?"

"Perhaps I'd like to, but I've never seen evidence that a God exists. Do you believe one does?"

"Certainly. My entire family are devout Catholics."

Rita viewed his hesitation to converse further on the topic as indication of at least moderate contempt.

"Hound, tell me what's on your mind at this moment," she said. "I'd appreciate knowing."

"Rita, I'm becoming very fond of you. I also respect your right to believe as you like. I don't want to do or say anything that might offend you."

"I'm growing fond of you as well. I allow you the privilege of being honest about your feelings with me. I want you to allow me the same. Please tell me."

"I couldn't claim to be devout in the Christian faith and live the life I've chosen. To do so would be a grandiose hypocrisy."

"I see your point and support it. I hope being a Christian who is a hypocrite is better than not believing in God at all. Even the slightest degree of hope is better than having none."

"Perhaps you have a point as well."

Hound felt it was time to change the topic of their discussion.

"What's on the agenda during my visit?" he asked. "We have a lot to do in a short time."

"My father suggested we give you a tour of a product production and warehousing facility. We'll visit the largest in Colombia tomorrow."

"Where is it?"

"About an hour flight by helicopter from here. It's well concealed in jungle terrain, far from civilization."

"So, you also have a helicopter."

"Three. We have to be assured one is operational at all times."

"How many such facilities do you have?"

"A few in Colombia, but we also have them elsewhere. Some are in other countries."

"Where?"

"Maybe someday you'll know everything about the cartel, but not right away."

Shortly after breakfast the next morning, Hound was waiting with Rita, her father and three bodyguards in a clearing at the rear of the estate property. The sound of a helicopter engine could be heard as it approached from the south. The sound reminded him of the times in Vietnam he listened for that sound and hoped the choppers would arrive early rather than late to extract him and his men to safety. He realized by the roar of the engine as the aircraft drew nearer it was large. The chopper landed in the center of the clearing. When all the passengers were on board, it lifted off and began flying south.

The craft climbed to the desired altitude and continued south. Within a half hour, the only thing Hound saw below as he looked out the window was a landscape of nothing but dense foliage with an occasional road winding through it. He was again reminded of Nam.

The chopper had been flying for an hour when it began a slow descent. A few minutes later, he saw the chopper was preparing to land in a cleared area just large enough to accommodate its size. He noticed a dirt road ran parallel to the landing zone that emerged from the jungle to the north and continued southward.

Two of the three armed bodyguards remained with the chopper. Hound walked with Rita, her father and guard to the road, where a truck was waiting to transport them to the facility they had come to visit. It was located a half mile to the south. When the facility came into view, Hound was again reminded of Nam. The layout of the operation was similar to Base Camp Bravo 127.

"Hound, you look as though you're upset about something," said Rita. "Is everything OK?"

"I'm fine — just having a bit of déjà vu."

The facility covered an area slightly larger than seven acres. The buildings varied in size. The two largest ones were used for manufacturing and packaging. The largest was a storage ware-house. Other structures included a mess hall, barracks, numerous supply sheds and a shower facility that was also used as a laundry. Water used for bathing and laundry was pumped from a nearby river. Drinking water and that used for cooking, along with all food staples, had to be brought in by trucks and stored on site.

No less than one hundred and seventy-five cartel workers were on duty at any given time. Shifts of work lasted twelve hours, six days per week. Half of the work force was on duty each shift. All the workers were armed with automatic rifles and plenty of ammunition. There were also other types of weapons including hand grenades and mortars. Two walking sentries constantly patrolled the outer perimeter of the facility on all four sides. All the other workers kept their weapons within reach at all times and were well trained in their use. The entire facility was concealed under the jungle canopy and surrounded by a fifteen foot fence constructed of heavy steel pipe set a foot deep in the concrete foundation, buried a foot below ground. There was a gate access at the front and rear of the compound, but the front was the only one large enough to permit entry and exit of large trucks.

Rita took Hound on a tour of the entire facility, which lasted until late afternoon. She made sure to visit with all the workers, individually or in groups. They all greeted her warmly and with enthusiasm. Hound was surprised at the type and quality of the food provided for the workers when he had lunch with Rita, her father and eighty workers in the mess hall.

When the tour was completed that afternoon, Rita and Hound returned to the mess hall to further discuss all he had seen.

"What do you think of the operation?" she asked.

"It's impressive."

"Can you make any suggestions on how to make it better?"

"Rita, this is my first exposure to any of your operations. I'm not qualified to make suggestions."

"How about security and defense capabilities? Your experience as a combat officer in Vietnam would certainly qualify you in that area. Anything you could recommend to improve the ability to defend property and lives would be appreciated."

"Well, you need to clear at least a hundred yards more of the jungle foliage beyond the perimeter fence. I wouldn't store your supply of weapons, ammo and other ordinance in a single location. You have mortars, but they're in a storage area. They need to be set up at strategic locations, ready for use at any time. Do your workers each have a designated defense position to get to in the event of attack?"

"Yes."

"Good. Should an attack ever come, it will play a big part in a successful defense."

"I'll get the additional hundred yards cleared outside the fence as soon as possible. The storing of ammo and ordinance will be taken care of before we leave. Will you specify where the mortars should be placed?"

"Sure. That won't take long. Are all your workers well trained in the use of all weapons?"

"Yes, very well trained."

"Who is the biggest threat to your operations?"

"The Sanchez cartel is the most successful from Mexico to South America. We grow and manufacture over fifty percent of the narcotics we distribute. To maintain our position as top dog, we purchase from producers in other countries. We do that in part to restrict our competitors' growth in size and power. We agree to purchase the majority of product manufactured by our foreign partners so the other cartels can't. These rival cartels are our biggest threat."

"You said you'd tell me later who these partners are. Why not now?"

"We've established facilities similar to this one in areas of the Middle East and Africa."

"Are your current rivals in Mexico and South America?"

"Yes."

"That will change. It's only a matter of time."

"What do you mean?"

"I think you're going to see competition from Russian and Chinese organizations sometime in the future. Drugs make big money. You know that. After you get it, never think it will be guaranteed the majority of the market in the U.S. can be retained."

"When do you expect all this to begin?"

"It already has, but it won't begin to grow until the war in Vietnam ends."

"How long do you think it will take the U.S. to win?"

"It won't win. I don't think it will take much longer to lose."

"Do you have any ideas how to prepare for future competition?"

"Maybe. I'll give it some thought.

Hound's ideas and plans for the future were focused on finally, once and for all, freeing himself from a life he never wanted. He wanted to become a wealthy businessman, but not in a corrupt, illegal business, especially drugs. He despised even the thought of it. He was trapped in a series of dangerous circumstances. The only way out was to carefully follow the plan he devised to rid himself of the plague that surrounded him. It would require time to yield positive results, but would there be enough to escape the inevitable consequences that drew closer as each day passed?

By 6 p.m., Hound had specified where the mortars were to be located. He, Rita, her father and the bodyguards were on board the chopper, returning to the estate at 7. A nice dinner was waiting for them when they arrived. After Carlos and Nita finished eating, they excused themselves and left Hound and Rita alone at the dining table to discuss business.

"Rita, you need to get the second shipment to me in New Orleans as soon as possible," he told her. "The sooner it's delivered, the sooner it can be sold. Time is crucial."

"I plan to send it on the day you return home."

"I plan to leave tomorrow. I need to get back as soon as possible."

"Are you worried about Jo?"

"I'm concerned about a lot of things. She's one of them."

"Why do you feel so obligated to her?"

"She's my wife."

"That's not the main reason. What is?"

"Rita, with all due respect, it's none of your business. I'd appreciate it if you would never make Jo a topic of our discussion again."

He hoped his demand, rather than request, wouldn't anger Rita, but it did.

"I think that's a splendid idea!" she said. "When we're together in the future, Jo will never be mentioned by either of us. Do you agree?"

"Yes."

"Good. I'm sick of being reminded of her, the daughter of the man who helped murder my brother. I'll always wonder if she was aware of her father's plan to kill Roberto."

Hound had just learned something he didn't like but needed to know.

"Rita, I'm damn sure she didn't," he said. "Ken would never allow her to know it."

"You can't be sure. How could you?"

"Ken never confided anything of that nature to her."

"Like I said, how can you be sure? My father confides everything to me."

"Your father is much different than Ken. Jo's relationship with her father was much different than you have with yours."

"How so?"

"Your father knows he can trust you with any information. Ken would never trust Jo the same way. He kept her in the dark about all family business so she could never be a threat."

"Is Jo really that weak emotionally?"

"Yes."

"Hound, I believe you. That's another reason to get away from her. How much does she know about our business arrangement?"

"Nothing. Like Ken, I will always keep her ignorant of any nefarious business I'm involved in."

"Hound, tell me the truth. Do you plan to stay with her indefinitely?"

"Rita, look at us. We agreed to not talk about Jo again, and we're both breaking our agreement."

"Answer my question. Then the subject is mute from now on."

He didn't know if he would stay with Jo another month, year, or always. However, telling Rita what she wanted to hear was in Jo's best interest.

"No, I don't plan to stay with her, but I won't leave until the time is right. I don't know when that will be, so I can't tell you."

"OK. I'm sure it will be sooner than later."

"I would think so."

Hound returned home the next morning. Rita ordered the second shipment of merchandise to leave by boat for New Orleans at 9 a.m. She sat and visited with her parents for a time after Hound left to be driven to the airport. He was the subject of their conversation.

"Rita, it seems you made the right choice in forming a business arrangement with Hound," said Carlos. "I believe he's quite capable and can be completely trusted. Have you discovered anything about him that causes concern?"

"Only the misplaced loyalty to his wife."

"What do you mean?"

"He's in deep water and she's an anchor around his neck."

"Does he feel that way about her?"

"I'm not sure how he feels, but I think she's not good for him. He has too much responsibility and danger facing him to be worried about a wife who is obviously messed up emotionally and depends on him for everything. She was raised to be a spoiled, entitled brat, never being taught or required to assume any responsibility of thinking or caring for herself."

"Rita, all that may be true, but she's still his wife. If he chooses to stay in the situation, then that's his decision."

"I'm concerned she might be a threat to the big business Hound and I are doing together. Maybe it would be best to eliminate her and not have to worry about it."

"Rita, this family has never, or ever will, take the life of anyone who hasn't threatened our lives or business. Are you certain you don't have another reason for wanting her out of the way?"

"What other reason could I have?"

"Hound is an extraordinary young man. He's extremely intelligent and charming. You and your mother agree he's very handsome — the most handsome you've ever met."

"Father, are you saying I'm interested in him for reasons other than business?"

"May I ask you a personal question and get an honest answer?"

"You can ask me anything, you know that. You also know I've never lied to you and never will."

"Have you asked him for more than a business relationship, perhaps a more intimate one?"

"I presented the possibility to him."

"What did he say?"

"Well, he said it wouldn't be wise to have a business and personal relationship at the same time. I agreed."

"Was that the only reason he gave?"

"OK! He also gave his marriage as a reason."

"Have you ever been rejected by anyone you were interested in?"

"Of course not! I've never been the one to ask either!"

"Rita, it's human nature to want the things we can't have. You've always achieved anything you wanted. Hound may be a challenge. Maybe you see getting his wife out of the way as your only way to win. I caution you, that would not be wise. Hound is a rare breed of man. I've seen his kind only a few times in my life. If you ever violate his moral code, he'll seek to balance the scale. You'll never see him coming in time to stop what he'll do. The only way to beat him will be to strike first. Either way you fail to win him."

Rita's mother, Nita, felt obligated to add her observation to the conversation.

"Rita," she began," your father is correct in all he has said. I wish to add my impression of Hound. He is a man of his word, always determined to honor it at any cost. Likely that is the reason for remaining with his wife, if he would prefer otherwise. Also, I believe him to be a man no woman can ever claim as solely hers. His very soul dictates otherwise. All any woman can hope to expect in a romantic relationship with him is the most satisfying time of their life for as long as the relationship lasts. It will take a very special, rare type of woman to capture his heart and hold it forever. Don't set yourself up to be hurt. If you pursue this man, be prepared to get only what he says he'll offer. Never expect more. For your sake, I hope you can be that special, rare type of woman should you ever come to love him as I do your father."

Rita valued the advice and counsel of her parents. Her heart told her they were right.

"Thank you. I'll consider all you've said."

When Hound arrived home, he was given a warm welcome by Jo, who was very intoxicated.

He said nothing to her about the condition she was in. After visiting a short time, she went to her bedroom to sleep for the rest of the day and all night.

"Hound, Jo has been drunk since you left," her mother said. "She won't eat, only drinks and sleeps."

"Sandra, Jo was very close to her father. It will not be easy for her to recover from his death."

"I know, but I'm afraid she'll become addicted to alcohol or drugs."

"We'll get her the treatment she needs before that happens. Sandra, how are you doing? I've been so focused on Jo and tied up with business, I haven't taken time to inquire."

"Honestly, I'm doing very well. Hound, don't think bad of me, but Ken and I had been drifting apart in an emotional way for a long time, years. I'm ashamed to admit it, but my grief is minimal. Please don't tell anyone. I just needed to confess my feelings to someone that could understand and be trusted to keep it quiet. I never want Jo to know what I really thought of her father."

"What did you really think of him?"

"Probably the same as you. He was a man in love with his money, power and image. His family was always second. He had Jo convinced otherwise, but not me. I resented the way he manipulated and used her to do things she didn't want to do, always making her feel guilty if she wanted to refuse. She never wanted to take the teaching job at your high school, or the position at the university. However, she did because he made her feel it was a family duty, a responsibility she had to assume. She didn't want to work in the family business, but she agreed for the same reason. I know you understand. He manipulated you to join the family business. I know you didn't want to. I was learning to despise him. Weren't you?"

Hound wanted to be honest in the way he felt to show the support she was seeking, but he knew better.

"No," he replied, "but I didn't know him as well, or as long as you."

The second shipment of merchandise arrived the next night. It was unloaded from the ship onto the trucks provided by Mike and transported to L.A. The delivery was completed without any problems. Hound felt some degree of relief, but now had to deal with Jo, who was continuing to drink heavily. He waited until she awoke after sleeping off the effects of her most recent intoxication to have a serious conversation.

"Jo," he began, "I'm sick of your bullshit! You're going to get and stay sober. If you can't, then we'll get you the help you need."

"Hound, you'd be devastated if it had been your father slaughtered. I can't deal with it without something to dull the pain. In time I will. The drinking will stop then."

"God damn it, Jo! It stops now! Right fucking now! Do you understand me?"

Jo broke into an episode of uncontrollable sobbing. Hound stood silent for a moment and then acted.

"Shut the fuck up! Get the fuck up and get your ass in the shower. You look like shit and you're starting to smell like it! I'm ashamed of you! I deserve better from my wife! You're no use to me the way you are now! Decide right fucking now whether you want me or the God-damn booze! Dinner will be ready in an hour. I'll expect you to be present, looking presentable, sober and ready to eat a healthy meal! If you're not, then consider me out of your life forever! Jo, I'm serious. I shit you not!"

Jo was still sobbing intensely when Hound left the room. He walked to the living room where he sat down to wait, hoping his method of intervention with Jo would produce the result he wanted. He had chosen the seemingly cruel, abusive approach, feeling it was likely the one to be effective. Jo was quickly relapsing into a similar emotional crisis suffered in the past due to trauma. Almost an hour passed before Jo appeared at the foot of the stairs and walked to where he was seated. She seemed tired but had bathed and groomed herself as he had demanded.

"Honey, is dinner ready?" she asked softly, smiling. "I feel a bit hungry and would like to eat."

"Yes. I'm hungry too."

Sandra was standing at the dining table when they arrived. They sat down to enjoy all of Jo's favorite dishes and have a casual family conversation. Jo ate a reasonable size meal, but it was apparent doing so was difficult. After dinner, Jo requested some private time with Hound. She suggested they go to the den.

"Sweetheart, do you know how much I love you?" she asked in a soft and breaking voice.

"Yes, Jo, I believe I do."

"You are the most important thing in my life. I don't want to lose you."

"I don't think you have to worry about that, but I want you to be happy and healthy."

"I want that as well, but I need to be honest with you about something. Can I do that without fear of you thinking I'm weak and spineless?"

"Jo, I'd never consider you to be either. What do you need to tell me?"

"Hound, I never completely recovered from the trauma I suffered in the past. When I was raped and became pregnant, you left, I aborted the baby and couldn't conceive your children as a result. The guilt of all those things never went away. I've been drinking and using prescribed medications since all that shit began. While we were separated, I became dependent on all of them. I was able to keep it from my parents, but how is a mystery to me. When you came back, but were still away so much, I was able to keep it from you. When dad was killed, I lost my control and desire to hide it any longer. It will be impossible for me to give up my habits without professional help. I'm so very sorry."

"There's nothing to be sorry for. Anyway, it won't help solve your problem."

"Will you stop loving me and leave now that you know the truth?"

"Of course not. You deserve a chance to recover and the support of your mother and I to do it."

"Thank you, my darling. I won't disappoint you. Where do I begin?"

"Let's get your mom in here to take part in the discussion."

Sandra was happy to be included. She'd been considering something that would benefit her and felt it might help Jo as well.

"We have relatives living in Ireland," Sandra began. "They've been asking us to visit for a long time. I think spending an indefinite time with them would be good for Jo and me. We both need to get away from everything in New Orleans that are reminders of Ken's death and the way life used to be. I have a brother there who is a prominent physician. He's helped many that suffered from alcoholism and other drug addictions. I'm convinced he could help Jo."

"Jo, how do you feel about that?" Hound asked.

"Would you come with us?"

"You know I can't leave the huge business responsibilities that are facing me. I'll try to visit if you don't return in a reasonable time."

"I can't leave you alone to do everything. I won't."

"Jo, don't worry about that. There's little you could do to help anyway. You know that."

"Do you want me to go? Won't you miss me?"

"I want you to go if it will help you. Your mom thinks it will. Of course, I'll miss you, but that's a price I'm willing to pay if you get well."

"Hound, I live in fear that what happened to dad will happen to us."

"That's all the more reason to get far away from here for a time. Besides, I hear Ireland is a beautiful country. I'll look forward to visiting you there."

Something Jo said prompted Sandra to offer Hound information that might interest him.

"Hound, I got a phone call from the Irish boss in Miami during the last time you were away," she said. "He said an offer could be made to buy our family business. The sum would be enough to provide us a very comfortable life now that Ken is gone. He said we'd be free from the stress of running the business. We could take his offer and all of us get the hell out of here. It might be the perfect way to start a new life, an honest and safer one."

Hound knew Sandra and Jo weren't aware of the new drug deal he arranged with all the bosses while they were in town for Ken's funeral. The bosses knew he didn't plan to tell her or Jo. He became instantly aware of three things that were certain. There would be no offer to buy a damn thing, making such an offer was meant to be notification that the drug deal had been reconsidered and rejected, and there was no time to waste in finding out why.

Hound didn't want to alarm Jo and Sandra, but they needed to be aware of what he'd concluded. This would be necessary in convincing them to leave for Ireland as soon as possible. He told them the bosses had no intention of buying what they could take by coercion. The offer was meant to deliver a message to the new boss of the O'Malley family business — that he was not acceptable as such and not to resist when his replacement was selected. He didn't confide his additional belief that the bosses would reject a drug deal that was certain to benefit them in a grand way financially. He concluded they had made a deal directly with a supplier and it sure as hell wasn't with the Sanchez cartel.

Jo became frightened after Hound's summary.

"Oh my God, Hound!" she said in a volume approaching a scream. "You have to come with us to Ireland! You can't stay here. It's not safe!"

"Jo, I'll be fine. I anticipated this and have prepared for it. However, I can't be concerned for you and your mom's safety. I want you to pack and book a flight tonight. You'll be leaving for Ireland tomorrow, as early as possible."

"I won't go without you! Why do you want to stay?"

"Jo, I'm not going to lie down for a bunch of bullies. Besides, I promised to get the ones responsible for your dad's murder. I'm going to keep that promise."

"God damn it, Hound! Are you saying it was the other bosses that ordered my dad to be shot down on a street in his own city?"

"That's right. Think about all that's going on. It makes perfect sense."

Jo thought and nodded in agreement. Her mother did also.

"I told you I wanted to personally be there when revenge was carried out," she yelled.

"I know, but that's not going to be possible. I'll act on your behalf. I swear they will at least get what they gave your dad. Now go book your flight and pack. There's no time to waste debating the issue further."

After Jo and Sandra left, Hound hurried to call Rita in Bogota. He told her there was something urgent he needed to speak to her about and it should be discussed in person, not over the phone, and there was no time to lose. She agreed to meet him in New Orleans as quickly as her private jet could get there, probably early the next morning.

Hound drove Jo and her mother to the airport early the next morning. Their flight left at 7 a.m. They would fly to New York, from there to London, and then to Dublin, Ireland. Jo was reluctant to leave, but she knew it was best.

"Hound, is it certain you'll be safe?" Jo asked with tears forming in her eyes.

"It is. I promise. Things will be back to normal when you return."

"When will that be?"

"When you're well and there's no longer a danger here."

"OK, but when will it be safe?"

"Jo, I don't know, but as soon as possible."

Jo gave him a long kiss and embrace. Her mother hugged him and told him to be safe. She also said not to worry about Jo, she would be well cared for. He watched their plane take off and soon disappear in the clouds.

He drove to the private airport where Rita would soon be arriving, if not already there. Her jet had just landed as he drove into the parking lot. He walked to where the jet stopped and waited. When the door opened and the steps came down, Rita led her entourage of twelve bodyguards down the steps. She greeted Hound with a hug and warm smile.

"The weather here is much colder than Bogota," she said. "I'm glad I dressed for it."

"It's unusually cold, ever for this time of the year."

Rita and her associates processed through customs with no problems. She was always prepared to travel anywhere at any time.

"Rita, my Corvette can transport only you and I," he told her. "We'll have to rent cars for your men."

"That's already taken care of. Three cars are waiting for us at the hangar where my plane is."

Hound and Rita got into his car and drove away with the other cars close behind. She told him the name of the hotel where three suites had been reserved.

"You and your men will be staying with me at the O'Malley estate," he told her.

"I don't want to impose on your family, especially Jo. Besides, it seems we have a lot to discuss that is delicate. We need privacy."

"You, your men and I will be the only ones there. I'll make sure the maid doesn't bother. The cook will prepare meals but won't interfere either. Jo and her mother are out of the country indefinitely. The estate isn't as large or elegant as yours, but it's big enough, and better than the nicest hotel in the city."

"OK, I accept your invitation."

After arriving at the estate, Rita was shown to the nicest of all the guestrooms.

"I suppose you sleep in the master bedroom," she said. "You are the new master of the estate."

"No, I stay in another room."

"Why?"

"The master room is reserved for Ken's wife. She wouldn't appreciate me taking it over."

"Would you take it if she offered?"

"Of course not."

"I didn't think you would."

Rita and her soldiers hadn't eaten since they left Bogota. Hound asked the cook to prepare breakfast. After the meal, the bodyguards relaxed in the living room and visited while Hound and Rita went to the den.

"What do you think is going on?" Rita asked.

"I'm not sure. I rely on my instinct at times like this. I feel some shit is going to happen. I just don't know what, or where or who it will happen to. I'm considering several possibilities. None of them are good for either of us."

"What's the worst we could expect?"

"Rita, which of the cartel competitors is your biggest threat? Who would likely be powerful enough to attempt a takeover of your business by force?"

"Do you mean go to war with us?"

"Yes."

"Hound, I suspect there's more than one. Do you strongly believe that's a concern?"

"I do. I can't prove it, but my gut tells me to get prepared."

"If you're right, what can we do?"

"We have to take the enemy out before it takes us. Our best chance is to be on the offense, strike first."

"OK, but what do we strike? We have no idea who the enemy is."

"You're right. Rita, there may be a way to find out, but I'll need your help."

Of course. What can I do?"

"If my instinct about what's going on is right, the Irish boss in Miami should know about it. I'll pay him an unexpected visit and get the answers we need. I'll need some heavy backup to get it done. I need you to provide me as many of your best soldiers as you can spare and still have enough to mount a defense in Bogota if an attack comes soon."

"You're not planning a peaceful visit with this boss, are you?"

"Peaceful wouldn't get what I want. It will take the right kind of coercion."

"The men with me are twelve of the best soldiers I have. How many more will you need?"

"Did you bring weapons?"

"We all have semiautomatic handguns, but no automatic rifles."

"We'll need rifles. I can get all we need. The men you have with you will be enough. I think I can get the additional crew needed from a source in Phoenix."

"What exactly are you planning to do?"

"Rita, there are twelve mob bosses in twelve states that are a party to what the boss in Miami has planned. I'm going to visit him, find out what the plan is, who all the players are, in addition to the other bosses. I'm going to kill that mother fucker in Miami, and then the other bosses and players as soon as possible after. If my plan works, I'll get all the bosses close to the same time. When we're finished in this country, we'll take care of any players in yours. Can all your soldiers back home be trusted?"

"None have ever shown otherwise. Why?"

"I hope I'm wrong, but there may be some traitors in your organization. If not, then perhaps friends or family, maybe an uncle or even a cousin. Is there anyone who feels animosity toward you and your immediate family?"

"Normal family disagreements, but nothing serious that I know of. Tell me how you plan to carry out your plan to take the bosses out. I know you realize how dangerous that is. They may be prepared for you."

"No, they don't suspect any threat this soon. They plan to kill me, Jo and her mother before we suspect any danger. If my instinct is correct, the same is planned for you and your family."

OK! Tell me how we're going to deal with this and not risk winding up in jail or dead. You're talking about assassinating twelve bosses who likely present themselves as prominent, honest businessmen in their communities. In addition, they'll surely be surrounded by security personnel. How do you plan to deal with that?"

"We'll kill everyone necessary to complete our mission. We'll move quickly and efficiently, get the job done, and disappear."

"What about innocent bystanders, witnesses, do we kill them too?"

"God damn it, Rita! I said everyone necessary! I sure as hell don't want any innocent, collateral damage, but we need to survive this shitstorm! We'll do whatever is necessary!"

"Hound, I don't like it, but I know you're right."

"Rita, don't be concerned. I could use help from your men, and the use of your jet, but you don't need to take an active part in the bloodshed."

"Bullshit! I've got as much at stake as you. I'll be at your side until you're done with the bosses. Will you be at mine when I take care of my enemies back home?"

"That's what I had in mind. Now, go check on your men. I need to make a phone call and recruit the rest of the help we'll need."

Rita left the den as Hound began placing a call to Maggie in Phoenix. She was happy to finally hear from him. After a short conversation of personal content, he focused on the importance of the call. Maggie quickly sensed the urgent need for the favor he asked. She agreed to learn the home addresses of twelve men unknown to her by the end of the day. She didn't ask his reason for wanting to know. She was delighted he'd be in Phoenix the next evening and they could spend some time together.

His next call was to Bear, who agreed to have Bill and Pony at the biker clubhouse the following day for an important meeting. He was happy with Bear's answer when he asked the number of automatic rifles and amount of ammunition available at the chapter headquarters.

15

Rita's jet landed in Phoenix early the next morning. She agreed it would be best if none of the friends Hound came to meet with knew she or her soldiers were with him. They checked into their hotel to wait until it was time to leave for Florida the following morning. Hound said he'd meet her at the jet around 8 a.m. He'd have all the weapons needed to complete their task in Miami.

Hound arrived at the chapter clubhouse on schedule. Bear was anxiously waiting outside. A big grin appeared on his face when his best friend showed up. He offered him a robust welcome.

"Hello, shithead!" Bear said loudly, continuing to smile. "I've missed having you around!"

"Go fuck yourself, you big, gross son of a bitch! Why have you missed me? I've been away less than three weeks! Well, shit! Guess I've missed you too. Are Bill and Pony here?"

"Yep. They're waiting in the clubhouse."

"Good. We have some urgent shit to discuss. I'm in one hell of a mess and need your help."

"I figured that! Tell me something I didn't expect."

"Don't sweat it, buddy. I will."

Hound explained his situation in detail to the three men. They listened with increasing intensity as the story continued.

"How do you plan to get out of this shit?" asked Bill. "What can we do to help?"

"Well, I'm going to kill all twelve of those fuckers. I need your assistance to hit them all around the same time. If I don't, then word of what occurred to one will reach the others. They'd have time to prepare for my visit to them."

"Hound, just how in hell can we help?"

"I need some shooters to be on site and in position to take out a boss in eleven different cities any time after dark three nights from tonight. I'm going to kill the one in Miami during that time frame."

"Well, fuck me! Is that all you need? Shit, I thought you needed something dangerous! Have you lost your God-damned marbles? Killing twelve mob bosses is insane! Even if we pulled it off, there's going to be payback! You're talking about starting a war with the Irish Mafia! That's a war that can't be won because it will never end!"

"It will never start if no one knows for sure who is responsible. What they'll know is the responsible party has got big balls and a lot of muscle. The entire Irish organization can't bring to bear the army I'll have at my disposal if we pull this off."

"What army?"

"Bill, how many members does your club have nationwide?"

"Why?"

"How many?"

"Well, I'd estimate at least ten thousand, but only a unanimous vote by all the presidents can commit them to a single task or cause. I can't commit to help you without that vote because it would impact the club as a whole. You should know that."

"I do, but I want you to contact them and see if they'll vote to help me after hearing what I'm prepared to offer in return. Do you have a secure phone line to conduct a conference call on with all the presidents at the same time?"

"Of course. What offer do you want me to present to them?"

"Not only can I guarantee exclusive purchasing of Sanchez cartel merchandise, but also at a fifteen percent reduction in price. Your club gets all the products, cutting out the competition to buy the highest quality shit on the market. In addition, the club can count on cartel muscle if any threats arise. The cartel can have a reserve army of no less than ten to fifteen thousand soldiers anywhere in the U.S. within twenty-four hours, if needed. That added to the number of current club membership makes for one hell of an army."

"Hound, that sounds good, except how can the club move all the merchandise produced by the cartel? We're breaking our balls to get rid of the shipments we just received in line with the terms of your last proposal. Our market simply isn't big enough to handle the volume."

"Shit, Bill! It's time for the club to start growing toward its maximum potential. Expand eastward. Open new chapters and increase the size of its membership. Tell the presidents that. Well, in three nights I'll kill the boss in Miami. If my offer is accepted, the eleven others will die. If not, then I'll deal with it the best I can. Maggie will be here any minute with the home addresses of all the bosses. I'll focus on the one in Miami. The others will be the responsibility of the club if the vote is in my favor. After Miami, I have to go directly to Colombia for an indefinite time. I hope we can celebrate the acceptance of my offer when I return."

"Hound, I hope so too."

Maggie was waiting for Hound when the meeting concluded. She gave him a big hug and kiss, both suggestive of things to come later. After, she gave him two copies of the information he requested. He put a copy in his pocket and handed the other to Bill.

"Bill, burn those names and addresses if you don't use them," said Hound. "We don't want them found."

"I will."

They all sat down to have a beer together before Hound and Maggie left. Nothing was said in front of Maggie about the meeting. She was dying of curiosity but wouldn't attempt to satisfy it. When they left the clubhouse, Bear followed a few seconds behind. He approached Hound to have more conversation. He asked Maggie for privacy to talk to his friend. She stood at her car while they took a walk around the parking lot.

"Buddy, I don't think there's any possibility of the club helping to solve your problem," Bear told him. "The presidents will feel it presents to much risk. Hell! We all consider you a brother, but what's best for the many takes precedent over one."

"Bear, I understand. I assumed as much."

"What will you do now? It might be wise to cancel your plan in Miami and devise a new one."

"I'm committed to Miami. There's too much in play to waste time on new planning."

Maggie sensed the seriousness of their conversation. She didn't like the concerned expressions both were showing. She walked to join them.

"OK, God damn it!" she said sternly. "I realize you don't want me to know what's going on! However, I assume Hound's in deep shit with a big problem to solve! Hound, tell me what's going on! Maybe I can help!"

"Maggie, I doubt you could help. Besides, I can't let you know, and it's something you don't want to get involved with."

"That's for me to decide. You don't trust me to know, so it must be something worse than the drug deal you let me in on. How many people do you need to kill, and why?"

Hound looked at her for a short time. He decided there was nothing to lose by telling her, on the chance she might be able to help. Bear nodded in agreement. Her mouth opened wider and wider as Hound explained his situation.

"Damn! Hound, you get out of a deep pile of shit and always

manage to jump into a deeper one. However, I happen to know some super bad boys who might help if the price is right."

"No shit?"

"No shit."

"Can these bad boys be trusted?"

"I've recommended them before. They've always proven trustworthy to get the job done and get away clean. These guys are the best professional assassins anywhere in the world. The government is their biggest client."

"Why does that not surprise me? How do you know them?"

"I have connections with all kinds of people who have connections with all kinds of people."

"Who are these bad boys and are there enough of them to do what I need the way it needs to be done?"

"Hound, I can't tell you who they are. That would cost me and anyone I told our lives. I assure you they are large enough in numbers to do what you need. You haven't asked how much it will cost."

"I don't care."

"OK, but the price is one hundred thousand dollars per boss."

"Do you have enough time to make what I need occur on schedule?"

"Of course. Give me the information on the eleven bosses. I'll set everything up before noon today. Are you sure you don't want them to take care of Miami for you? I know an additional one hundred thousand dollars is no problem for you. Besides, why take the risk of doing it yourself?"

"I don't have a choice. I have to get some important information from the boss in Miami."

Hound gave the information she'd obtained for him back to her.

"Hound, what shall we do this afternoon?" she asked.

"Whatever you want."

"Wonderful! I'll pick up some to go Chinese food we can heat for dinner and meet you at your estate around 3 p.m. I want to spend the rest of the afternoon and night enjoying your company. You're leaving again tomorrow. I don't know when, or if I'll see you again."

"What else do you get for helping me? I know there must be more."

"You'll owe me a big favor. I'll ask when it's needed."

Maggie got into her car and drove away. Hound decided to stay longer and visit with Bear.

"Hound, even though the club can't help, you know I'm ready to help as your friend. Could you use me in Miami and wherever you're going after?"

Hound decided to consider Bear's offer. There might be an advantage to having a friend at his side with Vietnam combat experience.

"Bear, how would the club feel about that?"

"I would just tell Bill I'm taking a leave of absence."

"You need to know we would be going to Colombia, if we survive Miami. I don't know how long we'd be there. I figure we might experience some combat, maybe equal to Nam. I have no idea what's going to happen."

"Count me in. Things are getting boring as hell around here. I could use some excitement. What are the women like in Colombia?"

"I only know two, Rita Sanchez and her mother."

"What is Rita like? I mean do you feel safe when you're around her?"

"I was apprehensive my first visit, but not now."

"I hope she never finds out who really killed her brother. How do you think she'd kill me if she found out?"

"You could bet it would be slow and very unpleasant. She has a thing about cutting off the balls of men that anger her. I'm sure that would be included in the many things she'd do to both of us. By the way, don't mention Carmella. Remember, Rita knows and is very fond of her."

"I'll guard what I say. Hey, do you need to get her permission to bring me along?"

"No, I don't think so."

"Well, I suppose we'll be leaving for Miami early in the morning. It's a long drive and we have to get there in time to get some rest before we take care of business. Even with my help, the two of us may not be enough to kill that fucker without getting shot to hell trying. Aren't you a little worried about that?"

"Bear, first of all, we aren't driving to Miami, we're flying. Second, I have thirteen more shooters to help out."

"Do you have all the weapons you need waiting in Miami? You sure as hell can't take them on the plane. I suppose the thirteen shooters there have all we'll need. Will they provide me a proper weapon, or will I be expected to go it hand to hand?"

"Shit, Bear! You worry too much. We're flying with Rita and twelve of her soldiers on her private jet. It won't be a problem getting the needed weapons and ammo your club is going to provide loaded on board. You can still provide them, can't you?"

"Damn straight I can! Son of a bitch, only you could get the boss of a cartel to back your play in such a big way. What the hell is she doing in the group?"

"She must have her reasons."

"You're fucking her, aren't you?"

"No, our relationship is strictly business."

"She must be planning more with you."

"I sure as hell hope not."

"Why? Is she a dog, butt ugly?"

"Rita is likely the most beautiful woman I've ever seen."

"How does she compare to Maggie and Carmella? They are two of the finest looking bitches I've ever laid eyes on."

"Rita beats them both."

"How about Jo? As I remember from seeing her at the grand opening of your nightclub, she was gorgeous."

"Yes, even better than Jo."

"Damn! Do you think Rita would fuck me?"

"Well, you are the poster boy for charm and sophistication. I think you should ask her."

"Why not! The worst she'd do is say no, like a lot of women I've asked, right?"

"The worst would be to cut your balls off and shove them up your ass."

"Maybe I should wait for her to ask me."

"Maybe."

Hound and Bear began to laugh so hard their eyes teared and breathing was difficult.

"Hound, do you think Maggie is making a good deal of money for herself from the amount you're going to pay those anonymous bad boys? Even if they're the best, one hundred thousand dollars for each of the bosses is way the hell too much!"

"I don't give a shit one way or the other as long as the job gets done. I need to get home. There are things to do before Maggie arrives later this afternoon. I'll meet you at the private airport in the morning. Be sure you bring all the weapons we'll need. Do you need any help to get them there?"

"No, I'll pack the weapons and ammo in crates. I've got help here to load them in the bed of my truck. I'll see you at the airport. Please make sure Rita is OK with me joining the crew."

"It will be fine. Don't worry."

When Hound arrived at his estate, he called Carmella at her home in Oakland. It had been days since they last spoke. He knew she'd be anxious to hear from him. She was relieved he was safe but upset he hadn't called sooner.

"God damn it, gringo boy! I've been worried sick something had happened to you! Why did it take so long to let me know you were safe?"

"Carmella, you wouldn't believe the shit that's going on. I've been putting out fires everywhere. I'm sorry, but I haven't had the chance to keep in touch."

"You know I understand and forgive you. I'm just happy you're OK. When will all the fires be out so we can spend time together? There's a lot we need to catch up on. I won't ask what the fires are. You wouldn't tell me anyway, would you?"

"No, I couldn't do that. However, as soon as the last is out, we're going to take a trip, get away and enjoy ourselves."

"Do you promise?"

"I promise."

"Do you have any idea when that might be?"

"I hope in time for your spring break at Berkeley. By the way, how's school going?"

"Terrific. Straight A's this semester. By taking a full load of courses and attending summer school, I'll graduate in a year. Can you believe it? I'm really going to get a college education."

"I'm very happy for you, and proud too."

"Thanks, but I couldn't do it without the financial help and moral support from you. Remember, I'm going to pay back all the money you've given me."

"Damn right you are!"

"Where should we go on our trip?"

"Anywhere you like."

They talked over an hour before the phone call ended. Hound changed into his workout clothes and began an eight-mile run followed by two hours of intense physical exercises.

Maggie arrived on schedule at Hound's estate that afternoon. She wasted no time in putting the carry out food in the fridge, and then suggested they take a shower together. He easily complied. It was his intention to humor her requests. She deserved it for the great favor done him. Besides, he was overdue for some sexual gratification, something she was excellent at providing.

What began in the shower was resumed in Hound's bed. Maggie's sexual appetite seemed insatiable for a long time. He enjoyed meeting her needs until she was completely satisfied and had neither the desire nor energy to continue.

At 6 p.m. they began to eat the Chinese food and drink cold beer, which seemed to perfectly complement the meal.

"Hound, what you're planning to do in Miami is very dangerous. I'm concerned for your safety, both physically and legally. Please let the bad boys take care of what needs to be done."

"Maggie, I told you information was needed from the boss in Miami. Otherwise, I'd be happy to let your boys take care of it."

"I'm sure they could get the information you need. It might cost more, but it would be money well spent."

"Information is power. I don't want them to have any that isn't necessary. I assume they don't know you hired them for me."

"Of course not! You know me better than that."

"Maggie, have you ever been concerned that if caught, I might implicate you in all this?"

"Hell no, but don't get caught!"

"I don't plan on it, but if that should happen, I know the right attorney to defend me, right?"

"Yes, just don't get caught!"

"How long will it be after you leave this time before I'll see you again?"

"I'm not sure, but as soon as possible."

After dinner, Maggie sat in the living room completing final preparations for a case she had in court the next day. Hound went to the den and called Rita in her suite at the hotel.

"Is everything going as planned?" she asked.

"A few things had to be changed, but all is fine. I'll fill you in tomorrow. I want to let you know I'm bringing a friend with me to Miami and Colombia. He's likely to be valuable in the things we're doing."

"We'll have all the help we need. I don't want a stranger involved."

"He's my best friend, a bit lacking in social skills, but I trust him with my life and yours. He saw a lot of combat in Vietnam. Another trained soldier might come in handy."

"OK, if you want him, you've got him. What's his name?"

"Bear is all he'll answer to. Like me, he prefers his nickname."

"The Hound and Bear! Well, that combination should make for an interesting time."

The next morning, Hound left Maggie asleep and drove to the airport. Rita and her men were waiting at the jet when he got there. A short time later, Bear arrived in his pickup truck. There were three crates containing weapons and ammo in the bed of the truck. Introduction of Bear to Rita would wait until after they were in the air. The crates were quickly loaded onto the aircraft and it took off for Miami. Hound was seated next to Bear.

"Shit, ole buddy," he said to Bear. "You look very different clean shaven and not wearing club colors. I've never seen you in a suit before. I appreciate the shave and no biker club reference, but you didn't have to wear a suit."

"I wanted to make a good first impression. You know how important that can be. Of course, I packed a supply of jeans and other casual shit for later. Do you think I made a good first impression?"

"I assume you did, pal."

"What makes you think so?"

Hound leaned close to Bear so he could hear his whispered answer.

"Your balls are still attached," said Hound, trying hard not to laugh.

"Damn, Hound! Do I have to worry about losing my nuts until this mission is over and I'm back in Phoenix?"

Hound laughed out loud at the seemingly serious question. Rita moved to a seat across from them and asked what was so funny. The look on Bear's face made Hound laugh harder. Rita insisted to know. Bear felt a bit strange and very surprised when Hound told her. He became somewhat relieved when she began to laugh.

"Bear, I think it would be an injustice to the human race if you were to lose your marbles," she said.

"Miss Sanchez, you have no idea how good it is to hear that. I lost my marbles a long time ago. I'm as crazy as a runaway road lizard, but I'm proud to keep what you're talking about attached and in good working condition."

When the jet landed, vans were waiting to take the weapons and personnel to the estate of a Sanchez family friend and business associate. They would stay there until their work was completed. After everyone got settled in at the estate, Hound, Rita and Bear drove to the home address of James O'Conner, the boss they had come to question and kill.

The boss's home was large and located in one of the exclusive neighborhoods intended for only the elite. Armed private security officers patrolled constantly, on foot and in cars.

"Hound, getting to the fucker at his home may not be possible," said Bear.

"It sure as hell won't be easy. Many places would be easier to waste him if we didn't need time to question the son of a bitch."

"How can you be sure he's going to tell the truth when you do?"

"Leave that to me," said Rita. "I guarantee he will."

"Hell, I'm sure you can! We have to get to him first. Hound, how do we deal with all this security?"

"I'm giving it some thought."

"How well do you think they're trained?"

"Not well enough to survive us, if it comes to a gunfight."

"Do you figure it will come to that?"

Shit, Bear! What the fuck do you think?"

"That was a stupid question, wasn't it?"

"No, an important one I wish didn't have to be considered."

After surveillance of the home and immediate neighborhood ended at 10 p.m. on the second night, all needed intel had been gathered. Hound, Bear and Rita returned to the estate to devise a plan for the next night. O'Conner and two bodyguards arrived home between 9:30 and 10 each evening. They entered the house together and then the bodyguards retired to a guest house in the rear of the main home. O'Conner's wife and one house servant were the only others expected to be in the home when the boss arrived.

When he'd discussed and carefully considered everything, Hound laid out what he believed to be the best option. He, Bear and Rita would be inside the home when the boss arrived. No vehicles would be used to deliver them in close proximity to the estate. They'd be dropped off two blocks away on another street by a new Cadillac, which would likely not draw suspicion. Dressed in ninja type attire, they'd make their way in a stealth fashion to the estate and gain access to the home. The wife and servant would be bound, gagged and made to lie face down, never to look in the direction of the intruders, lest they be killed. The bodyguards would be killed after entering, and the boss subdued for questioning.

When all tasks were completed, the three would make their escape in a manner to be picked up by the Cadillac strategically navigating the neighborhood. In the event of interference from the security force, or others resulting in a gunfight, Rita's twelve soldiers would be in radio contact, armed with automatic rifles and waiting in two vans outside the neighborhood perimeter to provide firepower assistance.

"Hound, I hope to Christ we don't need help from those guys," said Bear, "for a lot of reasons."

"Me too. I don't want anybody to get hurt but the target."

"Don't you think we should carry more than handguns?"

"No. Only the handguns have silencers."

They were successful in reaching and entering the home at 8:30 the following evening. The wife was in the master bedroom, recently dressed after her ritual soak in a bubble bath. The servant was busy in the kitchen finishing the late dinner she prepared nightly. Bear took her by surprise from behind, gagged and bound her, while Hound and Rita searched for the wife. She was quickly captured as she entered the living room to wait for her husband's arrival. The two women were placed on the floor in the kitchen.

Not a word had been uttered until Hound spoke in a low, soft voice to them.

"Neither of you will be harmed if you remain still, silent, and don't look in our direction until we are gone," he said. "To do otherwise will cost your lives. Do you both understand?"

Both women nodded in agreement.

Rita remained with them while Hound and Bear assumed offensive positions and prepared for what would come next. At 9:10 p.m., the car carrying the boss and his two men arrived. Two minutes later, the bodyguards walked through the front door. James O'Conner was a step behind them.

Bear shot twice. A .45 caliber round hit each of the bodyguards in the center of the forehead. They died before their bodies hit the floor. Hound also fired two shots. A round hit O'Conner in each of his kneecaps. He fell screaming in pain. He was quickly gagged and dragged to the kitchen. He saw his wife and servant. His expression showed a level of fear defined as nothing less than horrific. Hound picked the boss up, sat him in a chair and again spoke in a low, soft voice.

"James," Hound began, "I'm going to ask you some questions. You'll only have one chance to answer honestly before severe consequences are delivered. Do you understand?"

James nodded in agreement.

Hound put the barrel of the 45 between the boss's eyes.

"I'm going to remove your gag," said Hound. "If you yell, or even speak loudly, I'll blow your head off, and then do the same thing to those women on the floor. Do you understand?"

Again, James nodded. A mask concealed Hound's face. He removed it, and then the gag from the boss's mouth, and the interrogation began.

"Shit! It's you, Hound!" James said as he became more terrified and anxious. "The boss in New York said we shouldn't fuck with you."

"He did, huh. Tell me all he said."

James was suffering intense pain from the injury to his knees and hesitated to answer. Rita picked up a butcher knife lying on a countertop and cut the servant's throat deep, from ear to ear. Blood began to spurt onto the kitchen floor as the innocent woman started to bleed out.

"Your wife is next, mother fucker," Rita said forcefully, "if you hesitate to answer again."

"Holly fuck!" said Bear, surprised and shocked. "Why in God's name did you do that?"

"To show this cocksucker we mean to get what we came for without delays."

Hound was appalled but said nothing to support Bear's statement. James was trembling uncontrollably as the question was repeated.

"He had learned to read men and had met a few during his career that should never be fucked with," said James. "You were among them."

"I guess you and the other bosses changed his mind. Tell me what's going on regarding plans to take over the Sanchez cartel in Colombia."

"The big dog leading it is a guy named Francisco Bacca. He has at least a hundred of the Sanchez army supporting him. He feels certain when the Sanchez family is dead that all members of the cartel will support him taking over as boss."

"When is this takeover due to occur?"

"He said we'd be contacted a week before the coup began."

"Have you been contacted?"

"No, not yet."

"What kind of deal did Bacca make with you and the other bosses?"

"A fifteen percent reduction in price on all merchandise."

"Why was it necessary to take over the O'Malley business in New Orleans and kill me?"

"We didn't plan to do that if you'd step down and let another boss take over. That's why an offer was made to Sandra to buy her out. The amount to be offered was generous, enough for all of you to live very well for the rest of your lives."

Hound held the 45 tightly in his hand and sent it crashing into the left side of the boss's face, fracturing his jaw.

"How much do you weigh?" Hound asked him.

James was now in more pain but knew not to cry out. He endured the injuries to his knees and jaw and forced an answer.

"Around three hundred pounds," he replied.

"Well, sir, you are a lying tub of guts! You and the other bosses had no intention of paying a dime for the business. Your telling Sandra a generous offer was coming was nothing but a lie to keep us off guard while the plan to kill us was carried out. You bastards have already selected a boss to replace me. Who is it?"

"Shawn Mulligan."

"That makes sense. He was in line to take over when Ken retired. He was pissed off when Ken chose me. Shawn was easy to turn traitor and knew all the corrupt officials necessary to be boss in New Orleans. Who else in the O'Malley business knows what going on?"

"Nobody, I swear it."

"I believe you. Rita, I'm done with this piece of shit. Do you have any business to conduct with him?"

"You're damn right, I do! He was in on the plan to kill me and my parents. Gag him tightly and help me strip him from the waist down."

Hound signaled Bear to help with Rita's request.

"Hound, what is she going to do?" Bear asked. "Let's just shoot the fucker in the head and get the hell out of here."

"I'm pretty sure I know what she's going to do, and we're going to let her do it."

To see what happens next, read the beginning of "Dangerous and Deadly Hound" on the following page.

Dangerous and Deadly Hound

1

James was naked from the waist down, lying face up on the kitchen floor with his hands tightly tied behind his back. Rita picked up the butcher knife used to kill the servant. She promptly cut the wife's throat, then walked to where the boss was lying. He was devastated to have witnessed the murder of his wife and now knew his fate would be worse.

"Each of you grab a leg," she said to Hound and Bear. "Spread them wide so I've got room to work on this mother fucker!"

"Shit Hound! I'm not up for what she wants us to help her do," said Bear in a whisper only his friend could hear.

"Bear, be cool and go along."

To be continued.

www.ingramcontent.com/pod-product-compliance
Lightning Source LLC
Chambersburg PA
CBHW020328180626
46812CB00001B/100